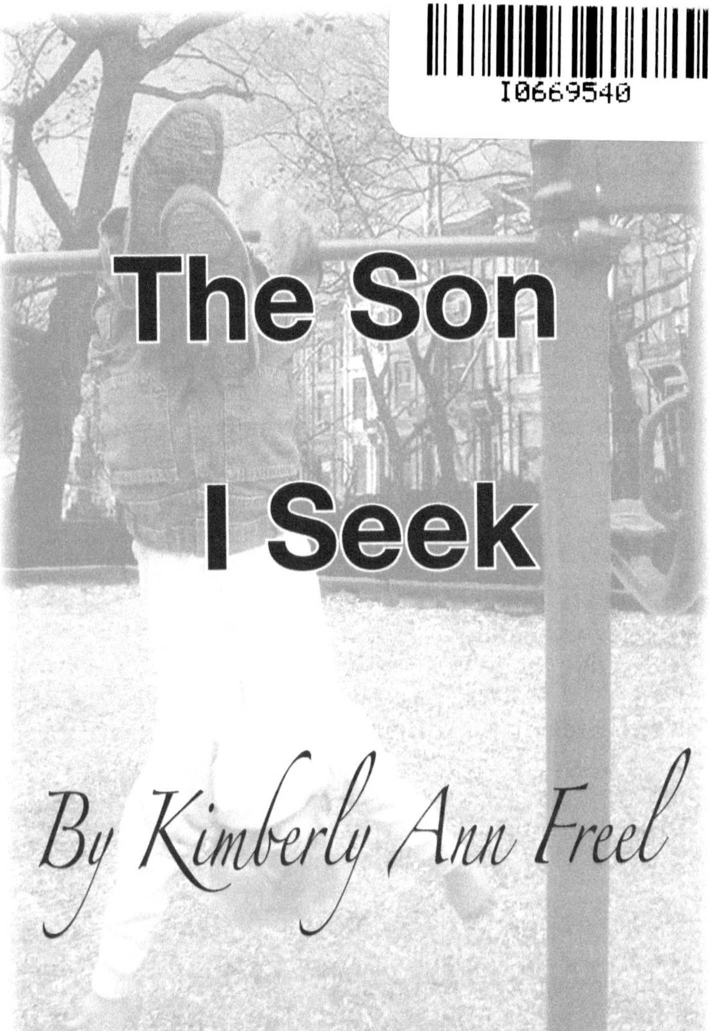

The Son

I Seek

By Kimberly Ann Freel

CMP Publishing Group, LLC
Okanogan, Washington

All inquiries should be addressed to:

> CMP Publishing Group, LLC
> 27657 Highway 97
> Okanogan, WA 98840

The Son I Seek may be ordered from CMP Publishing Group, LLC at the above address and at www.cmppg.com

The Son I Seek is also available at Amazon.com.

Contact Publisher for distributor information.

email: cmppg@cmppg.org
website: www.cmppg.com

ISBN13: 978-1-937162-99-3

Library of Congress Control Number: 2011961384

From The Author

Just as it takes a village to raise a child, it takes a family to spawn a book. The writing endeavor is not one I take on alone. I am indebted to my husband and kids for allowing me to 'escape' to my fictional world so that I can weave my stories. I'd also like to thank my special 'first readers', staid editors, who help me put my best work forward. I am forever grateful, also, to the people who read my books and continue to graciously demand an encore—you keep me writing even when it seems I'll never find the time. Finally, to my publisher, Edna, in your endless dedication to excellence in every aspect of what we do, and for being a dear friend and advisor through it all.

PART I

I can be changed by what happens to me,
but I refuse to be reduced by it.

—Maya Angelou

Chapter One

Holly

An unwelcome cry of pain issued from her core;
just like the guttural bawling of a calf when he's
been separated from his mother and castrated. She
chastised herself. The baby had to sleep. He shouldn't
see her like this.

Corey slept barely fifteen feet away, his nursery
separated from the main bedroom by a flimsy wall.
Corey was recovering from croup and it had taken
Holly nearly two hours to get him to sleep in the
first place. So far he'd slept blissfully through their
fighting.

Sweat beaded on Holly's brow, so she sought to
shed her sweatshirt, to cool her sudden flush. The
bones in her wrist ground together, something akin to
a dentist's drill bit hollowing out a tooth that hasn't
been numbed. She nearly bit through her lower lip to
keep another cry from surfacing.

It had been three nights since she and Corey had a
decent night's sleep. Pure exhaustion made her open
her big mouth; and that mouth had gotten her in a
heap of trouble, again, with Blake.

"Where were you tonight?" she'd asked,
perfectly justified, she thought, in verifying Blake's
whereabouts when he knew full-well that their son
was ill. He also knew that she'd spent the better
part of the early morning hours with their son in the
emergency room, getting Corey a shot of steroids and
a breathing treatment to open up his scanty airway
and ease the cough that sounded like a baby seal's

bark.

Blake's hackles had gone up the minute she asked the question. "Well, aren't you the curious one?"

Holly saw the cruel gleam in his eye and immediately backed off. "I just wondered, Hon, that's all…"

"I went off to work and some fairy godmother came along and made you queen, and now you get to go around and question all of your faithful subjects," he'd joked, but the words dripped venom and she immediately gave him wider berth.

"I'm not questioning you, Blake. You just know how tired I am and how sick Corey's been…"

"The hell you're not. You've sat here all day with one measly, sick eighteen-month-old. Yesterday's stinking dishes are still in the sink. You haven't even taken a shower. You smell like a whore's toilet, by the way," he paused to wave his hand in front of his nose dramatically, then he continued, "And me? I've been busting my ass all day at the department. To top it off, there was a bomb threat called in to Blondin's Foods right before my shift ended, so I told Sheriff Paul that I'd swing by and check on them on the way home."

"So you were at work?" Holly asked as she readied her apology. Blake, however, was already on a roll, and not about to be pacified off his high horse.

"Yes, *Holly.*" The way he said it brought gooseflesh to her arms, just like she'd gotten when she was a kid and he'd breathed her name in passion. Only now the hairs standing on-end meant fear— soul-stealing fear.

He was pissed that she'd asked and it didn't matter that she didn't know why he was pissed. It was a major transgression to question Blake, to verify his accountability, because, above all else, Blake was above reproach, above the demands of his stay-at-home wife.

"It's not that I thought you were at the bar or anything—" Holly defended. Wrong again.

"If I want to stop at the Watering Hole and have a brew with my buddies after a long day's work, after several nights of crappy sleep, then what damn business is it of yours? That doesn't affect you in the slightest."

"So *were* you at the bar?" Holly asked tentatively. Oh God, she was really asking for it, wasn't she?

So swiftly that she had no time to brace herself for the impact, Blake clasped his meaty hands around Holly's waist and tossed her to the side. He didn't account for the nightstand between her and the bed. Her right arm collided with solid oak and she felt a sickening snap.

"For Chrissake, Holly," Blake spat, as she yelped in pain. "Why do you always have to make me so angry? I swear you push my buttons just to see if I will lose my temper. If you're hurt, it's your own damn fault."

Tears sprang instantly to Holly's eyes, an assault that felt as if they'd been filled with acid. They were already bloodshot. Blake ignored her distress, ripped off his uniform shirt, tossed it toward the laundry basket, and pulled a bear-sized flannel from his closet. He grabbed a pair of well-worn jeans from the end of the bed and pulled them on. He picked up a pair of athletic shoes in one hand and pointed them accusingly at Holly who still sat in shock on the edge of their bed.

"Just for that, I'm going to do exactly what you've accused me of. I'm going to the Watering Hole to shoot some pool with Andy. That should give you plenty of time to clean up yourself and this pitiful house."

Holly pleaded, her voice barely above a whisper, "Just please be quiet when you go out, so you don't wake up Corey."

Blake glared at her, his normally russet eyes appeared black as coal. *Exactly when did he begin to hate me?* Holly wondered.

Police training had harnessed his wild teenage heart, yet after four years of wedded misery and unexpected fatherhood, he was defiant as always. Blake slammed the front door on the way out of their tiny rental house.

It was the crashing of the front door that elicited Holly's first cry of despair. She'd successfully stifled the second. Then Corey coughed, sputtered, and began to wail from the room next door.

"NO! NO, NO, NO!" Shouts erupted in waves. She scarcely recognized that they came from her, so foreign was the voice. Anguish rolled forth on an inescapable tide.

Chapter Two

Blake

"Hey Andy, want to catch a quick game of pool before the football game?" Blake shouted to the scrawny guy bellied up to the bar at the Watering Hole. Andy Sawyer had been his friend since they were both pissing their pants in Head Start. Still single, Andy was always up for a game of pool. Blake needed to decompress and smacking around a cue ball was just the way to do it.

God Almighty, his wife could be a bitch. She acted like she was the only one in the world who hadn't gotten a full night's sleep. Blake hadn't been able to sleep either, what with Corey breathing half the night like he'd swallowed a kazoo, and Holly wrapping Corey in quilts and packing him outside and back in again, starting the shower (like that wouldn't wake the whole household and the neighbors too), and sitting there crooning at the baby constantly to settle him down.

Not only had Blake suffered sleep deprivation too, he'd had to work all day and then some overtime, only to have his wife dish out grief about him being home late. And for Pete's sake, the house looked like a tornado had swept through. Empty baby bottles lined the sink and un-rinsed dishes with last night's food caked on, sat around in piles. Holly had let clothing and blankets and tissues fall where they may. The baby was asleep, finally. Would it have been so hard to clean up a little before her hard-working husband arrived home?

Andy raised his beer bottle in answer to Blake's inquiry about pool and sauntered over to the table where Blake joined him and began to rub chalk onto the tip of a cue stick.

"Thought you had a sick kid and couldn't make the game tonight," Andy commented as he racked up and rearranged the balls.

"He was dead asleep when I got home, snoring up a storm. His lungs still sound like a whistle got stuck in his gizzard, but Holly had it all handled, so I told her I'd catch up with you here."

"Oh yeah? You're so lucky, man. You should have taken advantage of the situation and banged her. What's wrong with you? What I wouldn't give to have my hands on your woman once in a while," Andy feigned ecstasy.

Andy knew how to push Blake's buttons almost as well as Holly did. "Shut up, Andy," Blake growled.

Andy knew he'd better shut up, because as long as they'd been friends, Andy had only kicked Blake's ass once and that was only because Andy had been the one wielding the hockey stick. And that was in the third grade.

They shot pool companionably for about fifteen minutes before Blake offered, with a chuckle, "You wouldn't think Holly was so hot if you could see her right now."

"Bullshit. There's no hiding that head of strawberry blond corkscrews or those cornflower blue eyes," Andy said earnestly. Andy had been half in love with Holly since her family moved to Okanogan in the seventh grade.

"Or the perfectly round ass and the tiny, perky tits, right?" Blake finished for him. He laughed again. "But she can, Andy. She can hide 'em. She looked perfect-ass ugly when I left her. She smelled like baby puke and body odor. Her hair was all matted flat against her head and she had her body buried in a sweat suit that was about three sizes too big. I think she must've worn it when she was pregnant."

Andy looked up from aiming his shot. His greasy black bangs hung temporarily in his dark eyes as he contemplated Blake. He stood his gaunt body up to its full 5'4" height. Beer had obviously stunted his good buddy's growth way back when. Even Holly was taller than Andy.

"You sound like you've been married for a century, Blake," Andy observed, then settled down to take his shot, "And that you weren't the luckiest guy in two counties to snag Holly right out of high school."

"Yeah, well, try livin' with her," Blake retorted as Andy's shot went wide.

"If I lived with Holly, I wouldn't get a whole lot else done besides bangin'," Andy replied with a grin.

Blake shot him a dirty look and repaid the offhand compliment by picking off the rest of his solids and sinking the eight ball. "Think we have time for another round before game time?" He asked Andy good-naturedly.

~~~~~~~~~~

Monday Night Football ended after nine and, by then, Blake had put a few too many away to drive home. He knew better than to operate a vehicle under the influence. It could cost him his job, and he liked his job.

Blake stumbled out the door of the Watering Hole into the star-filled October night. The moon looked huge from here. Coyotes howled from the edge of town. He breathed in wood smoke and musty leaves—the smell of a high desert hamlet preparing for the dredges of winter.

The Okanogan Valley was home to Blake. His great-grandparents had put down roots near a logging camp just twenty miles away from the very spot he stood. His grandparents had been orchardists two miles outside of town. His parents, Winston and Karen Dermot, were townies (as in, they lived in Okanogan Proper), and they worked together in the insurance business, a living that afforded their five children comfort, and a sense of entitlement.

Blake shook his head at that thought. He didn't act entitled, did he? Sure, his older brothers did. They had expected Dad to set them up with the car lot they ran north of town, and his dad did it without question. His younger twin sisters were still in high school, and word had it that both lookers had the boys at school by their balls. They dressed in designer clothes and drove matching Volvo's.

His parents hadn't known what to do with feckless Blake, the middle child, with the brawn of a lumberjack and the ambition of a tortoise. Blake's brute strength had made him a mark for every athletic coach in two counties, but he'd never liked working hard at sports. Weight-lifting was one thing. He didn't mind pumping iron, but football was all running, diving, and getting knocked around. Wrestling was simply too tactical. Plus, it was gross to have to writhe around on the floor with other guys.

They'd breathed a collective sigh of relief when Sheriff Paul recruited him right after graduation to go to the police academy and join the County Sheriff's office.

It wasn't until the academy that Blake realized what his size was meant for. He was The Enforcer. Perps took one look at him—at his muffler-sized arms, barrel chest, and his neck as big around as a coffee can—and surrendered readily. Blake had incredibly accurate instincts too, and the Sheriff often deferred to Blake's gut in hairy situations.

When Sheriff Paul had first recruited him, Blake had almost turned him down, because of Holly. He couldn't be away from his girl for three months. Some leach like Andy, or ladies' man like Troy or Tony, his older brothers, might put the moves on her. The thought of Holly going out with another guy nearly sent Blake into hysterics, but the idea of being a cop spoke to him like nothing else had. So he did the only logical thing he could think of—he proposed, and he and Holly got hitched in August right before he left for the police academy.

To this day, he wasn't sure what Holly saw in him when they were just sophomores in high school. She said it was his chocolate eyes and hefty muscles. God, but she had made him harder than a steel pipe in winter when she ran her hands over his muscles.

Even before she let him sleep with her, Blake had wanted Holly with an intensity that still scared him. Her peaches and cream coloring, effortless curls that hung nearly to her narrow waist, and her uncanny blue eyes all sent his senses reeling. If Blake hadn't had an ambition worth spitting at when he was sixteen, he did know one thing—Holly was meant to be his. She would always be his.

He was protective of her too. Her mother, Sissy Reel, was a white-trash, trailer crawler who barely came home to her teenage daughter. Who knew who Holly's father was? He'd been long gone before Holly and her mother had come to town.

Blake still looked after Holly. He hoped he hadn't really hurt her when he pushed her tonight. Sure, there had been other shoves and he'd raised his hand more than he cared to admit; but only when she'd irritated him beyond reason. Her mom had pushed her around and that had always incensed Blake. He forbade Holly and Corey from visiting his mother-in-law. She lived two towns to the south anyway and he was pretty sure she ran a Meth house. The Sheriff's office targeted the house in an on-going investigation.

Holly had one older sister, Susan, but she'd already graduated and moved as far away from their mother as she could by the time the Reels moved to Okanogan from somewhere in Wyoming. It didn't matter because Holly wanted nothing to do with her family anyway. Blake was her family. And now Corey and Blake were her family.

As he walked along the three blocks of Main Street, the crisp night air cooled thoughts of his fight earlier with Holly. She didn't have to be so abrasive.

That prickly crap had started after she had Corey. Corey, as cute as he was with his pudding brown eyes and white shock of baby-fine hair, was not planned per se. They knew they'd have kids someday, but they were both so darn young and Holly had tried to get a nursing degree. The pregnancy was a complete surprise. Holly had to quit school with only two quarters left to her RN. She had the baby in a fit of depression over crushed plans and servitude to a child who demanded every ounce of her time.

She'd had no time for eighteen months for her husband, and Blake knew it. He knew she'd lost complete interest in his needs when she went and cropped her breathtaking hair to just below her jaw. The thought of Minerva Jenkins sweeping those gorgeous curls into a tacit ponytail and lopping it off still nearly sent Blake into a frenzy.

He was pretty sure Minerva took great pleasure in doing so. After all, she'd been trying to get into Blake's pants almost as long as Andy had been lusting after Holly. They'd all been schoolmates. The binds and betrayals ran deep.

"Shit, Enforcer, don't you know it's nearly freezing outside right now? Where the hell did you put your car?" Deputy Harvey Morris broke into Blake's reverie. Blake hadn't really felt cold until the older man, a twenty-year veteran with the Sheriff's office, pointed it out. He shivered involuntarily.

"I shoulda brought a heavier jacket, I think," Blake admitted.

Deputy Morris took stock of Blake's slur and the stench of beer rolling through the cruiser window. How many times had Blake done the same thing with some other derelict? "Say, Son, can I give you a ride? You live at least six blocks away. I'd feel bad for the boss if I let his star pupil die of hypothermia."

A snort bubbled out of Blake's throat, delivered through chattering teeth. "I suppose." Blake went around to the passenger side and got into the front of the cruiser. The rules about putting passengers in the back didn't apply to fellow officers.

The cruiser was blissfully warm and familiar. Radio chatter flooded the airwaves just above the sound of the heater fan. The comrades rode in silence to Blake's neighborhood. Blake appreciated Deputy Morris' failure to pry or chastise. They all understood an officer's need to blow off steam.

"Which one is yours?" Deputy Morris inquired as he slowed in front of the row of diminutive, puce green rental houses.

"5-0-8," Blake replied, though he could already see that the house was completely dark and that Holly had not left even one light on for him.

"You know, son, you need to ask Sheriff Paul for more money. This here is a dive."

"I'm due for an evaluation and raise in about two months. I'll tell him you said that," Blake offered with a smile as he ducked out of the car, pushed the door shut, and waved Deputy Morris away. He stuffed his hands in his jeans pockets.

There was usually at least a night light on for the baby. Even when he worked the occasional evening shift and drove by at midnight, at least a little light shone from their low-slung picture window.

Something wasn't right. His heart skipped a beat. Where was Holly?

Chapter Three

Holly

Holly knew she was desperate when she asked the old lady from next door to call her mom. The feeble thing had practically broken down Holly's door to get to her and her distraught baby. Holly tried to stifle her own cries as the kind lady picked up the wailing, wheezing baby and held him to her sagging bosom.

"Oh my dear, the insulation in these houses isn't worth a penny candle," she offered with the slightest Irish accent. "I'm afraid I've been hearing you for several nights now. The baby's got you up in arms, does he?"

Tears streamed from Holly's eyes as she yearned to comfort Corey herself, but she couldn't let go of her wobbly wrist long enough to reach for him.

The neighbor lady noticed her cradling her injured arm. "Are you hurt, child?"

Holly nodded, then, retched with pain and, something else—fury maybe—uttered words that hadn't crossed her lips since she'd married Blake four years ago: "I need you to pl-please call my mother for me."

"I can do that. Certainly. What would you like me to do with the babe?"

Holly gritted her teeth against the pain. "I'll sit on the sofa in the living room if you will please lay him across my lap and prop him against my good arm," Holly shrugged her left shoulder and made her way slowly to the couch. The old lady complied and placed Corey gently into her arms where he immediately ceased his pitiful cries.

Holly looked deep into her neighbor's eyes as she backed away, "Thank you for being so kind."

The white-haired lady nodded and her gray eyes twinkled. "What are neighbors for? I'm Mrs. Jones. We've never met formally since you and your husband moved in. It's a pleasure to meet you. Now, what number would you like me to call?"

Holly ticked off the number in her head. It had been so long since she'd dialed it, she was surprised it came to memory, but then her mother had never been far from her mind, even though Blake barred Holly from taking Corey there.

Sissy Reel fit the description 'rode hard and put away wet' to perfection. Scores of useless men had abandoned her. Two louses left behind two infant girls. She'd had to do every menial, disgusting chore required of her to make money to support them. Sissy's heart was harder than the shell on a jawbreaker.

But Sissy, Holly was pretty sure, loved her daughters fiercely, even though blistering words and biting slaps had too often accompanied that love. Sissy stood her ground with Holly and Susan when they went wrong, when they defied her, and it was always for their own good—though that perspective was hard to see until Holly became a mother herself.

On Holly's wedding day, Sissy flatly refused to show up. Her baby girl was better than some rush wedding on a sweltering summer day. Sissy wanted Holly to go to college. It didn't matter that Blake was from a prominent Okanogan family or that he would soon have a good job to provide for the both of them. Sissy thought Blake a pushy, spoiled brute, plain and simple.

Sissy despised Blake so much by the time Corey arrived that she wanted Blake and Holly to stay away from her as much as Blake wanted to keep Holly from her mother. The ill feelings ran mutually deep.

Mrs. Jones held the cordless phone to Holly's ear.

"'Lo?" A gravelly female voice answered.

"Mom?" Holly measured her breathing to keep herself from bawling at the sound of her mother's voice.

"Holly? Is that you?" Sissy sounded confused, like she was trying to shake off a dream.

"It's me, Mommy," Holly's voice broke. "I need you."

"What has he done?" Sissy immediately blamed Blake, as Holly knew she would. Rightly so, Holly supposed.

"Can you come get me?" Holly needn't have asked. She knew Sissy would come immediately even if she had to fly out the door in her knickers and flip-flops. It was how her mom had always been—a bear to live with, but the most protective mother found in nature.

"I'll be there in fifteen minutes," Sissy replied. Holly heard the phone click. Her mom was on her way. They would need a diaper bag and formula for Corey. Holly looked up at Mrs. Jones, who stood examining Holly quietly. Holly wondered if Mrs. Jones had noticed the filth around them. Hardly a bare spot remained on the floor as the tatters of the last three days of illness and fatigue glared at Holly.

Holly flushed, embarrassed. "I normally keep the house a lot neater than this…" she offered.

"Of course you do, dear. I would love to help if you'll tell me where to start," Mrs. Jones replied sweetly.

If God sent angels to live on Earth, Holly imagined at that moment that Mrs. Jones could very likely be one.

~~~~~~~~~~

Sissy arrived in a fragrant cloud of Poison and pipe tobacco, her curly auburn hair billowing around her as she flitted from her car to the house and back again, taking as many of Holly's belongings as she could get her hands on in a few short minutes.

"When is the bastard due home again?" Sissy asked. Mrs. Jones did her best to bundle Corey while Sissy loaded the car.

"I don't know. We should leave sooner than later," Holly replied, her sense of urgency expanding now that rescue was so near. Blake simply couldn't find Sissy here. Holly couldn't imagine an uglier stand-off than that.

Mrs. Jones handed Corey off to his grandmother and, at Holly's instruction, went to place his car seat in the back of Sissy's zebra-striped PT Cruiser.

Corey had quieted down after taking his evening medications and he contemplated Sissy seriously as she propped him automatically against her hip. Holly saw unbidden tears pop into the corners of her mother's eyes as she held her grandson for the first time. Sissy bent her forehead into Corey's and gave him a winning smile. Corey smiled back wholeheartedly.

"Okay, little man, let's get you into the back of Grandma's fast car and race your mama to the emergency room."

Holly began to protest, but she knew her mother was right. Her nurses' training told Holly that her wrist was at least broken. She might even require surgical setting, judging by the instability of her arm.

Once Corey was strapped in, Sissy helped Holly slide gingerly into the passenger seat. Holly thanked Mrs. Jones and promised to update her on how she was doing.

Sissy at least held her tongue until they'd navigated two stop signs.

"Are you going to explain to me how you hurt your arm?" Sissy asked patiently. Maybe her mother had learned a little restraint in their time apart.

"I banged it on our oak nightstand," Holly said. The words sounded as lame as they were. Sissy could smell hogwash from a mile away.

Sissy pounced, just like Holly knew she would. She'd almost missed this—her spunky mom giving her the what- and where-for. "Don't give me that cockamamie load of crap, Holly. You wouldn't have called me if you'd just fallen down. I'm going to give you five seconds to tell me what that shithead husband of yours did to you; and if you don't, I'm going to turn my ass back around and find him myself."

Holly felt a nervous giggle bubble up in her throat. If she hadn't been in so much pain, it might have turned into a full-fledged laugh. "I missed you, Mom," she admitted breathlessly.

"You are not too old to turn over my knee and paddle, Holly. Now stop changing the subject," Sissy shot back, but Holly noticed the corners of her mouth turned up just slightly.

"I think he meant to throw me on the bed," Holly confessed.

"So, a man who's a foot taller than you and outweighs you by a hundred pounds grabbed you and chucked you across the room, and you're already making excuses for him."

"I honestly don't think he meant to hurt me," Holly argued.

"Holly, I birthed you after twenty torturous hours of back labor. I raised you on a pauper's dime. We've been through thick and thin. I know you, little girl, better than you know yourself. You are prouder than a male peacock about his tail feathers. There is no way you would have called me unless you were scared spitless."

Holly couldn't refute it. But the truth, once admitted, would bring her world crashing down around her ears. It had been Holly and Blake against the big, bad world for nearly six years now. Blake had pushed before, had reared his fist back and hit the wall beside her, had verbally eviscerated her. He'd never successfully hurt her, not physically anyway; yet, their exchanges had been increasingly heated since Corey's arrival. Blake was terribly short with her and of no help at all with baby Corey.

When Holly had walked down the aisle and taken Blake for better or for worse, she never imagined he would cease to adore her; to hate her, even. It couldn't be, but she couldn't think of any other explanation. Blake had always been about control. Holly's daddy-less self had been grateful to have a man adore her enough to surround her with love, demands and all. Sissy had pointed out the same failings to Holly before her wedding.

Somehow control had turned to violence, and that wasn't okay. It was time to admit that to herself as much as to her mother.

"Okay, Mom. You're right. I'm terrified. He broke me and then he walked right out to the bar, leaving me and a sick baby boy in his wake."

"Yeah, I noticed the kid is a little raspy," Sissy agreed.

"He has croup. We spent last night in the ER," Holly said.

"You two girls each had croup once. It's a real bugger, scared the hell out of me."

"It was scary," Holly granted, then took a deep breath. Here goes. "What's scarier to me, Mom, and I've never said this to another living being, is that Corey is going to be talking soon. What if he says something to aggravate Blake and Blake sends him flying into the nearest coffee table? You think I break easily? What in the world would become of a two or three-year-old?"

Sissy grabbed Holly's good hand awkwardly across the center console. "You've always been a smart girl, Holly. That is the absolute right question to ask; and I'll tell you the answer: If it's up to me, that jerk will never, ever get the opportunity to hear his son talk back."

Sissy put her hand back on the wheel and continued, "If there's one thing that doing every shit-job known to man gives you, Holly, it's connections. All you have to do is say the word, girly, and we can make you disappear faster than Blake threw you into the nightstand."

Holly closed her eyes and nodded, but said nothing. Another sharp pain shot through her injured wrist. She ground her teeth together and moaned softly. "Okay, Mom, but for now, can we please just see to this wrist?"

"Yeah, baby. I'm on it." Sissy punched the gas and shot toward the county hospital facility furthest from Okanogan.

Chapter Four

Mrs. Jones

She had once lived in a forty room mansion—in the servant's quarters, of course—but Mrs. Jones, nevertheless, took as much pride in her four hundred square feet as she had in the brassy West Berlin digs she'd been raised caring for.

An ounce of dust had no place among her treasures: A teapot that belonged to her grandmother circa World War I, Mr. Jones' war medals, one of each of her childrens' booties, which she'd had cast in copper, among other things. Shelves were lined with memorabilia and photo albums, memories of a life lived—one that had not always been easy.

Mrs. Jones, the child of servants at the Mueller estate, remembered acting in the role of servant from the time she was just four years old. She'd been trained to fetch pitchers of water for the ladies of the house, and to shine the boots of the men, young and old. As she grew older, her tasks became more complex.

Once she'd reached her twenties, Mrs. Jones was hired as the family's nanny, which was all fine until the mister of the house took a shine to her and began to slide his hands up her blouse whenever the children's backs were turned.

She'd escaped the Mueller's with the Polish gardener's son, Borys Ciszek, a blond, brawny, winsome sort. At least she hadn't minded *him* sticking his hands up her shirt. He immigrated to Ireland with her, impregnated her three times, and beat her senseless every time he returned from the Galway pub after gambling with his chums.

Borys had met with an accident, an unfortunate fall from a wind-shorn cliff, shortly after he gave their eldest son his first shiner.

Mrs. Jones met Mr. Jones via correspondence through an American agency which specialized in such things. Yes, she was a 'mail-order' bride, but in the late 1960's, that was a perfectly acceptable reason to be brought to America—as a companion to a lonely gentleman. Mr. Jones, ten years her senior, had no idea (for Mrs. Jones had been quite svelte back then) that she was mother to three children, then ages eleven, nine, and eight. She left the children with a trusted neighbor in Ireland amid promises that she would send them money until she could send for the children themselves.

About the eighth time she skimmed a twenty from Mr. Jones' meager wallet, he cornered her and demanded to know why the new Mrs. Jones felt compelled to steal from her own husband. She'd confessed her deception, by then completely sick that she'd left her dear children behind. As luck would have it, Mr. Jones had a soft spot for his petite bride: She cooked like a gourmet chef and she shined silver befitting a knight's servant. Plus, she was a firecracker in bed. Her time among the passionate Irish had taught her to value a good romp in the sack.

Mrs. Jones was allowed to send for her three offspring, two of whom moved the Jones' to the Okanogan area after they retired.

When Mr. Jones died, Mrs. Jones insisted that their lovely three bedroom house be sold. The profits were divided among her children, a gift to them for being so delightful to their parents. When she died, that way, there would be no complications about inheritance. She had enough money to live on and a tidy space to rent, close enough to her children to pop in on them almost daily. She also played a lively game of bridge at the Senior Center twice a week.

For nearly an hour after she had left that poor neighbor girl, Mrs. Jones sat quietly knitting, and wondered at the way her life might have ended up if it weren't for the love of   Mr. Jones.

Mr. Jones had taught Mrs. Jones so many things, the foremost of which was that love didn't have to come at a cost. True love was unconditional. One should never be made to pay for loving. Nor should one ever have to live in fear of a loved one.

That girl—Holly, that was her name—would apparently have to learn this the hard way. As Holly sped off with her mother in that ridiculous vehicle, Mrs. Jones wondered if it would be the babe who would finally teach Holly these lessons, as it had been for Mrs. Jones with her eldest and her first husband.

It was nearly nine-thirty and Mrs. Jones' eyes began to cross with fatigue. After she missed two loops, she decided to give up the ghost. She rose from her chair to turn in. Then she heard him—the bully next door—stamping about and hollering for his wife.

Mrs. Jones shored herself up and summoned her most serene, helpful old-lady look before journeying to the neighboring front porch and rapping her knuckles on the door. Blake opened the door in a flurry. "Yes?"

"Can I help you, young man? It's quite late and you've begun to shout, I'm afraid," she chastised gently, all the while smiling docilely.

Blake had the good grace to blush under the porch light and look sheepish. "I'm sorry about that, Ma'am. I've misplaced, er, someone."

"People are rather hard to misplace, Mr.—"

"Dermot, Blake Dermot. I don't think we've met since Holly and I moved in." Blake stuck out his hand politely. Okay, so he wasn't a complete ruffian. That made him all the more dangerous, as far as Mrs. Jones was concerned.

She took him in more keenly as she shook his hand. Her stomach rolled when she smelled beer on his breath. It hearkened back to her dreadful years in Ireland. She kept her expression carefully neutral. "Mrs. Jones… So, Mr. Dermot, whom have you misplaced this evening?"

As if she didn't know.

"My wife, Holly, and my baby boy, Corey. They were here a few hours ago. Maybe she told you where she was headed?" Blake said hopefully.

"Oh yes, I've seen your wife coming and going since you moved in. Lovely girl. So tiny and with those springy curls; she's fresh as an April rain, that one. And your little boy—was he bald as a cue stick when he was born? His hair's so white!"

She could see Mr. Dermot's patience stretch like a piece of gum between a hot sidewalk and a shoe. Oh yes, this man was dangerous. She'd be darned if she'd do anything to lead him to Holly now.

"Did you see any cars leave during the course of the evening?" Blake quizzed.

That's right, he's a police officer. Here comes the interrogation. "I'm afraid I had my TV turned up too loud to hear any cars along the drive. *Wheel of Fortune* was unusually rousing tonight. I turned the set off right before you arrived home and took to bellowing like an air-raid siren."

Blake flushed painfully again and shuffled his enormous feet. "Did you see her go for a walk or anything?"

"Oh no, dear, but these are lovely picture windows, aren't they? I was just telling my daughter Kelly how much light they let in even on a dreary day; then again, it's rather dark now and it has been for a couple of hours…"

"Thank you, Mrs. Jones," Blake interrupted, his annoyance scarcely concealed. "You will tell me if you see or hear anything, right?"

"Absolutely. I'm always happy to help. I'm sure myself and the other neighbors will appreciate it if you turn in for the night. What's lost can always be found in the sunny morn," Mrs. Jones smiled winningly, yet her hardened expression left no room for argument.

Blake Dermot's bluster deflated like a bike tire with a nail in it.

Holly had needed a head start and Mrs. Jones had just handed it to her.

Chapter Five

Blake

Blake's quandary was multi-layered. His buzz quickly dissipated as reality set in.

Holly had vanished and so had several items of her clothing, her pillow, her favorite fleece blanket, and her makeup bag. As far as Corey's stuff, well, honestly, there was so much baby paraphernalia that accompanied their son that Blake didn't even know where to begin to itemize what was missing.

Clearly, though, she was gone. Corey was gone. It was late and their absence could only mean trouble.

Holly had looked startled when she landed on the bed. He hadn't thought she was really hurt, though. If she *was* hurt, surely she would have said something, right? If she was hurt, finding her would be doubly difficult because he wouldn't be able to enlist the department. Domestic violence didn't sit well with fellow officers. Whether it was hearsay or not, Blake would get an unsightly black eye among his coworkers if Holly claimed in any way that Blake had hurt her.

It was possible that Holly had gone to his parents for help if, say, the baby woke up and needed to go to the doctor again. Blake had taken the only family rig, after all, when he went to the Watering Hole. Maybe that was it. In that case, his dad and mom would read him the riot act for abandoning his wife and son when they needed him.

Holly was friends with Troy and Tony's wives, Trish and Corrine. Both of his brothers had sworn off fatherhood, at least for the time being, so it was entirely feasible that Holly might have called up either young woman for help with Corey while she took a break.

The worst possible scenario Blake could imagine was that possibly Holly called her mom and told Sissy about their fight. Sissy's first reaction would be, Blake was sure, to whisk Holly and Corey far away from him. This option seemed least likely, though, because Holly hadn't gone anywhere near her mother since the baby was born. What would possess Holly to defy him now, especially when she knew Sissy hated him?

Where to begin to look? Who to call?

Blake looked at the clock: Eleven p.m.—past the decent time to call someone on a Monday night.

His mom would understand. Moms are on-call 24-7 anyway, so a call from her middle child would hardly cause her any distress. Of course, that depended on her mood. Before it could get any later, Blake picked up the phone and tapped in his parents' number.

A sleepy "Hello," answered.

"Mom? It's Blake."

"Blake? What time is it? My God, is everything okay?"

"Take a few deep breaths, Mom. It's not that bad," Blake soothed.

"Whew. Good golly, kid, you know it takes years off my life when one of my babies calls in the middle of the night," she chided.

"Mom, have you heard from Holly tonight?" Blake bit the skin around his thumbnail absent-mindedly. It was a nervous habit of his—good thing his mom couldn't see him.

"Well, no. She called me this morning to tell me about the trip to the ER with Corey, poor little guy."

"He's doing alright, I think," Blake replied, though he really didn't know for sure.

"What do you mean 'you think'? Are your wife and child missing, Blake, honey?" His mom sounded calm but Blake could already hear the edge in her voice. Hysteria never traveled too far from his mom's vicinity, and neither did drama.

Blake tried cutting the conversation short. He'd really only wanted to know if his parents knew Holly's whereabouts. Clearly, they weren't going to be of any help. "It's nothing, Mom. Really. I'm sure she went to get groceries and forgot to leave me a note—"

"Blake, you must be entirely aware of the hour," his mom interrupted. Her voice gained volume. His dad was going to love Blake for this. "Unless she ran out of diapers or wipes, there is no way that your young wife would haul your son to the store this time of night."

"There you go. Maybe she needed diapers," Blake reassured.

"Don't you go trying to placate me, not when my darling grandson has been carted off somewhere in the middle of the night—"

"Mom, calm down. Dad's going to be pissed if you wake him up," Blake urged.

"Your father sleeps in the next bedroom and he wears earplugs so that he doesn't hear that confounded oxygen machine the doctor insists he use. Let's not beat around the bush here, Blake. When did you see them last?"

"After work," he paused and added quietly, "We had a fight."

With yet more volume, his mom replied, "A fight? What has Holly done to upset you? I've warned you a thousand times about that girl and her type."

Blake jumped to defend his wife, as he had done so many times before to his parents. "Holly's a good girl, Mom."

"Yes, Blake, so you've told me, but that doesn't change the fact that you can't take the trailer park out of someone like her. You could have done so much better…"

"Do we have to rehash this, Mom?" Blake bit at another hangnail.

His mom mulled that over for a moment. "I suppose not. But you tell me, Blake. Has anyone else in the family seen or heard from her?"

"I don't know. You're the first person I called," Blake admitted.

"I will call your brothers so they don't skin you alive for waking them up this time of night. You need to check with the hospital to see if Corey needed to go back there for more treatment. Have you given any thought to calling work to make sure nothing's happened?"

"I didn't want to involve the department unless she's really in trouble. They discourage us from using police resources for personal problems," Blake covered. Truth was, his coworkers would be glad to help him look for his wife and son if he asked. But they might ask too many questions.

"I'll call you back after I talk to the boys so you don't have to ring again and wake up Dad," his mom offered.

"Thanks, Mom," Blake said gently and placed the phone back in its cradle. It really was just like his mom to go and blame this whole mess on Holly. It *was* her fault, though. She'd questioned him, made him look small, and there was nothing that irritated him more. Truthfully, he was sorry if he'd hurt her, but Holly had bought a good shove. He just hoped that the fallout hadn't gotten too messy to clean up.

~~~~~~~~~~

By midnight, the Dermots grew wary of the possibilities. No one among their ranks had any idea where Holly and Corey might be.

Blake's mom was furious—she definitely suspected Sissy and her drug-dealing cohorts. As far as Blake knew, his dad was still sawing logs to the beat of a sleep apnea machine. His brothers, Troy and Tony, expressed sympathy to their mom. They knew first-hand the incredible difficulty of beautiful wives, but they could really be of no help. His sisters had awakened to their mother's phone conversation and called to promise they would spread the word about Holly at school the next day.

Blake grew more apprehensive with the ticking of the Big Ben clock perched on the shelf by his front door. He sat for a time on their tweed loveseat and ran clammy hands over his exhausted face. Maybe he should just get some sleep. He didn't know who else to call.

Blake had gotten stonewalled at all three of the county hospitals since he called in an 'unofficial' capacity. They couldn't share patient information, so they could neither confirm nor deny the admission of either his wife or son.

A call to dispatch assured him of a quiet night in the county. No major car accidents, no accidental drownings, no abductions. They didn't need any extra hands for the night. Was that why he was calling? The dispatcher had wanted to know. Because she'd heard that some of the officers needed more hours. She could check with Deputy Morris to make sure he didn't need more help.

Blake rushed to reassure her that wouldn't be necessary. The last thing he needed was Deputy Morris to be alerted to his troubles after he'd had to chauffeur Blake home. The alcohol had worn off by now, and Blake would have walked back to his vehicle to go look for Holly himself if it hadn't been so som'bitchin' cold outside. The thermometer on the porch read thirty-one degrees. Blake was half-tempted to bundle up and make the trek to the car anyway. He didn't know where to look but at least he'd feel like he was doing something if he went patrolling. With or without a uniform and a squad car, it always relaxed Blake to have a look around.

He rose from the sofa and turned off the desk lamp on the end table. Through the side window, he could see that Mrs. Jones' light was still on in her living room. Well, how about that? He'd never noticed her to be a night owl before.

Blake traipsed around haphazardly arranged burp cloths and discarded baby clothes to gaze toward the neighboring front room. Mrs. Jones' shade was open. He could see her perched on the edge of her ruby red recliner as if she was about to rise. Yet her pink scalp shone through her snow white curls as the top of her head tilted toward Blake. Her chin rested on her chest which rose and fell steadily.

Poor old lady fell asleep in her chair. He could see her knitting on her lap. Blake went to pull his own shade. Something about the motion must have startled Mrs. Jones because her head snapped up and her nearly colorless eyes popped open.

Blake jumped despite himself. He moved to draw the shade. As he did, he found those cool eyes trained on him regardless of the dark. With a gleam that bordered on dangerous, Mrs. Jones sneered at Blake. The hairs on his arms stood up. What the—? She couldn't possibly see him. Why then, did her chin unmistakably move back and forth, just once, as if she'd sensed his intention to leave and warned him to stay put.

He pulled the shade hastily and turned toward the bedroom, suddenly not as eager to venture out as he'd been only moments before.

Chapter Six

Holly

Holly started awake from a dreamless sleep. Pain shot through her casted arm as she tried to sit up and look around. Jags of light filtered through broken blinds, eerily resembling the teeth of a jack-o-lantern. The dampened morning light fell on dingy blue, chenille bedding. It didn't register where she was until her eyes landed on her mom's brass-framed print of a 19th century burlesque. Cloudy glass nearly obscured the curled edges and cracks in the worn paper.

At least her mom's tastes hadn't changed despite the move two months ago to a newer home.

At nearly two a.m., after she and Corey dozed off in the car on their way home from the hospital, Holly had awakened to find her mother driving steadily north, toward home. Just the thought of being near home rattled Holly, but fear of Blake tracking her down changed immediately to relief when Sissy pulled her conspicuous car into a quaint garage just four miles from Okanogan.

Sissy had wanted to be closer to them. So, despite Blake's feelings about her, Sissy packed up her belongings, retained her phone number, and rented a two-bedroom bungalow in a development south of town—Blake's rich-bitch mama's town. Holly's town. Her sweet-smelling grandson Corey's town.

The deception of it all would have made Holly wary if it hadn't reduced her to tears to know that Sissy cared so deeply that she extended her work

commute to the Bridgeport Thrift Shop, nearly
thirty miles away, just so she could keep tabs on her
daughter and grandson, to be there if they needed her.

It shouldn't have surprised her. Holly felt the same
way about her son. A fierce sand storm in the desert
couldn't tear him out of her arms. She'd let the winds
bury her first.

Corey. She thought of his silky white head, the eyes
she could get lost in when they gazed into hers each
dawn. Where was he, anyway?

When they'd dragged themselves out of the car,
Sissy had taken them both directly to her guest room
where she'd struggled with the pack-n-play-pen for
nearly fifteen minutes before she declared it 'the most
stupid, friggin' conglomeration of metal and fabric to
ever grace the Earth'—Holly appreciated that Sissy
had moderated what she really thought for the ears of
the baby—and left Corey with a gentle kiss at the side
of his mommy in their full-sized bed.

But Corey wasn't there now. Holly struggled past
her half-drugged mind. She vaguely remembered her
mother handing her the painkiller and a glass of water
somewhere in the early morning. Maybe Corey had
awakened. Surely Sissy had him.

Holly switched on the bedside lamp and looked at
the Audubon bird clock hanging above the bedroom
door. It was after noon!

Holly heard Corey cough and heaved a sigh of
relief. Today, he sounded much less like a baby seal
and more like a cigarette smoker with a morning
cough. His airway was just fine—this she knew as he
let loose a hearty giggle, followed by another rattling
cough.

Holly padded over worn gray carpet toward the
sound of her son's laughter. Holly's hand flew to her
throat when Sissy popped up from behind her kitchen
bar, wooden spoons tied behind her head like Indian
feathers by a red checkered kitchen towel. Sissy's eyes
twinkled as she gasped and whispered, "There he is."

Corey erupted in giggles from his booster seat, his

chubby hands up in the air, grabbing—more!

Sissy winked at Holly and dropped out of sight again behind the counter. Louder this time, she shouted, "Where's the *baby*?"

Corey went dead still, his focus completely on the tile countertop those silly ears had just dropped behind. He didn't even see his mother as she perched quietly beside him and delightfully watched.

Up popped Grandma Sissy—the crazy hair, and the hideous ears—"THERE he is!"

Corey pealed with laughter, as if the game only got better each time. He sputtered and rattled afterward for just a moment, but he really sounded so much better. When Holly laughed too, Corey automatically reached for her.

Sissy knew that Holly couldn't pick up the babe with her fractured wrist, so she plucked him out of his seat and sat him on Holly's lap.

"Want some coffee, kiddo?" She asked, her wooden spoons lolling back and forth as she adjusted Corey on his mommy's lap.

Holly nodded and stifled a giggle herself. "That's truly distracting. You've got the whole '*Bugs Bunny* as Sushi Chef' thing going on."

Sissy smiled and gave her spoons an affectionate pat. Corey giggled some more as she walked away toward the coffee pot to pour Holly a cup.

"Don't you have to work today?" Holly asked. It was only Tuesday. The week had certainly begun unforgettably.

"I've earned a ton of sick leave. I'm never gone, so Sheila offered to let me have today and tomorrow off."

"Did you tell her why?" Holly wondered for her own sake. After all, Blake was a cop. He'd look for Sissy too, when Holly didn't turn up.

Sissy was no dummy. This had already occurred to her. "I told her I needed to leave Dodge for a while. You remember my old beau, Romeo?" Holly nodded and rolled her eyes—the man had certainly lived up to every aspect of his name. "He moved to Spokane about five months ago. I told Sheila that he needed help cleaning up his place."

"Does Sheila know where you live?" Holly quizzed. She took her cup of coffee black from her mom, took a deep sip, and sighed. Her mom still put a sprinkle of cinnamon over her coffee grounds. Back in the days when spices were a luxury, when Sissy had struggled to make ends meet, she'd persisted about cinnamon coffee—tradition wasn't to be a casualty of poverty. Holly's ancestors had been making cinnamon coffee since her family's side lost the Civil War.

"Is it just like you remember?" Sissy asked knowingly and smiled when Holly nodded. It was like so many traditions they'd had, Sissy and her girls. Holly had almost forgotten.

"Nah, Sheila doesn't know where I'm at, but there are a few other cronies down there who do," Sissy admitted. "It's not like I'm in hiding here."

Holly understood. Sissy made friends easily and often developed those bonds deeply. Holly had always been jealous of her mother's ease with people, her devil-may-care attitude toward life, her refusal to judge or be judged.

In fact, this last trait of her mother's was what gave Holly pause about the whole situation with Blake. Sissy had always worked hard, but she'd flatly refused to ever be pigeon-holed as a janitor or a maid. Nobody would ever tell Sissy what she did or didn't deserve, nor would anyone ever tell her how to live her life. So why was it that Sissy hated Blake so much?

Holly had always resented her mom's snap to judgment about Blake. Holly had always thought her mother couldn't see past the giant chip on her shoulder to get to know her son-in-law better. No wonder she rushed to Holly's aid—it was the perfect opportunity to further Sissy's anti-Blake agenda. Holly felt a raw twinge of guilt, again, for calling her mom in the first place.

Blake, by now, would be frantic to find them.

"I should probably give Blake a call," Holly mumbled and kept her gaze averted from her mother's suddenly harsh stare. "He's got to be frothing at the mouth by now. I wouldn't be surprised if he's already called in the troops at the department."

"He broke your wrist, Holly. How's he going to explain that to the big boss, Sheriff Paul, when he fesses up as to why you're missing?"

Holly winced at her mother's razor-sharp words. Truth was, she wasn't at all sure how they would manage if Blake got into big trouble at work. They barely made ends meet as it was. If Blake went off his rocker and lost his job, it would be her fault.

"You're not going to like this, Mom, but I've been thinking that maybe this whole situation could have been avoided if I hadn't been so pushy with Blake. His job really stresses him out sometimes—"

"Stop right there," Sissy's voice sliced through Holly's diatribe. Even Corey's head snapped up from the dry cereal he'd been eating. "I raised you to be so much better, so much stronger than that, Holly. You saw men come in and out of my life, that's true; but why do you suppose I kicked so many of those losers to the curb? Abuse is *never* the victim's fault. It is *never* okay for the injured person to take the blame. I know this for absolute certain: A man who will push, shove, or verbally belittle a woman will definitely eventually go a step further and strike her. Some will go even further and do the same to their children. Do you know how many women are killed by their 'loving' husbands every year? That would be a statistic to look up, little girl."

Holly's gut instinct was to defend her husband, as she always had. "Blake would never risk his career or his freedom to hurt me or Corey. This was an accident," she held her casted wrist out, earning a stab of pain as she moved too quickly.

Sissy noted Holly's grimace and shook her head ironically. "Are you telling me that he never shoved you or grabbed you by the arms and shook you or accused you of things you didn't do?"

Holly stared hard at the coffee cup before her. Words evaded her, because, in fact, he had done all of those things. How could her mom possibly know that?

Sissy tore the dish towel from her head. The spoons clattered to the floor. She swooped into the chair in front of Holly and Corey. Sissy's eyes, Holly noticed, were afire, her normally pea green irises rimmed by the burnt amber that appeared when her mood darkened. "I will *not* let you do this. I will *not* let you doubt yourself and put yourself and your baby boy in danger. You will put that child first. You will hide here with me until I can find a safe place for you and then you will take this precious boy and you will make sure his father never lays a hand on him."

Corey looked back and forth between his mother and the funny lady seriously, as if he was aware that his fate was about to be decided.

"But he's Corey's father. At least he *has* a father. I can make sure Blake doesn't hurt him—"

But Sissy would have none of it. "You did so well defending yourself last night, didn't you? Suppose Corey had started crying inconsolably and Blake had gotten annoyed. How far would he have gone to shut the both of you up?"

Holly couldn't bear to consider the possibilities, so she took a dutiful sip from her coffee cup and nodded with resignation.

Sissy laid a comforting hand on her daughter's shoulder and gave her grandson a smile and a tickle under the chin with her other hand, eliciting one more giggle.

In her tobacco-tinged voice, Sissy spoke calmly now, reassuringly. "Lord knows I wasn't the best mother, bringing men in and out of your lives, letting my words and hands fly at the smallest defiance.

"I haven't been there for you, Holly, though I've tried to be. It's felt wrong to me always, to have you with Blake. I know—he has a good name, and his family has money, and he's got a steady job—but he's a bad apple, truly. He laid claim to you years ago like you were a twenty acre parcel that he could squat on and gain ownership rights to. Even the way he steered you through town with his meaty hand on the small of your back screamed, 'This is my woman'. It made my skin crawl.

"He has also, however, given you this gorgeous son. I can't hate him because of that, but I'll be damned if I'll ever let him get another shot at you or Corey."

Holly nodded again and hugged her son closer with her good arm. "Just tell me what I have to do, and I'll do it. For Corey."

"So no crazy, 'I'm here, darling, come get me' phone calls, right?" Sissy quizzed.

"No, Mom. I won't call him again. I promise."

Sissy nodded her approval. With that, the pact was made, and Holly sensed, correctly, that there would be no turning back. The uncertainty of it all nearly took her breath away. Panic soured in Holly's core like a dose of arsenic as she steeled herself for the unknown.

Chapter Seven

Blake

"Deputy Morris said you wanted to see me." Blake leaned around the doorjamb of Sheriff Paul's office and spotted his boss enjoying his usual morning cup of joe and a copy of the *Seattle Times*. The Sheriff's black cowboy-booted feet rested on the desk before him as he absentmindedly rubbed his ample belly and chewed on his white mustache.

At Blake's greeting, the Sheriff groaned forward and set the paper aside, letting out an errant blast of gas. Sheriff Paul reddened, but said nothing as both men pretended they hadn't heard it. Sheriff Paul cleared his throat. "Yes, well, Blake, I got the strangest call this morning from a woman who says she's your neighbor."

Blake flushed, but kept words in check until he heard the Sheriff out. It was only nine o'clock, but it had already been a crappy morning. He hadn't fallen asleep until nearly dawn after tossing and turning for hours. Between his wife's disappearance and that crazy old neighbor lady staring him down, Blake couldn't lay his mind to rest until sheer exhaustion took over.

Then he'd awakened to the sound of a hedge-trimmer outside his bedroom window. Bleary-eyed, he had spotted the time on his digital alarm clock: Seven *and* it was *October* for Chrissake! Why in the world would the old bat decide to trim their bordering hedge at seven a.m. on a Tuesday? Hadn't anyone ever told her not to trim greenery during a hard freeze?

It was unreasonable. That's what it was.

He'd had it in his mind to be gentle. After all, he had never met this 'Mrs. Jones' formally until just the evening before and it hadn't been under the best circumstances. He had just discovered Holly and Corey's absence. He was distraught.

"'Morning, Mrs. Jones," he had greeted her; before he'd asked her what in the hell she thought she was doing waking him up. He didn't have to be to work until 8:30.

She had taken him by surprise, though. At his rebuke, that seemingly docile old lady narrowed her eyes, pulled her goggles back on, and with nary a return greeting, pointed that hedge-trimmer at his manhood and let it rip.

When he had jumped back, she'd simply smiled serenely and returned to her task.

Since there was no possibility of going back to sleep after all that, Blake had gotten ready for work. He needed an extra twenty minutes or so anyway so that he could go get his car.

He'd thought fleetingly about calling in sick so that he could look for Holly, but good sense told him that he'd get a lot further in the search for his wife and son if he used the resources of the department, inconspicuously. Gut instinct also told him that Holly hadn't run away for any good reason. She'd left him. He would do his darndest to bring her back.

Blake left the house with plenty of time to get the car. He lugged his huge frame over to the Watering Hole, all the while vowing to lose at least twenty pounds so he could walk his fat ass at a decent pace without huffing and puffing. Holly was way too good of a cook.

When he finally got there, the car—a blue Chevy Malibu that his brothers had made him a heck of a deal on—was gone.

The Watering Hole was locked. Blake peeked through the dusty window into the dark-paneled room. It was no use. The proprietor, John Henry, lived upstairs in an apartment overlooking the street, but the place never stirred before noon. He supposed that he could pull a 'Mrs. Jones' and make a bunch of noise, but then John would be as pissed at him as he'd been at his neighbor, and, well, friends just didn't do that to each other.

He reached into his pocket to pluck out his cell phone. Aw dammit, he'd left it at home in yesterday's uniform pants! Blake spun around in a fit of fury. What in blazes was going on?

It was only the good fortune of a county cruiser going by that saved the window in the door of the Watering Hole.

Blake had flagged the officer down. It was a guy who worked graveyards, so Blake wasn't familiar with him, but the officer sure recognized The Enforcer. Blake didn't exactly blend in.

The officer delivered him to work, nearly on time. The rest of the morning had been uneventful and then Deputy Morris told him that the Sheriff wanted to see him. That could only mean more trouble.

He regarded the Sheriff now, warily. "My, uh, neighbor lady?"

"Yes, son," Sheriff Paul replied, reflecting the affection Blake knew the old man truly had for him. "Come in, Blake. Shut the door."

Sheriff Paul's eyelids were watery, sagging red, giving him the look of an inebriated basset hound. Blake supposed the look lent his boss sincerity. The man must have been believable enough to be elected as County Sheriff six terms running. That was more than twenty years.

Blake respected Sheriff Paul more than his father and mother combined. His stomach did a jig as he considered that the man he most admired could be disappointed in him. What would Mrs. Jones have said?

"Mrs. Jones saw you rather early this morning, didn't she?" Sheriff Paul began.

"Too early."

"So you did have an encounter, then?"

"If you call an elderly woman cutting into much-needed sleep with a hedge trimmer an 'encounter', then I would have to say yes."

"She says you cursed at her and threatened her," Sheriff Paul admonished.

"Negative, sir. I did not threaten the woman. As far as cursing, I may have said 'hell', but I was still half asleep, so my recall is fuzzy. If anything, Mrs. Jones threatened *me*. She didn't say so in so many words, but I'm fairly certain she meant to strip me of my manhood if I took away her hedge trimmer," Blake held his meaty hands up in surrender.

Sheriff Paul laughed easily. "Sure, sure, I believe you, Blake."

Blake relaxed. That was easy. Then he tensed again as he realized that the Sheriff was not through with the conversation.

"That's not all she shared, though. Mrs. Jones told me she noticed that your beautiful young wife and son have mysteriously disappeared. Said that you might have something to do with that disappearance."

Blake blanched.

"Where are the lovely Holly and baby Corey these days?" The Sheriff asked delicately and took a sip of his coffee as he assessed Blake's answer.

"I don't know—" Blake answered truthfully as he examined the tile pattern in the floor.

"Has there been some trouble at home that you'd like me to know about?"

"Holly took off last night with Corey."

"I spoke with Deputy Morris. He mentioned that he'd given you a ride home last night…"

"He did. I watched Monday Night Football at the Hole with Andy. I didn't think I should drive."

"That was probably wise," the Sheriff offered. "So when did you last see her?"

"I saw her after work. We had a spat—"

"Yes, Mrs. Jones mentioned that. Those walls in

those houses must be awfully thin—"

"Apparently," Blake replied ironically.

Sheriff Paul leaned his ample frame into his oak laminate desk, which creaked in protest. He looked deeply into his protégé's eyes. If there was one man the Sheriff had ever groomed for his job when he finally retired, Blake Dermot was that man.

"Your affairs at home are truly none of the department's business, Blake. You know that. I would hope, if Holly is missing, that you would ask for our help. In fact, I would expect you to ask me for help."

Blake could barely stand the disappointment he heard in the old man's voice. He couldn't possibly tell Sheriff Paul why he hadn't entrusted him. After all, Blake didn't know if he'd actually *hurt* Holly. Perhaps she'd just had her fill of the exhaustion of caring for their sick son. Probably, Blake realized at that moment, she had enlisted the help of her mother in her time of need, though he hoped not.

"Blake?" Sheriff Paul asked expectantly.

"I want to be absolutely honest here, Sheriff. I don't know why she left. Corey was sick. I actually expected her to show up late last night or early this morning. If I didn't hear from her by this afternoon, I planned to call in the troops."

"So you didn't…hurt…her, as your neighbor suggested?" Sheriff Paul asked. His body language suggested that he was ready to believe in Blake's version of events.

"Not that I know of, sir." There. That was truthful, at least.

"Well, let's find her then. The sooner your wife and son return home, the sooner I can have my favorite deputy back in the saddle catching real criminals!"

Blake ducked his head, wary of his boss's enthusiasm, but Sheriff Paul couldn't know that. "I'd sure appreciate it, sir." All those resources at his disposal—his wife couldn't possibly hide for long. He just hoped that finding her wouldn't doom him in the end.

~~~~~~~~~~

"Are you sure you don't know her new address?" Blake quizzed the owner of the thrift store. He'd had to beg a favor of the neighboring jurisdiction to get help locating Sissy in the Douglas County area.

"I have a post office box number for her, only. It hasn't changed. The only reason I know she moved is because Bonnie, the weekend clerk, heard her mention the move during a coffee break," Sheila replied, annoyed about the employee in question and her absence.

"When does Bonnie work again?" Blake asked.

"Saturday. You know, on the weekend since she's the *weekend* clerk."

Blake seemed to sense Sheila's animosity, yet he didn't back off.

"Do you have Bonnie's home address?"

Sheila's hackles went up. She was not entirely unaware of Sissy's feelings about her son-in-law. She recognized the name Dermot on his badge. This brute was awfully pushy and she simply did not have the time. There were five shoppers and their three kids in the aisles to monitor.

"Do you have some kind of warrant, Officer?" Sheila quizzed. She was pretty sure he needed a warrant for her to give out employees' home addresses.

"I'm not asking to search through your employee files. I'm simply asking for some help locating Sissy Reel."

"Can I ask why?"

"That's police business, Ma'am."

"Well, my business is my business. So, if you will excuse me, I'm going to tend to it. Good luck finding Sissy."

Blake stood broadly in Sheila's way while the Douglas County deputy stood to the side with his hand on his taser, as if ready for an altercation. "Are you sure you want to be that way? I'm sure the deputy here would be more likely to be of help should you need it, if you cooperate fully at this time."

"Are you threatening me, Officer? What kind of help could I possibly need from this deputy?"

"Say, if one of these patrons tried to lift something? I'm much more likely to want to help a shop owner who has helped me in the past. That's all I'm saying," Blake reassured even as he continued to block Sheila's path back to the register.

"In case you hadn't noticed, Officer, this is a thrift store. Most things here are not worth stealing. Things that might be valuable are kept in a locked window case. The way I figure it, if a person is desperate enough to lift something at my store, then they need it far worse than I do. Now, if you will excuse me, I have a customer at the register."

The pinched expression on her face reminded Blake of his school librarian. *She* hadn't liked him either.

"Thank you, Ma'am," the other officer offered. He knew a stone wall when he met one. "We'll be in touch."

Blake could feel a glare staring holes in his back as he left the store.

~~~~~~~~~~

"I'm telling you, man, there eez no way she'd tell *me* where she going," the wiry, graying Hispanic man insisted.

"Were you not her landlord?" Blake asked, frustrated. It was six o'clock and this was the kind of reception he'd been getting all day from Sissy's acquaintances in Bridgeport. He was hedging his bets just to assume that Holly went to her mom in the first place. They'd checked all of the hotels in the area and Holly hadn't registered anywhere. There were no women at the county's only shelter.

He had learned one thing new, though. Holly had checked in at the hospital in Brewster at some point during the night. She had a broken wrist. Amid accusatory stares from the female detective who'd gleaned this bit of information, Blake had denied, denied, denied anything to do with Holly's injury.

So far, Sheriff Paul was wholly on Blake's side, but Blake could sense a waffling in the ranks of the department. A man as physically intimidating as Blake earned as many dissenters as fans, especially from the female officers. Holly's injury introduced doubt and Blake could scarcely afford that.

"I rent to her, jes," the little man replied, "but she don' like eet much when I keep her deposit. She peesed."

"Oh really? What, did she trash the place?" That sounded like Sissy. The woman crammed more stuff into her home than a baglady did her cart.

"No, not really. I jes keep deposit most times. I blame her cat. He carve up a few doorways, plus she have lightbulbs need replaced."

What a racket, Blake thought. He wanted the man to cooperate, though, so he remained sympathetic. "Yeah, I can understand that. We're renters too and I've seen how beat up some of the places can be from the previous tenants. It's good you keep a little extra to fix the place up."

"No, not really. I jes keep deposit most times," the man repeated. "The place look sheety anyway. Why fix?"

"Did she leave an address to send the deposit to after she left?

"No she jes tell me off and leave. The guy who help her move, though, he migh' know. He leeve here still."

"Can you tell me which apartment is his?"

"Two-oh-four."

"Thanks for your help."

"Sure. I help you, you help me. I'm smart man, you see?"

Blake laughed and shook the man's hand.

He and the Douglas County officer walked up the cast iron staircase to the upper deck of the apartment building. The fall sun had since set and Blake felt the chill of the night air sink through his jacket. The cold reminded him that his son was still out there somewhere. Damn Holly if she wasn't protecting him the way she should be. Corey was sick. She had better keep him out of the cold.

A short man with russet flowing hair and a beard like Moses opened the door. Oh yeah, he looked like Sissy's type—plaid flannel shirt, corduroy jeans, and Birkenstocks with wool socks. He smelled faintly of cannabis. Blake shored up his resolve to nail this guy, but only after he got the goods on Sissy.

"Good evening, Officer…Dermot." The man's eyes widened slightly at the name he read from Blake's jacket. Otherwise he kept his cool.

"Hello there. I'm Officer Blake Dermot. This is my friend, Hank Flossin, from the Douglas County Sheriff's office. I'm here to ask you a few questions about Sissy Reel."

"I don't know a Sissy. *Real*, did you say? What the hell kind of last name is that?"

"You don't know Sissy?" Blake was getting fully annoyed now. "The landlord downstairs told me that you helped her move just a couple of months back."

"I don't even have a car, man. It would be awfully hard to help someone move without a car."

"You could rent a U-Haul," Hank suggested helpfully.

"True, true, but have you seen the dump we live in? You tell me who here could afford a U-Haul, man."

"So you don't know Sissy at all? She lived five doors away from you."

"There was some curly-haired chick who moved out a while ago. She had a stinkin' tom cat that constantly took pisses on the railing in front of my place. Is that the one?"

Blake had enough fooling around for one day. He was tired and he was done beating around the bush. "I think you know full well exactly who we're talking about and you're going to tell me where you moved her to, or I'm going to get a search warrant and bust up the little marijuana fest you have going on in your pad."

The man's docile expression sharpened and Blake realized Sissy's neighbor merely channeled hippy pothead.

"Why don't you just go and do that, Officer *Dermot*? You do realize that medical marijuana is legal in this state? Why don't I just show my prescription to you? In the meantime, you can continue to bluster out here in this aching cold. Better zip up, Officer. It might take me a while." Moses chuckled evilly, then turned around and slammed the door.

Damn it. Blake cursed himself for his impatience. He'd just blown a chance to find Sissy.

Chapter Eight

Sissy

Sissy's first daughter, Susan, had been born of teenage stupidity—a romp in the back seat of a souped-up Chevrolet. That kind of shame she could bear, but Holly's conception had been an entirely different story.

What Holly never would know was that her daddy was the owner of a topless club in Reno, Nevada who had mickied and raped Sissy on a stifling midsummer night in the desert.

Sissy had never expected to love her youngest daughter. In fact, she'd kept herself busy to the point of being inaccessible for most of the time she was raising her girls. She called it making ends meet. Mothers who did everything right for their children would probably call it neglect.

Susan had certainly felt neglected and she'd done nothing but vocalize that from the time she could talk. She was five when Holly arrived and insistent that she didn't want a sibling. Sissy had been, of course, powerless to avoid this fate.

Holly arrived on a lovely spring day, tiny and quiet, with a capful of red hair and deep blue eyes. To the surprise of her mother and sister, she was as perfect as a baby could be.

Sissy and Susan were like balsamic vinegar and olive oil—they didn't mix, but they darn sure worked well together when it mattered. Despite them both and their self-centered battle of wills, they had fallen in love with sweet, little Holly.

Sissy's protectiveness of Holly unfortunately took on a shade of guilt too. Aren't you supposed to love your child, wholeheartedly, from the beginning? Maybe that's why she'd let Blake Dermot take her girl from her. She'd never really deserved Holly; never actually wanted her in the first place.

She wanted her to be safe now, though. That was certain. She didn't blame Holly for being scared, nor did she lack understanding as to why Holly might trust her husband more than she ought to. After all, Sissy had never exactly kept any valiant male role models in the girls' lives.

That was precisely why Susan vowed never to get married, ever. This also made Susan the perfect person to take Holly in, because Susan loved her sister fiercely, and she didn't trust men, at all.

Sissy sent Holly back to bed with another painkiller while Corey napped. As soon as they were both settled and Sissy had puffed away for fifteen minutes on her tobacco pipe, she picked up the phone.

"Mom?" Susan answered the phone breathlessly. Sissy could hear the hum of a treadmill in the background along with the thump-thump-thump of her daughter's running shoes.

"Afternoon workout time? You must be off work already."

Sissy heard the treadmill switch off.

"Yeah, I went in at five. I wanted to be off early so I could catch a horseback ride after work before winter hits in earnest. Can't though. It was raining like the Dickens when I got off work. The weather's turning foul pretty fast."

"It's been cold here too. No rain, though. That must be why it's so much greener down there."

Susan's breathing started to return to normal. "You didn't call me about the weather in Walla Walla. So what's up, Mom?"

Sissy sighed. Her older daughter knew that Sissy wouldn't call unless there was a reason. There were no 'hey, how are you's' between she and Susan. Their relationship was simply not that easygoing.

"Holly and Corey are here."

"What happened?" Sissy could almost hear Susan's claws being sharpened.

"He threw her into a table at the house and broke her wrist. She called me for help."

"Did they throw his ass in jail?" Susan demanded.

"Holly didn't press charges and I don't want her to. I just want her out of here, away from him. Can you help me arrange it?"

"He doesn't know where she is?"

"I haven't told you, but I moved a couple of months ago, so I could be closer, you know. He'll find us, Susan, but I'm hoping it'll take him a while. He'll never look here on his own. It's a nice place."

Susan snickered. "Yeah, the last place wasn't exactly 'nice'."

"I know, but you wouldn't believe the money I saved on rent there. I'm set for a while now. And I have enough extra to get Holly set up there if you will take her in."

"You know I will. How do you know Blake won't find her here?"

"Well it's kind of tough to get anywhere without a car. I called in a favor from a tow truck-driving friend of mine," Sissy replied, with a smile in her voice. "Plus, you and I are estranged, aren't we?"

"Oh, Mom, we're strange alright, but we'll just have to do," Susan replied and laughed.

~~~~~~~~~~

So it was by eight o'clock that evening that Sissy and Holly found themselves on their way to Walla Walla, Washington, the land of the sweet onion.

They traveled by the harvest moon among cliffs carved out by rivers over thousands of years to miles and miles of sage brush to the welcoming lights of the Tri-Cities. Then they turned east toward the farthest southeastern corner of the state and wound alongside the Columbia River and seemingly endless stretches of farms and wineries to the outskirts of Walla Walla.

It was after two a.m. when a sleep-addled Susan pulled them all into her arms and out of the light drizzle that had begun to fall.

Susan had just one guest room, so Sissy claimed the davenport after tucking Corey into bed with Holly for the night.

Sissy awoke at dawn with her eldest, who had always been an early riser. They took cups of cinnamon coffee to the breakfast nook where Sissy tucked her legs into the cushy gingham bench seat. She examined her daughter, her shoulder-length, burnt sienna curls such a mirror of her own and wild with sleep, her hazel eyes red-rimmed. Sissy wondered at the force of nature that took a grown child and turned her overnight into her mother.

Like her mother, Susan didn't beat around the bush. "So tell me, did Holly ever tell Blake where I lived?"

"I don't think she knew exactly. You went off to college at Brown. She knew when you moved back to Washington, but I don't think she knew precisely where. You don't send Christmas cards and she was already tied up with Blake by then. You know he considers us the riff-raff."

"I know. I know," Susan defended. "I've called her a few times, but Corey was always crying, or she was fixing dinner for Blake, or something like that. Plus, I stay pretty busy with my job."

"Are you doing sales now instead of accounting?"

"I do a little of both, actually. That's why I can go in so early, because I'm at work with books and numbers. I only go out in the field to do sales in the late morning."

"How's the nursery doing?" Sissy inquired as she sipped at her coffee.

"Since we expanded to include more types of grapes, we're doing a smashing business. I'm so glad I bought shares when I came to work here. If this keeps up, I'll be retiring before you do, Mom."

"Ha-ha. Retirement? What's that?"

"I thought I heard voices down here," Holly said as she padded into the room in a borrowed bathrobe and pink slippers.

"Where's that darling nephew of mine?" Susan asked as she rose to get her sister a cup of brew.

"He's still sleeping. I didn't think he would because he slept so much of the trip down here, but he's really sawing logs. He has a lot of lost sleep to make up for."

"I noticed the nasty cough when you came in last night."

"Oh yeah, he had croup. That stuff is miserable."

"I don't ever want to find out," Susan held up her hands in surrender. "I'll be leaving that whole child-rearing thing up to you."

Holly laughed. "It's good to see you, big sister. You've got a pretty fancy place here." She glanced around at the double-paned windows. Even with the earliest light of the day, she could admire the sweeping views of surrounding vineyards.

"It's quaint, but it works just right for me."

Holly caught on immediately. "It's going to be too crowded with Corey and me, isn't it?"

"No way, Holly. We'll make it work."

"Besides, it's not like you're going back to Okanogan," Sissy added for emphasis. "This ride is leaving this afternoon, so you'd have to walk and I'm willing to bet your stroller wouldn't make it that far."

"Mom, are you sure you're not too tired to set out today?" Holly worried her lower lip, looking like she was about twelve.

"I'm sure. I'll catch a nap here in a few hours. I need to get back, Holly, so Blake doesn't suspect anything is amiss. As far as he's concerned, you never hooked up with me."

"He could still find Susan, right?"

"If he knew Susan's professional name and where she lives," Sissy replied.

"Don't you use Reel like Mom?" Holly asked

Susan, curious.

"Nope. I had a professor at Brown tell me once that sometimes in business it's not what you know, but who you know. I planned to get a job in one of the major accounting firms in New York City. I changed my last name to Morgan—like the banking family— and I started applying for positions. That was the plan until I got a line on this job from one of my dorm mates and I saw the chance to build something big out of a little company. Plus, wait until you see Walla Walla. It's a gorgeous place. You'll love it. I had no idea all of this was here until I came to see it myself. New York City was history."

"Yet you were still Susan Morgan from Brown University," Sissy added.

"I still use Reel as my middle name, but my professional contacts would never know that."

"I'm safe here, aren't I?" Holly asked timidly, unsure whether the affirmative answer was really what she wanted to hear. It was all so unfamiliar, so scary, to be running from everything she knew. It too easily resembled the nomadic life she and her mother and sister lived before Susan left for college.

"You are," Susan reassured Holly as she grabbed her uncasted hand.

"He could still find you here if you call him or tell anybody else where you are," Sissy reminded both girls.

"I won't, Mom. I made you a promise, remember?"

"And I'll hold you to it," Sissy added her hand to her daughters'.

They heard a terrified cry from the guest room. "There's my little man," Holly remarked. "Life as usual, just in a different place."

"Oh, it's not usual at all! Let his auntie get him up," Susan offered.

"I'll go get the dish towel and wooden spoons," Sissy added.

Holly giggled and watched her loopy mother and go-getter big sister work. There was nothing at all to worry about anymore. They were safe now, away from Blake. He wouldn't hurt her or their son.

Why then, did she feel as though she'd just crossed the last person in the world she could afford to cross? Holly wiped away a confused tear and tried to prepare herself for whatever was to come.

Chapter Nine

Mrs. Jones

The lawn around her wee house amounted to a green patch about the size of a jail cell and a healthy Rose of Sharon hedge on either side to 'isolate' the houses from one another. Each house was backed up against a six-foot cedar fence that guarded the most stately brick house in town and its breathtaking, four-lot grounds. The front lawns of the six houses gently sloped down to a disheveled concrete sidewalk and curb to Third Street.

Mrs. Jones had no need to keep her lawn or hedge in order. The landlord, who lived in the grand brick house behind them, ordinarily hired that job out. That didn't stop her, however, from doing a little sprucing up here and there when their snotty teenaged groundskeeper neglected to do so—thus her intriguing encounter with Blake Dermot on a crisp fall morn.

She snickered as she prepared her after-dinner tea. Ha-ha, oh, the look on his face! Why, he had looked like a hunter who'd sighted in a bear, only to have the bear pull out a shotgun from beneath his belly and take aim! The surprise, the shock, when she'd pointed that hedge trimmer at him—she wished mirthfully that she could do it again.

Her reverie was interrupted by the sound of a car pulling up to the curb next door. The hedge was now nicely low enough to give her a clear view of Blake Dermot stomping from his squad car to his front stoop, all from her neat, cubicle-sized kitchen.

That was strange—normally Mr. Dermot arrived
home in a private automobile. She rarely saw him in
one of the county rigs, unless it was during his day
shift. Certainly he'd never parked one outside the
house and gone home for the night.

By the looks of it, his mood hadn't improved since
morning, either. She could see him flip on lights in
the living room and bedroom, then step to his kitchen
sink window, which faced hers, scowling. Their brief
face-off left Mrs. Jones with the upper hand as she
glared at him and closed her window shade.

She hummed and sat, curtains pulled, with her
tea, while she watched a re-run of *Two and a Half Men*.
Such insight into the heathens men could be, she
thought, as she watched bemusedly.

Her phone rang and she conversed with her
daughter for fifteen minutes. She made sure to
mention the events next door so that if there should
be any further trouble, Kelly could intervene, though
Mrs. Jones hardly thought the drama would amount
to that. Kelly complained, once again, about the slum
Mrs. Jones had chosen to live out her years in.

Mrs. Jones reassured her, yet again, that the house
was actually in quite a good neighborhood. After all,
look at the splendid house just several hundred yards
behind them. Besides, where else could she have the
perfect sized house for just her with precisely the
perfect sized lawn just the perfect distance from her
darling daughter and sons?

Kelly had wondered again at her mother's
remarkable good-sense and warned Mrs. Jones to be
careful about her brutish neighbor.

"Oh, you needn't worry about him, dear. I think
I've put him in exactly the place he belongs. I'll talk to
you tomorrow, sweetie. Good night."

The second she hung up the phone, knuckles
rapped upon her front door, startling her. Surely he
didn't have the nerve…

Mrs. Jones peeked through the peep hole in her
door. Blake Dermot hulked in her doorway. His breath

hung on the air as, hands on his hips, he waited for her to answer the door.

She took a deep breath and swung it open.

"Mr. Dermot," she scolded, "it's quite late to be paying a visit, I think."

"It's only eight o'clock," he shot back. "Of course, you were up pretty damned early, weren't you?"

"In my experience, polite men don't show up unexpectedly on doorsteps after dark—reeking of pissy beer and cursing—unless trouble is afoot." Mrs. Jones bolstered herself up to her full, five-feet and two inches.

To her dismay, it looked as though Mr. Dermot's brew-fest had infused his courage. She wasn't as strong as she used to be. (Nor were there any convenient cliffs nearby. A porch simply wouldn't suffice.)

"Any kind of trouble here, Mrs. Jones, would be the kind that you bought," Blake snapped back. "Where do you get off calling my boss and accusing me of hurting my wife?"

"Did you not hurt her, Mr. Dermot?"

"Just as I thought. I *am* a police officer, Mrs. Jones. I was nearly positive last night that you saw Holly before she left. Now, *you* are going to tell me who she left with."

"I never implied that I knew anything. These walls are terribly thin. It would be difficult to disguise the kind of cries I heard, even over the sounds of a television set. I'm not unfamiliar with the kind of anguish that came from your home last evening," Mrs. Jones chastised.

Blake scowled. "You helped her, didn't you? You helped her pack up and take my child away from me."

"In my opinion, whether I did or did not help Mrs. Dermot, 'tis entirely clear to me that it is help she'll be needin'," Mrs. Jones replied, nerves returning the Irish lilt to her voice.

"I love my wife," Blake replied defensively.

"Sure, and you love your little boy, too, am I right?"

Blake nodded, his monstrous face, to her surprise, falling to tears of frustration.

"Love, Mr. Dermot, should not leave a sick boy screamin' in his crib and his mother physically powerless to help 'im."

"Please tell me where they are," he pleaded as the tears left his coal black eyes. "I have to make this right. I know you know where they went."

"Your tears won't work on me, son. You see, a lifetime ago a man taught me these lessons. He was like you—masculine, powerful, and couldn't leave the drink alone—and I took every sort of punishment from him, because he said he loved me, said he loved our children.

"Mr. Dermot," she continued, gazing stubbornly into his eyes, "I will *never* tell you how your wife left last night. She deserves a chance to be away from you, to raise her child without fear."

"He's my child too," Blake retorted and wiped his tears furiously away. "She can't just take him. You don't know me, Mrs. Jones. You don't know Holly. Whatever happened to you doesn't make me the monster you think I am."

"Oh, you're him, alright. Any man who would snap his wife's arm the way you did and walk out the door—"

"I am a police officer, Mrs. Jones. Believe me when I say this: Sheriff Paul is on my side here. You are dealing with a man who has an incredible amount of power and resources at his disposal. You don't want to mess with me. You know where she went. Tell me."

"If you have so much power, Mr. Dermot, then why in the world do you need my help? I'm just the poor, feeble old lady next door."

"That's right, Mrs. Jones," Blake's eyes gleamed dangerously now. "You are old, and you are frail. If you're not careful, you might have an awful accident and fall down your stairs. Break your neck. Why, any number of things could happen to a poor old lady living by herself in a shady neighborhood…"

"Are you threatening me, Mr. Dermot?" She asked, her voice, against her will, suddenly shaky.

"Who did she leave with?" Blake asked again patiently, but the gleam did not leave his smug face.

Mrs. Jones pursed her lips and answered defiantly, "The thing about being old and frail, Mr. Dermot, is that it plays havoc with one's memory. I'm afraid that very detail has taken its leave from my shriveled-up, old brain. Now, if you will excuse me, it's time I turned in for the night."

With that, she shut the door right in Blake Dermot's livid face and turned the safety bolt behind her. She tottered over to her easy chair and sank into it. She could hear the man curse heatedly and trudge around the hedge back to his own house. She took a few deep breaths and picked up her knitting to calm her frayed nerves.

The minute Mrs. Jones touched her needles, however, a shiver overtook her that had nothing to do with the early winter cold.

Chapter Ten

Holly

The hardest part about leaving was watching her
son. Corey looked so much like his daddy—the shape
of his hands, the warmth of his eyes, his white hair—
the only thing he'd taken from Holly was his arresting
smile. Corey needed a father. Any kind of father was
better than no father at all.

Sissy and Susan didn't think a father was necessary.
Rather, to them, men were toys—not to be taken
seriously, not to be trusted, and certainly never to be
loved.

Holly felt differently. Sissy had never spoken of
Holly's father. She did share anecdotes with Susan
about her father, mostly disparaging, but Holly's
inquiries about her own father stealthily met with a
brick wall. Some immeasurable amount of pain had
been inflicted upon Sissy by whoever fathered Holly.

That did nothing to stem Holly's longing for a
father-figure of her own. Her early years, in fact, were
marred by the succession of Sissy's boyfriends whom
Holly tried to befriend, to endear, none of whom
would pay her any mind. When she turned thirteen,
though, Sissy's amours suddenly paid her the wrong
kind of attention. She felt cheapened, endangered
almost, by her mother's poor taste in men; so then her
tactic became avoidance.

It wasn't until Blake—big, strong, protective
Blake—that Holly felt completely drawn to any man.
Holly's friends balked at Blake's possessiveness,
his demands on Holly's time. Her mother loathed

Blake from the get-go. They warned her about co-dependence, about loving a man so focused on, so obsessed, really, with her.

At first with Blake, Holly had felt safe. She had felt enveloped in the kind of cocoon that she'd longed for her entire life—the kind that nurtured her, that looked out for her every need.

Blake had an interesting family. They were awfully spoiled, for the most part, and unappreciative of all their good fortune, but they loved each other fiercely. Family pride was a big thing for them. Being a Reel meant you were from the wrong side of the tracks, but being a Dermot meant prosperity. It meant you had roots in the community, and in a community as small as Okanogan, that was huge.

By leaving Blake, Holly was effectively robbing Corey of all of those things.

It was unconscionable, and it left Holly examining bus schedules and searching for jobs as a nurse's aide so she could buy a car and take them home again.

Susan was fully aware of Holly's internal conflict. Almost nightly, they sat on Susan's cushy davenport and rehashed the reasons why Holly left and why, after more time had passed, it would be even more dangerous for her to return.

Holly left the discussions resolved, but nightmares laid her raw again by morning.

October waned into an unusually snowy early winter, leaving Holly and Corey trapped by slick, winding, country roads, as Susan took her daily trek to work in her only car. Holly's injury began to physically heal even as her guilt and doubts grew.

She had plenty of time to play with Corey even as she kept the house up—she needed to contribute to her sojourn somehow, so she became Susan's housekeeper and chef. It was her direct time with her son that nearly sent her into a frenzy. How could she be so completely selfish?

By the time spring arrived, Holly was as strung out from guilt and lack of sleep as she was when Corey had been so dreadfully ill the fall before.

Sissy and Susan were at their wits-end because, while they could isolate Holly and Corey all they wanted, they both knew the seclusion did Holly no good. It gave her entirely too much time to think, to talk herself out of her resolve to stay away.

They agreed the best solution was to allow her some freedom, with the understanding that they trusted her not to go too far and flee back home again. Sissy decided to buy Holly a used car, but keep it in Susan's name, so that it couldn't be traced back to Holly.

Sissy drove up on a crisp March day, in a jawbreaker orange beetle. Susan followed in her beige Honda. She had tried unsuccessfully to talk Sissy into a less conspicuous vehicle. Holly pealed with laughter. Leave it to her mom to buy the gaudiest car on Walla Walla's ten used car lots.

Holly loved the car, and she was touched by the gesture of trust from her mom and sister. She wouldn't break that trust and hurt these women who had been there for her more than ever. Not with this car.

Instead, Holly used the car to drive into town for long, exploring walks and impromptu picnics with her son. She visited immaculate, historical neighborhoods lined by trees hundreds of years old and a myriad of city parks.

Corey neared his second birthday in April. His toddling had turned over the winter into full-scaled exploration of the world around him. Outings were a way to burn off his considerable little boy energy. He delighted especially in Pioneer Park—the maze of trees, the huge 'zebo', as he called the bandstand in the park, the birds and ponds, and, best of all, the enormous playground.

It was there, seated in the crook of a catalpa tree with her son, that Holly first met Vlad.

Vladimir Ivanov slipped into Holly's life with the ease of a sharpened knife through butter. He gazed admiringly up at Holly through ocean blue eyes, as if she was a goddess upon Mount Olympus. Yet the fine-boned hand he offered, words yet unspoken between them, was for her son.

When she shook her head no—she didn't hand her son down from a tree to a perfect stranger—he spoke in a British-accented tenor, his voice as musical as Blake's was deep. "I'd merely like to help the two of you down so that I might introduce myself to the most breathtaking woman I've chanced to lay eyes upon."

Holly blushed furiously and helped Corey down herself after she hopped stealthily to the ground. Forget his regal bearing and longish, silky, ash blond hair—the kind you longed to run your fingers through. She was a married woman, wasn't she? With no business seeking out a man?

He spoke so surely, so sweetly, though, wasn't it impolite not to at least introduce herself?

She held out her hand. "I'm Holly."

"Mmm, Holly, like the firmest, brightest berry found in nature. Nice to meet you. I'm Vladimir Ivanov."

"Isn't that name Russian?" Holly blurted out. She clapped her hand over her mouth. She might seem ignorant, worse yet, prejudiced. He sounded so cultured, and very British, like her high school science teacher had been. "I mean, you don't sound Russian. You sound like Mr. Phelps, my teacher. He was from Wales. He told us fantastic stories about our 'mother country'."

Vladimir laughed his fluted laugh and replied, charmingly, "I didn't expect to meet a woman in Walla Walla, Washington with such knowledge of the world. Yes, beautiful Holly, my name is Russian. Both of my parents immigrated to England when I was merely two, about the age, I'm guessing of this fine young gentleman."

Corey watched this exchange and then babbled joyfully as he began to chase a huge monarch butterfly.

Holly laughed. "He'll be two in a few weeks."

"He's delightful. I have several younger siblings back home. Seeing him makes me miss them."

"Oh? How long are you here?"

"I've begun graduate studies at Whitman College. There is still the better part of two years left."

"I have to ask this, because it is so random to see someone from halfway around the world in Walla Walla: Why would you come here, of all places?"

"I've a special interest in business and winemaking," Vlad replied easily. "This lovely area, Holly, has shown tremendous growth recently in both. I'll be getting my master's degree while I study under one of the original vintners in Walla Walla. In fact, I'm boarding at the winery. What better way to immerse myself in the culture?"

"My sister works for a nursery that supplies wine grapes."

"Well, then, she could tell you just how lucrative this wine business has become. Walla Walla is set to become the new Bordeaux region of the U.S."

"Really?" To hear Vlad tell of it, the whole business sounded rather exciting—much more so than when Susan had tried to explain her job.

"Have you had lunch?" Vlad asked.

"No. I was going to return home with Corey for lunch after we spent some time bird watching."

"Come out with me, Holly, and bring little Corey. I know a bistro just two blocks over. We can stroll there, get to know each other a little better, before I do my best to seduce you into a real date."

Holly was unable to refuse. For the first time in a long time, she found herself truly engaged and her guilt nudged aside for awhile. It felt good. It felt free. Freedom was what her mom and Susan had wanted to give her. Why not embrace it?

~~~~~~~~~~

The trouble with being merely twenty-two and

lonely was that reckless youth and good, old-fashioned longing made it impossible to be sensible about an affair.

Vlad was twenty-four. He had lived in Sussex, England for most of his life and moved to the States for undergraduate studies at Yale. His move to Walla Walla had been strategic, but had taken him much further from home. His parents had married young and had two sets of kids—three that were two years older and two years younger than Vlad, and three that were ages six, four, and two. Vlad, homesick, talked often about the family he left behind.

Holly tried hard not to make comparisons between Vlad and Blake, but she couldn't help herself. Vlad was graceful and willowy, the antithesis of Blake's bumbling girth and powerful strength; Vlad was educated and worldly, opposed to Blake's narrow-minded, small-town view of the world; Vlad flirted and teased, where Blake had always groped and hotly demanded. Vlad was gentle and complementary, and Holly's husband had been anything but sweet for a couple of years.

It was only a matter of time before Holly took to Vlad's bed—a lemon verbena-scented haven at the center of his eclectic picker's-cabin abode. Vlad taught her things there, brought her to new heights, and extended, beyond measure, her knowledge of love-making. Her Russian lover knew just where to touch, to taste, how to satiate her. Her previous life was all but forgotten while she was in the fold of Vlad's soft cotton sheets.

So she never told him about Blake. All he knew was that she wasn't with Corey's dad anymore. That was all he needed to know and he never cared to delve any further. Besides, they were too busy roving each other's bodies to talk about anything deeper.

Thus, it was a shocking surprise to Holly to find out Vlad hid deep secrets too.

Vlad ran his hand along the curve of Holly's hip after they'd made love on a rainy June Saturday.

Susan had taken Corey to a pizza parlor with an indoor play structure. Holly had insisted that she needed a break to do some summer clothes shopping at the mall.

Susan capitulated because she had no idea Holly was carrying on with Vlad. Holly had seemed much lighter and happier over the previous two months, but Susan assumed it was due to her extended freedom. Holly never let on to her sister that she was having a torrid affair.

"When do I get to meet this sister of yours? I keep thinking she must be interesting to have bought such a vivid car for you," Vlad teased, his breath soothing upon her flyaway hair.

"Believe me, that wasn't her idea. I don't know when you'll meet her, Vlad. Susan's so busy with work all of the time…"

"I've noticed she's been busy with Corey lately. You've left him quite often to come here, haven't you? Maybe you can invite me to your place sometime while he's napping so you don't have to make excuses to steal away."

"I'll think about it," Holly offered. "I'm afraid he might walk in or something, be confused."

"That's true. I understand," Vlad replied. He always understood.

He slid out of bed, his lithe body like a modern-day Dionysus in the dim afternoon light. "Can I get you a soda?"

"No, thanks, but I would love a glass of water."

He started toward his makeshift kitchen, a four-foot counter with a sink and a hotplate, when they heard the key in the deadbolt. His reaction to lock and key should have told Holly everything she needed to know. Vlad glanced toward Holly in a panic and threw a robe toward her, over her face, as he pulled a sheet around himself.

"Who—" she started to ask, pulling the silk robe from her face, as a statuesque brunette swept into the room.

"Vlad, what in tarnation?" The woman demanded as he ducked his head sheepishly. "You never lock the door. It's not as if this is the Ritz—"

With that, Wonder Woman, (who she uncannily resembled), noticed Holly sitting naked and bewildered upon the bed.

"Who the hell is this?"

"Veronica, it's not what it looks like..."

She eyed Holly keenly and Holly wondered nervously whether Veronica was the cat about to eat her canary.

"Bullshit. It's exactly what it looks like. Too bad your hearty, corn-fed American *wife* intruded upon your love nest with this delicate flower."

"You're *married*?" Holly blurted, incredulous.

Vlad went limp from the roots of his hair to his long, slender toes. "I am, Holly. It's true."

"Oh yeah, he's married. Vlad, here, and I went to college together at Yale. He got in a little trouble with customs over a package he tried to send home to his family. He thought it would be fun to export a few American-born goats to his little brother and sisters. He got in trouble with the embassy over trying to illegally send the animals. All in all, he was about to be shipped back to jolly old England before he could be off to graduate school. Instead, he turned to his good friend, V, to see if I would save his ass and marry him."

"So you're not lovers," Holly deduced. "Just friends, a marriage of convenience—that would explain a lot…"

"To the contrary: Vlad, as you know, is an incredible lover. Nope. We're married in every sense of the word. I just returned from visiting my family in Iowa. I've only been gone a month. You'd think he could see fit to keep his dick out of other females for that length of time, but, no, I've got me a regular Casanova."

Holly kept herself covered with a blanket while she began to gather her clothes. She willed the tears from her eyes. After all, had Vlad really meant more to her than just knock-out sex? She hadn't been entirely honest with him herself. She was married too. There wouldn't actually ever be any need for him to know this now. What she could leave with, though, was a little dignity. Wouldn't that make him sorry when she left him with his crass Amazon wife, never to see Holly again?

"Holly, I'm sorry—" Vlad offered. "Please, Holly, stay for a moment. Veronica, I'm sure you could leave us a moment while Holly dresses…"

"My ass, I'm leaving. You made me promises when we got married, Vladimir. Your little slut here is something else to look at, isn't she? I think I'll just wait here while she gets ready to go."

As intimidated as she was by men, Holly had no problem telling another woman off, as Sissy and Susan could attest. She felt herself flush at Veronica's ill-timed comment.

"If you lay those beady eyes on my body one more time, you're going to find out just how tough this 'slut' is," Holly growled.

"Holly, please," Vlad begged as Veronica backed up a step.

"Shut up, Vlad," Holly snarled. "You've said enough. You should have been honest. But then again, I should have been too."

"Veronica and I have a problematic relationship. You can see that," Vlad explained.

"Don't talk about me like I'm not here," Veronica warned, her mighty arms crossed in defense.

Holly pulled on her jeans and slipped her feet into leather flats. She grabbed her purse and headed for the door.

"Can't we please talk in a civilized fashion?" Vlad pleaded.

"We've gone so far beyond civilized, Vlad, you can't even imagine. Don't call me again. You won't even want to, because here's a news flash for you, Casanova: I'm married too."

Vlad's jaw hung slack. The raw hurt and surprise there was almost satisfying enough to ease Holly's embarrassment at how quickly disillusioned she'd been.

"See you around, Vlad," she said as she walked out the door without looking back.

Chapter Eleven

Blake

By the holidays, Blake knew that Sissy had helped Holly leave him. He'd tracked her down, followed her for a time, and even interrogated her at work. There wasn't anything legally he could do, though, to force Sissy to confess Holly's whereabouts. She had effectively stonewalled him at every turn.

He couldn't prove that she'd helped her daughter kidnap his son. He could only surmise. There was nothing traceable in Sissy's travels or with her friends or contacts to tell him where she might have taken Holly and Corey.

Sheriff Paul believed Blake when he said his gut kept leading him back to Sissy as Holly's accomplice, but they needed concrete evidence to bring her in and question her officially.

The only thing illegal about Holly's departure was that she had denied him access to his son, whom he had a legal right to see.

Lack of correspondence didn't give him legal relief either, because, for all Blake knew, the two of them had dropped off the face of the Earth. Holly didn't want a separation. She didn't ask for a divorce. She didn't let him know if Corey was well and thriving. She'd simply disappeared.

It was overwhelming enough to make him meaner than a hungry grizzly bear when he was asked about the situation.

His family did their best to try to help. Karen Dermot invited her son to move back home, and,

after the New Year, he finally agreed, simply so
the loneliness wouldn't be so stifling. Besides, his
neighbor lady, or some other nosey person had been
calling in anonymous accusations to the department
about Blake: His tendency toward violence, his
unnecessary intimidation of community members, his
lack of work ethic. Blake figured if he moved out, Mrs.
Jones would perceive his threat to her as neutralized.

Blake couldn't afford to lose his job. It was the
one thing he loved just as much as his misguided
wife. Thus far, Sheriff Paul had continued to support
and mentor Blake, but there was a faction of the
department who took negative comments at face
value. Their doubts about his public service abilities
were like a serious wound to Blake's heart. His size
and reputation for intimidation didn't preclude his
ability to feel. In truth, Blake was as devastated as a
man could be.

The Dermot family operated such that one family
member wounded meant an insult to the entire clan.
This was the center of the discussion as they sat
together around the family dinner table after Easter
dinner. Corey's absence meant there were no kids
for the Easter egg hunt in the five-acre Dermot yard.
The twin girls, Kelsey and Colby, were seventeen
and too old to hunt eggs any longer. So, it had been
an uneventful day, and Karen Dermot was furious
to see her family's Easter destroyed by Holly, as
Thanksgiving and Christmas had been.

Karen looked past the pale pink and yellow tulip
centerpiece on her antique oak table toward her
middle child. He looked thin; well, as thin as Blake
could ever look anyway—more like a Scot and
less like a Viking. His increasingly dark blond hair
standing on end was such a contrast to the white hair
he had as a child. Lines etched around his eyes told
Karen her child was hurting terribly. It was Holly's
fault, all of it: Blake's aging, the pit of Corey's absence,
the theft of joy at her Easter table.

"You know, Blake, it's a good thing Holly has

remained hidden so well, because if I knew where she was, I would have put a hit on her by now." Her sons' heads all jerked up in surprise.

"Mom, I'm a cop. You can't go saying things like that," Blake chastised. "It puts us in a bad light."

"Light? You think I give a flying crap what anybody says about me or my family? We are Dermots. We have traditions. Just look at this fine oak table and buffet that we've had in the family for one hundred years. It took your great-great-granddaddy on your father's side ten years to save up for the set his wife coveted. We take care of the things and the people we love.

"As I see it," she continued to rant, her own sandy blond hair aflight as she gestured, "There's one little Dermot who's been unwillingly taken from his home and his family. He should be here. I'd do just about anything to see that happen."

"You know, Blake," Kelsey said, as she twirled her purple-tipped hair around her finger, "at school they're saying that you broke her arm—grabbed it and snapped it right in two—and that's why she left you."

"That is not helpful," Karen chastised her daughter. "Blake would never have hurt Holly. She's trash, period, and that's why she left. You shouldn't go listening to rumors."

"That's what I told her," Colby, identical in looks to her sister except her blond hairdo, spoke up. "Blake's one of the best crime fighters this county has ever seen. He's a hero. That's what I tell people when they spread vicious gossip. Do you know how many drug dealers and thieves he's taken off the streets? That's what I say to them. I know you wouldn't sacrifice your career for Holly, Blake. She's not worth it."

Blake defended Holly, as he always had, though he was increasingly unsure why he did. "You all need to lay off on Holly. Whether or not she was hurt is irrelevant. What she did, by taking my son, is against the law and somehow I'm going to make it right.

Without any help from you," he looked from his mother to his sisters in warning.

"You know what you should do, Son?" Winston Dermot spoke up from his captain's chair at the head of the table. Winston, barrel-chested with a ruddy complexion, had all of Blake's physical presence, but a much softer demeanor. He so rarely put into these discussions that his sons all stopped tucking into their desserts to listen. "You'll need to consult a lawyer on this, but what I think you should do is start divorce proceedings. That way she'll be forced to respond."

"How will she get served if we don't know where she is?" Blake asked.

"As far as I know, she has a certain amount of time to respond to notices in local newspapers. If she doesn't, you get granted a divorce, no contest, by default. Then you can file for custody. If she doesn't respond to that, you can get the judge to grant you full custody. Then she'll be in contempt of court for denying you access. She'll be a fugitive."

"You really think that would bring her back to fight the petition?" Blake questioned as he chewed his thumb absentmindedly and Winston nodded. "I do have to admit that's the best strategy I've heard in a while."

It also meant divorcing Holly, an idea which he'd never even entertained.

"Blake, stop chewing your fingers," his mother admonished. "Can you get Ken Busby to check on that for us, Winston?"

"Ken's our business lawyer. I'm sure he avoids divorce like it's the bubonic plague, but he might be able to recommend a good local civil attorney. Blake needs to be on board for this, though."

"Do it, Blake," Kelsey urged, never one to shy away from a fight. She'd had enough of her brother acting like he was pussy-whipped.

"Only do it if you want to, Blake. I know how much you love her," Colby tempered, ever the reasonable of the twins.

"I'll look into it," Blake promised, his mood bolstered. "Maybe by next Easter we'll have a whole lot more Easter egg hunting going on. You girls can hide the eggs."

"Yay," they shouted in unison.

The men retired to Winston's study to strategize as Karen and the girls cleared the table, relieved after nearly six months that they finally had something to hope for.

Chapter Twelve

Sissy

"You've been a gem, Mrs. Jones, for keeping in touch with Holly," Sissy fingered the fine-boned china cup of the sweetest, full-bodied tea she'd had in a while. She wondered if Mrs. Jones had any interest in a coffee recipe.

The woman obviously had taste—each heirloom in the tiny, tidy space had a special shelf or table. Mrs. Jones' clothing was chaste and impeccable. She held herself like the finest Victorian lady.

What she must think of my leopard skin boots and lime fedora! Sissy thought as she uncharacteristically smoothed her skirt and tapped down her bushy mat of hair.

"I needed to know if the babe and his mother would be alright," Mrs. Jones replied. "I've never run across such a deserving pair for a new life, away, where they'll be safe."

"I know you understand why I've insisted that the letters be delivered by me," Sissy reasoned.

"Absolutely, I do. There must not be any reason for Mr. Dermot to know I've kept in touch with dear Holly. You've raised a delightful young woman, by the way. We don't want to give him opportunity to extract information of her whereabouts."

"That can't happen. I told Holly not to be specific about where she's staying."

"Oh, she's been quite careful," Mrs. Jones reassured. "I do believe she might have had a bit of a brush with an Englishman, though."

"I thought he was Russian," Sissy said.

"It's dreadfully complicated, isn't it? If we went by birth, I would be completely German, and I don't seem it at all, now do I?"

"No, as a matter of fact, I assumed you were Irish."

"My children spent the better part of their childhood in Ireland. Just to show you how complicated it gets: They consider themselves bona fide Americans."

Sissy laughed as Mrs. Jones rolled her eyes.

"Truly, though, Mrs. Reel—"

"Eee-Gad, Mrs. Jones—call me Sissy. My Reel was never a 'Missus', if you get my drift."

"Oh ,yes, I see, um, Sissy. Anyway, I think this son-of-a-Communist Brit might have put the hurt on Holly's heart yet again."

"You think so? Susan said she was dating someone, but neither of us thought it was serious."

"When has your Holly ever been anything but serious? Her letters during the winter while she was healing were positively gloomy. Your girl doesn't have a light heart," Mrs. Jones insisted.

Sissy shifted, embarrassed that this insight into her daughter came from a woman who had corresponded with Holly for less than a year. Mrs. Jones was correct, though. Sissy realized this astute lady might actually know her daughter better than she did.

"Don't look so mortified, dear. I never told my mother a thing either. She didn't even know I was moving to Ireland until I slipped a goodbye note under her servants' quarter door. I only wrote and told her I was pregnant when I'd nearly met the stork already." Mrs. Jones patted Sissy's knee reassuringly.

"Does your daughter confide in you?"

"Well, yes, actually, she does, but for the longest time she was the only one of my children who remembered much about our life in Ireland. Our closeness was born of hardship and heartbreak."

"Plus, I've got a hunch that you inspire confidence," Sissy admitted, grabbing Mrs. Jones hand spontaneously from her lap. "In fact, I'm about to spill my life story to you myself."

Mrs. Jones laughed wholeheartedly and sighed. "Why is it that women such as us must suffer so?"

"You're including me in this question?"

Mrs. Jones' clever, clear eyes soaked up their melancholy tears and zeroed in on Sissy. "Are you sayin', Sissy, dear, that your life hasn't been tough?"

With a hitch in her voice that surprised her, Sissy replied, "No, I wouldn't say that."

"Perhaps your Holly knows this and it's not in her nature to want to damage you any further."

"Oh…" This reasoning explained so many things. Again, Mrs. Jones was exactly right. Sissy had been around the block too many times not to know that Holly was keeping something from her now. Even Susan had suspected as much.

It wasn't that Holly was dishonest as much as she worried about hurting her mother and her sister.

"Can you carry another letter to Holly for me?" Mrs. Jones asked, interrupting Sissy's reverie.

"Absolutely," Sissy immediately agreed. Maybe Mrs. Jones would get to the bottom of things.

"I won't share whatever she writes back," Mrs. Jones warned.

"But you will let her say what she needs to say," Sissy reasoned.

"I will."

"Then that's all that matters."

~~~~~~~~~~

Holly sat motionless and watched the clouds gather and dissipate. The fragrant harvest wind blew thoughts of late summer thunderstorms into her troubled mind. She wished for the zen of floating upon one of those clouds, worries miles below.

She heard Corey and Susan inside the patio door going through their bedtime story ritual. Corey, already clad in a thin sleeper and smelling of watermelon bubble bath, chattered happily with his aunt, asking questions as the pages of the picture book turned.

Holly smiled despite herself. Blake was a brooding analyst—always quiet and pensive. Holly was meek, or so she thought—beautiful, but shy and difficult to approach—definitely not talkative. Corey was as outgoing and adventurous as the heroes in his favorite stories. He reminded her of Sissy—fearless—and everybody loved him like they loved Sissy too.

Holly admired the moon as it climbed above the horizon. She was Corey's moon: Attracted by his gravity, waxing and waning his tides. Yet she would always be content to hover in his orbit, because he would always be so much bigger, more significant than she.

As darkness fell, Holly mourned the sunset.

Night meant dreaded silence. Night meant stifling loneliness. Even after she began to bring Corey to bed with her to fend it off, his sugar-sweet breath and sleepy sighs reminded her all the more what it had felt like to have the weight and hum of a man in her bed.

Vlad had awakened Holly's deepest-seated passions. His absence fueled her resolve to cut off any other ill-intentioned man at the knees before she got in as deep. His deception, and hers, taught Holly that trust was as fragile as a newborn seedling. It could be easily snapped off and drowned by the very water meant to nourish it.

Surprisingly, this realization made Holly miss Blake too. Holly had never questioned Blake's loyalty or his ardor for her. True, he had become a danger to her and her child because of his temper, but ultimately, he had loved her.

On these cruelly lonely nights, the security of that kind of love was nearly all she longed for. It had been almost a year since she'd fled. Surely Blake still looked for them. According to Sissy, he'd never stopped. Wouldn't the simplest thing be just to drive back to their hometown and walk back into the fold of Blake's embrace?

Except that now she couldn't. She'd bungled things up too badly this time to reverse the tempestuous decisions she'd made. There would be no going back to family, Blake's family, however much they'd always hated her, because now they'd hate her more. There was no telling what Blake would do.

When they saw her ample breasts and thickening waist, saw the way her cheeks had grown perfect red dots on the apples, saw her run for the bathroom at the sight of grease or the smell of tomato sauce—the way she had done when she was pregnant with Corey—every single person in her past would realize that there was no going back to life the way it once was.

Because now there was a new life involved.

Holly wiped away a rogue tear. She was happy, damn it. Hormones were the source of this raw despair, that and isolation, she assured herself. If the only thing that had come of her tryst with Vlad was the opportunity to love and nurture another child, then she was blessed. After all, this child would be her own. She'd never have to run away and hide with it the way she'd done with Blake's child. Vlad had vacated town shortly after Holly met the Amazon wife. She didn't know what had happened to his marvelous educational opportunity, but Holly didn't much care.

Vladimir Ivanov was merely a sperm donor. He wouldn't ever know that he'd fathered Holly's child. She thought heated, unwelcome thoughts of Vlad's chiseled body and impossibly blue eyes. It occurred to her that she couldn't have picked better baby-making stock. There was no denying that this child would be gorgeous.

"Are you crying?" Susan asked suddenly from the doorway, interrupting Holly's reverie.

"Um, not really," Holly wiped away another naughty tear and rubbed her nose. "It's just such a gorgeous night. Would you look at that harvest moon?"

"It looks almost close enough to touch, doesn't it? Too bad it's full, though. That means I won't sleep a wink. Might as well start scrubbing the floors right now, because that's inevitably what I'll do at midnight when I'm through with tossing and turning."

Holly laughed. That was true of her big sister. There were mornings that Holly would wake up to a pristine house and a sister with twin tea bags beneath her bloodshot eyes, and know that Susan had lost the battle to turn off her thinker.

"Where's Corey?" Holly asked.

"You must have worn him out picking grapes today because he went from babbling to yawning to snoring in about ten minutes flat. I put him in your bed."

Holly detected the note of disapproval in Susan's voice. "I'll put him back in his own bed when I can finish my nurse's degree and get a job, so I can pay for a big boy bed for him," she defended.

"You know Mom has offered to buy one for him several times."

"I'm tired of making Mom buy everything for us. Don't you think it's time I got a job?"

"Your job is here with the house and Corey, plus you've done wonders for my garden and flower beds. You're a modern-day Alice," Susan quipped.

"I'd feel better about that if I didn't know you could do it yourself. Susan, when are you going to reclaim your sanctuary? It's been almost a year. You've got to be tired of us by now."

"You can't just go and get a job and move out, Holly. Blake would find you quicker than a bloodhound on the trail of a jackrabbit…"

"Is anybody home?" Sissy's voice rang out from the foyer at the front of the house.

Susan and Holly exchanged perplexed looks. This was an unexpected visit. Sissy almost always called before she showed up.

"We're out on the patio," Susan called to her

mother. Sissy came rushing through the door, newspaper waving, breathless with her news. The stench of tobacco smoke flooded their space and Holly had to swallow back a surge of bile.

"Blake has really done it now!" Sissy declared.

"What? What has he done?" This from Susan, who watched her mother with her hands on her hips. Something definitely had Sissy in a dither.

"Read." Sissy ordered Holly.

"SUMMONS BY PUBLICATION Case No. 2011A55555. In RE: The marriage of Blake Corbin Dermot and Holly Lynn Reel Dermot, Holly Dermot is hereby notified of the final contested divorce hearing as follows: Before Judge Vern Lucas, at Okanogan County Courthouse, 505 3rd Avenue, Okanogan, WA 98840 on September 30th at 10:00 am. Failure by the party named above to appear may result in the court entering a judgment of divorce in her absence... What does that *mean*?" Holly screwed up her face in confusion.

"It means that your soon-to-be-ex-husband put a legal notice in all of the papers in the state to notify you that he's divorcing you," Sissy responded.

"It means that you either appear or he gets granted the divorce anyway," Susan added.

Holly felt her stomach clench and fought the urge to gag again. "Well, that's good, right? Why do you two look so ate-up about it? You've wanted me and Blake apart since we were dating. And why, Mom, would you rush five hours down here to show me this when Susan could have read it in our local paper?"

"If Blake gets granted the divorce in your absence, he can make whatever kind of custody arrangements the judge will agree to—" Sissy said.

"—and if you aren't there to argue, he may get full custody," Susan added.

"But I have Corey," Holly argued. "How could he have any kind of custody at all?"

"If you still have Corey after all of this goes down, then you are in contempt of court. I consulted a lawyer friend of mine. If you keep Corey away from his father after he has a custody order, you will, Holly, officially be a fugitive who has kidnapped her child. Blake will have every law jurisdiction in the country on his side." Sissy waved her arms about dramatically.

Holly felt her mouth go dry. Her hands shaky, she put them on the arms of the chaise lounge and pushed herself to her feet. "Can you excuse me for a minute?" She asked weakly and made a run for the toilet.

"That wasn't the reaction I expected," Sissy puzzled as she nervously wiped newsprint on her jeans. "I expected tears, maybe fury, but I didn't expect her to run for the house like a mouse who'd got her tail chopped off."

"Yeah, well, I'm pretty sure you didn't expect her to be pregnant either," Susan replied sarcastically.

Sissy stared, open-mouthed, at her older daughter. She plopped on the chaise as if somebody had set an elephant upon her shoulders.

"Oh, God. No. I didn't expect that."

Susan sat next to her mom and took Sissy by surprise when she wrapped her in her arms. "Well we've got ourselves a fine mess now, don't we Mommy?"

Chapter Thirteen

Mrs. Jones

The click-click-click of the propane burner annoyed Mrs. Jones as she attempted to light it. Must let the landlord know about that too, she thought as she waved away a whiff of gas and rummaged through her drawer for a match.

"Ah, there," she said aloud as she prepared to burn the letter and its envelope in her stainless steel kitchen sink. The sound of her own voice startled her. She felt her heart palpitate, once, twice, then resume a more normal rhythm.

"I've got to get young Dr. Scot on that one," she said aloud again. "The ol' ticker doth protest. Of course you know, Mrs. Jones, if you would quit talking to yourself, you would stop hearing voices entirely." She giggled at her own silliness. If her children were to watch her now, they'd sock her away in a retirement facility straight away.

Still, her faculties weren't what they used to be. Thus her urge, before she lit it up permanently, to read the letter one more time:

Dear Mrs. Jones:
You have been so kind to keep writing to me and asking about Corey and myself. We're as well as can be expected. As Sissy must have told you, I've gotten myself into what you'd call a 'fine predicament' with my 'young man'. Somehow Susan knew before I had even come out with the news. Something about all of

the getting sick before breakfast and sleeping
endlessly, I suppose. Did you ever feel, when
you were having your kids, as if your toenails
were pulling your eyelids shut? I swear I could
fall asleep sitting on a metal lawn mower
seat. It's a good thing it's autumn, because I'd
probably run myself over mowing the lawn if I
were to try it now. Raking is much safer.

I've got other news too. I realize how discreet
you are about my notes, so I know you will
guard this information. I understand that Blake
has moved into his parents' place. I hope he's
not still sniffing around there and harassing
you. I want to warn you that it might get worse.
Blake has summoned me publicly to appear
in court by the end of the month. If I show up,
I'll most likely have to give him Corey, plus
I'm honestly not sure what Blake would do to
me, whether he might send me to jail or break
another arm.

Truthfully, I'm terrified to come back there.
I probably made a mistake when I ran, but it's
not one I can undo. I've spent so many nights
lying awake (before pregnancy intervened)
wondering how I could go back, what I could
change or make up that would take the past year
away. What could I do to make up for what we
all lost when I ran? Would Blake really have ever
hurt me again? Couldn't I just have turned him
in and gotten my son all to myself on the up and
up instead of on the lam?

Whatever the answers, I've screwed up, Mrs.
Jones. You, my mom, Susan—you've all tried to
reassure me that protecting Corey and me could
only be done if we ran away. Honestly, at the
time, I didn't feel as if I had a choice. Well, now I
have a choice to make again: Do I return, or do I
stay on the run?

The one advantage I have is that Blake still
doesn't know where I am. My name hasn't

surfaced anywhere because I haven't used my identity to do even one thing since I moved away. I've dropped hints in some of my other letters as to the things Corey and I do to stay occupied, but you don't even know where I am, do you? That's good and I'm going to have to keep it that way until the whole custody thing blows over. I hate to be in limbo for years—no job, no house, nothing public in my name—but if it means keeping my son, then I'll do it.

I've become so attached to you, Mrs. Jones, almost like you're my lifeline. I hope that we can stay in touch, but there might even be a time that Sissy can't come to me for fear of leading the wolf into her sheeps' den. So if you don't hear from me again, I want you to know that I appreciate all you've done to communicate with me. You've boosted my spirit, if nothing else. I don't take that lightly.

You take good care.

Love, Holly

The dear girl, Mrs. Jones thought, so forlorn, yet with all of these people who love her. Even if the shiftless husband hadn't taken action, Holly would have continued to torture herself just as much.

In a way, Mrs. Jones figured, it had been easier to have her husband die, because then she'd never had to share her children, nor fear whatever retribution he would seek for her actions.

No matter what she decided to do, Holly would never stop looking over her shoulder.

Mrs. Jones put the stainless Dutch oven in the sink to contain the letter once she'd lit it with a kitchen match. She watched the flames caress Holly's careful script, mesmerized as she always was by the beauty of fire and the permanence of ash.

"Stay away, sweet Holly. If I never get to tell you, at least your secrets will be safe with me," she murmured into the whispering fire. After several minutes, the flames died off and Mrs. Jones waved away the curling smoke. She looked at the clock. It was nearly seven: time for *Wheel of Fortune.*

As she headed for her TV set, a knock upon the door sent her heart's rhythm into a terrific tailspin. She clutched her chest and willed herself to breathe normally. Perhaps it was her son dropping by to challenge his mother in the word contest.

Her heart refused to settle when she swung the door open to find Blake Dermot, all official and terribly intimidating in his uniform.

"C-can I help you?"

As if he noticed her pallor, Blake seemed genuinely concerned when he asked, "Are you okay, Mrs. Jones? You look like you need to take a seat."

She coughed and waved at him as if to put the kibosh on such nonsense. "I'll take a seat when you leave me to my television program, Mr. Dermot. Whatever are you doing here?"

Blake scowled. "Your new neighbor reported seeing a fire over here and I was on my way home from my shift, which made me closest. I volunteered to check it out."

"Apparently the new neighbor isn't any less nosey than you were," Mrs. Jones retorted.

"It does look a little hazy in there," Blake replied patiently. "Maybe you'll let me in to look things over…"

"And let you confiscate my one-of-a-kind, blown-glass *bong*? Not on your life."

Blake snorted despite himself. "Nice try. I know darn well that you have a fully-propane range in there, because I did too. I can't go letting some old lady burn her house down, even if it is a stubborn, conniving old broad like you."

"Conniving? You wouldn't be goin' on about your cute little wife again, would you, Mr. Dermot?" As always, Mrs. Jones' Irish brogue came out when she was about to do some tongue lashing. "You'd think with a year gone, that you'd be about findin' another young lady to torture. I wish to the Almighty you would so you'd stop knockin' on my front door."

Blake turned just a hair shy of crimson, but Mrs. Jones stood toe to toe with him nonetheless. She just wished she could will her heart to settle down.

Still, he had a job to do, and Mrs. Jones almost admired his cool when he ignored her jabs and asked patiently, once more, "Sheriff Paul would shish-kabob me if I let you burn this house down and get yourself killed in the process. Your neighbor said she saw a glow and smoke in your kitchen window. Can you please let me in to check out the kitchen?"

"Since you asked so politely, I suppose it wouldn't hurt," she capitulated, but she made sure to step to her right in front of her tiny framed portrait of Holly and Corey before she let him through the door. With her hands behind her back, she tipped it over on her shelf subtly.

Blake peered around as he stepped over the threshold. She wondered if he was keeping his eyes peeled for a shotgun or a machete (or a *baseball bat*, she thought, barely repressing a snicker at the thought of the look on his face if she untucked *that* from her sofa cushions.)

"It sure smells like something burned in here. What's the pan for?" He asked, as he checked out her sink. She wished she'd run water in the pan for good measure.

She tried her best to look embarrassed. "Well the truth is, Officer, that I might have let a pot of cooked greens run dry. It was all I could do to get the burnin' mess to the sink before I was truly sorry."

"Why didn't you run water in it?" Blake sounded skeptical.

"Didn't your mother teach you never to pour water on a flaming mass of food? Why, if there was any grease in it, then I really might've caught the curtains on fire!"

"I don't see any salt either, though."

"All I have is in the shaker. I figured the sink was

the safest place, and, as you can see, the fire burned itself out just fine there." She shifted uncomfortably, hoping her story would gain purchase just so she could at least settle down and breathe a bit.

"Mrs. Jones, I'm going to be perfectly frank here. I know we go back to some messy stuff, so you may question the place this advice comes from. You see, I think, um, that it might be time for you and your children to discuss the wisdom of you living at home alone…"

Wasting no time, Mrs. Jones got in Blake Dermot's face and shook her gnarled index finger. "Now you just wait one minute, *Mr.* Dermot. I'm more capable than the Women's League when it comes to cookin' and cleanin' my humble abode. Plus I'm sharper than the blade on a Ginsu. Now, I wouldn't want to go so far as threatenin' an officer of th' law, but if you finish sayin' what I think you're tryin' to say, don't think I won't find the latter and stuff it into your nether regions."

Blake flushed again, violently, his anger now past the point of patience. "I'm going to pretend you didn't say that."

He walked stiffly for the door, but he didn't leave without his parting shot. "I've been a police officer long enough to know the difference between burnt food and paper ashes, *Mrs.* Jones. All of your bluster won't protect you when I find out what you're hiding from me."

Now that she could have done without, she thought as she dropped, leaden, into her favorite easy chair.

Chapter Fourteen

Blake

The Watering Hole had a surprisingly majestic burled wood bar complete with mood-lighting and ample mirrors. Blake caught a glimpse of himself as he reached for his pint of beer. He held his glass up to his reflection as if to toast.

It was November and he'd been divorced for over a month. Plus, just that Friday, he'd been granted full custody of his and Holly's missing child. This was the victory he had expected. Still, the outcome felt hollow as he laid claim to a child he didn't even know anymore, and let go of a woman his heart would yearn for the rest of his life.

Christ, he thought, after he put his glass down and summoned John Henry for a refill from the tap, he looked like a craggy old soldier just back from a tour of duty. His eyes were bloodshot, glassy, and gray-rimmed. Weight loss had left unexpected hollows in his cheeks. Divorce, abandonment—guilt—had turned him into an old man overnight.

Yet, he wasn't even twenty-four years old. He knew as he stared into the amber of his new beer glass, that he had to find a way to start living again, even if the life would be one that he'd never imagined for himself.

As if she'd heard his thoughts, Minerva Jenkins materialized next to Blake, smiled amiably at John Henry, and ordered one of what he was having.

The thing about hairdressers, Blake thought, is that they rarely go out in public without every hair in place—color perfect, stylishly cut, and lacquered carefully into place. Minerva was currently wearing her hair blue-black and pixie cut. The short 'do normally wasn't Blake's cup of tea, but it suited sassy Minerva and sent her cat-shaped, tawny eyes leaping out of her carefully made-up face.

"Blake Dermot. Fancy meeting you here," she purred. "You look like shit."

"You don't," Blake replied blearily, already half-gone into the pit of drunkenness he allowed himself every Friday night nowadays, whether in the company of his brothers or at the Watering Hole.

"Why thank you, Blake. The rumor mill has been positively humming about you lately. Nearly every client I've had this week has wanted to chew the fat about you. I guess you finally gave mousy little Holly the boot, huh?"

"Holly's never been mousy," Blake growled. "She's gorgeous and you hate her for it."

"Well, I admit she was cute in high school, but you have to acknowledge she went downhill after motherhood. I'd never let that happen to me. I'll be more stunning the more kids I have, you watch."

"I don't plan to watch you do anything, Minerva."

"You watched me plenty before you and Holly started dating," she pointed out and leaned in so close Blake could smell the earthy scent she wore behind her earlobes. "In fact, I remember your meaty hands in a few unmentionable places in the back seat of your Mustang. I still get wet when I think about it, Blake."

She nodded as his euphoria cleared enough to let him swallow nervously.

"Wet," she repeated, and he barely suppressed a needy moan. It wasn't natural for a hot-blooded man to go without a woman as long as he had and Minerva just offered herself up like a holiday ham.

"Let's get out of here," he choked out, and led her by the elbow toward the door before he pulled her skirt up and buried himself in her right at the bar.

~~~~~~~~~~

Several hours and just as many rutting sessions later, Blake and Minerva rested upon her bed in the apartment above her beauty shop. The space was a contradiction to the woman lying with him. Her clothing and hair were hip and modern, but Minerva's decorating tastes veered toward chaste Victorian linens and furnishings. While her persona was impulsive and bold, her color scheme was pastel and calm.

Lying here, her hair tousled, her makeup faded by sweat and sleep, Blake found himself curious about the woman in his arms. She made love like the wildcat she appeared to be, but now she looked almost child-like. Minerva had been vicious with Holly, but then she'd been transparently clear that her problem lay with Blake. Minerva had always wanted Blake. Blake wasn't entirely oblivious, but he'd pigeonholed her as an abrasive bitch with wicked scissors and a forked tongue.

After their lovemaking, she curled into his embrace like she'd longed to be there forever. Her body was silky soft and curvy in the right places, but her arms and abs were like iron. Her lips felt like feather pillows and he longed to explore them again. Instead he let her sleep. There would be time for more love in the morning.

Lord, it had been so long. Yet, every moment had felt so right. He felt the dead weight of fatigue drift around his satiety, so he wrapped his arms tighter around Minerva and gave in to sleep.

~~~~~~~~~~

"Wake up, Blake. You're snoring," Minerva chastised as she plopped on the bed, freshly showered, and crawled immediately back onto his chest. Her smile belied her rebuke.

"Mmm. You smell great. What is that? Jasmine?

You should have let me wash your back for you."
Blake stroked her damp body and felt himself
growing hard again.

"I would have if you would ever wake up."

"What's the hurry? It's Saturday," he rolled and
looked at the digital clock beside her bed, "and it's
only seven…"

"And I have clients starting at nine! Nobody ever
wants to get their hair done on a weekday."

"That sucks." Blake kissed her for emphasis. Her
mouth tasted of toothpaste.

"You need to borrow a toothbrush," she
commented.

"Your brutal honesty is one of the things I've most
admired about you," Blake joked. "You're right,
though, I have morning beer breath."

Minerva backed away from him and went to her
bureau to draw out white lace panties and a matching
bra. Great—now he'd be thinking all day about how
her neat triangle of black pubic hair shone behind
the virtuous lace and the dark areolas of her ample
nipples strained against the cups of her bra.

Blake groaned and she ignored him.

"By the way, Blake, I realize the beer might have
been a factor when you came home with me last
night…"

Blake shushed her with a kiss. "You could have
come home with me, but I'm not sure mom could've
taken you swinging from her ceiling fan."

Minerva giggled nervously. "You're exaggerating.
I'm not that talented."

"I'm beginning to think you might be talented in
ways I know nothing about. The beer has naught to
do with how I'm feeling now."

"Which is?" She came over to the edge of the bed
and leaned into it.

"I'm just marveling how you were right under my
nose all of these years. I thought I had you pegged for
who you were when we were just fifteen years old. I'll
be the first to admit that you might have changed a

smidge."

"Yeah? And you've been a little *married* in the meantime. I knew that was a mistake, by the way."

"Can we just not go there?" Blake asked gently.

"Sure," Minerva shrugged. "So what do you want from me, Blake?"

"Not just this," he replied, gesturing to her four poster bed. "I'm too complicated a person to have one night stands and we're both too old to pretend that's all that this was."

"So…"

"So, I'm offering you more, Minerva. Let's go out on some dates. Let's borrow my Dad's Mustang and take a few cruises out to Omak Lake so I can paw around on you again."

She laughed and threw her balled up shirt at him.

"Let's see where this goes. I can't make any promises, because, truthfully, I'm just a little bit raw from everything that's happened. Plus, I still have my son to find."

"I'll help you look," she offered seriously.

"Would you do that?"

"He's yours, Blake. You should never stop looking, Holly be damned. You need to bring your little boy home. I would never, ever get in the way of that."

"I just wish I knew where to start looking," he admitted, his frustration killing the amorous feelings he had been having just moments before.

"She'll make a mistake. When she does, you will be there to catch it. I'll be by your side every step of the way."

Blake nodded and embraced Minerva gently.

"When I asked what you wanted from me—" she added as she ran her hands over his bare muscles, "I meant that you can have it. You can have whatever you want from me, Blake."

Blake moaned and lifted Minerva's lithe body, depositing her on the bed where he gently peeled her lace aside and explored her hollows and folds with his mouth and hands. She gripped his shoulders greedily,

readily accepting what he was finally ready to give.
Her Saturday clientele would just have to wait.

Chapter Fifteen

Mrs. Jones

Mrs. Jones sighed with satisfaction as she held up the bonnet and booties she had just completed for Holly's baby. She'd chosen fine angora yarn in a spectrum of greens and the result was as irresistibly soft as it was functional. In fact she like the yarn so much that she planned to buy more and add the blue and pink spectrum yarns to make a crib blanket.

Too much time had passed since she'd had a babe to knit for. Even though it was a child she'd likely never lay eyes on, Mrs. Jones anticipated the February arrival of Holly's baby as anxiously as his own mother.

This was Holly's chance for a fresh start. When they had exchanged Christmas letters and cards via Sissy, Mrs. Jones could almost hear the excitement in Holly's words.

Holly also sent the gift of a framed portrait of Corey. My, but he had gotten big. His lengthening neck and thinning cheeks were evidence of his transition to boyhood from toddlerhood. He still looked an awful lot like Blake Dermot. He had only one dimple, in his right cheek. Though it appeared Holly had done her best to smooth down his white shock of hair, cowlicks stood at odds with the combed strands during picture time.

The new babe would surely be just as handsome. Holly went to a private clinic run by midwives out of an old mansion, where deliveries were performed. Holly's midwife had never seen the need for an ultrasound in the case of Holly's pregnancy, so the gender of the little one remained a mystery to them all. But Mrs. Jones had it in her mind it would be another boy.

Holly had taken care to mention that she used an alias at the clinic. They had never required an ID, nor had they delved into questions that might have given Holly away. Since the custody trial, Sissy had only taken two trips to her daughter; and both times she'd visited Mrs. Jones after, it had been on-foot and she'd arrived at the back door in case she was under surveillance.

Mrs. Jones didn't understand all the fuss, really, because it appeared as if Blake Dermot had finally moved on. Okanogan was a small town and a friend of a friend had told her daughter that Minerva Jenkins, the hairdresser behind the Pharmacy on Main Street, had taken up with Blake shortly before the holidays. In fact, their engagement announcement had hit the paper just last week, after New Year's, in anticipation of a March wedding. If Mrs. Jones hadn't been so completely disgusted by now by Blake's face, she might have had to admit they were a rather attractive couple—he craggy, yet powerful; and she, polished and petite.

If Blake was remarrying, surely he had moved past his continual hunt for Holly. But then, as Mrs. Jones remembered from her own separation so long ago from her children, it is nearly impossible to set aside one's desire for a child. Holly still had Blake's child. That was the bottom line and that still made him dangerous.

Mrs. Jones burned Holly's Christmas card and letter and gave the framed picture an obscure position on her shelf—just in case.

She decided to stretch and walk around a bit before sitting with her tea. She had been knitting most of the morning. After tea, she'd give a call to Kelly to see if she'd drive her to the Superstore for more yarn in the morning.

Too bad it was January. She'd have enjoyed a brisk walk right about then, but ice on the sidewalk below her house prohibited such a jaunt. She wouldn't ever want to burden her children with a crippled, broken-up old mother. That meant no walks outside in inclement weather, no nightgowns or robes with floor-length hems, and no wet floors.

So she puttered about lovingly dusting her belongings instead. She accidentally knocked over the vase of flowers on her kitchen table. As she rushed to find a cloth to clean it up, she became unexpectedly breathless. She leaned over to pick up the flowers and water and felt a foreign and unwelcome arc of pain through her chest and left arm.

Vision blurred and brow sweaty, Mrs. Jones remained on her hands and knees and made her way to her coffee table, where her cordless phone rested. By now, the pain shot up her neck and through her left fingertips. Something squeezed her chest like a vise. She grabbed the phone and lay on her back while she dialed the numbers she knew by heart. Good sense told her to call 9-1-1, but instead she automatically dialed her daughter's number.

"Hello?" Kelly's voice rang out like a lighthouse beacon on a stormy night.

"Kelly…"

"Mother? Mother, are you all right? Mum?"

"I'm…something's not…right…it…hurts…"

"Mum, did you call 9-1-1?" Kelly asked calmly, and Mrs. Jones just had to smile. That was her girl, ever-ready in crisis. She'd know what to do.

"No…just…you."

"Mum, I'm on my way over. You're only five minutes away, so I'll be right there. When I hang up, I'm dialing emergency and I'm sure they'll be right behind me. Hang on, Mum. Hang on."

"I…love…you…"

Mrs. Jones could hear the tears in Kelly's voice when she replied, "I love you, too. Just hang on."

Then Kelly was gone.

The abruptness of her journey's end had taken her by surprise. Still, as the darkness cocooned her, Mrs. Jones felt tremendously at peace.

Kelly was on her way.

Mrs. Jones was on her way out.

Chapter Sixteen

Sissy

"I'm so sorry for your loss," Sissy offered to the slightly taller, younger version of Mrs. Jones who stood before her. The funeral had been beautifully simple. A picture of a striking twenty-something Mrs. Jones had presided over the sea of lilies and gladiolas at the front of the room. Her remains lay in ashes, encased in an urn below.

A consortium of gray-haired friends spoke fondly of their bridge playmate. Her fair sons and their wives, and her daughter spoke eloquently about the kind of mother she'd been.

Mrs. Jones had been as loving as she was fearless. The funeral home had been packed to the gills with people eager to say she had touched them too.

"Thank you for coming today. I know you and Mum weren't close until the last year or so, but she spoke fondly of you and your daughter," Kelly Jones replied graciously.

"She would have been here, you know?"

"Who? Holly? Isn't she expecting a baby anytime now?"

Sissy looked around quickly to make sure no one was listening. She lowered her voice. "She told you about Holly and the baby?"

"My mom and I shared just about everything," Kelly lowered her voice to match Sissy's. "I apologize. I forgot in the stress of everything that your daughter is in hiding."

"And her ex-husband has deep roots here. There

are ears everywhere, if you get my drift."

"Speaking of that, my mother had some pictures your daughter sent framed on her bookshelf. Perhaps you might want them, since none of us would lay claim to them. They're hardly family artifacts."

"Has anyone else seen these pictures?" Sissy asked in alarm. She didn't know Holly had been so careless as to send updated photos of herself and her son.

"The only people who've been in the house are us kids and the emergency personnel who came on the afternoon of her heart attack," Kelly replied matter-of-factly, though Sissy could tell thoughts of that afternoon still haunted poor Kelly.

"Were there any police officers?" Sissy quizzed.

"There were a few, but, to be truthful, I was in a daze after I got to the house and found out I was too late. I sat with her until the coroner arrived and held her hand until it went cold." Tears slid gracefully down Kelly's cheeks.

"I'm so sorry to bring that pain up again, Kelly. Mrs. Jones would chastise me something fierce for asking about that day."

"No. It's okay. I've had trouble thinking about anything else since."

Sissy patted her shoulder reassuringly. She guessed Kelly Jones to be about her age. Under other circumstances, they might have become friends.

"Can I come by and get those pictures later?" Sissy asked.

"We'll be clearing out the place tomorrow, giving the basic things away to charity: her clothes, dishes, pots and pans, and such. Then we divide the heirlooms. My brothers won't be a problem, but I'm not too sure about the wives."

Sissy laughed. "Isn't that always the case? Good luck. I'll drop by about noon, if that works for you."

Kelly smiled too. "Thanks, Sissy. For being here."

"I wouldn't have missed it. Your mom was intrepid. She would have haunted me if I was a no show."

~~~~~~~~~~

The next day dawned and stayed the same misty gray until noon. Looming clouds threatened snow, but only a few flakes flew here and there. Sissy pulled up in front of Mrs. Jones' house. The low-slung houses looked even shabbier in the gloom. She shivered as she pulled her raspberry parka tighter.

She knocked on the door and hoped they could hear her through the mayhem on the other side.

"Sissy!" Kelly threw open the door and exclaimed. "You sure look like a warning flare on a dank day! Is it noon already?"

Sissy peered around Kelly and saw the household abuzz with her brothers, their wives, and her nephews and nieces. The space teemed with boxes, plastic bins, and newspapers. Kids bickered with kids while the adults did no less squabbling. No wonder Kelly had such a flush in her cheeks. Stress oozed from the place.

"I won't take up too much of your time," Sissy reassured Kelly. "If you have those pictures handy, I'll be on my way; and we can visit about your mom some other time."

"I'd like that," Kelly replied warmly and rolled her eyes toward her family. "Let me get them for you. You know, we also found the cutest little hat and booties among Mum's knitting. I'll bet she intended those for the baby."

Kelly retreated to the set of shelves by the door. She grabbed a tiny set of green knit booties and a cap, and a pewter four by six frame. Sissy could see from where she stood that the frame contained one of the professional pictures they'd had done of Corey before Christmas. Of course Holly would have wanted Mrs. Jones to see that one. Corey had looked so happy, fresh from visiting Santa Claus.

Kelly frowned and gestured to her brother. "Did you see the other picture of this little boy and his mom? It was a tiny gilded frame toward the back.

They were in some kind of park."

"Did anybody pack it?" Her brother asked. Each adult passed the information around. No, nobody had seen it.

Kelly came to the door. "I can't find the other picture. I'm sure it's lost in the transition and we'll find it when we unpack the boxes we're taking home with us."

"Nobody else has been in the house since the day Mrs. Jones died?" Sissy knew she was being redundant, but she wanted to be sure.

"No. Just us. I saw the picture too, the day before the funeral, which is why I thought to mention them to you yesterday."

"Oh. Well, it has to be here somewhere then, right?" Sissy reassured Kelly as she accepted the framed recent picture of Corey. At least Blake or his family couldn't get a hold of that. Knowing them, they'd post it immediately to a missing persons' website or social network.

"Mother has your phone number in her address book. I'll be sure to call when the photo turns up."

"I'd appreciate that. You've been so kind, Kelly, to offer me the pictures back in the first place. Thank you."

"Absolutely. It feels good to spread a little of Mother's treasure around."

"It'll bring closure at the very least."

Kelly shrugged her shoulder at her chaotic family in the background. "We could certainly all use a little of that," she quipped.

Sissy laughed, waved goodbye and returned to her car.

Time to borrow another car. She patted her Cruiser lovingly before she hopped in. She had to take another inconspicuous trip South in two weeks. The Cruiser was anything but ordinary.

Over the past year, she'd borrowed a few vehicles from her old friend Ross, who owned a used car lot in Brewster. With the baby's arrival so close, Sissy was going to go for several weeks this time—on a planned vacation from her job. She would have to do some smooth talking to get the car for longer than a weekend.

The problem of the picture temporarily forgotten, Sissy mulled over where she would get a fresh batch of cinnamon rolls for her friend Ross before she went to talk to him.

Chapter Seventeen

Blake

There were thousands of towns in the U.S. that had gazebos in their parks, which was why Blake had taken the risk and broken into Mrs. Jones house to steal the framed picture of Corey and Holly.

Actually, as it turned out, he hadn't needed to pick the lock or bust a window. Someone had left the rear bedroom window unlocked. Holly and he had used the same portal themselves a few times when they'd forgotten their keys.

He doubted that anybody in Mrs. Jones' family would miss the picture, since Holly wasn't a relative and the diminutive frame hardly bore noticing anyway.

Not that he hadn't noticed it immediately when he glanced around the day Mrs. Jones died—he would recognize Holly's strawberry blond corkscrews anywhere. They had grown longer. Corey's shock of white blond hair had also been a dead giveaway. They looked bumble-bee sized in the middle of a giant gazebo that stood about ten feet off the ground.

He thought about pocketing the photo as Mrs. Jones' was getting stiffer by the minute and the daughter grieved with as much dignity as she could muster at her side. He was afraid someone, either an EMT or another cop would notice, though, so he left it alone.

For all he knew, they'd visited the park on their way to somewhere else. Still, it was the first clue Blake had of Holly's location and he wasn't about to let it go by.

"Hey, Enforcer, whatcha got there?" It was Harvey Morris. Both of them had recently been promoted to detective and that officially made them partners.

"It's a picture of my ex and my son," Blake said honestly, handing it over.

"Whew-ee," Detective Morris exclaimed. "I'm not going to even *ask* how you got this one. I'm assuming it's not from before you two busted up."

"No, it's well after. Corey was only a year and a half when she took off with him. He's at least two here, I think. He looks bigger, at any rate."

"So you two never visited the Bandstand with him then?"

"Bandstand?" Blake perked up immediately. "You call that a bandstand? Why? I thought it was a gazebo."

"Ordinary parks have gazebos. If you're a native of Walla Walla, you know this one's special. We call it the 'Bandstand'. You can see all of Pioneer Park from up there."

"You're from *Walla Walla*? I always assumed you were from Idaho or Southeastern Oregon or some other hick place by your hayseed accent," Blake jabbed.

"Walla Walla *is* a hick place, smartass," Detective Morris shot back. "It's just a little bigger, is all."

"So you're saying to me, without a doubt, that this picture was taken in Walla Walla, Washington?"

"Oh, absolutely. I'd know the Bandstand even if they painted it fluorescent green and hung a Confederate flag on it. It's a bona fide landmark."

Blake laughed.

"They could be miles from there now, you know, Enforcer," Detective Morris reminded him in all seriousness.

"Of course I know that. It's been over a year since they left and it's been quite a while since that was taken. Corey is at least six months older than that now." He didn't let on that he'd seen the more recent picture of Corey too, but he'd left that one behind because it was more obvious and might be missed.

"Still, it's a lead, isn't it? You sure you want to pursue this one? I mean you've got Minerva and everything now. Rumor mill has it that you mighta knocked her up before the old nuptials, if you get my drift." Detective Morris smiled conspiratorially.

"You shouldn't listen to rumors, Harv," Blake chided, but there was no hiding his prideful blush. Yeah, he was going to be a dad again—again unplanned—but he and Minerva were over the moon about it. She was such a sparkplug, it would take a whole lot more than an unplanned pregnancy to upset her applecart. She was already researching nursery plans for the back of her beauty shop.

Between that, and her mother and *his* mother planning the event of the spring, Minerva and he were plenty busy, and, surprisingly, deliriously happy.

He hadn't told her about the picture. Because as much as she wanted him to find Corey, he knew it would hurt her to know he might have gotten closer to finding Holly too. That was the double-edged sword they lived with; because finding Corey meant finding his mother and Minerva would forever be overtly jealous of Holly.

She didn't need to be. He loved Minerva perhaps more deeply than he'd loved Holly because everything about this new relationship was openly honest. He'd actually told her about his last fight with Holly, when he accidentally broke her arm. Minerva scolded him for his bad behavior, told him it was his own fault then, that Holly had taken off, and warned him that if he ever laid a hand on *her* 'accidentally' or otherwise, she'd castrate him under the light of the moon and hang his jewels from her beauty shop mirror for all to see.

That was the kind of honesty he expected and would always get from his bride-to-be. There'd be no sneaking away with his child, no quiet suffering. She'd simply let him have it and he'd be done for. He respected the hell out of Minerva for that.

Holly might have had him by the heart, but Minerva, she had him by his manhood. That, to a guy, meant everything, or nearly anyway.

Detective Morris broke into his reverie. "Why don't you hop online and cross-reference Walla Walla with Holly Dermot?"

"She might be using her maiden name," Blake pointed out.

"So cross-reference Holly Dermot and Holly Reel with Walla Walla," Detective Morris rolled his eyes impatiently.

"I think I will," Blake answered and took a deep breath. "Here goes…"

Both of them watched Google do its magic, but the search didn't come up with any matches.

"You know you can do the same thing with law enforcement agencies down there, right?"

"If she hasn't been in any trouble, though, it might be hard to find a match-up."

"Let me try something." Detective Morris grabbed the keyboard and logged onto the state patrol website for licensing. "I'm just going to enter the name Reel and see what I find."

"There's Sissy," Blake pointed out as her name flashed up toward the bottom of the list.

"Well, well. It looks like Sissy bought a car last spring in Walla Walla, Washington. Now why in the world would she do that?"

"And look here," Blake added. "She registered the car under the name Susan Morgan. Holly has an older sister named Susan."

"Looks like the address, though, is the one Sissy uses for Bridgeport."

"Damn it." Blake pounded his fist on the desktop, making the keyboard jump.

"Well, hey, Enforcer. You have a town. You have two names. I'd say that's a start."

Blake nodded and ran his fingers through his short, spiky hair. "I'm a lot further than I was a week ago, even. I should be grateful. The whole thing has just been so frustrating."

"I get that, man, but if you can keep it cool now, your head will stay more level. You'll find your son and get to keep him. Lose that cool and the outcome might be a little different," Detective Morris warned.

"I hear you. I'll keep working on this. Thanks, man."

"Anytime. I'm happy to help out my ginormous partner and his pea brain," he teased as he grabbed his coffee mug from his desk and headed for the community pot.

Blake picked up the phone. Maybe this was premature, but he felt like he might add a few years to her life if he made this call.

"Hello?"

"Hey, Mom. I think I might have found her."

He could hear the tears as his mom choked out, "Don't you dare blow this one, Blake. You get my grandson back in my arms. I don't want that bitch to ever see it coming."

Chapter Eighteen

Holly

"I thought the focus here is on *natural* childbirth," Sissy spat at the midwife, who held up her hands in surrender.

"For the most part, we try to avoid any kind of monitoring of the fetus, but our proctors—the physicians who back us up in difficult births—want routine monitoring strips at least twice during the labor process."

"Yes, but Holly has been monitored repeatedly. More than twice. Try tripling that. She vomits every time you lay her down to take another 'strip', as you call it."

"Unfortunately, in Holly's case, her strip has been abnormal several times, so we're forced to do repeat monitoring."

Sissy examined the nurse midwife who happened to be on-call the evening Holly's water broke like the river Nile just as they'd arrived home with Chinese take-out. Two weeks early. The woman appeared professional enough with her burgundy scrubs, hair pulled back neatly into a bun with a matching scrunchy, and tortoise-shell glasses perched on the end of her nose; but it increasingly irritated Sissy that Holly was made to lie uncomfortably and be sick for the sake of 'monitoring'.

When was the baby going to make his appearance, for Chrissake?

"Her water broke hours ago. Shouldn't we be seeing a little progress by now? And what do you mean by an abnormal strip, anyway?"

"Mom, I think Karissa knows what she's doing. Maybe you should give her a break and let her do her job," Susan suggested with a nudge and a warning glance toward Holly. Sissy's worry and stress weren't helping her daughter to stay calm during what was turning out to be a nightmare labor and delivery.

"I'm going to be completely transparent with the three of you right now, because you'll find out soon enough anyway: Holly's baby has failed the last three strips because of 'decelerations'. What this means is that every time Holly's uterus contracts, the baby's heart rate drops dramatically. When the contraction ceases, the heart rate comes back up. This means, usually, that either the baby is lying on the umbilical cord, that the cord is wrapped tightly around the neck, or that the cord is prolapsed, which means it's between the baby's head and the birth canal."

"Holy crap," Sissy breathed, "So he's choking off his blood supply somehow…"

"Sshhh," Susan chastised her.

Holly pursed her lips and tried hard to breathe through the next contraction, which meant ignoring the undercurrent of panic.

"Any of these scenarios can be difficult in the home birthing situation which is what we try to simulate as much as possible here at the clinic. We are going to do one more strip right now with Holly in a different position on the bed. If the results are the same, she'll be transferred via ambulance to the county hospital to be delivered there."

"Take me now," she whispered as her contraction began to lighten up.

"What was that, honey?" Susan asked, brushing Holly's hair back from her forehead.

"I said, take me NOW."

"I'm rather hoping that won't be necessary," Karissa argued. "The baby might have shifted when you got up to go to the bathroom. Let's put you on the monitor on your left side for twenty minutes…"

"Bullshit." Holly's face turned the crimson of Karissa's scrubs. She rarely swore and especially not in front of Sissy, who would have promptly taken a bar of soap to her mug for such language when she was a kid. "Something is really wrong. I can feel it. I've had nurse's training and I've already had another child. It's not like this is my first time. I'm not lying here for another twenty minutes to find out what I already know. Get me to a real hospital, will you? Now?"

"I don't think you should be so hasty…" Karissa tried to argue.

"Holly is anything but hasty," Sissy sputtered. "She is intelligent and her instincts have always been spot-on, except when she married her ex-husband—"

"Mom—" Susan interrupted.

"Oh, right. That's irrelevant. I know. The thing is: You should believe my daughter here, er, Karissa. If you don't, then believe *me*. I haven't heard my girl say the word 'bullshit' since the night before her wedding when I gave her some cockamamie excuse for not showing up. She means business."

Karissa turned and began to put the elastic straps around Holly despite their requests.

"Karissa, may I please speak with you outside?" Susan requested reasonably, since it didn't appear the woman was inclined to believe the outrageously disheveled redhead or the emotional mom-to-be.

When the two of them returned, Karissa walked stiffly over to Holly and removed the straps. "I've had my nurse put in a call for ambulance transport to the hospital. They should be here in five to ten minutes. I'm sorry you couldn't have had a more fulfilling natural birth here at Hannah House."

Holly grabbed Karissa's wrist in earnest, looked her in the eyes, and said, "Thank you."

"Yes, well, we're all just doing our best…" Karissa replied hotly.

When she left the room to complete her paperwork, Holly reached for Susan. "Whoa, she's pissed. What did you say to her to change her mind?"

"I just made her see reason—I told her I had an expensive-assed attorney on speed-dial if she ignored your gut and mucked up the delivery of my precious niece or nephew. I think she saw at that point that time was of the essence."

Holly laughed and winced as the vise tightened again around her middle.

"Now why didn't I think of that?" Sissy deadpanned as she gripped Holly's other hand and encouraged her to breathe.

"We have one more problem," Holly choked out as she felt the pain lessen again.

"What's that?" Susan and Sissy asked in unison.

"County's going to require an ID."

"They are still legally obligated to protect your privacy," Susan argued.

"Still, it's the first time Holly has had to use real documentation since the divorce hearings," Sissy replied nervously.

"She'll have to anyway when and if she enrolls Corey in preschool."

"I'm going to have to face the fact that I either can't go on being me in any legal sense, or that I'm going to be caught eventually," Holly reasoned.

"I might have a guy who can get fake ID's for the two of you, but he'll need a month or two," Sissy offered.

"That won't do me any good tonight."

"This is the point at which we all need to be thankful that it's a hospital you're giving the ID to. They can't release anything to police agencies or the media without your consent," Susan reassured Holly.

Two medics entered the room and lifted Holly handily onto a stretcher for transport. They took a fat manila envelope with Holly's records and copies of the 'strips' and before Sissy and Susan could even step outside, the ambulance was on its way to the hospital with Holly.

Susan and Sissy had stayed level-headed until now,

but anguish lightened their steps to Susan's Honda as they rushed to catch up and find out whether little baby Reel was going to be okay.

~~~~~~~~~~

"Actually, you can list his last name however you want," the delivery nurse, Bonnie, offered helpfully. "I see here that your last name is Dermot. Am I to assume that you and the father aren't together?"

"That's a pretty good assumption, yes," Holly answered. She was still fuzzy around the edges from the dose of anesthesia they'd given her before rushing her to an emergency c-section. There had been no time for an epidural.

The worst of the three scenarios the midwife had presented—cord prolapse—had been the case. There was no way for Holly to have a natural delivery once the hospital OB/GYN figured that out. Plus, by the time the information was gleaned—roughly ten minutes after she'd arrived at the hospital—Holly had nearly fully dilated and the baby's heart rate had dropped dangerously low and stayed that way.

As she cradled her six pound baby boy, Holly thanked God that she, her mom, and sister had been so insistent on her transfer. Otherwise, Tristan Sidney Reel might never have seen the big wide world that he seemed to want to squall at constantly.

"Oh dear, he is kind of fussy, isn't he? Can I take him while you sign these papers for me? Maybe he'll find me interesting enough to ponder, instead of giving you the what- and where-for."

Holly smiled a mellow smile at Bonnie and handed over Tristan for the time being. He'd settle down after she got paperwork out of the way and concentrated on nursing him.

"Weren't your mom and sister here right after you came back from the OR?" Bonnie asked.

"Yes, but it's nearly three in the morning. I know they're exhausted. I insisted they at least go for a coffee in the cafeteria. I'm in good hands, I think."

"You bet you are. Now, if you have any questions about those forms, you be sure to ask."

"I'm having a little trouble concentrating," Holly admitted.

"That's the drugs talking. You're sure to be extra tired for a few days. Such a bummer when you have an infant to deal with."

"And a three-year-old," Holly added, as she shuffled through the documents: consent for vaccination, eye drops, birth certificate papers…what else?

"Oh really? You have another little guy too? Did you have an uneventful delivery with him?"

"Extremely uneventful. This one was a shocker." Not surprising though, Holly thought, when everything in her life had held a higher level of difficulty for the last year and a half.

"What's Tristan's brother's name?"

"Corey."

"Who has him if your mom and sister are here?"

"Susan has a coworker, Maggie, who's in her fifties and opted never to have children. She's everybody's aunt, though, and makes a super babysitter. I swear that woman owns more toys than we do."

Bonnie laughed. "Crazy, isn't it? I'm forty and I've never had kids either, but I own every Beanie Baby ever made."

"I can't believe you haven't had kids! You're such an awesome delivery nurse, so at ease with patients and you explain everything so thoroughly. I would've thought you'd pushed out five yourself!"

"Thank you for the compliment," Bonnie responded warmly. "I guess one doesn't need experience to feel compassion."

"And to really know one's job," Holly added. "I went through RN school. I was a hair's breadth from graduating when I had Corey."

"You should finish what you started now that you've had this little one." She gestured to Tristan, who had finally fallen mercifully asleep.

"I might, but I may never have your touch," Holly laughed.

"Are you finished with all of that?" Bonnie asked as she tucked Tristan into his bassinet. "I imagine that Tristan isn't the only one who's pooped. You should get some rest before he wakes up and wants to eat."

"I am definitely ready to shut my eyes. They keep rolling back in my head."

This time Bonnie laughed. "I have that effect on people—babies and mommies."

Holly reached for the string on her overhead light and shut it off, leaving just the ambient light from the hallway. "Good night, Bonnie. Thanks for everything."

"My shift ends at seven. I probably won't see you before then if you and Tristan get the kind of rest you need. If not, Holly, it's been a pleasure. Remember what I said. You can't forget your dream of being a nurse. I'd bet you could do it better than most. You have a knack for people, I can tell."

Holly snorted quietly. "That would be my mother. She's the people person. I'm sort of quiet and shy."

"Don't you dare," Bonnie warned. "Whatever you've ever told yourself about your people skills, I can tell you that you're quite wrong. There's something about you that's not shyness. It's quiet reassurance. It's calm. Your presence is soothing. You'll make a fantastic nurse someday."

Holly felt herself tearing up. Hormones. "Thank you, Bonnie. Yes. Someday…"

"Good night, Holly."

Holly waved to her idol nurse as she walked out the door into the dimly lit hallway.

"Someday," she repeated as sleep finally came.

~~~~~~~~~~

A fierce snowstorm blew in the next morning. The portal-type windows in the mother/baby unit revealed horizontal streams of enormous snowflakes, as if God had opened the toll bridge and let all the cars through at once. Holly hardly dared to look outside, besides she was just a little too sore to venture out of bed just yet.

"That's some snowstorm," Sissy remarked. "The news says we got four inches overnight and at least a foot more is expected."

"It's a good thing they put a fold-out sofa in here for family members, because your relatives just happen to be snowed in," Susan quipped.

"What about Corey?" Holly asked sleepily.

"I've already talked to Maggie. Corey's missing us, but her pooches are keeping him occupied. She's okay with keeping him at least for today. Our boss doesn't have much for us to do anyway since everyone's holed up for weather."

"I can't wait to introduce Corey to his little brother," Sissy said. "You can hardly tell the two of them are brothers. At least I think so. Corey's got such bold bone structure and huge brown eyes…"

"…And he was bald as a bad tire when he came out," Holly added.

"Well I didn't see him then," Sissy jabbed, earning herself a dramatic eye roll from Susan. "Tristan, though, is so fair and fine-boned. He looks like a porcelain doll."

"Have you looked under his cap yet?" Susan asked.

"Can I?" Sissy asked and moved to Holly's bedside where Tristan rested in her arms.

"Of course," Holly insisted.

"Why his hair is almost a reddish-blond, isn't it? And curly."

"Like his mommy," Susan commented.

"That's not his most distinguishing trait, though, is it?" Sissy finally acknowledged what all of them had avoided talking about.

"There is the birthmark, yes." Holly admitted.

"Do you think it'll stick around as he grows?" Susan asked, her concern obvious.

The three of him examined him again. Yep, there it was, a taupe mark on his left cheek shaped like the African continent and about the size of a dime.

"Will it get darker?" Sissy asked.

"Maybe it's his Russian blood," Susan suggested. "Russians have a lot of moles, don't they?"

"Geez, Susan, why don't you just throw that one out there?" Holly asked, annoyed now. "Tristan has a beautiful face and, frankly, I think his birthmark just makes him more unique and gorgeous."

"Right," Sissy affirmed. "It's a beauty mark. Not everybody gets one of those from the get-go."

Tristan opened an eye tentatively to find his mom, grandma, and aunt staring intently at him. As if he'd heard their contemplation, he let loose a howl and proceeded to berate them for it.

"Well his lungs are perfect, that's for sure," Sissy laughed.

"*He's* perfect," Holly insisted as she readied her gown to nurse her son for the third time in an hour.

"That he is," Susan agreed.

"He's a miracle, just like his brother, and we're going to keep you all safe, no matter what," Sissy declared as they watched him dig in greedily.

Holly sighed with contentment, secure in her cozy hospital room with her new son and the two women who had come to mean so much to her. What could possibly be any safer?

Chapter Nineteen

Sissy

Sissy plopped a bowl of congealed oatmeal onto her tray and reached for two pats of butter and a handful of sugar packets.

Susan clucked her tongue in disapproval as she selected a non-fat yogurt and a banana.

"Yeah, yeah, Miss I-Eat-Only-Health-Food. Lucky for them they don't have eggs and bacon. I'd be all over that," Sissy declared.

"Mother, it is truly due to your enormous energy and your tobacco pipe that you stay so stinking skinny. I, however, would not want to guess about the insides of your arteries."

"Given that my blood is two-thirds vinegar and I'm too damn mean to ever die, I'd hazard a guess that the ol' pipes are pretty clean."

Susan laughed. "You sound like that old codger on *Grizzly Adams.* What was his name again?"

"Wasn't it Jack? Or was that the name of his ass?"

"I don't remember his ass having a name," Susan quipped. They scooped up their trays and headed for the cashier.

They took a window table and contemplated the continuing storm.

"Did the doc say when he expects Holly to go home?" Sissy asked as she stirred butter and sugar into the gray matter.

Susan cracked open her fresh banana and talked around a healthy-sized bite. "If all goes well, she can go home tomorrow afternoon. Normally, they try to keep C-Section patients at least three days. Hers was particularly hairy, so that's the best-case scenario."

"We're going to have to brave this weather to go get Corey. Besides, I'm starting to smell like Sly Stallone's armpit."

"Oh, I don't know, Mom. I always thought Rocky's armpit would smell sexy—male sweat and body odor—you just plain reek."

Sissy giggled. "Yeah, well your hair looks like you massaged it with shortening."

Susan snorted. "We're pretty dedicated broads, aren't we, sticking around like this? It's not like the house is that far away."

"It would take at least a half-hour to get there in this weather. Besides, Holly has needed us. That Tristan is a handful already!"

Susan chewed thoughtfully. "He's adorable, though. I missed all that snuggly, new-babyness with Corey. I could stare at Tristan sleeping for hours. His eyelashes might be blond, but they're at least a half-inch long. Plus, he works his lips like he's eating even when he's asleep!"

Sissy examined her older daughter's face. There was fatigue there, but something else too. Susan had grown incredibly close to Corey and she was already gaga over the new guy too. "You know, kiddo, it's not too late for you to have some little ones of your own someday."

"You mean you don't want me to continue to live vicariously through my little sister. You forget—I've never thought signing on for the single mom gig was very smart."

"So go meet Mr. Right. Have a family. You have the space for it."

"But not the desire," Susan insisted. "Where's this coming from, Mom? You know I was perfectly content before Corey and Holly came to live with me. I'm a career woman. Plus, now I have a growing family that includes my sister and my nephews. Why are you pushing this?"

"They could be gone tomorrow," Sissy offered quietly, admitting what neither of them were prepared to discuss.

"As in, Blake finding them, locking Holly up, swiping Tristan to put him in a foster home, arresting the two of us for aiding and abetting, and taking Corey to live with the rest of the spoiled Dermot clan?" Susan asked ironically, but she could scarcely conceal the hysterical edge to her question.

"As in, I'd run him over with a stolen semi-truck before I'd let him get that close to my little girl again. I can't let him get that close, Sus. If this name thing with the hospital becomes an issue, we're going to have to hide them. They can't stay here in Walla Walla to hide."

"She can't run with them right now. Holly just had surgery. She has a newborn. Besides, Corey would be as devastated to be taken away as I would be to see him go," Susan persisted.

"Nothing could be as devastating as having his father blow this whole thing to smithereens…"

The conversation was interrupted by a blaring riff from 'Stairway to Heaven'.

Sissy rolled her eyes skyward. "God help me, I hate those things."

Susan scrambled to dig the phone from her purse. "This is Susan. Oh, hi, Gertrude. Say, thanks for running by to put the newpapers inside for me. They would have been mush by now with the snow… What's that?"

'It's my neighbor,' Susan mouthed at her mom who nodded and busied herself with emptying their trays.

"Yes, yes, she's had the baby. His name's Tristan. He's beautiful… Yep, like his momma… No, I don't think you'll be able to look him up online," she paused and glanced up at her mom, "What do you mean? Does this hospital do that?"

Sissy tuned back into the conversation, as she instantly sensed Susan's distress.

"So you're saying that the hospital website posts

pictures online of the latest newborns? Don't they have to have some kind of permission to post people's private baby pictures…? Right, that makes sense. Maybe they don't list the parents' names either… Oh, no. No particular reason. I just had no idea there was such a thing… Say, thanks again, Gertrude. We'll be back this evening or tomorrow morning. Bye, now."

Sissy's eyes narrowed. "What the hell was that?"

"*That* was my neighbor lady informing me that this hospital posts daily lists and photographs of its newborns."

"Do they put the parents' names on there too?" Sissy asked, fully alarmed now.

"Gertrude's granddaughter had her baby here about a year ago. They do list the parents' and newborns' names, but only with written authorization from the parents."

"Thank goodness, then. Holly would never have signed any such thing."

"Still, I think we should check."

"Where will we find a computer…?"

"I have a smartphone, Mom. I don't need a computer. Give me a minute."

Susan spent a few minutes navigating the Web. Sissy's heart dropped to her toes when Susan's face registered what they already knew.

"He's there, isn't he?" Sissy asked, as tears popped into her eyes.

"Worse. He's there and so is Holly's full name and his."

"It's a mistake, that's all. We can get that taken down. Come on. Let's hurry over to administration."

"What if it's too late, Mom? What if he's already seen it?"

"Well, it just can't be, can it? It just can't be," Sissy contended as they hustled from the cafeteria.

~~~~~~~~~~

"Corey needs to meet his baby brother," Holly

insisted, exasperated that her mother and sister
still hadn't left for home. They at least needed to
shower and change before they picked up Corey. She
imagined the childless Maggie's patience wearing thin
by now. Her oldest boy was inquisitive and energetic,
enough of a handful for Holly—let alone a near-
stranger.

Sissy flitted about the room like a swallow stuck
in a church vestibule. Her mom was nervous about
something. That much was obvious.

Susan, on the other hand, was the epitome of calm,
as she pretended to study the evening paper.

What were they up to?

Holly knew the plan: As of that afternoon, Mom
and Susan were to have left to shower and retrieve
Corey so he could have supper with his mom and
Tristan; then they were all to return home for the night
and pick up Holly and Tristan after their discharge the
following day.

It neared dinner time and Holly's mom and sister
hadn't budged. The crappy weather hardly warranted
any huge delay in the plan.

"So you should be going now, right?" Holly kept
on. She shifted Tristan to her other arm as he stirred
in his sleep. "We're doing just fine here, as you can
see. I've even taken several walks with Tristan in his
bassinet this afternoon. The nurses have insisted that
the more often I get mobile, the sooner I can breeze
out of here."

"I don't know why you're in such a hurry," Sissy
argued. "These guys feed you regularly, bathe your
baby, change his diapers. Why it's twenty-four-seven
pampering around here!"

"I want to start doing some of that for myself.
I'm incredibly bored right now. At least at Susan's,
nobody swoops in and rescues me from my fussy
baby. It's pretty hard to get to know him when I can't
respond to his needs on my own," Holly complained.

Neither her mother nor her sister responded to her
grievance, so she continued. "Are you going to leave

already? The snowstorm let up hours ago."

Nobody moved. Holly slapped the bed in frustration with her free hand. Tristan startled and twisted his face into a blistering scowl before he let loose a shriek.

"That was uncalled for," Susan remarked blandly as she reached for her nephew.

Holly held firmly to her baby. "Enough. You two are stalling and I want to know why, pronto."

"The road crews are still clearing the snow from earlier today. Honestly, Holly, is this hormonal, your newfound impatience? You've always been so tolerant," Susan chastised.

"Pardon me, but my tolerance escaped me the day my ex-husband threw me into a bedside table," Holly replied, furious.

Susan raised her eyebrows at the assertive tone in her sister's voice. The Reel women all had a bit of the devil in them, Holly included.

Sissy stopped her pacing long enough to rummage through her purse. Holly could see her grasp her tobacco pipe and lighter. If Sissy was going for a smoke in this weather, in the middle of this sort of a confrontation, something was most definitely up.

"Oh no you don't," Holly swung her legs over the side of the bed, ready to bodily block her mother from leaving the room. She winced at the sudden movement as her abdominal staples twisted and pulled.

Susan hissed, "Damn it, Mother. Can you not just stay still for a few minutes? Holly's no idiot. She knows something is up."

"And you, Mom, are not exactly subtle," Holly added.

"We can't get Corey yet," Sissy offered.

"Because…" Holly waited for Sissy's reply.

"He's safe with Maggie. She's not in any hurry to give him back, if that's what you're worried about."

"And why wouldn't he be safe here with us?"

Susan and Sissy's eyes met as Holly rose to her

feet to confront them both. She put Tristan, who'd calmed down as she rubbed his cheek, gently into his bassinet.

"Why isn't Corey safe with us?" Holly asked again through clenched teeth.

Before her mother or sister could reply, the three of them heard a muffled commotion from the nurse's station. Bonnie, the venerable obstetric nurse, clearly sounded off, "I don't care who you are, or what kind of uniform you wear, you should never have made it past admitting, to this floor."

The raised voice that replied could not have been more familiar to Holly's ears if she'd heard it just yesterday. "You are interfering with a legal investigation. I could arrest you right here…"

"Then arrest me," Bonnie argued. "You will not crack open a single one of these charts on my watch. Not without a warrant or a patient release form."

"Blake…" Holly croaked out. Susan saw Holly falter and caught her arm before she crashed to the floor.

Sissy blanched. Knowing that her next move could be critical to her daughter's safety, Sissy pushed the door shut very slowly and put her back against it. She looked helplessly at her two beloved daughters— brave women she knew she would put her life on the line for. "Lord, have mercy. What are we going to do now?"

Fat tears slid gracefully from Holly's eyes as they awaited an answer.

Chapter Twenty

Blake

The steel sky deepened to pewter as Detective Blake Dermot and his partner, Detective Harvey Morris, stood on opposite sides of the cruiser and drank lukewarm coffee from the dredges of their thermos.

"We've been here three days, Enforcer. I hardly think staying here on the county's dime can be further justified."

"This isn't personal," Blake reiterated. "A fugitive is hiding here with a kidnapped and missing child."

"That this fugitive is your ex-wife and the child is yours bears nothing on your determination to stay here?" Deputy Morris quizzed.

Blake grimaced as he choked down a mouthful of coffee. "I'm close, Harv. I can taste it."

"What you are tasting is rancid coffee."

"That's not funny," Blake remained serious. "That nurse was hiding something from me. I know she was."

"That was two days ago, Blake. She said Holly was already discharged, right?"

"It would have been an awfully fast recovery if she was. She'd only had the baby the day before according to the website."

"That's the way of hospitals nowadays. So long as you can swallow and get up to pee, they'll let just about anybody go home. Childbirth isn't any different."

"She had Corey so easily, I'd bet this guy shot right

out too." Blake shook his head.

He still couldn't quite process how Holly could have a *baby* already. The ink was hardly dry on their divorce. Never mind that he, himself, had moved onto similar circumstances. He'd never thought of Holly as promiscuous, but the term 'slut' leapt to mind anyway.

For several weeks, his daily habit had been to cross reference Holly's name and maiden name to Walla Walla. When the hit showed up—for county hospital baby announcements—Blake was justifiably stunned. Jealousy welled up like a crimson handprint after a roundhouse slap, occurring just as quickly and stinging just as much.

Until that moment, Blake had no idea Holly still had that kind of hold on him. It shouldn't have mattered that she'd moved on with her life. He had Minerva. He had a wedding and a baby on the way. He had domestic bliss and a promotion. As a matter of fact, talk around the department had been about Sheriff Paul's retirement in a few years, and he was shocked to find that most people considered him a viable successor for the position.

Blake had strong community ties, a good family name, respectability, physical prowess, and the approval of the Sheriff himself. He had every reason to be happy.

He tried to tell himself that he couldn't possibly move on from Holly because of Corey—his little boy needed a father and to grow up in a town where his name would matter, where his status would always be assured. Blake increasingly realized that Corey's well-being was just an excuse. He hardly knew the boy—when they left, he was just a baby and a fussy mama's boy, at that.

Finding Corey meant finding Holly; and until he'd spotted her name alongside her brand new baby boy's on the Walla Walla County Hospital website, Blake hadn't known that this mattered.

Now he knew that it mattered a whole lot.

"So what do we have here?" Harvey Morris asked, interrupting Blake's reverie. "She's discharged from the hospital, so you're not going to find her there…"

"…and we know where the sister lives, but we've surveilled the residence for most of the past two days and nobody has returned home," Blake added, sounding as frustrated as he felt.

"The neighbor lady talked to the sister two days ago, but hasn't heard from her since. She knows your ex fairly well, sounds like, but has no idea where else she would go with the new baby and Corey."

"I still think we could get a search warrant for the house if we leaned on Judge Henry some more," Blake added.

"Do you really think we'd find anything there? It's obviously unoccupied."

"We could find out where the sister works. There are three Susan Morgans in town, but unless one of the employers is lying to us, none of them works at the places we've interviewed," Blake replied.

"Right. If we were to go into the house, we could find a paystub, which could possibly lead us back to the liar, who would possibly stonewall us from finding out anything further."

"Why is everyone so damned protective of these Reel women, anyway?" Blake spat in frustration.

"Maybe the Reels are careful who they're friends with."

"You'd think their associates would at least cooperate with the law," Blake reasoned.

"Enforcer, you need to work on your demeanor. Unless someone's from Okanogan County and he knows what a sweet, fuzzy teddy bear Blake Dermot can be, all a guy sees when he walks into the room is a big-ass, madder-and-meaner-than-stink grizzly bear in a cop's uniform." Detective Morris finally did the wise thing and dumped out the last half of his thermos cup for emphasis.

Blake shifted and peered at the sliver of moon outlined by the branch of a dormant elm. His size had never been his friend. In fact, his brute strength had shattered his marriage.

"It's not like I can just be smaller." His admission was a hair's breadth above a whisper. "I am what I am, Harv."

"You think size is what this is about? You are as dumb as you are tall." Harvey Morris put his hands on his hips and looked frankly in the waning light at his partner. "Word has it that you might be favored to be the next sheriff someday. I've been around the department way longer than you, but you don't see anybody tapping me for the position, do you?"

Blake shook his head.

"I'm a foreigner there because I grew up in a different town. Sure, I'm well-liked, but I don't have the presence you have, Blake. I don't have the name. I don't have the stature, but I'm damned good at my job because I so easily fly under the radar. I think. I plot. I research. No one ever sees it coming when I come after them.

"Therefore, I feel qualified to give you this advice: You need to develop some finesse. Stand less behind the law and your uniform. Shoot, stop wearing a uniform. You don't need one to be a detective. Start wearing flannels and khakis like a small-town sheriff would do. Flash your badge only when you truly need to. Earn respect and admiration from people through your carriage, your dignity, not your name. Your reputation and longevity as a Sheriff is going to rely on people thinking you're a *good man,* not on toughness, intimidation, or anything else.

"The closest you came to finding Holly and Corey was when you approached the nurse who took care of her. I watched that whole thing transpire, Enforcer, and you were all about bluster, your rights, and the law, and your power to make her tell you. Step back and look at this with me now: What do you think would have happened if you had gone to her quietly at the nurse's station and sat down eye to eye with her, no uniform or badge, and explained who you were and that you've been missing your wife and child for more than a year? Maybe you nearly shed a tear or two? You explained that you meant them no harm but that you just want to be reunited, for the good of your family, for the good of your child? Now you and she are friends, right, allies in putting your family back together? Unless she's got a hate on of some kind for men, you're in like Flynn. Suppose after all that explaining, then you pulled out your legal documentation and explained that her cooperation wasn't required by law, but that you would sure appreciate it if she could help you out? What would have happened then?"

Blake rested his arms on the top of the squad car and laid his enormous head on them. Detective Morris was right. He'd blown his shot again—with the nurse, with the neighbor, with Susan's employers. In fact, his attitude problem extended all the way back to his dealings with Mrs. Jones. Finding Holly was not about the law when it boiled down to needing people's cooperation—it was about whose side they would take. Nobody would take his side with the way he'd been behaving.

"I can't leave it like this, Harvey. This is the best lead I've had. Holly is somewhere here in your hometown. Help me out, will you?"

"I've exhausted my contacts. I've watched you obliterate yours. Unless we stake out Susan Morgan's place for the next week or so, I'm not seeing progress anytime soon. We could have the local cops do surveillance there just as easily."

"So let's do that," Blake insisted. "Let's stick it out."

"What about Minerva? What about the wedding plans? What about the strict budget we work within? Are you going to start funding this investigation out of your own pocket, because you know the Sheriff isn't going to sign off on this trip past today? He gave us three days."

Blake scowled. "I made a promise. I promised I would see this through."

"A promise to who?"

"To myself, to my family," To my mom, he thought, silently. She wouldn't understand when he returned to town without a child to place in her arms.

"How much money do you have?" Harvey asked, pulling out his wallet and opening the car door to illuminate its contents. He was divorced. Beyond paying child support once a month for his teenage sons, his money was pretty much his own.

Blake flattened his paws on the hood of the cruiser. "I can't let you do that, Harv. Put your money away. Minerva would kill me if I cracked open my wallet to stay here longer. Fact is, you're right. Until we get another lead, this case is cold."

"At least with local law enforcement on the case, the Reel women won't be able to hide long. Plus, Sissy got fingered by the neighbor as abetting her daughter. We can nab her for questioning when she returns home to Okanogan County. You use some of this finesse I'm talking about, Enforcer, and you'll find them. Guaranteed."

"Who knows? If I'm to believe you and your methods, they might just fall right out of the sky onto my lap, right?" Blake teased. "Seriously, though, Harv, I think you might be right. I appreciate the advice."

"No problem. Now let's go home. I've seen enough of this flat, farmland sinkhole to last me another decade."

Blake chuckled. "Well you sure as hell aren't Dorothy in ruby slippers. 'There's no place like home; there's no place like home…'"

"Shut up, Enforcer."

"Sure thing," Blake agreed, but he still tapped his heels together three times, to the eye-rolling exasperation of his partner, before he took his place in the driver's seat of the county cruiser.

Chapter Twenty-one

Sissy

Sissy couldn't put her daughters, her grandson, and his new baby brother on any kind of airplane—a stunt like that could be traced—but she sure as hell could drive them as fast and as furiously away from Blake Dermot as her borrowed Chevy truck would allow.

Thank goodness for Bonnie, the angel from heaven posing as a nurse, who had bodily kept Blake from barging into any of the hospital rooms on her ward. Thank goodness for security who had seen to it that Blake and his fellow cop were sent packing when Bonnie reported to administration that the police officers had violated important privacy rules. Thank goodness for Susan's neighbor—nosey busy-body that she was—that she had known very well where Corey was staying, but hadn't revealed that information to Blake. Thank goodness for Maggie, who upon viewing the very pale Holly and fussy Tristan, had immediately offered the bedraggled fugitives a place to stay for the night while they laid out their plans, no questions asked.

Thank goodness for Ross, who understood that his dealer plates would be crossing a few state lines, but only because his dear friend Sissy would reward him copiously—and he wasn't talking cinnamon rolls—as soon as she returned to town. Plus, Susan had already mailed him a money order for the down payment on the truck, so long as he agreed not to try and transfer ownership until a few weeks after Sissy's return.

Thank goodness for Montana, where wide open spaces attracted the likes of Stanley P. Diddredge, ex-con, ex-boyfriend (with the hottest pockets this side of the Rockies) of Sissy, and master counterfeiter. At one time, Sissy had actually lusted after Stanley to the degree that she would have married him if he'd asked—except that he got arrested and spent ten years in the joint, abruptly ending Sissy's gleeful romp and prompting her to move to Okanogan.

Susan intensely disliked Stanley Diddy—as she had always called him—for many of the same reasons Sissy loved him. He was as disarming as he was dishonest and as talented as he was shifty. He was suspiciously charming, using his looks to his best advantage. She'd never liked the way Sissy fawned over him and his needs the way she'd never paid attention to her daughters'.

Susan was not happy at all that they needed to turn to Stanley Diddy for help. Holly was too tired and strung out to care.

Thus, the climb to the top of the snowy Beartooth Mountains, on the journey to the tiny town of Red Lodge, was frought with the dread that Blake might still be following them, and the unspoken frustration between mother and daughter that they needed to come this way at all.

While the day before had held wonder and delight for little Corey with great maws of bubbling mud and imposing columns of steam bursting from the center of the diamond-encrusted Earth, they'd scarcely taken any time to enjoy Yellowstone Park. The Beartooths jutted skyward at the Northeast corner of the Park, an area still surprisingly scarred by a wildfire two decades prior. Still, Corey's chubby index finger pointed out elk scratching themselves on burnt-out snags and buffalo foraging on spikes of grass that jutted here and there from piles of snow. A jackrabbit and a skunk each took its turn crossing in front of them, the latter with a litter of kits scurrying close behind.

Smiles of approval for their observant boy,
murmurs of encouragement, accompanied hours
of palpable tension. As if feeding from it, at least
every hour, Tristan balled up his fists, his face turned
crimson, and he let loose a guttural howl. The women
were forced to pull over and allow Holly to comfort
and nurse her youngest.

When the winding uphill climb to the summit left
Sissy nothing but guardrail and snow-plow berms
on the shoulder, they ignored his cries until a safe
place to pull over revealed itself. During these times,
Corey's face reflected his annoyance at the newest
addition to his family.

"Tistin cwy all time," Corey complained from his
car seat perch. Aunt Susan comforted Corey, unruffled
his jealous feathers, and cuddled him while his
mommy nursed Tristan.

Sissy watched them and wondered if the rapid
shift in elevation could help prevent a broken heart.
Sure, Susan's cranky disposition had to do with
Stanley Diddy—her childhood feelings were hardly
something she could easily overcome just because
he had agreed to help them—but the root of Susan's
problem was the inevitability of Holly and the boys
departing, possibly forever, from her life.

They stopped at the summit at a quaint variety
store labeled 'Top of the World', and after the
harrowing winter roads and endless switchbacks
they'd just traveled, as far as Sissy was concerned, it
was. Holly got out and wandered around the store
while she cradled a mercifully asleep Tristan on
her shoulder. Corey toddled happily behind. Sissy
corralled Susan before she could follow them.

"How are you doing, sweetheart?" Sissy asked
tenderly, putting her arm around Susan's shoulders.

The question—posed so sweetly by her so usually
matter-of-fact mother—caught Susan off-guard. Tears
sprang to her eyes and her hand flew to her mouth to
catch the hiccup of grief in her throat. For once, she
was speechless.

Sissy held her daughter tighter and let her own tears go. "I know," she pronounced rawly, "it's like somebody took a weed-wacker to my emotions all day today. I just keep plowing forward, but I'm all at once wanting to scream and cry and drive us all off a cliff. This cannot end badly, Sus. We've worked too hard to protect them."

Susan nodded through her tears. She hiccupped again. "C-can't we go with them?"

"You'd give up your home, your job, your identity, to go with them?" Sissy quizzed.

"Why not? It's not like my life before Holly and Corey had any kind of color or texture. All I can remember is career satisfaction, yes, but at home I yearned for more. I can't fathom a bathroom that doesn't smell like baby lotion or a pantry without cheese crackers and fruit snacks. Also, what about that wet-haired baby-boy smell that tickles your nose when you read him a bedtime story? And who's supposed to have a snow-ball fight with me this time next year?"

Sissy fished around in her purse and pulled out her pipe and tobacco. She handed Susan a stick of peppermint gum. "It'll help with the hiccups."

Susan nodded and popped the gum in her mouth compliantly.

Sissy puffed on her lit pipe for a few minutes sending its rich aroma into the air around her. It settled her frayed nerves as she debated what to do about Susan's dilemma.

"It would be easier for Holly if you were there to help," she admitted.

"Have you ever thought about coming too, Mom?"

"We'd be adding ourselves to the list of fugitives," Sissy reasoned. "It's not like I'm all that attached to the Bridgeport Thrift Shop. Shoot, I'm pretty sure I'll be gone long enough this time that I can kiss that job goodbye. I do kinda like my little house, though."

"I love my house, and my garden, but I can't live there knowing that I might never see them again.

After tomorrow, it might not be safe to have contact
with them at all." Susan gazed at the horizon as if
she were trying to visualize her life in Walla Walla
without Corey and Holly. She shook her head as if she
were erasing a piece of sand art gone awry. "I have to
go with them."

"Oh no, you don't," Holly interrupted, her voice
lowered to a hiss as she put Tristan back into his
baby carrier without waking him. "That is just about
enough from the both of you."

Corey froze and looked wide-eyed at his mom,
who almost never acted cross when he was around.

"Corey, honey, could you please get in your seat for
Mommy? I'll come open your juice and crackers in a
minute, okay?" He nodded and did as he was told.

As soon as both boys were contained in the truck,
doors secured, Holly whirled on her mother and
sister. She glared at Susan whose eye makeup ran in
icy rivers down her cheeks. "Get a grip, will you?"

Sissy jumped to her defense. "She's only thinking
of you and Corey. Your sister is willing to give up
everything for you two…"

"Oh, hogwash," Holly spat. "You don't think
her motives are selfish at all? I've seen the way she
coddles Corey as if she were his mother instead of me.
Well, he does have a mother, Susan."

"I realize that, but you're busy with the baby…"

"And Mom, you don't think I see how ready you
are to enable my sister to take over that role in Corey's
life? As if I'm too weak or stupid or strung-out to take
care of my own children…"

"We don't think that at all…" Sissy argued.

"STOP. Just, stop. Hear me out, once and for all:
It's not that I don't appreciate your help. When I left
Blake, I really needed your help. Corey needed your
help. I was a mess. Having Tristan, I was a mess too,
but you know what? I had a heart-to-heart with nurse
Bonnie. She got me to thinking about how, in reality,
I can control my own destiny. Sure my ex-husband is
chasing me and I'm a fugitive from the law, but do I

really have to accept the role of victim for the rest of my life? What does that teach my boys? That women are frail and need to live in fear and have someone to help them take care of their problems?"

Susan started to hiccup again as if her diaphragm gauged her level of distress. Her eyes pleaded with Holly.

Holly's resolve broke when she saw how strung out Susan really was. She put her arm around her sister. "I won't do it, Sis. I can't ask you to give up your life as you knew it."

"But I w-want to. I love y-you. I l-love C-corey," she blubbered.

Holly sighed. "I know you love us. We love you too. Honestly, though, it's going to be so much more difficult for me if you disappear too. The authorities will take to looking for two women, sisters, traveling together, which is slightly more conspicuous than a woman traveling alone with her children. We'll have to explain why we live together with the boys and no husbands around. It's not so rare to have a single woman raise her children, but it is unusual to have a live-in aunt."

"I could be the n-nanny."

"Only if you've got some way to make it appear as if I'm rich too."

"That's not going to be possible for a while until you get back on your feet," Sissy reasoned.

"So then it's settled. I'm no wimp. Nope, don't argue or try to defend yourselves," Holly fended them off with her raised hands. "I can do this on my own. Once Stanley Diddy does his magic, I'm out of here and we're on our own."

"I'll never see C-corey a-again," Susan sniffed miserably.

"I'll find a way, big sister. I promise. He'll miss you terribly too, you know."

"I kn-know."

The three of them embraced, forming a cocoon of frizzy hair and saltwater. As they left the embrace—

resolved, but frightened and immeasurably sad—
Susan, Holly, and Sissy felt almost a physical fissure
between them. It was as if the rubber band had
snapped and they began to scatter, like fine wisps of
paper that were never meant to drift apart.

Chapter Twenty-two

Holly

Stanley P. Diddredge dealt in crime as a form of art. Not only did he intend to obliterate Holly's former identity, he decided that her best chance for escape was to become wallpaper: so non-descript as to be part of the landscape. Holly defied the very principle with her glossy ringlets and doll-like face.

Stanley scowled as he examined Holly for any flaw he could exploit. Even her body sprang back from her recent pregnancy like a tightly coiled spring. Instead of being flabby anywhere, she simply looked voluptuous. Her breasts would be the envy of any centerfold model.

He put his hands on his lean, Levi-clad hips and muttered something derogatory in his deep Southern drawl about 'old girlfriends'.

"See, Mom," Susan said under her breath, "I told you he was all smooth moves and tight butt cheeks. His tongue is sharper than a razor blade."

"Yeah, well, that tongue does some other rather interesting things," Sissy replied wryly.

"Ew."

"Sorry, babe, but he's even gorgeous when he's perturbed."

Susan gagged and went to look after Corey, who'd found Stanley's cat and stood beneath his scratching post perch, trying to coax the feline down.

Sissy admired Stanley as he alternated running his fingers along his silken mustache, and flexing his biceps as he gestured with his hands at Holly's hair and face. His bleached blond hair was longer than she remembered, giving him a Fabio-like appearance. He even had an aquiline nose and strong, dimpled chin like the model. His eyes, though, were unique—they shone like pools of silver at the moment, but Sissy knew they grew dark as a thundercloud when he was angry or, she blushed, in the throes of passion.

His tattoos had grown more numerous and creative, she noticed, since his time in the joint. She realized with a jolt that he wore an 'S' like Superman's on his left forearm. 'S' for Sissy? Then she remembered, 'Stanley'—'S' for 'Stanley'. She chided herself for her juvenile fantasy and let out an indelicate snort.

"Whatcha thinkin' about, Curly?" Stanley quizzed, a master of nicknames, though Sissy's was hardly an original.

"Just thinking, Stan," she replied smoothly, but turned crimson, nonetheless.

He raised his eyebrows at the woman he knew didn't readily blush and the sexual tension between them rose another notch.

Holly wasn't exactly oblivious. "Oh, good God, you two, get a room already," she fussed. "Give me that hair color box, Stanley, and I'll go in the bathroom and work on this while you get re-acquainted."

"Yeah, okay," Stanley shrugged, his attention still riveted on Sissy. He shifted his gaze back to Holly for a second. "Take that whole grocery bag with you. There are a few other surprises for de-beautification in there too. I didn't buy a muu-muu, though, and that's about the only thing that's gonna hide those magnificent tits of yours. Do your best, will you?"

Holly fled to the bathroom to administer the regimen before Tristan woke up and needed to be fed.

Stanley leaned in closer to Sissy.

"Not on your life," Susan protested, as she barged between them, packing Corey, and headed for an afternoon snack from the kitchen.

Stanley's doublewide was surprisingly modern

and cozy with worn red-leather sofas and vinyl-record-shaped throw pillows scattered about. Windows framed by crisp gray linen revealed snow-blanketed evergreens on all four sides of the house. Crystal prisms hung in each window, dispersing late-afternoon rainbows throughout the kitchen and dining area.

Dishes stood neatly in a row in the white dish drainer next to the kitchen sink. As Susan rummaged for a box of graham crackers or a slice of bread and peanut butter, she realized that even the cupboards were tidily arranged. In fact, she could actually live in this house of Stanley Diddy's.

"Can I help you find something, Suzy Q?" Stanley asked teasingly.

Susan ground her teeth together and ignored his jibe. She'd always despised that nickname, but then, he didn't like her moniker for him either.

"I'm looking for a snack for my little buddy here."

"There are whole wheat crackers in the pantry and organic peanut butter in the fridge. Or, I have some Brie in the bottom drawer if he likes cheese."

Susan couldn't help herself. She cleared her throat and said what she'd been thinking since the minute they'd pulled into the driveway. "Um, Stanley, what exactly happened to the beer-swilling, mama-stealing hippy that I used to know back when I was a pre-teen. You're actually, um, kind of *refined*. It's unsettling. I keep waiting for your wife to walk in."

"For one thing, Suzy Q, when you spend ten years livin' in a six by eight cell, you develop a sense of order, neatness, if you will. You also become starved for color. That's what the crystals are all about. I got a sweet deal on the red couches from my brother.

"Plus, darlin', we all gotta grow up sometime. I definitely drank too much beer when I was puttin' the moves on your mama. But I still wanna put the moves on your mama, so I haven't changed all that much. And, I got too many tattoos to be refined."

"That's for sure, Stanley," Sissy rubbed her fingers

over his forearm. "But I sure like your 'S'."

Stanley leaned his forehead into Sissy's, locking in her gaze. "You could get one to match if you want. I know an artist back in town…"

"Can you just wait until I've settled in front of a movie with Corey before you start canoodling, so I don't have to be sick?" Susan slammed the fridge door shut.

"Hey, Curly, do you wanna come in my office and check out my, um, computer?" Stanley asked as he tugged on Sissy's hand and pulled her up from the dining room chair.

"Is it big and powerful?"

"You know it is."

"Ack, God, I just vomited in my mouth," Susan deadpanned, but the two of them completely ignored her as they went to check out Stanley's computer.

~~~~~~~~~~

Forty minutes later, Corey dozed in front of *Disney Channel* re-runs. Susan pored over the first few chapters of a mystery she'd found on Stanley's chock-full bookshelf. Tristan remained asleep in his portable playpen, finally taking a decent nap after days on the road of car seats and pure exhaustion.

Sissy and Stanley emerged from Stanley's office disheveled and subdued, like two kids who'd made out in the backseat of a Buick for hours.

"How's that computer, Mom?" Susan asked without looking up from her book.

"You are a good sport, Susan. It'll be great for achieving the purpose of changing Holly's identity and the boys'. It's a marvel, really."

"I'm sure it is."

"I hope you've got a good camera for my new picture I.D." The three of them swung their heads around at Holly's voice and the room stood still.

Sissy's hands flew to her mouth and she actually started to cry.

"Now, Curly, don't get all emotional. The idea is for her to look different…"

"Different, Stanley, but isn't this sort of extreme? Her son is not even going to recognize her when he wakes up," Susan protested.

Holly remained silent as they perused her, her chin up in the air, defiant, as if she expected them to challenge this new person she'd become in less than an hour's time. Medium ash brown hair hung just to her shoulders, straight, thanks to a flattening iron. Her sea blue eyes had disappeared into mud brown lenses, framed by golden, wire-framed glasses. She wore no makeup and a frumpy sweat suit hid most of her curves.

"I borrowed your sweats from the bathroom hamper."

"I could get you a clean pair," Stanley offered.

"Actually, these have enough wrinkle to them to be convincing. They smell like men's cologne, though, so maybe I'll take you up on that."

Susan laid down her book and walked a circle around her sister, her arms crossed. Holly watched her sister, waited for her reaction.

"I think you actually did it, Stanley. You've turned our golden child into an ugly duckling."

"He didn't do it by himself," Holly argued. "Besides, I'm not ugly—just different. Do you know what it feels like?"

Susan shook her head and waited for Holly to continue.

"It feels like I'm passing through the night in a black cloak. I could brush past someone and they would know I'm there, but they'd never actually see me."

"Invisible." Stanley clapped his hands in satisfaction.

"Invisible." Holly agreed.

"You'll have to color about every four weeks to keep those blond roots covered. The contact lenses are disposable, but there are enough pairs there to last you at least six months," Stanley advised.

"That was the hardest part—poking something into my eye. I've never had to do that. That took longer than straightening my hair."

"You'll get used to it."

"I can get used to a lot of things as long as the boys and I are safe." Holly sat gingerly next to Corey and ran her hand over his spiky hair. He sighed and rolled into the curve of her arm. "That's right, big boy, you stick with me. Your mama's going to give you a whole new life. We're going to find an exciting place to live where nobody will ever even look for us. We're going to make friends and make memories and we'll stop looking over our shoulders, and just, live."

Susan hiccupped again and fled with Sissy on her heels to the rear bedroom.

Holly measured her annoyance at her sister. She couldn't blame Susan for being heartbroken, could she? After all, she couldn't bear the thought of leaving either one of her boys behind, even for a few days. They were a team. For over a year, Susan had played catcher to Sissy's pitcher.

Holly cleared her throat. "Okay, then, Stanley. You have more work to do. Have you thought of a name for the new me yet? I've always liked Claudia."

Stanley bared his white teeth. "You're kind of a tough chick like your mama, ain't ya? You only look soft and feminine. I think there might be some grit there. Don't you worry none, Claudia. I'll fix you up."

PART II

Continuity gives us roots; change gives us branches, letting us stretch and grow and reach new heights.

—Pauline R. Kezer

Chapter Twenty-three

Blake

"I, Blake Dermot, do solemnly swear…"

He took his oath with as much trepidation as pride. This was his county now and he, personally, took responsibility for the safety of every individual who resided there. Blake shook the hand of the superior court judge and turned to his family.

Minerva sat in the front row on a polished oak bench, tears streaking what had been a gloriously made-up face moments before. Her pearly white smile shone like the sun as she clapped her hands around the body of their youngest child—a stunningly pretty two-year old named Camillia whose chocolate curls bounced with her mommy's claps. Minerva paused for a moment to settle their five-year old son, Jonas, who'd climbed up on his chair to show his enthusiasm.

Blake smiled at his radiant wife—pregnancy made her glow even more than usual—and wondered if she would pass on her unusual, caramel eyes to this one too. His reverie was interrupted by the whoops and hollers of his siblings, their spouses and their kids. Everyone roared their approval for the new county sheriff, Blake Dermot. All except, of course, Blake's father, Winston Dermot.

Winston, a man of great dignity and few words, had been rendered powerless by a stroke just a year before. Unfortunately, the incident had also robbed him of much of the self-respect he treasured. He mustered a thumbs-up for Blake from his motorized wheel chair, but as soon as the ceremony ended, he grasped the control knob, turned the chair about and headed discreetly away from the court room.

Blake's mother, Karen Dermot, shrugged her shoulders helplessly at Blake and hurriedly followed her husband out the door.

The twins scarcely noticed as they rushed the bench, their long-suffering husbands in tow. Kelsey, her hair a halo of lime green spikes, enveloped Blake in a jasmine and ketone-scented cloud. He tried mightily not to stare at her row of diamond lip rings as she grinned at him, her cheeks hollow from her latest crazy diet scheme. "That was so worth the drive from Seattle, Sheriff Blakey."

"Watch it, little sister," Blake warned as he grinned back and completely ignored her equally pierced and emaciated vegan husband.

"Yeah, show some respect, Kels. Our big brother is an elected official now," Colby swept into Blake's arms, her gray Chanel wool coat soft enough to pet. Her loaded lawyer husband, a fifty-year-old father of two almost-grown children, gave Blake an official handshake and a murmur of congratulations as his wife continued to gush. "Oh my gosh, Blake. You looked so tall and debonair up there. It almost makes me wish my hubby wore a uniform, not that I don't love your designer suits, sweetheart." She smiled at her husband coyly and Blake shifted his weight to try and stomach the disgust he felt for the man who'd made his littlest sister into a twenty-something, mid-life trophy wife.

"Why don't you put on a few more airs?" Kelsey groused. "By the way, sis, how many sheep do you suppose they imprisoned to make your get-up?"

"Not as many as the number of needles you've poked through your face to try and look weirder."

"Okay, girls, that would be quite enough," Minerva announced as she handed Camillia into her daddy's arms and took Jonas' hand, placing herself bodily between the twins. "Sheriff Dermot has some important dignitaries…"

Blake snorted.

"…Okay, maybe not dignitaries, but definitely VIP's, to talk to. Now run along and beat each other over the head with insults somewhere else."

The girls rolled their eyes and complied.

"Thanks, honey," Blake said and planted a kiss on Minerva's raspberry lips.

"Absolutely. I am so proud of you, babe."

"Not as proud as I am to have you by my side as I do this." They beamed at each other.

It hadn't been easy. Blake had largely been the favorite to replace Sheriff Paul for a good five years before the old man finally retired, but a rogue candidate—a tough, beautiful female cop, also a county native—had come into the mix, and Blake—a family man, ruthless, yet tender—had won by a slim margin.

"You realize it's only because you made me pretty, don't you?" Blake teased. Actually, Minerva had put him on a brutal, low-carb diet and encouraged him to grow his formerly spiky hair into a longer blond, youthful, Dennis-the-Menace sort of 'do. Blake was still tall. That he couldn't change, but he appeared slender and his more relaxed hairstyle made him appear approachable.

" And are you ever pretty." Blake's next oldest brother, Tony, gave him a high-five after the jibe and walked away with his wife and two small kids to find the buffet line in the hallway. The oldest brother, Troy, didn't bother. He just waved and led his wife and their squalling newborn to the doorway. Blake understood.

At the rear of the room, Detective Harvey Morris raised his punch glass to his new boss and Blake excused himself to go greet his crew, as Camillia tagged along.

"You did it, Enforcer," Harv clapped Blake on the back affectionately. "I had my doubts. Therise Loden gave you a run for your money. Did you hear she took a job up at the city police department?"

"That's probably best. I could've kept her on with us, but after she pulled the dirty campaign tactic of looking into my past with Holly and Corey and all of that, and implied abuse, I don't know how charitable I'd be, you know?"

"I don't blame you. It's not like you needed all that dredged up again."

"It dredges, Harv, anyway. I think it always will as long as they're missing. Anyway, that's neither here nor there. Life is good again. Let's celebrate."

~~~~~~~~~~

The last of Blake's supporters left and Minerva took the kids home for their requisite naps. The courthouse had grown quiet and Blake contemplated running over to the office building to clean out his old desk so he could move into Sheriff Paul's office first thing Monday.

As he passed the holding room normally reserved for witnesses, he heard his mother's voice.

"Blake will be done soon, honey, and then we'll get you home. I wanted to congratulate him before we left…I know. I know. You're ready to leave. You're tired. Blast that Troy. He was supposed to help me…"

"I think Bess had different ideas," Blake spoke softly from the doorway.

"Was the baby acting up?"

"Oh yeah, and the wife practically dragged Troy out by his ear when he suggested she might go home by herself and take care of the baby while he hung around with me and the guys."

Karen's eyes lit merrily, softening the lines that had become indelible around them since her husband became an invalid. "I thought he and Trish never would have babies, so if Bessie gives them fits, so be it. It's good to see your oldest brother settle down some."

"Just look at all these grandbabies you have now.

I wondered sometimes if you'd ever have any after…
you know…after…"

"After Corey was viciously taken from us?"
Karen's eyes darkened into onyx cabochons.

"Don't get worked up, Mom, please."

"I don't care if you give me a hundred more
grandchildren, Blake. My first will always be missing.
Do you really think I'll ever forget that?"

"I can't forget either," Blake admitted, shoving
his hands in his pockets so he wouldn't bite his
thumbnail. "Without Corey's disappearance, I would
never have married Minerva. I wouldn't have taken
the anger management and leadership classes I
needed to do this job well, and you know how much
they've changed me for the better. Can we appreciate
just how far we've come since then?"

"I'll appreciate it more when that conniving wench
pays for bringing distress to my family like she has.
Your father would never have become so ill without
the stress she caused us."

"You can't blame Dad's stroke on Holly…"

"*Don't.* Don't you speak her name to *me*."

"I won't stop looking for him, Mom. I'll always
look for him. He's my son, my firstborn."

Karen patted Blake's cheek reassuringly, placated
for the moment. "It is such a pleasure, let me tell you,
to see your son grow up, to succeed. I want you to
have that someday with Corey, so he can make you
proud, like you've made me proud."

Winston grunted as if he agreed and then began
to hum and gesture, flailing, toward the door. A
string of saliva escaped down his chin as he became
increasingly agitated.

"I think Dad wants to go." Blake's heart tugged at
its moorings to see the patriarch of his family in such
a state.

"Will you walk us to the car, Sheriff Dermot?"

"It would be my pleasure, Madam Citizen," Blake
replied as he pushed the button for the elevator.
"Where did you park?"

Chapter Twenty-four

Holly

Holly re-read the flimsy, dog-eared letter.

Dearest Holly:
You've had the hardest jolt a young mother will ever face, realizing that the life she lived must no longer exist, and that the pattern must be broken. I, like you, took matters into my own hands so long ago I can hardly remember. My children got the best benefit from it, and the worst. I remember the horrific guilt I felt, having denied them of a father, however mean-spirited and abusive he was. You can't be both, you know: Mother and father. But I know you will try. Lucky for me that I had Mr. Jones come along not so many years later. He filled that hole for all of us. You need to have faith that you, too, will love again.

In the meantime, love your sweet boy. Take care of him and make something of yourself that he can admire. Remember that all of your sacrifices came from your desire to be unbeaten, unafraid, and to protect your son. That is the kind of woman he will always admire. You've escaped all possibility that he will ever believe a woman should be subservient, or worse, worthy of ridicule and physical abuse. I'm proud of you, Holly, and someday your son will be too.

It's truly been a joy to continue correspondence with you. I didn't know you

*before that terrible night, but our friendship
means a great deal to me now. I'll look forward
to your next letter.*
Love,
Mrs. Jones

Holly swiped at a rogue tear, put the letter tenderly
back in its envelope, and placed it in the vintage hat-
box she'd reserved for precious valuables. So many
links to her former life had been obliterated. She felt
at once comforted and saddened by Mrs. Jones' letter.
She wondered briefly if Mrs. Jones would be proud of
how far she'd come.

Holly shrugged and rubbed the chill from her
arms. Why was it that the hairs on her neck stood on
end whenever Mrs. Jones was on her mind? Of course
Mrs. Jones would be proud of her. Mrs. Jones was
Holly's guardian angel, and an ever-present one at
that.

It was Mrs. Jones' characteristic twinkle that she'd
seen in the eyes of New York City's very first angel,
Yvonne Plough, a woman with the blackest skin
and the whitest smile Holly had ever seen. Yvonne
directed a women's shelter in Brooklyn. Holly could
have sworn Yvonne had an Irish lilt in her voice when
she'd said to Holly, "We've been waitin' for you, child.
Come on in…"

It was the capable hands of Sugar O'Donnell the
first time they reached for Tristan—so much like
Mrs. Jones withered, yet adept hands, when she'd
plucked Corey from his crib that awful night—that
told Holly it would be okay to leave her boys with the
highly recommended babysitter when she went off to
nursing school that first day five years ago.

The occurrence that stymied Holly the most,
though, was Dr. Howard Young, dean of the Mid-
Queens School of Nursing. He managed a merry smile
so reminiscent of her kindly neighbor that it nearly
took her breath away when he called her to his office
to offer her a full scholarship to their Master's degree

program. That smile virtually guaranteed that Holly would jump at his offer three years later to teach his nursing professionalism classes while she worked on her doctorate.

So, five and a half years later, she had an apartment on a tree-lined Brooklyn street close to the best elementary school in the borough. She had a fulfilling job—students who continually challenged and inspired her—and in eight short months, she would have her doctorate degree. Thanks to Dr. Young, she had received letters of recruitment from Brigham and Women's Hospital in Boston and UCLA Medical Center to come teach.

Holly gazed out the window and sighed—so beautiful out. Late September had turned the trees into a cacophony of crimson and gold, and a squirrel chattered as he worked at gathering his winter store.

Holly and the boys could very possibly be leaving New York in less than six months. She needed to stick to task—if she didn't de-clutter before it came time to pack, the move would be a nightmare. It was Saturday, thus she needed to take advantage of her free-time.

Tristan, her bounding, enthusiastic, soccer player son, had other ideas. His cerulean eyes twinkled from beneath strawberry blond bangs that had grown too long, again. "Let's go, Mom. Anthony said he'd go to the park today. We gotta go to the park."

Holly reflexively touched her index finger to Tristan's honey-colored birthmark, a gesture of greeting as familiar to the both of them as an embrace. Then she brushed the hair out of his eyes. "You need a haircut, son."

"Mo-om," Tristan whined. She *always* changed the subject. "You promised we'd go meet Anthony and his mom at the park today. Remember?"

"I do remember. Angela and I agreed we'd meet up at one sharp. It's only eleven."

"Couldn't we go get pizza at Joe's beforehand?" Corey chimed in. Holly never failed to marvel at the changes in her older son. She looked up at him expecting to see a shock of white hair and pearly baby teeth, but instead saw a helter-skelter patch the color of sand, so similar to Blake's, and a whole mouthful of grown-up chompers that seemed out of place in his still little-boy face.

Corey's were rugged, tanned good-looks that contrasted his brother's ivory-skinned, pretty-boy appearance. They were polar opposites in personality as well. Tristan was a sporty guy. Holly kept him active and occupied from dawn until dusk, lest he get bored and do something awful, like smearing lipstick on the neighbor's dog or making snow out of toilet paper (both of which he'd already tried.) Tristan even ate like a terror, wearing as much as he consumed, and with his gangly arms and legs, he looked like a knobby kneed gazelle on the soccer field.

Corey, on the other hand, read books voraciously like a famished person consumed food. At eight, he could read and understand classic works like *Moby Dick* and *Grapes of Wrath*, though he much preferred *Harry Potter*.

He tended to be stocky because he enjoyed food and he only went out for football in the spring because Holly believed he needed the physical stimulation. Corey towered over his classmates and the coach had practically swooned when he met his newest player. What the coach soon learned, though, was that Corey's gentle nature belied his stature—he played center because he could hold his ground, but aggression was completely beyond him.

As both boys stood before her, bright-eyed and eager to enjoy the last vestiges of clement weather for the year, Holly's resolve melted. "Get your jackets. It'll get cold later this afternoon."

They grinned and ran for the hall closet.

Holly paused in front of the foyer mirror to re-adjust her scrunchy. She finally let her shoulder-length, natural curls do their bidding these days, though she dutifully touched her blond roots brown once a month. She'd switched the shade from ash to sable, which was far more dramatic with her pale skin and commanded sometimes more attention than she'd planned. She still wore brown contact lenses. Corey caught her putting them in one day and asked, wide-eyed, why her eyes were blue, and mostly, why she covered them up.

Holly had made up a story about blue eyes being more sensitive to sunlight. (He knew her propensity for sneezing in the bright sun.) She swore that wearing the lenses kept her from sneezing as much. Luckily, a kid had no trouble buying that without brown contact lenses, she would sneeze in bright sunlight nearly constantly, and that would be truly awful.

An unfortunate side-effect of her story was Corey's insistence to every blue-eyed sneezer he encountered that they needed to try brown contact lenses. She only rolled her eyes and shrugged at strangers when his 'bless you' included this authoritatively-delivered advice.

She pulled a lime-colored fleece over her t-shirt and jeans. No sense dressing up for a jaunt to the park. Mommy-hood was no fashion show—that was for sure.

Holly and the boys chatted about school while they walked the short four blocks to the pizzeria. They giggled over a large pepperoni pizza and rootbeers. By the time they reached the park, Holly was relieved to watch her amped up boys stretch their legs and start to run it off. Her friend Angela waved to Holly from a wrought-iron bench.

"Hey, Ang." She plopped next to her newest friend whose unguarded smile had first drawn Holly to her at a school orientation meeting. There were very few people Holly trusted enough to befriend even after all of these years. She had never let her guard down when it came to her tightest circle—she and her boys.

Angela had disarmed Holly to the point of play dates and occasional coffee breaks, but neither woman had ever seen the other's home. Yet, they made easy comrades when the boys could act as a centerpiece to their conversation.

"Hi, Claudia. How are you? How are the boys?"

Holly's pseudonym never really fit her like her given name. Too German, or too many syllables—she wasn't sure which it was—but she'd grown accustomed to it. It had va-va-voom, if nothing else.

"They're jet-fueled right now."

"Cotton candy?"

"Rootbeer," Holly replied as they both laughed.

"I swear I have to peel Anthony off of the deli ceiling if I let him have soda." Angela's parents owned one of their neighborhood's freshest delis and one of Holly's favorite places. *Heroes* was aptly named because the walls were adorned with memorabilia, signatures, and hand-painted quotes from the 9/11 massacre in New York City. Angela had lost a brother—a firefighter—and a cousin, who worked in Tower One, to the tragedy.

"Too bad diet drinks give them such a bellyache," Holly said.

"Oh yeah. *Bellyaches* suck. I do love how you talk," Angela teased, her Brooklyn accent such a contrast to the fake Texas twang Holly had adopted.

"You're the one with the accent," Holly shot back good-naturedly.

"I can only imagine the lazy, wide-open spaces that must produce such a drawl. Promise me someday you'll take me to that grassy field with a stream running through it where you got knocked up with Cody."

Holly nudged her friend playfully, "I'm not ever goin' back *there*, that's for sure." She grinned outwardly, but grew quiet inside. She never would go back where *Corey* was conceived, not willingly. Pangs of homesickness besieged her far too often. Would that ever fade? She wondered.

"I'll bet it's beautiful," Angela breathed. "Fresh, clean air; hardly any cars; room to run…"

"It's overrated. This park is a lot prettier than any patch of sagebrush." It was true, too. The high desert climate of the Okanogan held its own brand of beauty, but it was untamed, ill-manicured, rusty-old-car-type beauty.

"Was Taylor born in New York then?" Angela asked. Holly wondered, too, if she would ever think of her boys as Cody and Taylor instead of their given names. It was like she was a native Spanish speaker whose thoughts were in Spanish, but she voiced them in English. She spoke and acted like Claudia, but her thoughts were unfailingly translated by who she was deep inside: Holly.

"Taylor's a New Yorker, yep."

"He acts like a New Yorker."

"That he does," Holly agreed as she watched her confident city dweller do a penny drop from the middle monkey bar. She gritted her teeth as she prayed he wouldn't land on his head.

"That's a neat trick." Angela clapped for Tristan's benefit as he smiled toward the moms and took a bow.

It was then that Holly noticed the guy with the camera.

Her hackles went up instantly. This was no ordinary point-and-shoot. The guy had a telephoto-type lens on what looked like an expensive digital camera. He was no bird-watcher, either. The fancy camera pointed rather obviously at the kids playing.

Holly felt her pulse quicken. Was this a private detective? Had Blake finally located her and the boys?

That was impossible. Even Sissy and Susan didn't know exactly where she lived, even though she convened with each of them separately each alternating winter break in a warm location. Communication came via Stanley. Stanley kept tabs (among other things) on Sissy. Sissy sent updated pictures and reassurances to Susan, though Holly's big sister was busier these days with a new husband and delightfully unexpected baby boy of her own.

Holly kept her cool for the sake of Angela. If Holly

panicked or jumped to conclusions, she only risked their safety more. "Are the parks guys carrying cameras now?" She asked calmly as she wiped sweaty palms on her jeans.

"Not unless the parks guys also run around in wheelchairs," Angela pointed out.

It was true. The cameraman was in a wheelchair. She'd only noticed fine-boned hands and one intimidating camera. Now she noted salt-and-pepper hair cropped neatly around the ears and a crimson oxford shirt topped by a down vest. He backed away from the camera long enough to smile and Holly realized that he was rather young, this voyeur. Prematurely gray. Interesting.

Not interesting enough to let him keep snapping away at her kids-in-hiding.

"Well, wheelchair or not, I'm going to find out what he wants with our kids."

"Good idea," Angela concurred, though Holly could tell Angela was puzzled by her sudden nervousness.

The cameraman watched Holly approach with keen eyes and she couldn't help but notice they were large and deep-set, the color of roasted almonds. She felt suddenly self-conscious in her frumpy clothes. He looked friendly, and cute, yet she kept her guard up.

"Get some good shots?" She gritted her teeth.

"Incredible. They don't even know I'm watching. That towhead there? He looks like the cat that ate the mouse right before he flings himself into space off those monkey bars."

"What about the darker haired blond? Did you get him too?"

"Sure, I caught him passing the football with the dark-haired kid. The all-American boy. Let me guess. You're his mom."

"How'd you know? We don't look anything alike."

"Maybe it's the way you stand with your hands on your hips, looking like a mother cougar about to rip the head off a hunter who sighted in her cub."

"Perhaps if you weren't hanging around kids at playgrounds, us mother cougars wouldn't have any desire to pounce."

"Touché," he laughed. He had a manly laugh, deep and rich like his baritone voice. He held out his hand. "Tanner Grafton."

Holly took his hand hesitantly. Fine boned, yet strong. She kept her face neutral even though she felt the instant undercurrent between them. "Ho…um… Claudia…Brown."

"You sure?" Tanner grinned, his front teeth pearly white and straight, though she noticed his left front tooth had a chip out of it.

"Yes. Now…" she cleared her throat and took her hand back, "I'm wondering why you feel the need to stalk playgrounds and take pictures of young boys at play."

"I'm a professional photographer. My agent wants pictures for a set of children's museum ads back in California."

"So why are you in New York taking these pictures?" Holly crossed her arms.

"Have you noticed the fall foliage around you? Palm trees weren't what the client ordered."

"Isn't it illegal to take pictures of minors for publication without the consent of their parents?" Holly persisted.

Tanner raised his hands in surrender, leaving his camera on his khaki-clad lap. "Do you see any kids here without parents around? I happen to have consent forms here in my satchel. Would you like to look one over?"

"No way. I won't give consent for my boys…" By now Angela had wandered closer to see if Holly needed her assistance.

"So you have more than one child here? Let me guess again. That big-eyed, dark-haired guy digging in the sandbox—he's your youngest, and all-American boy, he's the older one."

Holly wanted to wipe the smug look off of his face,

but she took some satisfaction in that Tanner believed her hair and eye color to be real enough to have passed on to her child. "Nope. I'm the mommy of the towheaded daredevil. Now, can you kindly delete any pictures you have of my children?"

"I'm sorry. I can't."

Holly prepared to mount her protest. He stopped her.

"Even if you don't give your permission, I can keep the photos on my memory stick. I just can't submit them for publication. I'm an artist. I don't erase my work."

"How do I know you won't sell them?" Holly tapped her foot testily.

"You'd have to trust me…" At her raised eyebrows, he shrugged and grinned some more. "Will you at least see some of my work before you rush to judgment?"

Holly felt her resistance crumble. Tanner was nothing but charming, and it appeared he had a job to do. How would she handle somebody standing in the way of her doing her job? The same way, she thought—diplomatically and irresistibly.

Plus, Angela, by now, stood mesmerized by Holly's hostility. She would ask questions. Holly knew this for sure.

Tanner held out a glossy card. "My cell phone number is on the back. Please say that you'll call, Claudia—you wouldn't want to disappoint a good-looking guy in a wheelchair."

Holly snorted. That was a cheap shot. She stuffed the card in her back pocket. "We'll just have to see about that," she said crisply before she turned to corral her boys.

Chapter Twenty-five

Sissy

It wasn't so bad visiting a tropical location every other winter. It *was*, however, enormously taxing to arrange the whole thing on the sly. She couldn't wait to get things under way. Sissy glanced out the skywalk as she hustled out of the terminal to board her plane. 'God, I hate snow,' she thought as she prepared to sit and meditate thoughts about warm, sea-salt scented breezes and ice-cold mai-tais for the six hour flight.

Co-passengers smiled ironically and whispered to each other as she floated past them in her island blue caftan and beach hat. What? At least she'd left her rhinestone-studded sunglasses in her sequined, pineapple-shaped carry-on until she reached sunnier climes.

This year they were being particularly adventurous—Orlando, Florida. Tristan had finally gotten old enough to navigate the amusement parks properly. Sissy knew he'd have no problem keeping up with the rest of them. Plus, they were going to a water park, and she'd arranged for a tour of the Everglades on a swamp boat (Corey's idea.)

It was all so intoxicatingly thrilling, the prospect of this year's meet-up with Holly, Sissy, and Sissy's grandsons, that Stanley P. Diddredge had decided to go along. After all, Sissy couldn't communicate with Holly without Stanley's help, so he was privy to the whole plan. In fact, his involvement was crucial.

Yet, they planned to share a hotel suite—she and

Holly and the boys. How would Sissy ever keep her hands off Stanley for a whole friggin' week? She hadn't seen him in months. The precious man had done so much for them. She needed to reward him properly. She wondered briefly about a separate hotel room. No, too expensive. She'd already spent a good month's earnings on her plane ticket!

At any rate, she anticipated the sight of her daughter and the boys keenly. They had surely grown up so much in the two years since their last meet-up in Lake Havasu, Arizona. Back then, Tristan had just become a motor-mouth and poor Corey could hardly get a word in edgewise.

Corey had been missing both of his front teeth and Sissy remembered how they had laughed and laughed when they bought him a gourmet caramel apple—at his insistence—and he tried to figure out how to bite into it. They finally took mercy on him and cut it into pieces.

Sissy couldn't imagine how she lived the two years in between without seeing everybody's shining faces. It was for everybody's safety that they didn't make the trips more frequent, but for Sissy, it was as if she scarcely ate or slept or even *lived* properly for the duration of that time. Each day without them was torture, but the alternative—their discovery—was terror, so they settled for this winter week of paradise instead.

The deepening lines on her forehead told the tale, as did her sylph-like figure. Even her flaming mass of hair had been dulled by mischievous, increasingly gray strands. She'd taken to wearing bandanas and hats over her roots to disguise signs of aging that had nothing to do with years passing.

She fastened her seatbelt and put her hat dutifully on her lap, so as not to disturb her seatmate. She wondered if someday she'd learn to like flying. For now, it felt too much like careening calamity—wheels, wings, and fuselage on course, but completely out of her control. She began to inhale and exhale vigorously through her nose. Time for a little of that meditation.

~~~~~~~~~~

"Grandma!" The boys yelled simultaneously from the baggage claim area when Sissy finally navigated her way to it.

"It's my boys!" She yelled back and held out her arms and all their billowy fabric for the boys to run into them. They hugged her vigorously, then Tristan stood back a ways while he reassessed just who this woman was that his brother was so excited about.

Holly chuckled. "Did Grandma Sissy suffocate you in her muumuu, Taylor?"

Sissy remembered the code names as soon as Holly said it. The boys didn't really know themselves by any other names, plus she needed to remember that 'Claudia' was incognito too. *Claudia,* she thought, with distaste, was a name she *never* would have given her daughter.

Sissy also couldn't reconcile this dark-haired beauty before her with the golden child she'd raised. She'd changed the shade of her hair. "I love what you've done with your hair, *Claudia,*" she offered before she enveloped her daughter in a cloud of *Poison* for that long-awaited hug.

"What's this?" Holly quizzed. "I don't smell pipe tobacco curling through your wave of *Poison.* Can't have it in the airports, huh?" Her eyes twinkled at her mom.

"No, sweetie. I gave it up. The doc told me I have high blood pressure and, between that and smoking, I wouldn't be around to see these guys grown if I kept it up. I need to see them grown and you free of this nightmare. So I quit."

"Wow," was Holly's amazed reply.

"Grandma, grandma, have you seen the car we get to take to the hotel?" Corey grabbed his grandma's hand and led her toward the doors.

"Wait, I need my bags…"

"Oh, I've already got those," Holly reassured her. "You're still using the same leopard print suitcases you had two years ago. They beat you here." She gestured to Sissy's tattered, yet durable bags.

Each boy grabbed a hand and led Sissy to their waiting 'car'. Except this was no car, it was a Hummer limousine—candy apple red. Her jaw dropped.

"No plain old taxi cabs for you, missy," Holly teased, then before her mother could voice her concern about money, she continued. "Stanley sprang for this one, Mom. I'm not sure what kind of business he has going over there in Montana, but it's lucrative. He wanted us to have a classy ride."

"Isn't he here?" Sissy peered inside to see if her amour awaited her.

"He's not, but he sends you his love. He told us all to have an amazing time."

The four of them slid to the back of the limo's bench seat and Holly helped buckle the boys in while the driver loaded Sissy's luggage.

Sissy cursed the tears that defiantly popped into the corners of her eyes. It wasn't like Stanley had ever joined them before, but she had so looked forward to seeing him, dammit.

Holly took her hand. She understood. Being a woman meant your heart would be broken at some point—probably at several points—in a lifetime. She had taught her daughters that, sometimes the hard way. She fought tears for several miles until she saw the spires of the castle that was their hotel.

Oh, this was going to be fun. The boys' faces lit and there were oohs and aahs all the way around. Sissy tabled her feelings. She could get to those when she was alone in her room later. No sense spoiling everybody's fun on account of a man.

They pulled into the roundabout where a uniformed concierge with a French accent greeted them like VIP's. "Madams, we have your room ready. We'll have the bellhop deposit your bags there, but you will first please accompany Miss Carroll here to the salon," he said, gesturing to a spritely girl in a pillbox hat and white gloves. It was as if they'd been transported in time.

"This young woman," he said, pointing to a twenty-something Snow White, "will take the young gentlemen to our play area. I assure you that they will be safe, but for good measure, we will give them a bracelet with your pager number on it, and you will wear the pager. No one else will be allowed to take them this way, see?"

Holly nodded obediently. The boys whooped in excitement and followed Snow White.

"Maybe we're the actors in an impromptu movie and they're waiting to see how we'll react," Sissy murmured under her breath.

Holly laughed nervously. "Or maybe Stanley Diddy feels bad that he couldn't be here and he's trying to make up for it."

"Maybe…"

Sissy didn't have time to contemplate as they were whisked to the salon for facials and mani/pedis. The pampering didn't stop there, though. Sissy felt like a girl again as a young man built like a Greek Adonis clucked about her gorgeous curls and talked her into coloring her roots to match. Holly added caramel highlights to her crown, which brought out the chocolate in her contact lenses—however unnatural they seemed to Sissy, the overall effect was gorgeous.

They were made over until Sissy scarcely recognized the old woman she'd been when she hobbled off the plane. Instead in the mirror sat an Irish goddess—shoulder length ringlets of gilded red, eyes rimmed by russet kohl and shining like emeralds, lips lush sienna red.

Miss Carroll rejoined them. "Are you pleased with your salon day, ladies?"

"Are we ever?" Sissy waved at her face. "Do you believe this?"

"The transformation is stunning, ma'am."

"We've been here for hours, though," Holly

worried. "Are the boys okay?"

"They've played and snacked the whole time. To be quite honest, I don't think they've missed you."

Sissy clapped her hands, delighted. "So when do we get to the martinis?"

"Martinis?" Miss Carroll looked confused.

"It's been a perfect day. The only way it can get better is if I get a martini, three olives, just a spritz of Vermouth."

"You'll wear your lipstick off," Holly chided.

"What am I keeping it on for?"

"Will you please follow me again, ladies?" Miss Carroll requested, as if in answer to her question.

They were led to a boutique and instructed to pick out whatever they might like for an evening out.

"Is this just a rental?" Sissy whispered, wide-eyed, as she took in the racks of sequins and furs in every color imaginable. Holly just smiled and walked over to a shelf to run her hands over the exquisite silks and cashmeres before her.

"You get to keep whatever you'd like," Miss Carroll informed them.

"Oh, I've got big suitcases, missy. You don't know what you're saying," Sissy warned.

"A certain Mr. Diddredge told us not to spare a thing."

"If Stanley thinks all this pampering is going to make up for the fact that he skipped out on me on my vacation…he might be right," Sissy giggled and dove into the mountains of clothes.

~~~~~~~~~~

Of the five outfits she picked out, accessories and all, Holly talked Sissy into wearing the classiest, and most demure, for their evening out—it was fire engine red. The silk blazer fitted her streamlined figure like a glove over a camisole of stretchy satin. Her skirt, fitted through the hips, billowed out in alternating layers of lace and silk. Peep toe pumps with five inch heels showed off toes that matched her lipstick.

Holly wore a black cocktail dress with faux mink accents on the bodice and skirt and black patent flats.

"Are you ladies ready for your evening out?" Miss Carroll materialized on cue.

"But my boys, they're…"

"…waiting for you in the car. They've been dressed for the evening as well."

The women looked at each other and mouthed 'wow'. What couldn't money buy?

They slid back into the Hummer, too full of the day to do anything but watch the passing scenery. The boys, however, had no trouble jabbering about their adventures for the fifteen minute drive. Open-air restaurants, interspersed with hotels and shopping centers, whizzed by them.

When they finally stopped, Sissy stared at the building before her in bewilderment.

"It's a church."

"It's charming, don't you think? Mission style. Look boys, those are real flamingos around the water feature," Holly said.

"But it's a church," Sissy insisted. "How am I gonna get my martini in a church?"

"Come on, Grandma, let's check it out," Corey grabbed Sissy's hand as he bounded out the door. She struggled to follow him and stay upright on her huge heels. She ran her hands down her skirt to smooth it. When she raised her eyes, she saw the most beautiful thing she'd seen since she arrived in Florida—Stanley P. Diddredge stood in the open doorway of the church. He stared so intently at her, she feared she might vaporize.

"He's here," she breathed.

"Come on, Mama," Holly encouraged her.

Sissy looked away from Stanley long enough to look back at her daughter. "You knew, didn't you? You knew he was here?"

"Yes, Mom, I knew," Holly took her hand, as Corey grasped her other elbow and she climbed the four stairs of the church to where Stanley awaited.

Stanley held out his hand and Sissy took it in a trance. He dropped to his knee. His eyes shone like sterling in the early evening light. He'd trimmed his hair—it barely brushed his shoulders now, she noticed fleetingly. He pulled a tell-tale box from behind his back and she realized what Stanley was about to do.

"Sweet Jesus, you know I'm no princess, Stanley…"

"Shhh," Holly breathed.

Stanley's laughter rumbled forth from his chest. Whether it was nerves or mirth escaped them all, but once he caught his breath, he finally spoke. "I shoulda known you'd never make it through the whole fairytale scenario without lippin' off."

Sissy smiled back. "You love me anyway, don't you?"

"Ah, Curly, I do. I can't live without ya no more. I did all this so you'd say yes. This preacher here," he gestured inside, "just happens to have a few minutes for us. So whatdya say?"

Sissy hesitated, but only for a moment, because the one thing that held her back melted away when she heard a familiar voice behind her say, "Go on, Mom. I know you always wanted to marry Stanley Diddy."

"Susan." Tears flowed freely down Sissy's cheeks.

"Hi, Mom. You are ruining your gorgeous make-up," Susan chided as she climbed the steps of the church and joined them, with her babe in arms.

Sissy cleared her throat. "In all my life, I've never been broad-sided like this, Stan, well except maybe when you had to go to jail. You've ganged up on me. Just what am I supposed to say?"

Stanley's mouth dropped open, but he clearly had no argument. He looked at the ground for the answers.

Sissy took his chin and lifted his face to hers as she stooped down next to him. "Did you really think I needed all of this in order to say 'yes'?"

He nodded, near tears himself.

"Stan, I would say yes to you standing nekked in

the laundry room at your house. I would say yes to you in a seedy bar. I would say yes to you standing knee deep in a creek, fishing. Yes, you silly man. Yes."

Stanley smiled and kissed Sissy greedily. He scooped her up in his arms as he rose to carry her into the church where she could say 'yes' to him again in the presence of the most precious people in her life. The perfect ending to a perfect day, martini or no martini.

Chapter Twenty-six

Holly

"So we spent the entire day together getting pampered, I got *married* and, yet, you didn't say one word about this guy?" Sissy admonished Holly over a cup of joe two mornings later.

"I didn't think it was important."

"You've assumed a new identity to escape the first guy you married with a brand new baby from the second guy you slept with. Of course it's important if you've met somebody new."

"Because I normally choose so badly, that's what you're saying?" Holly chopped furiously at the banana on her buffet plate.

"Have mercy on that banana, will you? No, I'm not saying that. You've grown up a lot since then," Sissy admitted.

"Anyway, this guy is no big deal…"

"Hol-, um, Claudia…I may not see you very often these days, but I'm your mother. I know your heart. I also know you wouldn't have started a conversation with 'There's this guy…', unless there was something special about him."

"I've only seen him twice. That's hardly serious, Mom."

Sissy's eyes commanded Holly's, so she abandoned her breakfast for a moment to look back at her mom.

"It's just that, watching you and Stanley so in love, so happy, it makes me realize that maybe that part of me isn't dead; that I don't have to avoid men for the rest of my life just because one or two made me miserable. Of all of life's bitter lessons you've taught me, I have to say this redeems them all."

Sissy's eyes welled up with tears. "It does, doesn't it? I never imagined I'd marry the one man I've dreamed all my life of catching and holding on to. It was perfect—my daughters, my grandsons, my love—I still can't believe you all pulled it off."

"Susan had to fly into Charlotte and drive down with the baby to avoid the same travel pattern as you, in case the powers that be are still tracking that."

"It's too bad she had to leave already. Keegan is beautiful, isn't he? … So, will you tell me about him?"

"Keegan? You just saw him yesterday…"

"No, silly, the photographer," Sissy smiled slyly and cradled her coffee cup as if she'd settled herself for a long talk.

Holly sighed. "It's nothing, really. He was taking pictures of the boys in the park," she began, careful to avoid telling her mom the park's location or a specific description. "Taylor was doing penny drops. Remember those?"

Her mom nodded. "You two used to scare the pants off me when you flew off those bars. He's a chip off the old block. Go on."

"Tanner snapped away, unbeknownst to me and, as it turns out, caught some breathtaking pictures of my son just before he let go and in mid-flight. I wouldn't give him permission to publish them, for obvious reasons, so he invited me over to his studio to see them. That's it. I just saw him those two times…"

"That's it? Oh, puh-lease. You're turning the color of a ripened strawberry. That is *hardly* it. What does he look like? Did he publish those pictures? Most importantly, did he get any pictures of Corey that he wants to publish?"

Holly shifted awkwardly, like she was fifteen again and her mom was lecturing her about sex.

"He's handsome, I guess. His eyes are sort of an amber brown, really warm—inviting, like his personality. I'm guessing he's in his early thirties, but he's already got a ton of gray hair. It doesn't make him look old, though, just worldly, sophisticated. His hands look like a musician's, narrow and graceful. He's really not my type at all…"

"Like you have a type…" Sissy said wryly, captivated by Holly's discomfort. Holly's love affair with Blake had been defiant; with Vladimir, illicit and secretive—this light in her daughter's eyes, and uncertainty, were new things altogether.

"He didn't have any decent pictures of Cody," Holly defended, automatically using Corey's false name out of habit. "I still haven't decided if he can send Taylor's to his agent or not. I promised to meet him for coffee when I return from vacation."

"So you have another date?"

"It's not really a date. It's business. Besides, Mom, he's in a wheelchair," Holly blurted out.

Sissy reacted as if a hurricane-force wind had blown her back into her chair. "Permanently? He's crippled?"

"I don't know him well enough to ask him that yet," Holly admitted, "but I did see several pictures of him with less gray in his hair with friends and, quite frankly, some rather famous people, on the wall of his studio. He was in a wheelchair in all those photos."

"So he's successful too?"

"Well, yes, Mother, he appears to be. Being handicapped doesn't preclude being successful."

"Don't get snippy with me, Holly," Sissy shot back, forgetting to use the code name. "I'm just trying to sort this out. What I've got is this: This good-looking cad has pictures of a child you've got in hiding from your abusive ex-husband. You're on the fence because he's handsome and charming, and you feel sorry for him because he's in a wheelchair…"

"And they are fantastic photos. As someone who appreciates a professional being good at his job, I can totally see why he'd want to use them."

"So you don't deny that you sympathize with him also?"

"It's got to be incredibly difficult to navigate life as a young man, wheel-chair bound—dealing with ramps, elevators, narrow doorways—but, yet, I didn't get that from him. He used the cripple card the first time we met to charm me, but he's never acted handicapped since. He tools around his studio like there's nothing unusual about his disability at all. He appears to lead a full and satisfying existence just the way he is."

"Yet, he's single."

"A lot of guys in their early thirties are single where I live," Holly jumped to Tanner's defense.

"Precisely why you should probably move on from this one," Sissy concluded.

"I don't get you, Mother. You say you want your daughters to be happy. You've finally found a man in your own life who proves the gender worthy of love. Yet, you've shot me down every time in my life that I believed someone could make me happy. Are my choices truly that poor, or is your judgment skewed by all the times you've been disappointed?"

Before Sissy could open her mouth to answer, Holly pushed her plate away and fled to the hotel's recreation area to seek out her boys. Her boys loved her, free of judgment. Why couldn't her mother and her sister? Susan had been similarly unenthusiastic about Tanner.

She thought of the day ahead of them. Stanley planned to take them all to the water park. Holly would have to endure her mother, her silent disapproval, for hours. She considered fleetingly begging off, claiming a headache, or something of the sort, but that would only disappoint the boys.

She sat on a suede sofa in the reception area while the assistant retrieved her kids. She plucked absent-mindedly at the lint balls on her lemon capris. Why hadn't she just worn a new sundress from her 'Stanley Diddy' collection?

She shifted restlessly. That wasn't the question at all she should be thinking. Her boys came running to her, sweaty and smelling of chlorine and Florida sunshine, and she hugged them both to her briefly. A mother's intentions were always pure, weren't they?

What she should have been asking herself was whether her mother was right.

Chapter Twenty-seven

Blake

With Christmas only two days away, Blake marveled again that he hadn't received his normal holiday greeting card from his mother for his desk. Come to think of it, she hadn't called and made dinner plans yet either. The Dermot family Christmas dinner was a given. So why hadn't she called with the details? Who was in charge of mashed potatoes? Who got to pick up the dinner rolls? If someone didn't take control of this, they might end up with five cranberry Jell-O molds.

Something was definitely wrong with Blake's mother. Minerva tried to convince him it was stress. It couldn't be easy to look after his dad. Not only was Dad unable to communicate, he'd become physically cumbersome and more unhappy with his situation.

That unrest reflected in the briskness with which she ended their phone conversations. "I have to go help your father." *Click.*

Even his brothers and sisters had noticed how short she was with them on the phone. His brothers gave their parents monthly stipends from the auto and insurance businesses, even though they weren't contributing to the business operations. Dad had skimped on retirement savings and Social Security wasn't nearly enough for them to maintain their household. At least the state had come in with nursing care and a housekeeper a few times a week to provide his mother some relief.

Maybe it was financial stress that had gotten to his

mother. What if she couldn't afford to provide the ham this year, and she was afraid to ask her children for help? Blake chewed his thumbnail behind the same oak desk Sheriff Paul had used. At any rate, he should probably go over to their house sometime and hash it out with her. He slapped his hand on the desk suddenly; but, *dammit,* he had four other siblings and none of them shouldered the responsibilities Blake did.

He had a whole county to police. Christmas time meant drunken drivers and horrible roads. Why should he be the one to sort his parents' mess out?

His sisters would do a whole lot better job, anyway. Well, Colby would. He wasn't so sure about wild-child Kelsey. Woman to woman. He'd give Colby a call later and sweet talk her into making a trip over the mountains to help them all out.

Blake contemplated his half-empty mug of green tea and heard his stomach growl. That seven a.m. bowl of Cheerios hadn't gone nearly far enough. His mind turned to the carton of doughnuts his secretary had plunked down on the conference table earlier.

No. He'd promised Minerva. Since his swearing-in nearly a year ago, he'd kept his body lean. Minerva had birthed another gorgeous baby boy in June, so her exercise and diet regimen was as strict as his: Early morning workouts, cholesterol and fat-burning foods for breakfast, salads for lunch, chicken-something for dinner—all the more reason to crave a loaded Christmas dinner at his mom's. He'd even managed to avoid the glut of Christmas goodies adorning every desk and spare table in the office.

He needed a big ol' slice of his mom's old-fashioned pumpkin pie with a dollop of real whipped cream.

His stomach nearly clawed its way out of his gut. He picked up and dialed his phone before he dove straight into the nearest maple bar.

"Hello?" The voice sounded tinny, like a door hinge in need of greasing.

"This is Sheriff Blake Dermot. May I please speak to my mother?"

"It is your mother, Blake Dermot. Since when don't you recognize my voice?"

Since you never call anymore, he thought. Aloud, though, he said, "You sounded, uh, a little higher pitched than usual."

"I had to run for the phone."

Blake detected the note of annoyance. When wasn't his mother annoyed nowadays? Enough was enough, wasn't it?

Except that he had no finesse. Even the best coaching from his former partner, his wife, and his anger management counselor couldn't squash the idiot he could be when it came to delicate matters.

"Aren't you getting enough help there, Mom?"

"Why? Are you offering to help? If you actually are, it would be a first from you or any of your siblings," she snapped.

"I've been super busy, Mom, with work, with the new baby…"

"I don't particularly want to hear that, Son. Now, I left your father in the shower, so I really don't have time to talk…"

"It's Christmas…"

"That's right. It's Christmas. And I gave birth and thirty years of blood sweat and tears to five children, and have any of them shown up at my door to see if they could visit with their father while I do some shopping or write Christmas cards? Has anyone thought to bring my grandchildren's bright faces by this house so I could see something besides misery and pain in a loved one's eyes? For that matter, has the love of my life even once stopped his petty demands so that we might enjoy the quail eating from their feeder in the front yard, or sit holding hands quietly in front of the fire while it snows?"

Blake didn't know what to say, so he said nothing. His mom hiccupped indelicately. Then he heard the muffled click of the receiver as she placed the phone back in its cradle.

~~~~~~~~~~~

"I'm sure you just caught her in a weak moment," Minerva reasoned with Blake as she waved her wooden spoon like a conductor. "I get like that sometimes with a brand new baby—she's overwhelmed."

"Oh, honey, you're never overwhelmed. I haven't seen anyone else who can nurse a baby, talk on the phone and wipe a two-year-old's bottom all at once."

"Don't forget the curlers in my hair—that's true multi-tasking if I'm curling my hair at the same time as all that," Minerva laughed wickedly and turned to stir her fajitas.

"Seriously, babe, I think Mom might be pulling her Mercedes into the driveway of the loony bin pretty soon." Blake picked up Camillia's crayons. She grinned. The bulk of the coloring game involved the test of gravity and of Daddy, the picker-upper.

"Boo, Daddy?" Camillia asked, holding up the green crayon.

"That's *green* nimrod," Jonas scolded.

"Like you're some kind of Einstein just because you're in kindergarten," Blake rushed to Camillia's defense as she glared at her brother. "Where in the world did you learn the term 'nimrod'?"

"Never mind where he learned it. Those kindergartners say a lot worse words than that. I've heard 'em when I go and monitor recess. The point is, son, that you do not call names. You don't want to visit the naughty chair, do you?"

Jonas' eyes got huge as he looked down the end of his mom's wooden spoon and shook his head slowly from side to side.

Blake chuckled at his son's suddenly subdued bravado. "That worked pretty swell. I think I might need to borrow Mommy's naughty chair for work."

Loud protests issued from the playpen in the living room as the new baby, Samuel, realized he'd awakened alone.

"I'll get him," Blake offered so Minerva could finish cooking dinner.

Sammy stopped crying as soon as he saw his daddy. Blake's heart always skipped a beat when he first glimpsed his new son: No matter how different the times and circumstances of their births, Corey and Sammy could have been twins. From the cue ball head to the serious dark eyes, both boys looked breathtakingly like their father.

Blake rested his chin on his hands at the edge of the playpen while Sammy sat himself up and chattered happily. "Come on, little man. I'm sure your mommy has something even better than chicken fajitas in store for you."

As he leaned in closer, Blake realized the little guy had more for them than smiles. Solid foods in a baby belly churned into waste toxic enough to burn off nose hairs. Blake's empty stomach rolled—this, he was not good at. He headed toward the kitchen with the babe dangled delicately away from him.

"Mommy, Corey has a little surprise for you in his pants…" before he could finish his sentence, Blake realized his mistake.

Minerva froze. When she turned, it wasn't anger he saw in her eyes. Anger, he expected. Instead, he saw pity.

"I-I'm s-sorry," Blake stammered as he did the hand-off.

"Blake Dermot, don't you apologize. Do you know what just occurred to me when you called your baby boy Corey instead of Sammy? This guy, you, our other kids—they're never going to know their brother. They'll never know Corey like they do each other. That is incredibly sad, isn't it? Honey?"

Blake had already busied himself at the stove, dishing up plates for Camillia and Jonah, so Minerva left him alone to go change the baby's diaper. He paused for a moment, leaned into the counter, and breathed away the threatening tears. Between his mom's deal and one carelessly misspoken name, it had been a hell of a day.

"Daddy, who's Corey?" Jonah asked cautiously.

"He's your brother," Blake admitted as he put Jonah's plate in front of him.

"Sammy's my brother."

"Yah, Thammy bruddah," Camillia reiterated, holding her index finger high in the air while she expressed her point. "He a baby."

"You have another brother, from before Daddy and Mommy got together and had you."

"I do?" Jonah was enthralled.

"Nudda bruddah?" Camillia inquired.

"You all do. When he was smaller than Camillia, his mommy ran away with him and I never got to see him again."

"Does that make you sad, Daddy?" Jonah's serious gaze forced Blake's tears back to the surface.

"You don't miss much, do you, buddy? Yeah, Daddy's sad. I'm sad for you and for me. Maybe someday you'll get to meet your big brother. He's eight years old. Sammy looks an awful lot like him."

"He does? Is that why you called him Corey?"

"Probably. Now, can you both eat your dinner for me, like good kids?"

Blake went to see if Minerva was ready for her dinner and ask if she wanted him to heat up some baby food for Sammy. Instead of finding her nursing their son in the rocking chair, as he expected, she was bundling him into his one-piece snowsuit.

"Whatcha doing, honey?" Blake put his arms around her waist and hugged her to him while her hands worked.

"I'm taking Sammy to see your mom."

"Now? It's dinner time. She wasn't in a good way earlier, like I said."

"All the more reason for me to go," Minerva concluded. "For one, she obviously needs someone healthy and happy to pay attention to for a few hours. For two, I haven't seen her in a while, and I need to know how she's really handling Winston. Third, Blake, if you're struggling with the whole Sammy/ Corey likeness thing, just think how she's doing with it. It's no wonder to me that she's going off her rocker. Between the loss of the husband she's always known and her first-born grandson, your mom has some serious pent-up grief."

"You really think she pens that kind of stuff up?" Blake asked wryly. "In my experience, Mom usually blurts out whatever pops into her head, and she means it."

"Why do you think she never calls anymore?"

Blake nodded. Guilt gnawed again at his gut and he was reminded that he needed supper too.

Minerva grabbed him by the lapels of his flannel shirt and planted a kiss on his lips. "You've had a rough day, Blake. You go eat and watch out for the other munchkins. I'll get to the bottom of this stuff with your mom."

"Can I fix you a fajita to take along?"

"Oh, I'm not hungry. I probably ate a whole red pepper while I was chopping them up!"

Blake looked into her eyes—the eyes of love—and he knew every bit how lucky he was. "Have I told you lately how amazing you are?" He asked tenderly as she swept the baby into her arms and he kissed her forehead.

"I'm afraid it's been a few days," she teased, "but yeah, I know. I love you too."

Chapter Twenty-eight

Karen Dermot

Christmas meant so little when one had no desire to share it with anyone: No greeting cards to draw distant relatives into her home and family; no pumpkin pies cooling on the breadboard; no sparkling packages under the tree for glowing-eyed grandchildren; no mistletoe for Winston to sweep her under and steal a kiss.

The Dermot family Christmas had died a sudden and tragic death when Minerva Dermot declared at Thanksgiving that Karen had worked way too hard on the meal, and that she should next time think about buying turkey and accompaniments prepared from the local chain grocery store.

Minerva had slid under Karen's radar for the first five years of her and Blake's union, popping out gorgeous babies and looking immaculately pretty on Blake's arm. Minerva had even created a comfortable home for her brood, clean and functional. Until that moment a month ago at the Dermot family's blessed table, Karen had quite happily embraced her youngest daughter-in-law. Karen should have known Minerva was nearly as much of a low-class redneck as Blake's first wife.

If Karen had given up on planning Christmas this year, well, it was entirely Minerva's fault.

Which was why she nearly choked on her spearmint gum when Minerva showed up on her doorstep the evening of the twenty-third.

There she was, looking svelte as ever, as if having

three babies didn't qualify as a reason to leave five pounds of padding alone. How could Minerva possibly have time to properly care for Karen's precious grandbabies if she was exercising and dieting all of the time? Those glossy ebony curls? They took time away from the children.

But then, Blake had always gone for the beautiful and the vain.

There was Sammy, too, bundled like the Michelin man. Oh sure, it wasn't enough that Minerva had come to chide her about Christmas, or the lack thereof. She'd brought her Corey replica to rub salt in Karen's ages-old wounds. As memory had it, the last time Karen considered cancelling Christmas was after Corey disappeared.

True, Karen wanted to see her grandbabies. They shed light onto what had become a dreary existence, so dark in fact, that color nearly ceased to exist.

Not this grandbaby, though. This little boy made her heart tumble into an airless crevice. He grinned to spite her, and she felt her hold on reality slip. *Get a grip, Karen,* she thought, *This isn't Corey.*

"Karen?" Minerva interrupted her reverie. "Can we come in?"

"Yes, of course," Karen remembered her manners. Regardless of her state of mind, she'd always been an impeccable hostess. Thus, she kept her home tidy and the potpourri burning.

"Well, it smells like Christmas anyway," Minerva offered. "Is that Bayberry?"

"Pomegranate."

"Right. Well, Sammy and I were out doing some last minute shopping and we thought we'd stop by to see how you're doing." Since Karen didn't take her coat, Minerva took it off anyway, hung it neatly on the hall tree, and proceeded to unbundle Sammy.

Karen panicked. They surely weren't planning to stay! "Cut the crap, Minerva. Blake sent you to look after me after I hung up on him, did he not?"

"I thought you might want to see Sammy. It's been

a while…"

"Jonah and Camillia, I would love to see. I have coloring books for them so they won't think I've forgotten the holiday entirely. The baby, though, well, you might as well have left him at home with Blake. I don't care to see him, actually."

Minerva froze. Karen normally doted on her grandkids. Hostility toward one of them wouldn't set well with Minerva. True to form, Karen could almost see Minerva's mommy teeth lengthen and grind together.

Minerva held fast to Sammy, but didn't continue to undress him. "How is Winston?" she ground out civilly.

"You don't need to concern yourself with my affairs, Minerva. Winston and I are just fine."

"Blake and I are worried about his father, about you…"

"Yet I've heard almost nil from any of you since Thanksgiving. My goodness, my daughters are all of the way across the state, and my sons, well they might as well be," Karen declared.

"If you need something from us, I wish you'd call," Minerva reasoned. "I'm home every afternoon after I close up the beauty shop. I could get groceries for you or come by and entertain Winston…"

"Winston abhors anyone sitting around gawking at him. It takes me hours to pacify him after a visit."

"Talking to him and setting kids on his lap is hardly 'gawking'."

As if he heard their conversation, Winston sounded off from the living room. Guttural and pained, the call sounded sub-human, more like a wounded sea lion. Minerva winced and Karen fixed her with a glare.

"Well he *was* taking a nap."

"I'd like to say hi if that's okay with you," Minerva persisted.

Since she couldn't bodily block Minerva and the baby, Karen was forced to let her past. Minerva sucked in her breath at the sight of Winston Dermot.

Hair uncombed and waving about like prairie grass, Winston was a disheveled shell of the man Karen had married. To Karen, he was a simpering lunatic, not only physically disabled, but unhinged. She sat to feed him his meals three times a day—soft foods only—and two-thirds of the time, he managed to upset the tray onto her lap or fling an arm into a glass, shattering it against the wall. She thought she'd foiled him when she bought clear plastic tumblers, but cranberry juice and iced tea stains on the wall disproved her victory.

To Minerva's eyes, Karen imagined Winston's emaciated, unkempt appearance looked like she had ceased to care for him. Quite the opposite, his care took more and more of her time. She had no hobbies, no clubs, no naps—Karen simply existed to take care of the man she'd signed on with for a whole lifetime, for better or worse.

That his worst meant he hated life even more than he hated her made Karen wish he'd fall asleep someday and never wake up. Better yet, she had half a mind to look up Jack Kevorkian and see if he'd come out of retirement for her. Winston could manage to push the button, she was sure of it.

"Hi Winston, how are you?" Minerva warbled as if she spoke to a four-year-old. "I brought Sammy over to see you!"

Winston gurgled and managed to raise his arm a few inches from his lap.

"I know, I know, it's been too long. Your boy, the Sheriff, works some hellacious hours. You'd be so proud of him, though. Okanogan County thought crime had no deterrent until Blake Dermot became the sheriff. Now the bad guys are practically holding out their wrists to be taken away. They don't want to mess with the Enforcer."

A half smile lit Winston's face. Much to Karen's chagrin, Minerva took this as a sign to continue her dimwitted, one-sided conversation.

"Jonah told me to tell you hi too. He wants to know

when he can ride on your scooter around the yard again. I told him that the snow needs to melt first. Camillia doesn't care about the ride, though. She just wants to come sing you her ABC's. She's finally got them down and she's so proud of herself…"

"Winston, aren't you tired?" Karen interrupted.

"Didn't you say he just woke up from his nap?" Minerva hedged, as if she had a right to challenge Winston's caregiver, as if she knew what he needed.

Karen flushed, but she held her ground. "Why don't you just go and dispute the way I take care of him, just like you questioned all of the work I did on Thanksgiving dinner."

Non-plussed, Minerva sputtered, "I never questioned your work on Thanksgiving! I just thought it would be nice for you if you didn't have to work so hard."

"You don't think this is hard work? Taking care of all of this? Taking care of *him?*"

"Karen! Should we take this conversation somewhere else?" Minerva asked through clenched teeth as she gestured to Winston.

"No…no!" Karen fumed. "I want Winston to hear exactly why the sounds and smells of Christmas he loves are absent this year."

"I'm the reason you haven't planned Christmas dinner here?" Minerva sounded incredulous.

"If you know so much how it should be done, why don't you just do it yourself? I don't need Christmas. I don't need my children here doing nothing but feeling sorry for me and their father. Not if all you're going to do is exclaim that I work too hard."

"I wanted to help…"

"If you wanted to help, you would have realized that the work I put into the holiday was done out of love. I don't love anything else about my life right now except for providing special food and a festive atmosphere for my family. You, Minerva Jenkins, took those traditions and threw them back into my face," Karen finished her tirade, breathing heavily.

Minerva's Latin temper finally got the better
of her and she sat Sammy down on the floor with
a magazine so she could turn and face down
Karen more effectively. Hands on hips, topaz eyes
flaring, she bit back. "It is obvious to me that your
responsibilities here have outgrown your ability
to handle them. Look at Winston, Karen. Does this
man look well-cared for to you? If I suggest you do
less, it is because you've let so much else slip to do
something as trivial as putting a bird on the table for
your sons to eat."

"Feeding my sons is not trivial…"

"Oh come on, Karen. If you had to choose between
folding a linen napkin into a friggin' tent and giving
your husband a bath, where would your priorities
lie?"

"The nurse can give him a bath on Tuesdays when
she's here…"

"Once a week? How often do you brush his teeth?
Every other day? It's no wonder Winston's unhappy!
I'd be unhappy too if I sat in my own filth for hours
while my wife shaved chocolate curls onto her
mousse!"

Karen gasped and Winston made a grunt that
sounded curiously like a shout of encouragement.

"Get out," Karen breathed, low enough that
Minerva almost didn't hear her. Except that Minerva
did take note of the candlestick that Karen had
grasped as she said it.

"Oh, so now you're going to beat me over the head
in the parlor with a candlestick?" Minerva said with
bravado, yet her eyes reflected her uneasiness.

"I said, get out," Karen reiterated.

Minerva scooped up Samuel and thumbed out the
piece of magazine page he'd managed to gnaw from
the edge. She pulled on his hat and grabbed her own
jacket in just a few movements. Without a word, she
tore out the door and slammed it behind her.

Karen did a rare thing and moved to her husband
to smooth his hair. If he was upset with her, he said

nothing, but then there wasn't much he could say anymore.

"It's probably best that they just all leave us alone, don't you think, Winston, honey? Our children always were just way too demanding. Everybody but that Blake. That Blake, if he had a spine at all, he'd quit marrying these petty, stupid women who prance about with his children like they're possessions. If he had any grit, he'd have found Corey ages ago." She did her best to make Winston meet her gaze.

"It's true, honey. If only we had Corey, none of this ever would have happened. Not any of it."

Chapter Twenty-nine

Holly

Unfortunately, comparisons to the other men in her life were inevitable. After all, there had only been two.

Though Blake's mother had surely taught him better, his meals had always been accentuated with unapologetic belches, never a napkin in sight. He'd wiped his hands down on his jeans. He had basically been a heathen for all of the years Holly had known him.

Vlad, well, Holly didn't honestly know whether she'd ever sat down to a polite meal with him—they were too busy hustling into positions that even now made her blush.

It was Sissy's fault that Holly thought of Blake and Vladimir as she watched Tanner wipe his mouth graciously and place his linen napkin neatly back in his lap.

After all, was it entirely necessary to compare her real life with this bubble she and Stanley had constructed five short years ago? Claudia scarcely knew Holly—the immature, naïve girl who fled instead of fighting, who succumbed to life instead of chasing her dreams, who let bullies and cheaters call the shots.

A confident, cool Claudia faced Tanner Grafton, mirroring his impeccable manners. Yet, he caught her lost in her thoughts—those pesky comparisons.

"I swear sometimes you look like the entire galaxy weighs on your mind," Tanner jibed, pulling her back to the present.

"Oh, no," Holly defended immediately. "No worries here," she twanged as she picked through her penne pasta.

"Are you sure? It took some serious persuasion to get you to sign that consent form. No second thoughts?"

Actually, she thought, she'd had second and third and...twentieth...thoughts, but Tanner couldn't know that. These pictures were too critical to the children's museum campaign they were intended for. Tanner had already voluntarily donated the money they would have paid him back to the museum, an inner-city, non-profit play mecca for underprivileged children and their families.

The museum taught children real-life skills through role-playing in areas like veterinary medicine, theater, art, retail, food-handling, and construction. Tanner's money would help make after-school programs available for kids whose parents couldn't greet them at home or who couldn't afford admission costs.

But, was the threat to Holly, Corey, and Tristan worth the risk, no matter how good the cause? That was the question that gnawed at her gut. Had she signed consent for release of just Tristan's images because she believed in the museum and wanted to contribute to its advertising? Release of Corey's pictures had been out of the question simply because he looked so much like his dad. Blake didn't know what Tristan looked like, so it seemed like a safe venture. Yet the question nagged: Had she signed to make Tanner like her better?

Oh, for Pete's sake, she wasn't a starry-eyed freshman in love with a senior boy, was she? She was a grown-up and Tanner certainly was no movie-star-heartthrob. He was a real man with real problems and a real job to do. Why, then, did her heart do cartwheels when he grinned at her just now and asked about her thoughts?

"Claudia?"

"Hmm? Oh. No, Tanner, I'm not having second

thoughts. Those pictures of Taylor were perfect for the campaign. I told you I was fine with it."

The waiter approached the table. "Can I get you anything else tonight? Coffee? Dessert?"

Holly shook her head nearly imperceptibly and Tanner replied, "No thank you. Can I please have my check?"

"No mudslide for you?" Holly teased.

"Nope," Tanner hedged. "We're going to take this on the road. Time for a walk."

The irony of his statement didn't faze Tanner. To him a walk meant fresh air, not feet on the ground. Holly had yet to ask him about his need for the wheelchair. She figured he'd offer the information in good time. Until then, they were just getting to know each other. This was the second time he'd taken her to dinner.

The South Street Seaport teemed with other couples fresh from their early dinners and bundled in their New York uniforms: tailored wool pea coats in shades of gray, boots, wool hats, and scarves of every color. For February, the air was unusually warm and Holly found herself wishing she'd dressed lighter—maybe a skirt instead of twill khakis.

Tanner wheeled alongside of her for a few minutes, then suddenly veered off toward one of the Seaport's antique battleships. She followed in long strides—his wheels were much faster than her legs. He turned a corner to a wooden ramp and she raced to catch up to him. Was he trying to lose her?

Suddenly, Tanner's arm shot out and caught her off balance. Before she knew it, she'd tumbled into his lap. He held her fast as her face turned a color of crimson in harmony with the breathtaking sunset they now had before them.

"You blush like a natural blond," Tanner said as he crooked a finger under her chin and pulled her face toward him.

"I..um…" Holly stuttered as she struggled in his arms. What could she say? That she was a natural blond? "I mean, I'm…sorry…I didn't mean to fall on you…"

"I won't break. Relax," he commanded and she took a few deep breaths. "Besides, you didn't fall on me. I pulled you into my lap." His eyes twinkled mischievously.

Holly stilled. She knew Tanner was playful, but this physical side of him, she didn't expect. What if he kissed her? What then?

As if in answer to her question, Tanner cupped his graceful hand beneath the curls at the nape of her neck and pulled her face to his. Gentle lips on hers yielded to glorious heat like their mouths had burst into flame. Goose flesh rose on Holly's arms and she felt her core glow like a candle flame as she pooled into his arms.

Tanner pulled away, his eyebrows raised, breath coming fast. "Wow…" he breathed. "You're like dynamite that's gotten wet. One tiny spark…"

Holly got hastily off Tanner's lap, embarrassed at her wantonness. She knew now how badly she wanted him. How wrong was that, though? For all she knew, he couldn't fulfill any of those needs for her, nor could she fulfill his. She turned away from him and walked a ways further down the pier.

"Claudia? What's wrong?" Tanner came up behind her.

"I didn't expect that," she admitted and tears sprang to her eyes.

"Are you *crying?*" Tanner wheeled around her so that he could look at her more closely. "You are!"

"It's not anything you did…" she said, swiping at her face with her sleeve.

"I was just trying to have a little fun," he said, and then a cloud moved over his face in the waning daylight. "But you don't think of me that way, do you?"

"I do, Tanner. That's the thing. I don't know how to want you. We've gone from you coaxing me into a business transaction, to you coaxing me to have dinner, to me anticipating those dinners like a schoolgirl with a crush, to you possibly wanting me back. I don't know anything about you except that you're a successful photographer and you have incredible hands, and now your mouth… Look at me. I'm like a violin string beggin' to be plucked."

To her surprise, Tanner laughed heartily. She put her hands on her hips defiantly as he struggled to regain control. "I'm sorry…it's just…I've always thought you were kind of high strung, ever since that first day in the park with you and your boys… it just struck me funny that you think of yourself as a violin string. It was all the more cute with your Texas drawl."

She snickered too, at that, and the mood lightened again. Chumminess had returned, but that kiss still lingered between them.

"Can we go back to my place? SoHo's closer than Brooklyn and it's about to get real chilly as this sun goes down." Tanner held out his hand.

"Just to talk?" Holly raised an eyebrow.

"Of course."

~~~~~~~~~~

Tanner's apartment boasted a handsome cast iron façade, characteristic of SoHo. His huge windows overlooked a busy street three floors below. In true loft style, the only interior door opened into a bathroom. Even his bed lay behind a veil of chocolate chintz curtains. Holly spotted it and her pulse quickened.

Tanner missed nothing. "Don't see an elephant?" he asked wryly.

"What do you mean?" Holly asked, plopping down on one of the tailored black leather armchairs.

"I mean, you were expecting to talk about that elephant, right? The elephant in the room?" He moved to face her.

"Tanner, you're going to have to help me out here."

"Claudia, it's no secret that I'm in a wheelchair. We need to talk about it. Obviously."

"Is it painful for you to talk about it?"

"Sometimes," he admitted, "but it's not like you think. It's not about the way people look at me with pity. It's not about the way it's difficult to go everywhere because not everything is wheelchair accessible. I'm not big on self-pity, if you haven't noticed. It is a little painful to have someone I like— like you—judge me without knowing all of the facts."

"I'm truly sorry if you think I've done that, Tanner." Holly grasped his hand.

"Why don't you just ask me?" His eyes pleaded.

"I can just ask anything?"

"That's how it usually works, isn't it?"

Unless you're me, Holly thought. She ran her sweaty palms down her slacks, refusing to make eye contact.

"What do you want to know?" Tanner persisted.

"How did you get hurt? Or have you always been in a wheelchair?"

Tanner took a deep breath and began to tell his story. Only he told it like it wasn't his story, but that of a folk hero: "This is the way it goes: There once was a mighty sixteen-year-old boy who could beat any of his classmates at thumb-wrestling and who could palm a basketball even if he couldn't jump high enough to slam dunk it. He was as wiry as he was tough, and he was smooth with the ladies. Not only was he a stud, he was king of knowledge, an ace at trivia and computers. He got straight A's and, because he was his parent's only child, they hung on his every accomplishment.

"Nothing could knock this invincible lad down. That was why, that warm spring day, when his friends dared him to, he dove head-first into a canal before anyone else could show him up. Alas, that spring had been unseasonably warm and the canal, concrete-lined and devoid of fishes, didn't have nearly as much water running through it as any of them remembered.

"Just before he jumped, the boy remembered thinking that the water looked farther away than it ever had before, but then he'd been a whole year younger the last time he'd ventured in through a locked gate to take a dip. He thought perhaps his memory had served him wrong; but then when his head struck the concrete bottom of the canal and his neck snapped nearly in two, he knew his mistake.

"It was by sheer luck that his friends were able to reach him before he was swept too far downstream, before he drowned, for he couldn't feel his arms or legs well enough to fight the current and swim. It was weeks before they knew for sure how much damage had been done and how much use he'd have of his arms. They knew for sure he'd never use his legs again, and he hasn't felt them since.

"His dad, once so proud of his son, took to a Jack Daniels bottle, for he knew that the responsibility couldn't be borne by his son alone. It wasn't long before his dad ran himself off the freeway into a ravine so deep it was only by chance that a transient spotted his car a week later. Luckily, the boy's mom stayed by his side every moment of his recuperation and she's still his biggest cheerleader.

"That boy spent a good five years feeling sorry for himself, wallowing in self-pity, getting addicted to pain medication, and wasting time. Then he met a girl who wanted to be an actress—she had the looks for it, if not the brains—and followed her to L.A. She found work in commercials and bought him a camera for his birthday. Eventually, she dumped him. Fortunately, he found out he had an eye for what people wanted pictures of and it wasn't long before he had a passel of cameras and a full-blown career.

"Before he was thirty, that boy had a fulfilling life despite himself and his handicap, so he vowed to never let self-pity claim him ever again. He'll never be invincible, because now he knows better, but he's a whole lot braver than the boy who dove headfirst into one-foot-thick concrete."

Holly wiped her quiet tears away. He'd told this story before, she knew, because it wasn't long before he lost the distant look in his eyes he'd had while he told his story. His words didn't haunt him like they did her.

"What else?" He asked, his voice husky.

"This girl, was she the only one you ever loved?"

"No. I've loved a few others. They always break my heart, though. My lifestyle means I jet-set a bit. Not everyone can cope with long absences. I always stay in love, though, until they let me down easy."

"Did you and these girls, you know…?"

"Is this conversation about sex?" Tanner asked frankly, but a smile played about his lips as Holly blushed furiously again.

"Maybe," she hedged.

"I may not be able to use my legs, but pleasure can be obtained in many ways, Claudia. Would you rather talk about that or have me show you?" Her body quivered despite her reservations and Tanner's eyes lit appreciatively. "That kiss was hot, you know? I could go for more of that."

"What if I have more questions?"

"Can you ask them while you're sitting on my lap?" Tanner hefted himself handily from his chair to the chair next to Holly's and held out his arms.

"That might be a little distracting," she bantered back, but settled into his lap anyway. "Tanner?"

"Hmm?" He asked as he ran his hands up and down her back, lighting little fires along the way.

"I'm not going to be that easy," Holly admitted, though Tanner had no idea how deep that statement went.

"Oh I hope not," he replied as he reclaimed her lips.

~~~~~~~~~~

It was much later, when to Holly it seemed like they'd been making out for hours—in the kitchen, on the sofa, and finally on the bed—that Tanner came up for air long enough to ask her what she meant by that.

Actually, how he put it was, "I've told you my sad

story. Now, when do I get to crack the mystery that is Claudia Brown?"

She stiffened and Tanner noticed immediately.

"What's that about?" he asked.

"Oh, nothing, it's just that I noticed what time it is on your alarm clock. Angela will be wondering just exactly what could be keeping me so late."

"It's eleven o'clock."

"I have little boys. They're probably both conked out by now."

"Call her. Let her know they might have to have a sleepover," Tanner suggested in all seriousness.

"Why don't I just call up my friend, who doesn't know me that well, by the way, and tell her I'm planning to bed a man I've only been on two dates with?" Holly's eyes flashed angrily. "And exactly what am I supposed to say to my two little boys when they want to know why I left them overnight?"

"Why are they with a friend you say you don't know that well?" Tanner shot back at her. "I thought you were the overprotective-type mother."

"Are you kidding me? You think refusing to let my sons' photos be published in a state-wide campaign is overprotective? I know Angela a lot better than I know you and I've given you way more liberty with their safety than I've given her."

"I don't get that, Claudia. Why would an ad campaign endanger them? When are you going to tell me why? If you don't know me that well, then why don't you give me a chance to know you?"

"Nobody knows me."

"I'll bet your boys know you."

"Are you jealous of that?"

"Maybe I am," Tanner admitted as he sat himself up on the edge of the bed. "I've been an open book with you, Claudia. I've told you some very painful things about me, about my past. Something beautiful happened between us tonight, didn't it?"

Holly nodded, the pain of her predicament written on her face.

"Claudia, when will you let me into your world too?"

She replied as she was walking away to get into her coat, and he almost didn't hear her say, with not a trace of a Southern accent, "When I can also tell you why my mother would never have named me Claudia."

Chapter Thirty

Blake

Blake's mother and wife had taken the 'strange' in estrangement to an incomprehensible level. Neither woman would agree to share the same space, no matter how much coaxing Blake did. They also weren't fessing up to the Sheriff about what had rifted them in the first place.

A tacit peace treaty was in place which would allow Blake to associate with one or the other—no bad-mouthing allowed—with the opposite party's complete cooperation. He didn't need his mother telling him constantly that he had married an ignorant tramp, *again.* Nor did he need his wife espousing to him how *truly scary* his mother had become and how neglectful she was of his father.

Blake needed a vacation to restore his equilibrium. Lucky for him, he and Minerva had the perfect get-away planned—if only they could find a way to ditch the kids. He chuckled to himself.

That wasn't fair, though. After all, they'd picked this destination for Jonah and Camillia specifically. Sammy would be too young to appreciate mouse ears and princesses, but if he didn't believe they'd ever taken him, the digital photos would prove him wrong.

Blake had wrapped up work and turned things over to his second-in-command, Harvey Morris, for his time away. After all, even a busy elected official deserved time to decompress. Just one more stop to make—his mother's house (and he steeled himself)—before they departed for the Spokane Airport and a blissful ten days away.

The Dermot house sat among a burst of mid-Spring tulips, golden and royal purple mingled with petal pink and bold reds, all neatly bordered by a trim lawn and shrubs of canary yellow forsythia. Blake stepped around the gnome holding the welcome sign on the concrete steps and rang the doorbell.

"Blake, honey! What a surprise…" His mother exclaimed. He tried not to be taken aback at Karen's emaciated appearance. She'd never been heavy and he remembered grueling workouts and fad diets throughout his childhood. Now, though, she didn't look fit; she looked starved and shriveled. Since her hairdresser became her nemesis, her hair had grown grayer and more unkempt.

Karen patted his cheek just like she'd done when he was a child. Forever his mom. That's what made the divide between Minerva and her so painful, as much as Blake tried to shrug it off.

His dad was all but lost to him. Blake could scarcely stomach the company of Winston nowadays between his disheveled appearance and his miserable attitude. None of them liked Winston's circumstances, but the man himself was the one who'd least accepted it.

His mother, in her fragile state, was the only person who kept him from being an orphan. And, well dammit, he'd lost too much to let her go too.

Blake heard a grunt from the front room. "Hey Mom, Dad," he nodded toward Winston on his way through the foyer.

"How are you? It's been forever since you've dropped by. Is work being good to you?" Karen quizzed.

"It's a lot of responsibility," Blake admitted, "but I kind of like calling the shots. I think we're doing a lot of good. We have a whole new department called the 'Preventative Law Enforcement Division' or PLED for short. They're going into schools and the jail and honing educational strategies that prevent crime from happening in the first place."

"Won't criminals just do their deeds anyway?" Karen asked.

"So much crime occurs out of desperation— someone hooked on drugs who needs money for more, a mom who doesn't have enough baby formula or diapers, or a teenager trying to impress his friends. If we prevent the drug addiction, the shoplifting, or the effects of peer pressure in the first place, just think how far we could go to prevent crime."

Karen's eyes shone. "See, I knew you'd make a difference as Sheriff. I'm so proud of you."

Blake ducked his head modestly. She was his mom. She had to say that. He changed the subject. "What do you hear from my sibs? I haven't seen either Troy or Tony for several weeks."

"They're busy holding down the office and the dealership. Without Dad around to help, I think the boys are at work most of the time. You should drop in on them during your lunch hour sometime."

"Have you seen any of the kids lately?"

Karen snorted. "Like any of my daughters-in-law care about me spoiling their babies…"

"Maybe you should pop in on them when you have a caregiver over," Blake suggested helpfully.

"If they wanted me to see the little ones, they'd show their faces once in a while," she countered stubbornly.

Blake shrugged it off. "How about the girls? Is Colby tired of playing society wife yet? Have you any idea what color Kelsey's hair is?"

"I know about as much about those ungrateful money-suckers as you do. Colby may have a rich husband, but he sure won't buy her a decent car. We're still footing the bill for her Beemer and her insurance. Go figure. Kelsey, our pauper of a peace-child, will always be 'on-the-take' as you law enforcement people put it. You'd think they would have figured out by now that your father and I aren't made of money anymore."

"You shouldn't have to deal with that, Mom. Cut them off. Seriously. Do you need their big brother to school them?"

"That's sweet, Son, but I'm afraid I'll have to be the one to strip the sheets from the beds I made with them. I keep waiting for them to grow up."

"You do remember how long it took me, right?" Blake offered wryly and they both chuckled.

"So are you off on that much-needed R and R, then?" Karen asked amiably.

"Yep. I stopped by to see if you and Dad needed anything before I jet off with Minerva and the munchkins."

At the mention of Minerva, Karen's lips pursed as if she'd bitten off a chunk of lime. Blake would have found it funny if the rift hadn't proven so damned uncomfortable over the last few months.

"Actually, I do have something for you, Blake. You can drop it in the official mail at the Sheriff's office for me. I'm sure Deputy Morris would be happy to put his stamp on it in your absence."

"What's that?" Uh-oh, Blake thought.

"I've written a letter for Sissy Reel, complete with a current photo of your father and me. I had Colby's photographer come all of the way from the coast to get a formal picture of the two of us, before it's too late, you know."

"Did you at least make sure to wipe his chin first?" Blake asked bluntly below Winston's ability to hear them.

"Would it have the same effect?" Karen retorted stubbornly.

Blake shook his head. Oh crap, he could only imagine how forlorn the two of them looked in portrait form right now.

"And this letter, it wouldn't contain any threats or distasteful language, would it?"

"For God's sake, Blake, the woman helped take my grandson away. She aided and abetted a known fugitive. She may have hauled herself off to the wilds of Montana recently, but I know you're fully aware of her new address. YOU should be threatening her plenty."

"I can't do that, Mom. That would be harassment. You would be harassing her if I sent her that letter. If it comes officially from the Sheriff's office, I would be doubly indicted," Blake tried to reason with her.

Karen sighed impatiently. "Okay, so I didn't seal it yet. You can read it if you want and see if it would be suitable."

Blake fingered the envelope as if it were pipe bomb wires. What could it hurt to read it? He removed the parchment stationery gingerly and read.

> *Dearest Sissy:*
>
> *I've recently learned of your relocation to Montana, I'm sure influenced by the fact that my son can't keep as close a watch on your activities from afar. Regardless of that, I wish you well with your new marriage. Spending a lifetime with someone is a special endeavor, and I can honestly say that to grow old with your favorite companion is a privilege few of us receive. I, for example, will never grow old with my Winston. As you can see by the enclosed picture, he is not well these days. Life has chewed him up and spit him out. His heart was broken six years ago and that heartbreak eventually deadened a good portion of his brain. You may deny responsibility as long and as insistently as you want, but I will always know the truth. That's why I've written, Sissy. To tell you that I know the truth. You know the truth. It's time for it to eat at you like it's eaten at us.*
>
> *Sincerely,*
> *Your Mortal Enemy,*
> *Karen Dermot*

Blake looked up from the note and the accompanying journey into a freak show that was

Karen and Winston Dermot's portrait, and raised his eyebrows at his mom, who looked at him expectantly, chastely. "You don't think the 'Your Mortal Enemy' part might be a little dramatic?" he asked with little humor.

"It's not a threatening letter, Blake. I think you can see that at least."

"It's plenty dark…"

"But only a glimmer of the darkness I experience every day," Karen argued, now toe to toe with her son.

He held his hands up in surrender. "Okay, okay, I will mail this. I will have Harvey look up Sissy's address at the department, but it will be mailed from the post office. I can't send this out as official Sheriff's office mail."

"I'm telling you, Blake, you have to be more forceful with these people…"

"And I'm telling you, Mom, that's the best I can do. I've kept Sissy and Susan on my radar since Holly's last disappearance. I've done a weekly search on her, Corey, and her youngest on the FBI database. I even have the local authorities in Red Lodge, Montana doing regular drive-bys at Sissy's new place and reporting on her travels. Other than those things—and any good cop could say I'm doing my best—I have duties I've sworn to uphold!"

He ran his hands through his hair in frustration and to resist biting on his thumb like his mother detested.

"Sometimes I think you believe that I don't want to find Corey. Moves like this scream that you still think that."

"I'm not sure you have the spine to do what it takes to find Corey."

"Like what, would you propose?"

"Arrest Sissy Reel. Arrest Susan Reel. Hold them until they say where you can find Holly and your boy. If they have to be in your holding cell for years, find other reasons why they need to be there, but make it clear that if they cooperated with you, they could regain their freedom from the highest law enforcement authority in the county. Put them in Hell, son. Like we've been in Hell."

"None of that is 'by-the-book'!" Blake protested. "You want me to misuse my power and put my job on the line."

Karen took both of Blake's hands and looked deep into his eyes. "No, Blake, honey, I want you to find our boy. Do whatever it takes. His grandfather needs to lay eyes on him again. I need to wrap my arms around him. Stop letting the women you've chosen as your life's companions to call the shots. They've neutered you. They've softened you to the point where you don't even try to be tough anymore."

"So I should let my mother control me instead?" he hedged as he took his hands back.

"I'm merely making suggestions. You can take them how you want."

Blake felt his nose start to run as he held back emotions—pain, frustration, horror at his parents' impossible situation—he had to get out of here before he really lost it. He never had been entirely graceful when he 'lost it' and that was precisely how he'd misplaced Corey and Holly in the first place.

The airport had never seemed so inviting.

"Okay, well," he cleared his throat. "I'll see to it that this gets in the mail."

"Thanks, son." Karen hugged him briefly, just a wisp in an ill-fitting housecoat. "Just do your best, my sweet boy, that's all I ask. Don't give him up. Please." She pleaded.

"I'll always do my best, Mom. I promise." Blake let the door click shut softly behind him. As soon as he reached his rig, he realized he hadn't even really looked in on Winston to see how he was doing. Sometimes it was as if he'd already gone. If only things could be so easily ignored with his mom, he thought as he fled the Dermot house, a place that had always meant home to a tight-knit clan. Blake glanced in his rearview mirror as the Dutch colonial shrank from view and thought how ironic it was that with nary a shrub or blade of grass out of place, the place— and their once invincible family—was in shambles.

Chapter Thirty-one

Tanner

A native of California, and the son of farm workers, Tanner had spent much of his childhood shifting between towns and farms in the central and northern parts of California. He was a teenager before his father took permanent work as a foreman on an avocado farm south of Fresno. His childhood morphed so often that he had little recall of the schools he'd attended or the early friends he'd made. Memories, when they did surface, often associated in his mind with the type of harvest his family sought.

He was roughly nine the first time they traveled far enough north to harvest cherries. It had been years since he'd had any, but he could still taste the tart, sweet juice of the ripe fruit and recall the stains on his face and hands from the blistering late spring day when he ate as many cherries as he put in his bucket. Torturous bellyaches and punishing trips to the bathroom broke him of such lunacy long before the foreman could reprimand him for eating the crop.

However, the uneasy boil in the pit of his stomach and how something so completely delicious could cause so much misery, taught him the lesson of a lifetime. The lesson: Don't eat too damn many cherries.

So it was, as Tanner left Claudia off at work, and flagged down a cab, that he recognized immediately the unsettling ache that gripped his gut as he sat and waited for the cabbie to load his wheelchair in the trunk.

He thought back. Nope, he hadn't had any cherries at lunch. Just a corned beef on rye and a kosher pickle—salty, but innocuous. The conversation, though, had been sweet and cheek-bitingly tart, like cherries:

Claudia had been fresh off teaching an ethics class with a particularly rousing group of students. She swept, rosy cheeked from the brisk spring breeze, into the deli and greeted Tanner with a rare kiss square on the lips.

"Maybe I should skip nursing altogether and just teach philosophy," she declared as she tossed her hobo bag on the floor and settled into the booth next to him. She shed her navy blazer to reveal a gauzy cornflower blue dress that brought out caramel tones in her unruly curls. Tanner affectionately tugged at one and Holly smiled.

"Are you sure? I find Sartre and Nietzche kind of dry."

"I don't mean that kind of philosophy, silly. I mean the practical kind. The kind that can be applied in real life," she giggled.

"I don't think they teach that kind of philosophy in college."

"You could be right, but I so enjoy philosophizing with these young idealists! Why, if the powers that be listened to them, we might just solve world hunger! Hey, did you order for me already?"

"It's not like you're old and worldly, my dear, and yes, I did order you a turkey and cranberry on sourdough just as you like."

Claudia's eyes clouded over like blue sky yielding to a thunderstorm.

"What? I thought that was your favorite. At least it was the last time we had lunch…" Tanner faltered.

"Hmm?" Claudia looked confused. "Oh, the sandwich. No, that's fine, Tanner."

"Was it the 'old and worldly' comment?" Tanner pressed. "Don't tell me you feel old when you just swept in here looking as perky as the Easter bunny."

Claudia laughed, bitterly. She never replied.

Oh no, here we go again with the 'you'll never know what I've been through and I'm not gonna tell you' nonsense, Tanner thought. Before he could blurt out how he felt about that, though, Claudia rendered him speechless with a kiss that could silence a Piccolo Pete.

That had been the sweet part. That kiss had held all the promise of a lifetime—raising kids, going to ballgames, growing old together—Tanner had felt that kind of power radiating from Claudia's embrace. He wasn't the only one either. When they came up for air, the owner of the deli caught Tanner's eye and gave him a rousing thumbs-up. As Claudia pulled away, she looked victorious, not because she'd felt it too, but because she knew she had successfully changed the subject. That was the part that roiled in the pit of his belly, on the cab ride home, like a bucketful of cherries.

Tanner wasn't one to play games. He didn't mince words. He was completely forthcoming with his past, his career, and his intentions—to most people, not just with Claudia. It was how he'd earned a reputation as an excellent businessman, who just happened to take exceptional pictures. His talent was instinctively knowing how to read someone well enough to know which portrait would best capture him or her.

He had yet to figure out Claudia's ideal portrait. He could try to capture the haunted fear in her eyes when he tried to press her for details about her past. He could snap a color photo of the painful blush that appeared when she hadn't gotten her fake accent right and she knew it. He could click a picture while she looked down at her hands and the part in her curls showed just right the pinkish blond roots that peeked out stubbornly from between them.

Claudia was fake from the colored contacts that made her eyes painfully red after ten o'clock, to the nicknames she used for her boys. A fool could hear the start and stop in her fabricated stories as she mistakenly dropped the first syllable of the wrong name or hinted at a place or animal from her childhood that sounded like nothing he'd ever heard of from Texas.

So his quandary was how to approach a liar who had no idea he'd cracked her ruse. Claudia, or whatever her name was, clearly thought she'd gotten away with it, which meant one of two things: Either she'd never let anyone else close enough to notice the holes in her story; or nobody else was as observant as Tanner.

What stuck in his proverbial craw was: Why should he care? Tanner didn't routinely associate with liars. He had no patience for it. Why didn't he just call a spade a spade as he would normally do and kick Claudia to the curb? They'd only known each other for four months. Their relationship had deepened physically, and they had fun when conversation stayed light. Claudia matched Tanner's playful banter with quick counter-remarks. She was an attractive, intelligent, confident woman, devoted to her two sons. She also seemed dedicated to him. They spent several evenings a week together.

Her easy acceptance of his disability also took him by surprise. There was no pity there. Sometimes she asked a technical question or two when it came to his comfort, and to his pleasure.

Perhaps, he thought, as he hoisted himself back into his chair and absentmindedly paid the cabbie, he clung to Claudia because of his immense physical attraction for her. After all, the last time he'd been this stupid about a woman, he'd moved to Los Angeles on a whim. He was, however, getting far too old for that nonsense.

But, his movie star girlfriend had never made him physically sick with worry. Nor had she ever lived up to his expectations about fidelity and honesty.

Claudia unknowingly twisted that knife in his gut every time she evaded his questions, not because she made him angry, which would be understandable.

No, it wasn't anger. It was worry—mind-bending worry; because the girl he'd slowly, but surely gotten to know, had chosen him carefully. She'd grown weary of hiding from him. He could tell by the frequency of her mess-ups. She loved him, he was pretty sure, and it was killing her to hide from him.

Tanner was worried sick about Claudia, because whatever she hid terrified her to the point where she would go completely blank, like a newly washed blackboard, at the prospect of revealing any of it. She'd run to one of the largest cities in the world to make herself invisible, and Tanner, of all people, had actually been able to see her. He was also troubled that when she realized how well he really knew her, Claudia would run from him. That prospect he couldn't handle. As bad as his mid-section felt worrying about her, he feared that *losing* her would steal the very air he breathed.

Chapter Thirty-two

Minerva

Vacation with three kids was a balancing act between the need to relax, and the drive to have as much fun as possible in a short span of time. Well, actually, Minerva was the driven one. Everyone else wanted to relax. If she spent one more lazy afternoon by the pool, she would go crazy!

They were in Southern California! There were six major amusement parks and several smaller operations within an hour of their time-share condominium! According to her calculations, they had six days left, and they needed to hit at least one major activity per day to see everything they could possibly see. Why else would they have come all this way except to see everything?

Yet, Camillia wanted nothing more than to collect seashells at the beach and Jonah was content to do cannonballs into the condo pool all day long. The parks wore them out. Sammy, he was cool—satisfied to hang out with his mama as long as she whipped out the milk jugs on demand. Blake, well, he wanted to make Minerva happy, so he mustered when she snapped her freshly French-manicured fingers. God, she loved that man.

She hoped today's activities would be a little lower key for the kiddos so she and Blake could do some hand-holding. Minerva's cousin had grown up in L.A. and dropped her a load of brochures in the mail before their trip to tell them about some of the lesser known tourist traps. Fun could be had off the beaten path, or so her cousin told her. Today they ventured to the heart of L.A., where there were no castles or water features.

"Holy nuts, Minerva," Blake exclaimed, because he was in earshot of the kids, "Where the heck are you taking us? This looks like stuff I saw on films of the Watts' riots."

Minerva looked around at the storefronts with steel bars on the windows, vagrants hanging around with bottles covered by paper bags, and punk kids pushing each other as they attempted to play soccer on the sidewalk. A lot of the kids were Latin, like her. There were a few blacks mixed in, yet she saw a red-headed Irishman sweeping his shop stoop—diversity teemed from the place. The Okanogan had never seemed further away.

"It looks peaceful enough, however I don't suggest you stop if this museum is inside one of these storefronts," she offered.

The kids remained silent. Jonah sat wide-eyed, but his sister and brother dozed.

"No kidding. My law-enforcement hackles are standing at attention right now. This neighborhood reeks of trouble waiting to happen. Keep the windows rolled up and try not to stare at anyone. They might pull out an oozie."

"That's not funny," she retorted, but her gut instincts started to hum anyway. Yeah, this might have been a bad idea. Ahead of her, however, she noticed the first of the banner signs she'd been looking for. "Look, honey. There are those signs the brochure said to look for."

Dilapidated storefronts gave way to bistro restaurants with tables out front and updated old warehouses with huge picture windows punched into the sides. About every half block there was a wrought iron light post with a colorful canvas banner anchored on the top and bottom. Each depicted a child at play and read, in bold Kelly green, *Inner Los Angeles Children's Museum.*

Apprehension turned to delight as Minerva pointed out the signs. "Gorgeous photography," she murmured as she rolled down her window to get a better look.

"I guess this isn't so bad. Their neighbors suck, but this looks like it might be a neat place," Blake admitted.

"Look there's a parking garage," Minerva pointed out and then strained in her seatbelt as Blake slammed on the brakes. Cars behind them honked in protest. "Blake! What the heck?"

"Do you see any parking on the street?" He asked through gritted teeth.

"Just go to the garage…"

"Just look up the street, would you?" He asked in irritation.

"Okay, but I think it would be safer to go to the garage," she argued again, but started looking. There were meters anyway, so God knew what Blake was thinking. Miraculously, she saw a spot for their rented crossover SUV on the right just a half a block ahead.

They were no sooner parked when Blake tore out his door, heedless of the traffic, earning himself more angry honks. Minerva realized, with major piss-tivity, that Blake had taken off on foot without even helping her with the kids. She wasn't about to leave them in the car by themselves, nor did she have three hands so that she could hold a baby on one hip and keep track of the other two.

So she sat there and ruined her manicure while she kept an eye on Blake in the rearview. If he went into a building and left them to their own devices, so help her, she would string him up by his toenails.

Instead of going inside, he walked back a block and a half and crossed the street at the crosswalk. Minerva shifted into the driver's seat and watched him from that side. Instead of going into the business there, a shipping store, he stopped at the banner overhead and stared at it with a mix of wonder and anger on his face. She'd seen that look before. That was an 'aha' look. What in the world could be on that sign?

Blake pulled his cell phone from his pocket and hit something on speed dial. He talked rapidly into it. A smile played about his mouth for a moment, but then his brow furrowed as he hung up. Minerva could think of only one thing that could have Blake so emotionally torn. Suddenly, she needed to see the sign too.

"Mommy, why did we stop? Are we going to see the museum you told us about?" Jonah finally inquired timidly from the back seat. He'd been watching his dad too, she knew, because he sounded as confused as she felt.

"Yes, baby. As soon as Daddy comes back to the car we'll go. You see, he's walking back here now," she reassured him. Camillia remained conked out in her car seat, which was a blessing because she would definitely be hollering by now.

Blake walked lightly back to the SUV, coming to the passenger side window, so Minerva rolled it down. He'd left in such a hurry that the keys remained in the ignition.

"I'm so sorry I left like that. It just occurred to me that I probably scared the daylights out of you," Blake put his huge hands on the door and rested his loving face on them. "Forgive me?"

Minerva put on her best mean mommy face, even though her core melted when he looked at her like that. "We are in the downtown of a city that neither one of us is familiar with, and you just took off and left me and your three children to our own devices…"

"Not for very long!" he defended.

"…Well you're not going to get off that easy. Not until you tell me what it is you think you saw on that sign. I saw your face, Blake. It was huge, wasn't it? Was it Corey?"

His face changed then—the anger, the wonder, the possibility, the joy—all registered at once. Minerva put her hand on his cheek to wipe away a tear that escaped his eye. "Tell me, sweetheart."

Blake put his hand over hers and choked out the next words that set her heart pounding, "It wasn't Corey, but I think it might have been his brother."

~~~~~~~~~~

"This is what we have," said Deputy Morris over the cell's speakerphone later that evening, "We have the name of the photographer. Tanner Grafton divides his time between New York and L.A. We have a time of the photo. According to his agent, it was taken last fall and the signs were put up in January. The cell phone photo you sent me shows fall foliage which, by deduction, means the photo was taken in a northern climate…"

"Which means it may have been taken in New York," Blake finished. "That gives us a city anyway."

"Not so fast, though, Enforcer. I have to admit this birthmark on the kid's cheek is a ringer for the one you have on the baby photo you saved. We turned the daredevil's picture over with the Photoshop program at the office and put it side-by-side with the baby picture you stowed in your file cabinet six years ago. I agree with you. That mark has gotten a little bigger and a little darker, but it's pretty recognizable. You know the possibility still exists that this is a coincidence and that two kids could have similar birthmarks."

"Harv, I noticed it with the kid upside down and grinning, while I was driving in L.A. traffic. Besides, the kid looks just like her. His hair is straighter, but it's the same color and I'd know that smile anywhere."

Blake tried to ignore the smear of pain he saw cross his wife's face. This wasn't about Holly. Minerva had to know that by now. It was about Corey.

"Grafton has a studio in Manhattan. The guys at the nearest NYPD precinct agreed to check it out for me, though it's pretty low on their list of priorities. Our best bet might be if you hired a private detective to scope him out instead. It might cost you," Harv admitted.

"Up until now, I've used mostly law enforcement resources. You're right. If this photographer guy knows Holly and he knows she's in hiding, the cops won't get anywhere. We need something a little more covert."

"We have some money in savings, Blake. We can use that to hire a private eye," Minerva offered quietly, her words surprising him with their powerful intention.

"Okay…" Blake agreed tentatively.

"I'll see if the guys at NYPD can recommend someone good," Harv replied, sounding excited as he rang off.

"You know this is just a shot in the dark," Blake admitted, as he rubbed his wife's back. The kids had already crashed and it was just the two of them and a cell phone out on their veranda.

"I know that you believe it's your best shot in six years," Minerva replied wearily.

"We need to talk about this, sweetheart. You and I have worked hard for those savings…"

"Yes, and they paid for this trip. We thought the rest might be for Hawaii in a year or so or a new minivan or a remodel," Minerva finished. "But, Blake, if you could use that money to find your child, does any of the rest of that matter?"

"You do realize that finding Corey means finding Holly?" Blake asked gently as he began to plant blazing kisses on her exposed shoulders.

"Blake, honey, you divorced her years ago. Whatever you guys had when we were all kids is hogwash now. You've known me long enough to know how confident I am. Holly and her delicate little curls and her non-stop cute body and her poor-me attitude, well, she doesn't hold a candle to me, now does she?"

Blake merely chuckled and pulled a spaghetti strap aside for better access.

"You deserve to have your boy back, Sheriff.

I've seen how hard you've worked to become a better man. I know how desperately you miss him," Minerva caught Blake's face in her hands and stared deeply into his eyes. "I love you and I can't stand for you to be in pain anymore. We do what we have to do to bring him home. Period."

Blake stared back, a man who had once been a naïve, giant boy and chased his first family away. She could see the doubt in his eyes. He could beat himself up forever over Holly. Well, she wouldn't let him. The time had come for them to fix things, together.

Minerva kissed Blake with all of the fire he'd kindled inside her. He moaned and lifted her easily, carrying her over to the shadowed corner where the deck storage closet met the wall of their condo. He ground into her pelvis shooting lava through her middle as she fumbled with his belt. When they joined, she melted into the wall and they exploded into the rhythm that defined them: Tender passion and scorching chemistry that no old flame could ever hope to compete with.

Chapter Thirty-three

Holly

Crunch time, she thought mirthfully as she fingered benefits packets from the three hospitals who had offered her jobs.

June had arrived in a spate of unseasonable heavy rains and high winds, making the offer from Columbia Medical School all the less desirable. She loved her Brooklyn digs and the boys were comfortably ensconced in their school and activities, but a part of Holly believed that she was running on borrowed time if she stayed in New York too much longer. A runner needed to run, didn't she? Could she conceivably stay here for the rest of the boys' childhoods and expect to remain hidden? She left the packet on the bed.

There was Brigham and Women's in Boston, by far the best offer she'd gotten. Her boss would be another woman who considered Dr. Howard Young her mentor. She would hire Holly to be an associate professor in the nursing program and a clinical instructor in the hospital itself. She'd get the chance to work directly in patient care, but also mentor others in their direct-care skills. The amount of money and benefits they'd offered her were excellent, enough to allow she and the boys to live in a more affluent area of town or she thought about commuting by train from Cambridge or Worcester. She and the boys had taken several 'field trips' there on the bus and all three of them were enthusiastic about the more compact city.

Then there was UCLA Medical Center. At UCLA, Holly would be doing a similar job to what she did now, teaching ethics and professionalism as a full-time professor. While she found teaching rewarding, she missed the patient interaction she had while working in a hospital setting. She wouldn't see very many patients directly in the L.A. job. Plus, she'd be back on the West Coast in much closer proximity to home. Yes, it was a huge city and she could still maintain a level of invisibility, but L.A. was also a major media capital and only two days' drive away from Washington State. Holly wondered about her psyche more than anything if she decided to go to L.A.

She shuffled the UCLA packet to the bottom of her pile. It was the least lucrative offer. Holly sighed. There had to be an easier way to make this decision. Her lease ran out at the end of June, so she needed to give notice on the apartment if they were leaving. Plus, she and the boys had a lot of packing to do, now that they were out of school. She looked over at Tristan and Corey playing their video games, still comfy in their pajamas, and envied again the simplicity of a child's life.

Today was finally a sunny day, so she'd promised them a trip to the park after lunch. To speed up her process, she decided to make a list of the pros and cons about each job and city, so she got out a yellow legal pad and drew three neat columns with a straight-edge. She wrote Columbia, UCLA, and B & W in the three columns. Against her will, and her better judgment, she wrote the first thing that popped into her head when she looked at the first column: Columbia meant New York. New York meant Tanner.

But, then she could put that at the top of the list in the UCLA column too because he spent most of his spring and summer out there. Tanner enjoyed four seasons, so he endured the fall chill and winter snow of New York and brilliant springs and summer tans of Los Angeles. Plus, those were the best times for photo opportunities in each place. Tanner loved his bicoastal life. In fact, he'd left in May to go back to his Malibu home, and as much as Holly tried to put him out of her head while he was gone, he inevitably crept back in. They talked daily and she remembered with a heavy heart last night's conversation:

"So when are you making the move to L.A.?" Tanner teased. He thought she'd love the sunshine and fresh air of the West Coast. He'd even offered to rent a beach house to her on Malibu. He owned three and rented the two out that he didn't occupy.

Holly wasn't sure, though, that she wanted him to exert that kind of control over her life. "The boys prefer Boston or New York so that they can stay in touch with their friends," she countered.

"The boys are young enough to adapt to whatever their mommy decides," Tanner pointed out, teasingly, but Holly could hear the edge in his voice.

"Maybe so, but Tanner, you know my best offer is from Brigham and Women's."

"I do know this, but I've already got places in New York and L.A. Are you suggesting I add to my real estate empire and find a Boston home too?"

"I'm not suggesting anything of the sort, Tanner. This is my life to figure out."

She could hear the raw hurt in his voice when he contemplated that and replied back, "So what you're saying is that you don't need me to be a part of that life once you've got it figured out?"

"Oh, Tanner, you know I could never say that. You're an amazing friend…"

"Ouch."

"…and there are other benefits to our friendship…"

"I should say so," he countered, the intimate tone in his voice heating her as it always did. Tanner had a sexy voice.

"…but do you realize how many times we fought this spring about me and my past and me letting you in and, just, all of that hogwash, Tanner? I can't make you see that my past doesn't matter. Who I am now is what matters. You can't just accept that, ever, and that just plain wears me out."

She heard him breathe into the phone for a few moments, but she couldn't read what he might say next. "I would accept you for who you are now if that person was truly you, but you've hidden you, behind a ruse."

"This is precisely what I'm talking about," Holly replied heatedly. "Just because I won't tell you about my past, you think that makes me a fake?"

"You are fake, *Claudia*. Otherwise, why would I find no record of a Claudia Brown of your relative age from Lubbock, Texas? Every story you've fabricated about your childhood is a lie, isn't it?"

"You've been checking me out? What, did you hire a private detective? I thought I saw a guy scoping me out the other day at the park," Holly shot back angrily.

Tanner's reply was acid. "No, I did not sick a detective on you. I simply did an online search for you. I was curious, okay?"

So who was the guy? Holly wondered briefly. To Tanner she retorted, "No, it's not okay, Tanner. If you cannot take me at face value, I'm certainly not going to make a move across the whole country for your benefit."

"I think it might be best if we continued this conversation some other time," Tanner countered. "I'm sorry you think I'm too nosey. It happens to be because I care."

Yeah, Holly thought, a little too much. She hadn't allowed herself the liberty of caring as much for a man she admired more than she'd admired any other man. Her relationship with Tanner was perhaps the most honest relationship she'd ever had—less about sex or necessity, and more about respect and friendship. Ironic, since he didn't know the slightest truth about her. Also ironic that he knew her well enough to sense that.

She bid him goodbye wearily, glad that he couldn't hop into a cab and show up at her door. Though he'd respected her wishes and avoided coming by while the boys were home, Tanner was more than familiar with her apartment. She blushed when she thought of the last time he'd been in her bed.

Her reverie was interrupted by Tristan, who stood in her bedroom doorway, beautiful and eager. "Mom, there's someone at the door! Can I answer it?"

"Thank you for asking, baby. You know it's not safe for you to get the door by yourself. I'll get it since you're still in your jammies."

"Aw, Mom."

"Well, if you would ever get some clothes on, you would be presentable to the neighbor lady or the florist or whoever might be at our door," Holly laughed at the sour expression on her son's face.

Holly smoothed her hair and looked through the peep hole. She recoiled in horror when she saw the uniformed policeman waiting expectantly at the door.

"Um, yes, can I help you?" She called through the blessed protection of the door.

"NYPD, ma'am. I need to ask you a few questions," came the reply.

"May I please see your I.D. before I open the door?" She asked shakily.

He held the badge up to the peep hole and it looked legitimate enough.

"Can I ask what this is regarding?" Holly still refused to open the lock to a man who could mean the end of life as she knew it. By now, both of the boys had dropped what they were doing and stood behind her expectantly.

"I've come by at the request of a distant colleague, a county sheriff from Washington by the name of Blake Dermot. Now if you would please open the door, ma'am, I do need to ask you a few questions."

Holly's mouth went dry as she felt her breath leave and her world tilt on its axis. She looked at her boys. She'd failed them again, when all she'd ever wanted to do was protect them. Wait, Blake was *sheriff*? Oh God, that meant she would never see either of them again. She looked over her shoulder toward the fire escape.

"Mom?" Corey sensed her panic.

"Cody," she said as calmly as she could, "will you please take your brother into your room and get the two of you dressed?"

"Is everything ok...?"

"Cody, I need you to do it right away," she interrupted and he knew from her expression that everything was most definitely not okay.

"Just a minute," Holly called out to the officer.

"Just in case you're thinking of stalling and leaving through the back exit, miss, we've got that covered too. Sheriff Dermot thought you might consider such a thing. I'm beginning to sense that he's right. Now, I'm going to ask one more time calmly for you to please open the door."

Holly's hand shook uncontrollably as she reached for the chain lock and opened the door. The officer was young, perhaps early twenties, and Italian. He looked wary, as if she were a hardened criminal about to put a move on him.

"I'm Officer D'Angelo. Do we get to talk calmly and rationally?" He asked evenly.

"Y-yes," Holly replied. She could see both boys in the threshold of their room getting dressed as fast as they could. The officer glanced over toward them.

"Good boys, getting dressed. Would you like to go for a ride in a police car?"

"Yah," Tristan yelled excitedly and Holly couldn't help but smile through her sudden tears.

"Why?" Corey asked suspiciously, simultaneously. He could sense Holly's distress and he was, after all, the man of the house.

"Does the name Corey Dermot mean anything to you, son?" The officer asked kindly.

"Sounds familiar," Corey admitted, "but I don't know why you're here asking that."

"Ma'am, would you like to explain to your boy who Corey Dermot is, or shall I?"

"Don't you want to know who I am first?" Holly

asked, stymied that this officer should make so many assumptions based on a demand from an officer of the law so far away.

"Oh, we've already made you, ma'am. Your ex-husband identified you from photos taken about a week ago. And this boy, here, well he just happens to look exactly like the little boy you took from Mr. Dermot when he was less than two years old. We did an age-enhanced drawing of what he would look like from a photo he had taken back then. It seems you have a lot of explaining to do."

There was another knock at the door and Officer D'Angelo opened it to reveal a mousy-looking woman in an ill-fitting gabardine suit. She wore her gold-rimmed spectacles on the end of her nose. She peered over them at Holly, large-eyed and suspicious.

"This is Ms. Hart. She works for Children's Services here in the city. We've asked for her assistance in placement of your boys…"

"What? My boys? You're not taking them anywhere!" To Holly's horror, Ms. Hart pursed her lips tartly and went straight over to the boys whose faces had glazed over with confusion. The woman bent down and introduced herself quietly, then took both boys' hands and led them back to their bedroom.

"They'll be perfectly safe, I assure you," Officer D'Angelo replied soothingly. "Sheriff Dermot has already made arrangements for them."

What the hell? Holly held up her hands. "My ex-husband has nothing to do with these boys. If he's in charge here, I'm sure he's told you all about how he shoved me and broke my arm before I ran away from him."

This earned raised eyebrows from Officer D'Angelo, but he didn't budge.

"He can't be allowed to have these children at his disposal, you see. No matter who he says he is," Holly insisted. "He could hurt them. Tristan isn't even his. How am I supposed to trust that they'll be well-cared-for if you tell me that my former abuser is to be left in charge of their care?"

"Regardless of what went down wit' you and Sheriff Dermot," Officer D'Angelo persisted, "he has paperwork proving you and your boy are fugitives. You kidnapped the boy and kept him from his rightful father, according to the law. That's all I'm sworn to protect. Now, if you will kindly put your wrists forward, I need to put these cuffs on them."

Every fiber in her being told Holly to resist, but she'd mentally prepared so many times for this moment, that she clung to good sense and obeyed. After all, if she resisted, the boys would see further need to panic and all hell would break loose.

As soon as the cuffs were fastened, and she was read her Miranda rights, reality set in and Holly could no longer hold off the sobs that issued forth from her chest. The boys were led out, their duffel bags packed with what they needed, and Officer D'Angelo guided her with his hand on the small of her back to follow them.

At the bottom of the stairs, Tristan suddenly broke away from Ms. Hart, ran back to his mother, and threw his arms about her neck. "No, Mommy, no!" he shouted.

She sobbed all the harder. Corey followed suit and though she couldn't hug them back, Holly planted kisses on their heads and took in their scents, locking them into her memory.

"I love you, Taylor and Cody, no matter what. We'll be together again soon, I promise."

Her boys. Her heart disintegrated as she wondered if she'd just told them a terrible lie. They were pried gently away in the harsh light of the foyer.

Holly looked up as a huge figure filled the doorway. He moved closer and she caught the first glimpse of a face she'd hoped never to see again.

"It's him! It's my boy! Corey!" Blake shouted and fell to his knees in front of her oldest son, who gasped and took a step backwards. Blake's joy turned quickly to dismay. He stood, thinner than she remembered, but even more imposing than he'd ever seemed in their years together. With his first glance at Holly— anger, betrayal, resentment in eyes black as coal—she realized she'd told the biggest lie of all.

In fact, she'd be lucky if she ever laid eyes on her boys again.

Chapter Thirty-four

Stanley

"Do you want this bad boy above the fireplace mantel or over here behind the dining table?" Sissy roused Stanley from a Sudoku puzzle as she carried her treasure from one place to the next for demonstration.

"Must we have lovers *en flagrante* adornin' our livin' space?" Stanley quizzed, unconvinced that the flaming crimsons and passionate purples of Sissy's abstract painting distracted the eye enough to disguise the purposeful intent of the central figures. They were about to 'get it on' if you asked him.

"Leave it to a man to see something phallic within a completely abstract embrace. I just don't see it, Stanley. All I see is the color. It's beautiful. It makes me hot."

"Well, if it makes you hot…" he chuckled. "On second thought, maybe you should put it above our bed."

"The painting looks great in here, though. It brightens up your gray curtains," Sissy argued.

"*Our* gray curtains," Stanley corrected, planting a kiss on her bare shoulder, and relieving her of her burden. "Okay, I know this was a bargain at the flea market and you did somehow match the red in my couches by accident, so I guess I'll make a concession and get rid of the cowboy portrait above the dinin' table…"

"The frame sucks anyway." Sissy sealed the deal with a rousing kiss.

Stanley laughed. "I'll go get a hammer and a heavier nail."

"You could use the one I tapped through Karen Dermot's forehead on that picture she sent me. It's hanging on your bulletin board."

"I would never disturb that one. That was nice work. I have a nail in my desk, I'm sure."

He went into his office to rummage for a nail and was caught mid-task by the ringing of the office phone. That was odd—in his business, he got calls at all hours of the day and night, so a mid-Sunday afternoon call wasn't that unusual—but this one showed up on caller ID as 'OKCTYJAIL'. Stanley smelled trouble. He propped the painting against the wall and answered the phone. "Stanley P. Diddredge."

"I only get one phone call, Stanley. Let's make it count."

"Claudia?"

"Claudia is history. Apparently the powers that be have decided that I get to be Holly Dermot again. I haven't seen her in years, and from what I can tell, she's a dead-tired broad—jet-lagged and looking like hell in an orange jumpsuit."

"Let me guess, they wanted you to get 'settled' 'fore they let you call me." Stanley knew the drill, unfortunately. If his guess was right, Holly had probably already been in custody for a good twenty-four hours, but then if she'd already made it to Washington, maybe it had been longer.

"I could've called a lawyer right away, but I refused to until I could talk to you and mom. So I had to wait. I got the good 'ol first class escort with Blake and one of his cronies on almost the first flight out of New York. You do know a good lawyer, don't you Stanley?"

"Well for a girl whose cover has been blown, you sure are in a chipper mood," Stanley offered.

"I can't go serious just yet. I'll go crazy. Certifiable. They'll lock me up. Oh wait, they already did." An ironic laugh bubbled out of Holly's throat. "I don't know where the boys are. Ah, God, what are you going to tell Mom? She'll go apeshit."

Stanley realized Holly rode on a razor thin edge of hysteria, so he sought to calm her. "I'm sure the boys are in good hands. Blake just got his boy back, right? He'd want to make sure they were well-taken-care-of. Don't you worry none about your mother. I'll take care of her."

"You'll take care of who?" Sissy rounded the corner into the office, red hair and flip-flops flying. Apparently his search for a nail had taken too long. "Who is that, Stan?"

Stanley's mouth went dry. Holly was right. Sissy was going to freak. There was no pretty way to tell her that her baby daughter and grandsons were in the hands of Holly's abuser, a man who also happened to possess all the winning cards in this poker game.

"Listen, dear," he spoke to Holly as if she were a client playing the changey-name-game, because while he wanted to reassure Holly, he surely didn't want her on the phone when he shared this news with Sissy. That most certainly would not calm Holly. "I can help you do this, but you need to give me a day to gather my resources. After that, I can and will meet with you in person to try and resolve this matter."

"She's standing right there with you, isn't she?" Holly deduced.

"That's correct, ma'am," Stanley replied. "Thank you for calling, though, because I can see that you need my help."

"Can you lock her in a padded room before you tell her?" Holly asked in all seriousness.

"I don't want you to worry none, girlie. I'll fix you up right. I will."

"Just break it to her gently and then get your butts out here, will you?"

"That I can do, sweetheart. That I can do. Alright, then, I'll be talking to you soon." Stanley replaced the phone in its cradle like it was a scorpion with its tail reared back.

Sissy stood before him, arms crossed, tapping her foot impatiently. "Stanley P. Diddredge, I've known you way too long to be fooled by your doogie dance."

"Doogie dance?"

"Yeah, you know, when you've stepped in a pile of steaming dog doogie and you're trying to rub it on everything to get it all off your shoe."

"How was that phone call a doogie dance?"

"Whatever was said before I came bounding into the room clearly stunk because your face was bunched up enough to stay that way if someone came along and pinched you on the butt."

"What in the hell are you saying, woman?" Stanley tried to appear confused. "That one's face freezes in place when one gets pinched on the butt?"

Sissy didn't budge. "Don't change the subject, Stanley. You spent the rest of that phone call trying to wipe crap off your shoe. Was it so that I wouldn't notice how worried you were by that call? Well I did notice. You haven't looked that worried since you thought I was gonna turn you down at the altar."

Stanley blew his air out in a rush before he knew he'd been holding it. "That was Holly," he confessed.

"Holly? Is she okay?" Sissy sat down in Stanley's office chair, hands on her lap, waiting for him to continue.

"She's in jail."

"She's WHAT? Where?"

Really, there was no way to pull this punch. "Okanogan County."

Sissy's hands flew to her mouth as the color left her face. "He has my babies, doesn't he?"

"She sounded fine, Sissy. Not hurt, but plenty worried."

"She better not be hurt. I don't care what I have to do to protect her from Blake Dermot. I will not see him break her again," Sissy banged her hand on his desktop as angry tears sprang to her eyes.

"We probably need to get out there. I can take my business on the road for several days. My friend

Rummy has a private plane. We could be there in a few hours."

"Ah yes, Rummy. Such an inspirational name for a pilot," Sissy breathed, but nodded her head vigorously. "When can we leave?"

"Give me a half-hour. You can pack. Leave out the 44 Magnum too, Sissy. I mean it."

"It's not like we have to go through airport security…" She started to argue, and then saw that her hubby meant business. Besides, Stanley thought, she would need more than a pistol to break Holly out. She'd need the whole Gestapo and an armored tank, and then they'd probably only land their own asses in jail too.

Nope. They were going to have to do this one on the up and up. By the book. Stanley hated the goddamn book. He cursed under his breath as Sissy fled to their bedroom in a scarcely concealed panic.

Just how in the devil had Blake Dermot caught up to Holly? Did he somehow trace phone records or have someone follow him or Sissy to Orlando? Why wouldn't he have nabbed her six months sooner, then?

As Stanley picked up the phone to call Rummy, his gut twisted wretchedly. Obviously, he'd failed the love of his life in the most basic of ways. Somehow her daughter had been caught. In a case where he thought he'd done everything right, Stanley knew he wouldn't rest until he found out just what in the hell had gone wrong.

Chapter Thirty-five

Karen Dermot

The way to describe how she had felt when Blake called her from New York and said he had their boy? Well, she'd been simply giddy.

The lightness she felt hadn't faded, either, even when it took four endless days for Blake to arrive home with Corey. He had offered to bring their boy by on his way into town, but she would have none of that. She and Winston planned to meet them at the airport, just two hours away, in Wenatchee. They'd been far too house-bound as it was and she didn't see why they couldn't have a little outing.

She'd bathed Winston and fixed him and herself up like they were going out on a date. She had even put on a hat. It took the help of both of her other sons to get Winston loaded into the car, but load him they did. Winston protested the whole time, but she was, no way, going to let him stop her from getting her first good look at her grandson since his babyhood.

Half an hour into the trip, Winston shat himself. Karen nearly wanted to vomit with the stench, and, with every moment, imagined the smell seeping into her hair and clothes. Why, that would ruin Corey's and her reunion for sure. She didn't have the resources to clean him up that she would need, nor had she thought to bring a change of clothes—after all, Winston was hardly a baby—so she'd made-do at the nearest restroom with paper towels and personal sanitizer.

Another half an hour into the trip, Winston started

to moan like a bad radio signal. She asked him
politely to please be quiet, but this only made him
speak up louder. Karen decided that her husband
must be hungry, so she whipped into a middle-of-
nowhere fruit and coffee stand and bought him a
hand-stirred chocolate milkshake. His favorite, or at
least so she thought.

Winston complacently took two sips of the shake,
and then with that spastic, evil way he had with soft
food in general, he flung the cup into the windshield
of the Mercedes. Near tears, Karen wished fleetingly
that she had windshield wipers on the inside of the
window so she could wipe the shake away and get on
with it. Instead, she pulled to the side of the road and
used her hands and suit jacket to get the worst of it off
the window and dash.

Winston gestured and postured the whole time.
She could tell he was upset, but then what did that
make her? She was well beyond upset, after all. Yet,
she couldn't just pile him onto the shoulder of the
road and leave him to fend for himself, as she was
wont to do.

Instead of turning around, though, which was
obviously his aim, Karen decided to stay her path.
She ignored his annoying protests and the sudden
pungent odor of fresh urine, though how she even
detected the latter over the smell of chocolate
milkshake and shit, she did not know.

Forty-five minutes from the shake wipe-down,
Karen heaved a sigh of relief as she pulled into the
airport terminal and parked her car in temporary
parking. She couldn't possibly load Winston into the
chair by herself, so rolled down all four windows and
put the sun shade in the front window to protect him
from the oppressive summer heat.

She noticed people departing from the terminal so
she rushed inside to greet Blake and Corey before they
could be whisked away with the posse of sheriff's
vehicles parked at the terminal curb.

The sight of her son, his arm draped loosely about

the shoulders of a tall, full-bodied miniature of himself brought her to a sudden halt. Her hand flew to her mouth. Corey. She blinked back tears that had waited years to fall.

Blake spotted her and waved enthusiastically as he and his son approached. He stopped short of embracing her and cleared his throat. "Um, hi, Mom. Where's Dad?"

"He's in the car."

"In this heat?"

"Oh, I've shaded him and left the windows down," Karen waved his questions away. "Now, can I please get a proper greeting from my son and grandson?"

Blake pulled Corey out from where he'd hidden behind him and introduced him. "Son, this is your grandmother, my mom, Karen Dermot."

Karen pursed her lips before she could blurt out that she should hardly have to be introduced. The boy should just know his own grandmother, right?

Corey looked at her sternly and she could hardly repress a grin when she remembered all the times Blake had regarded her so seriously. He moved slightly closer, assessing her, then his nose wrinkled up as if he'd happened upon a pig pen.

"I'm Corey," he offered her an outstretched hand. So, he wouldn't get close enough for a hug, but he'd learned some manners along the way. "Or at least that's what they tell me."

The last part felt like a slap. "Who else would you be?" Karen demanded.

"His mom called him Cody," Blake explained.

"Why in the world would she confuse poor Corey that way?"

"They were on the run, Mom," Blake replied honestly, far too gently as far as she was concerned. As if running with her grandchild was perfectly understandable. She bit back a retort, though, when she detected a look of warning in her son's eyes. They could talk about this later.

She had no way of curbing her reaction, though,

when a spritely blond ruffian came bounding from behind Corey and held out his hand enthusiastically. "I'm Taylor!" he pronounced.

Karen recoiled in horror. What would the other child be doing *here?* Didn't he belong in some New York foster home until his mother could reclaim him? He was, after all, her spawn, her problem, as far as Karen was concerned. She pretended to ignore Taylor's outthrust hand.

"Your name is Tristan, numbnuts." Corey pulled his little brother quickly next to him and flashed Karen a suspicious look. He hadn't taken kindly to her rebuff of his younger brother, she could see.

"Hey, watch the name-calling," Blake admonished. Blake had taken in her discomfort as well, but he, as always, tried to smooth things over. "Tristan is going to be staying with us while we get this all figured out."

"With you? But why?" Karen blurted.

"Corey needs his brother right now," Blake replied through gritted teeth, brooking no argument.

Yet argue she did. This just wasn't right. "Corey needs his *real* family right now, not the fake-out he's been fed for years. Couldn't you just let the authorities handle this…this boy?"

Tristan had already moved on, paying no attention to the stinky, mean lady in the stained blouse. He'd already begun to chat up the deputy near the entrance.

Corey, however, had caught every word exchanged between Karen and Blake. His jaw hardened and she could tell he fought back tears. The kind of separation she suggested was just the kind that terrified him. "Tristan *is* my real family. As far as I know, you're just a smelly, nasty bitch who needs to change her clothes."

Blake and Karen gasped collectively as Corey ran over to join his brother, passing a baleful glance over his shoulder at Karen Dermot.

Karen's mascara turned to rivulets coursing down

her cheeks. Blake put a hand on her shoulder. "Mom,
I'm sorry…"

"Don't," she struck out at his arm viciously. "I have
had one hell of a day. Just to be here with you. With
Corey. I don't want to hear that you're sorry."

"I didn't expect him to react that way," Blake
soothed. "I'll talk to him later about manners…"

"Yes, well, you know this is not your fault," Karen
replied, trying mightily to collect herself. "You don't
have to apologize. After all, the blame for this rests
in their mother's hands. She will be the one who has
to pay. And you're going to make her pay in spades,
aren't you darling."

Blake nodded solemnly, but the ill-concealed
shudder that accompanied his nod was what set
her nerves humming. She sensed doubt. She sensed
weakness.

He would make this right, wouldn't he? She would
be damned if someone didn't make this right, for all
of them.

Chapter Thirty-six

Corey

Corey felt as if he'd been bitten by a rattlesnake—
an animal he'd only seen in an aquarium in the
Central Park Zoo—and the doctors had done
everything they could to stop the flow of poison into
his system. They'd sucked out what they could, put
ice packs everywhere, and even injected anti-venom,
but the enemy still surged through his body with
every heartbeat, wasting his flesh and swelling his
head to the point where he thought it would explode.

He shivered despite the one hundred degree heat
and pulled himself further into the corner of the
dugout where he hid, from them, from everything.
Only one short week and he wondered how he could
possibly feel any sicker.

First his mom had been dragged away in
handcuffs, crying out to them how she was sorry, how
much she loved them. He believed her. The pain of
watching her go away like that stung still just like a
snake bite would.

Then the poison: Your name isn't what she told
you it is. Your name is Corey. The giant of a man
standing over there talking quietly to your mother,
who does nothing but cry—he's your father. You are
actually from Washington State and your mother stole
you away when you were just a baby. Your brother's
name isn't Taylor either, but Tristan. No, the big man
isn't his father too. He's only your half-brother. I'm
sorry, son, but you can't stay here, and, no you can't
see your mom and see if she's okay. By the way, we

need to decide if your brother and you will have to be
separated too.

The horror, the confusion, seeped into his skin.
Then they brought him to hell, or a place at least as
hot, and as out-of-the-way. His welcoming committee
was a one-woman portable toilet, who claimed to be
his long-lost grandmother, and who put the hate on
his brother right away. Now, jetlag had allowed the
poison to grow even stronger. He wanted to scream.
He wanted to rail. He wanted to run away. But he was
entirely too sick, too confused, too angry.

He ignored the crunch of gravel as a police cruiser
pulled up to the baseball field and the officer got
out and yelled for him. The cell phone in his pocket,
they'd insisted he carry, sounded off again, so he
chucked it under the bench. He waited for what felt
like hours and finally silence was his again.

His stomach protested the fact that he'd skipped
out on dinner. He wished he'd brought a book to
distract himself with.

Finally, dark ate up the bitter sun and the crickets
sang their relief. Heat turned into the sweet smell of
cut grass on a gentle, soothing breeze. Corey loosened
his grip on his frustration long enough to fall asleep.

Chapter Thirty-seven

Sissy

Miraculously, Blake hadn't arrested Sissy yet. She and Stanley had arrived in Washington merely hours after Holly's call, thanks to Rummy. Since their arrival had been after visiting hours, though, she'd had to spend a fitful night in a hotel on the outskirts of town. Hotter than blazes by day, the Eastern Washington summer heat hadn't slacked off enough to let in sleep, not that she could have slept anyway.

Morning had dawned hotter still, making Sissy yearn for her new mountain home, in lieu of this furious desert.

Her reception at the jail, while glacially overseen by her ex-son-in-law himself, had been nothing short of professional. She did not get the third degree, but was allowed to see her daughter while Stanley consulted with an attorney friend who'd driven from Spokane to meet them.

Holly knew their conversation would be monitored, so she did her best to pretend like they hadn't seen each other all those years. Sissy played along, because her involvement , as far as Blake was concerned, was clearly foggy at best; and because it would do no good for her grandsons if she was thrown in the slammer as well.

Holly had looked frazzled, the shadows under her eyes a testament to her lack of sleep. One thing was immediately clear: Holly wasn't worried for herself. She was terrified what would happen to her boys. Sissy played her cards to win when she lied through

her teeth and said she'd already seen them and that
they were doing fine.

Where were they? She'd asked. Safe, Sissy had
replied. With who? She'd asked. Good people, Sissy
had responded quickly. Then she'd changed the
subject. They needed to talk about bail, arraignment—
legal things. Holly needed to entrust the boys' well-
being to Sissy.

By the time she'd hugged her daughter goodbye,
Sissy was near panic herself, wondering just how
she would fulfill that responsibility. She could tell by
Blake's impenetrable gaze, as she exited the jail to find
him standing by his police cruiser: Hell could freeze
over before she laid eyes on those boys again.

That was why she nearly keeled over when he
approached her immediately and asked for her help.

"Sissy, I know we're on terrible terms here. Shoot,
we have been since I showed up on your trailer
stoop for my first date with Holly when we were
only sixteen years old. Clearly, you hate me. Even
more apparently, I suspect you have been involved in
criminal wrong-doing in Holly's case…"

"You better have some proof before you lay those
overgrown paws on me…" Sissy recoiled, since
Stanley was still inside with Holly and her lawyer.

"Now, just a minute," Blake held his hands up
in the classic sign of surrender, and that's when she
noticed the worry playing about his expression, like
he hadn't slept either. "I'm not stirring up trouble
here. I've taken a backseat in this investigation to my
deputy, Detective Morris. My personal involvement
in this case could cost me my job if I play it wrong.
In short, I'm not going after you, Sissy, as much as I
might want to."

Sissy relaxed, but only slightly. There was still
something terribly wrong. She could tell by Blake's
discomfort. "Well, if we're being all civil-like, Blake,
why don't you just go on and tell me where I can find
my grandsons."

"The boys have already had one grandparent

reunion go completely afoul. You folks are strangers to these boys." And this was where Blake started watching her carefully for her reaction. "This reintroduction thing may have to go a little slower than you grandparents like."

Sissy cleared her throat and smoothed down her curls—the heat sprang them out like coils of smoke from a dying candle. Dammit, she wanted a pipe right about now. "I'm not sure they'd think of me as a complete stranger, Blake." There. She'd said it. *Should she hold her wrists out now for the cuffs?* She thought.

Blake's somber expression lit with something she hadn't expected to see—hope.

"What exactly is going on with the boys, Blake? Where are they?" She demanded, because something was off-kilter.

"Tristan is at home with Minerva. We've taken the boys into our home to join my three other kids."

"And Corey?" Sissy asked, scarcely concealing her shock that Blake and Holly's former nemesis would take in her other child so readily in her time of crisis.

"Well, there's the rub, Sissy. He ran away yesterday afternoon and we haven't found him just yet. I'm sure he's just upset and confused, but with this godawful heat, I'm getting worried…"

"Where have you looked?" Sissy interrupted. Why Corey had run away was obvious. What she wanted to know was how she could help find him.

"Everywhere we could think of for a kid to hang out. Plus, we think he'd try for some shelter. He's got to be getting hungry by now. Minerva said he wolfed down a turkey sandwich and an apple before he split after lunch yesterday. None of the local eateries have seen him, but they've got my direct line if they do."

"There are two things that kid loves most—reading and soccer. Have you looked at the local library yet?"

"Yep, we've checked there. I did notice how he loves to bury his nose in a book. He certainly didn't get that from me," he chuckled ironically.

"Did you check the local soccer fields?" Sissy

continued. She refused to believe Blake's civility, as he attempted to smooth over a rough situation.

"We have a sports complex over the bridge, just east of town. My deputies did swing by there, but we could look again, if it would make you feel better. I'm willing to look anywhere if you think we might find him."

"Do I get to drive?" Sissy quizzed, eyeballing the back seat of the cruiser. No way, un-uh, that wasn't going to happen.

Blake repressed a smile. "I'll navigate," he offered and hulked behind Sissy to her borrowed car.

~~~~~~~~~~

The clever boy had sheltered in a dugout, not at the soccer field, but at the baseball field nearby. Still, he'd given them a scare. Calling for him hadn't yielded an answer, so Sissy had decided to snoop around anyway. It didn't take her long to find him stretched out on a painted wooden bench, beads of sweat covering his face, mouth hanging slack as he slept.

She shook him gently while his father looked on. Corey started awake, took a moment to focus on her in the shade of the dugout, and then shouted "Grandma!" and gave her a big hug. He seemed okay by all appearances, so Sissy hugged him back gratefully. She was also fully aware that this greeting left no doubt in Blake's mind about her continued contact with Holly and the boys.

"What are you doing here, Cody? It's hotter than blazes outside, don't you know that?"

Blake cleared his throat loudly. "Um, we're not calling him Cody anymore. It's time he used his real name."

"Well, that's got to be awfully confusing for him and his brother, don't you think?" Sissy sat next to her grandson on the bench.

"There's no use pretending they're on the run anymore, is there?"

Blake shifted uncomfortably as Sissy chastised him again. "Their names are not pretend to them, Blake. Their real names probably sound more made-up to them than the fake ones. They don't know themselves any different. It's no wonder Cody here ran away. The information about 'reality', as you call it, is probably overwhelming."

Corey cleared the sleep from his eyes and leaned into his grandma's shoulder. She patted his knee.

Blake had no argument. Yet he fidgeted, biting his thumb, tapping his foot, his body language nothing short of frustrated. "It's not like I'm working in familiar territory here, Sissy," he admitted.

"Cody, honey," Sissy said, eyeballing Blake warily, "do you want to explain why you spent the night on this hard bench?"

"I couldn't take it anymore, Grandma. That's all."

"Couldn't take what anymore?"

"The poison. Every time I turn a corner there's someone new telling me some all new thing about me or my past or my family or my brother. 'Cept now he's not really my brother anymore, did you know that, Grandma? Did you?" Corey's jaw worked against threatening tears.

"Taylor will always be your brother. I don't care if you have different daddies. Your mom doesn't care if you have different daddies. She is mommy to the both of you, and you two are as close as brothers can be."

"But if Mom's in jail, 'cause she kidnapped us, then will that mean Taylor has to go to his dad too?"

Sissy didn't know how to answer that, so she looked helplessly at Blake.

"Tristan's dad isn't in the picture. She didn't take him away from anybody." What remained unspoken was that the boy didn't really belong with anyone if his mom stayed in jail. Blake sighed and knelt down in front of his son. "I've tried to explain this to you, Corey. I always wanted you. Your mom is in trouble because she didn't care whether I wanted you or not. She didn't take my feelings into consideration…"

Sissy rushed to her full height immediately and stamped her foot at Blake. "Well it's no wonder he ran away from you, Blake Dermot. That load you're feeding him about his mother makes me feel like I swallowed charcoal too. Would you kindly try a more neutral approach?"

"These are the facts, Sissy."

"Would you like him to know the truth about why Holly really ran away?" Blake flushed like a turnip and shook his head curtly, and Sissy knew she had him on that point.

Corey assessed her seriously. "You might as well tell me everything, since everyone else seems to be putting their spin on things too."

A smile played the corners of Sissy's mouth. Wouldn't that just frost Blake's cookie? She remembered the night they ran away with baby Corey like it had happened only the night before—Holly's wrist broken, Corey wheezing wretchedly, Blake swilling beer at some bar. Yes, she could share this all with Corey; but then where would that leave the boy? With a mom in jail and a dad he could no longer trust?

She couldn't do it, so she ruffled Corey's hair instead and pulled him to his feet. "What I'd rather do is feed you breakfast while we catch up. Past is past, Cody. What you and I really need to do is talk about how you're going to cope with your new digs, and not spend any more nights in baseball dugouts."

To Blake she offered, "You can join us if you want."

If she hadn't known him better, she might have thought Blake looked grateful. Perhaps the guy had changed after all.

The tendril of trust she'd sensed got hacked off abruptly soon after that, though. She'd no sooner rounded up Stanley and filled all their bellies at the local diner, than Deputy Morris showed up, Blake's 'man-in-charge-of-the-investigation'. Blake stood and put his hand on Corey's shoulder and pulled him over to the jukebox, while Harvey Morris invited Stanley and Sissy outside.

Before the proud old clock on the historic courthouse tower turned twelve, Sissy had been installed as Holly's neighbor on the county cell block.

Chapter Thirty-eight

Tanner

Tanner returned to New York on business—an opening for the first of a series of his photography displays at a new *galleria ristorante*. Generally, Tanner avoided New York in the summer. It was too muggy for his taste. Summer air in New York City tasted of asphalt and freight truck emissions. Yet, Tanner needed to be there to reassure the restaurant owner about his feature artist.

That he was also in New York to ferret out why Claudia hadn't called him back was just an aside, or so he told himself. She couldn't so easily brush him off just because he'd hassled her about her past and about moving to L.A.. He needed to settle this issue of Claudia once and for all. It had been nearly two weeks since they'd talked, and ignoring his messages was just, well, childish. He planned to tell her so as soon as he could get the business day out of the way.

He'd taken the red-eye, arriving at JFK Airport at seven a.m. Eastern time. First thing, Tanner wheeled into his studio, bossed around his assistant for a few minutes, and then sent her out for coffee. He cradled his head in his hand while he rang Claudia to see if she would answer when a local number popped up on her caller ID. He hung up, frustrated, at the, 'I'm sorry, but the mailbox you are trying to reach is full.'

Rather than dwell on her repeated rebuff, Tanner called his client to make sure all of the pieces had arrived intact, framed properly, and to see if there was anything in particular he should bring to the opening that evening.

With any luck, he'd have a date on his arm.

Tanner took the proffered paper cup of steaming coffee from his assistant, balanced it between his knees, and wheeled out the door as quickly as he'd come. He hailed a cab to haul him to Brooklyn.

Because their meetings had been planned around Claudia's boys, it was a rare pleasure for Tanner to visit Claudia's apartment. He knew exactly how to get there, though, because he'd memorized everything there was to know about her. Everything she would tell him, anyway.

The brick façade on Claudia's building teemed with petunia blossoms from the dozens of flower boxes adorning the windows. They invited him in. Yet, she hadn't. Tanner felt his heart thud in his chest. Would she be angry when he just showed up without invitation? Would she have thought he'd gotten the message to leave her alone when she didn't answer his calls? All he knew was he couldn't get her off his mind.

The building was too old to accommodate anything but a freight elevator, so Tanner rang the manager and patiently waited for him to answer the outer door. He was thankful for the shade of the hundred year-old trees above him.

"What you want Ms. Brown for, anyway?" The height-challenged Puerto Rican looked at eye level at Tanner in his chair. "She not home 'tall dese days. Some friend help get her stuff out 'fore end of month's rent."

"What do you mean 'get her stuff out'? Is she leaving?" Tanner's annoyance with Claudia turned to panic. Was she running from him? Or just leaving for her new job without telling him?

"She gone. Boys too. Dese ladies tell you da story." The manager pushed Tanner out of the elevator courteously and took him to Claudia's door which was wide open. Boxes lined the hallway.

An African American woman, tall as a birch tree,

but who looked like she'd disappear if she turned sideways, regarded Tanner seriously. Joining her at the doorway was Aunt Bea, or at least an exact replica. She spoke first.

"Can we help you, young man?" She even sounded like Aunt Bea.

"Yes, I'm Tanner Grafton, a…um…friend…of Claudia's."

The African American woman smiled broadly. "Oh, yes, indeed you are a friend, Mr. Grafton. Claudia worried that you would show up. She had an associate of hers write you a note, should you appear. I'm Yvonne Plough, also an old friend of Claudia's." She held out her hand and he shook it.

"Sugar O'Donnell," the matronly woman offered her hand in greeting as well, but kept a more suspicious eye on Tanner. "I kept Claudia's young men in my charge for years. She did speak giddily of you, alright."

"Pleased to meet you both, but I am anxious to hear why you're here rearranging Claudia's things for her. Is she indisposed?"

Yvonne's laughter tinkled through the hollow apartment. "You could say that. Only that sounds so much more sophisticated than saying 'she's in jail'."

"Yvonne!" Mrs. O'Donnell exclaimed, nonplussed. "I'm sure she wouldn't want Mr. Grafton here knowing all of that business."

Yvonne snorted, but drew her explanation short. "You're right. I should let Claudia explain. I really should. Here's the note on the window seat. I left it there for the manager in case you showed after we finished."

"May I?" Tanner asked politely, but his heart had dropped to his toes when Yvonne had mentioned jail.

Both women nodded and Tanner made his way to the window seat. Tearing open the envelope without further ado, he read:

Dear Tanner:

There's almost so much to tell you that I think it might be better if you knew nothing at all.

That's not fair, though, and as much as you've meant to me, I can't leave you at that kind of loose end. You've been after me so long for the truth, it's almost a relief to be able to tell it.

My current residence: Okanogan County Jail, Washington State.

My real name: Holly Lynn Reel Dermot

My sons' real names: Corey Dermot and Tristan Reel

My ex-husband's name and occupation: Blake Dermot, Sheriff of Okanogan County

Amount of time I could be in jail: Indefinitely

So you see, it's a simple story. It's happened to thousands of moms before me—I ran with my kids. I got caught. I get to pay the price. My dear friends who have helped me since I came to New York, Yvonne and Sugar, will try to get this letter to you. I understand why you'll take this letter, tear it up, and bid me goodbye. There's no excuse for what I did. I'm a child-stealer, certainly not worthy of any kind of love or trust from a man like you.

You see, when it comes to men, I've always chosen badly. Somehow with you, I picked right, which is why fate made it impossible for us to be together. I'm not meant to be loved. Except by my sons—they still love me and look where it's gotten them—as far from my arms as they could possibly be.

So, goodbye, Tanner, my love. I have loved you, you know, even though I never told you. I guess I didn't want those words to come from 'Claudia'. She's not me, but that didn't make my feelings any less real. I hope you can remember me fondly.

Sincerely,
Holly Dermot

Holly. Now that name suited her right down to her reddish blond roots, Tanner thought ironically. Just as he had suspected, she was a big, fat liar. Also, just as he'd suspected, she'd brushed him off, though not in the way he'd anticipated.

What hurt him more than anything was that she didn't know him better than that. He wasn't unfamiliar with adversity. If she wanted him to see her through this crisis, he would. Instead, she'd cut him off at the knees.

Well, in case she hadn't noticed, he thought, gritting his teeth, he was wheelchair-bound. He didn't need legs to pursue her, so cutting him off at the knees would never work.

He looked up to find Yvonne and Mrs. O'Donnell examining him thoughtfully. "Could she possibly think it's this easy?" He asked angrily.

"What could be easy about losing your kids and getting thrown in jail?" Mrs. O'Donnell looked near tears.

"No. I mean that she thinks it could be this easy to get rid of me."

"It's not, is it?" Yvonne's eyes lit merrily as he shook his head. "I told her months ago that you were a keeper."

"Well, we agree on that point," Tanner grinned back. "She's a keeper too, you know?"

"Yes, we do know," Mrs. O'Donnell replied seriously. "Are you going to help her then, young man?"

Tanner looked out at listless Brooklyn streets, heat radiating from the pavement in the places not shaded by trees. New York really was miserable in the summer. He wondered what Washington State might be like this time of year. "Where the hell is Okanogan County, anyway?"

Yvonne shrugged dramatically. The three of them laughed and began to rummage through boxes for an atlas.

Chapter Thirty-nine

Minerva

"Camillia, you do not have to whip your horsey
to get him to go," Minerva warned as she watched
patient Tristan cart around her pert little girl, who
held a magic wand 'crop' in her hand. He winced
when she slapped him on the flank with it, but kept
riding her around as if she was a princess, and he, the
drudging draft horse.

Minerva shook her head, amazed that he put up
with Camillia. Tristan was such a bright spirit. Was
it any wonder he had a knack for making everyone
around him happy, kids included? "Would you guys
like lunch now?" she asked. "Should we have mac
and cheese?"

"Yeah!" yelled Camillia, Tristan, and Jonah. Sammy
sounded off from his playpen as though he agreed.
Minerva laughed and went over to the sink to wash
her hands. She looked out her garden window into
the yard below. Corey was there, tossing a basketball
listlessly toward the hoop. Her mood dimmed again
as she saw that the sky threatened rain, but Corey
obviously would rather have been anywhere than
with them.

It was like this every day at the Dermot house:
Minerva cajoled, coaxed, and tried to make nice with
her husband's long lost son. Yet, Corey did more
than hold her at arm's length—that she would have
expected—he retreated from Minerva like she emitted
a stench he couldn't stomach. He'd even run away, on
her watch, and gone missing overnight.

Blake hadn't blamed Minerva. After all, she had to deal with four other children under the age of six. Plus, Corey had been dealt a huge blow. They all navigated unfamiliar waters and, as of late, they did it without the help of the moon. No amount of guidance or wisdom from counselors, therapists, family judges, or lawyers had helped them sort this mess out.

The closest person to Corey all of these years, besides his mother, had been Tristan. Yet, even Tristan couldn't penetrate Corey's hell. Minerva remembered the blistering words they'd exchanged just yesterday.

"You can't talk to Minerva that way, Corey. She takes care of us," Tristan had defended when Corey berated Minerva for undercooking his eggs and 'burning' his toast.

"She's not your mom, Tristan. You need to stop acting like she is," Corey had spat back, scraping his chair across the floor and severing Minerva's last thread of patience.

Before she could scold him, though, Tristan had piped up. "Well Mom isn't here, is she? She *can't* take care of us."

"She always took care of us, you little jerk, until *they* threw her in jail." Jonah and Camillia looked at Minerva wide-eyed for her response when the 'they' appeared to be directed at her.

"Corey. That is enough," Minerva said calmly, though she didn't feel it. "Can you please clear your plate if you don't want to eat anything, and take your brother's plate too?"

Corey's face bunched up in anger, just the way his father's did when he was about to say something stupid that he would pay for later. "He's NOT my brother."

His parting shot had hit his brother like a slap and Tristan teared up immediately.

Minerva had gone straight to Tristan and cradled him while he cried. The age of six was way too young to understand the complexities of things like biology. Minerva knew quite a bit about biology, but she also knew that it didn't matter when it came to Tristan. The child was golden—cheerful, sweet, daring—and she already loved him like a member of her family, biology be damned. She scarcely even remembered, after one month of having him, that he was Holly's child.

Corey had spent the remainder of the day in the yard, refusing to come in even to eat until Blake came home and demanded that he join them for dinner.

Minerva felt guilty now as she prepared lunch and started to tick the days off in her head until school started again. Bliss would be just two small children and no mouthy nine-year-olds. She could ramp up her beauty shop schedule again and lose herself in the business of making women stunning.

The phone rang. She set the pot of boiling noodles aside so they wouldn't boil over while she answered it.

"Hello?"

"Is this Mrs. Blake Dermot?" It was a lilting woman's voice. She said 'Dermot' like a foreigner.

"It is."

"This is Kelly Jones. My mother was a neighbor at one time of your husband's."

"That must have been a while ago. He's been here with me forever," Minerva offered, her curiosity certainly piqued.

"I'm sure he's come quite a long way since living there. Those tiny little houses left a lot to be desired. I always told my mother so."

"Jones. Wait, was your mother *the* Mrs. Jones?"

Kelly Jones laughed musically. "Oh, she was indeed. She'd be completely nonplussed to know that her former nemesis is the county's very own Sheriff."

Minerva's defenses hummed. Blake was not that man anymore, not by anyone's standards. As far as she knew he no longer had a nemesis. "Yes, well, we've all come a long way in the last seven years, Ms. Jones."

"I am aware of that. Actually, the reason I called is

because Mr. Dermot is the sheriff now. My brothers and I moved away after our mother died and I've just begun to go through some of the boxes of her things. I have come across a 'confessional', if you will, and I'm entirely unsure what to do with it. I thought Sheriff Dermot might be able to make some sense of the information. Certainly, I think he should see it."

"Why didn't you call him at work?" Minerva asked coldly. This wasn't the first time she'd gotten a call on their personal phone regarding Blake's job. They were listed by Minerva's maiden name, but that didn't stop people from tracking them down. She would never understand why people felt the need to skirt the normal channels.

"I have left him several messages. He's a busy man. Plus, I'm sure he recognizes my name. The name Jones must make him quite nervous considering the trouble my mother put him through. Oh, my, but she was a firecracker!" Kelly paused to suck in a fortifying breath. "I called you to reassure you both that I mean no harm. I simply need to lay something to rest. I'll be traveling back to the Okanogan from the west side of the state next week. Will you consider meeting with me?"

"I can have Blake call you…"

"You don't know his schedule then?" Kelly interrupted. "It's just, I don't believe he'll want to meet with me if he thinks I mean trouble."

"But you don't mean trouble?" Minerva quizzed.

"No, no trouble. Really."

"We've had enough trouble to last us forever, Ms. Jones. That's for sure. Why don't we just meet you at the Sawtooth Diner on a convenient morning for you? I'll make sure I get the Sheriff there."

Minerva realized she'd just stuck her neck out. She hoped Blake would forgive her for it, but she was thoroughly enchanted with what Kelly Jones was up to. Plus, she needed a break from the kids. She could get a teenage babysitter to come watch them for a few hours.

"Shall we say Tuesday, then? At nine a.m.? And, please, call me Kelly."

"I look forward to it, Kelly." Would she ever? Just to have a few hours respite from a sullen boy and her naughty minions, she'd listen to just about any spiel that came at her. Minerva chuckled and returned her noodles to the stove. Blake was going to kill her.

Chapter Forty

Blake

Blake leaned back in his leather chair and ran his face over his hands. Life in limbo simply did not suit him. Nobody was happy. Nobody.

They had looked forward to this for years: Corey's return, the jubilation of a family finally at peace, a reunion with a long lost son. Yet, Corey wasn't a chubby toddler anymore, nor was their family unit the fortress it used to be. The Dermot clan had ruptured irreversibly with his father's illness and his mother's subsequent misery. Corey refused to go to the Dermot home. Blake had done everything short of threatening bodily harm to try and coax him to go see his grandparents.

Karen Dermot had been by Blake and Minerva's house a few times while Winston's home health nurse visited. She'd refused to come inside Minerva's territory—whether it was pride or spite that drove her, Blake would never know—so her visits with Corey had been limited to the confines of the fenced back yard. Karen left each time, bereft, no closer to recapturing the spirit of the sweet baby boy she remembered from so many years before.

Minerva wasn't happy either, with a boy around who loathed and avoided them. He ate and slept inside, but all other hours were spent outside. He hadn't run away again because of a promise he made to Sissy, but Blake wondered when that fine thread of good behavior would wear away.

The younger kids were confused by the attitude of

this 'big brother'. Didn't big brothers automatically love their little brothers and sister? Jonah and Camillia wanted to know. Tristan loved them. Why couldn't Corey?

Blake grew frustrated with his inability to communicate with Corey. He'd tried everything: Counseling; family therapy sessions; and meetings with a family court judge who'd granted sole physical custody to Blake of both boys, given the incarcerations of the boys' mother and grandmother. Corey would not have a civil conversation with his father. It was as if Corey drew the shades on any kind of emotion when faced with his father or any other authority figure.

Blake asked himself on a regular basis: If he would have known how fully miserable his son would be to come home again, would he still have sought him out? After all, he loved a little boy he'd idealized in his mind. This sullen adolescent, he did not know.

He contemplated the map of Okanogan County on the wall to the right of his office window. He had all the power in the world, or his part of it anyway. Yet, he did not have the power to change this. He beat his fist on his desk angrily, making the clay paper weight Jonah had made him jump like a kernel of popcorn. This was all Holly's fault. Every bit of it. He understood how his mother felt.

Detective Morris appeared in his doorway with a bemused look on his face. "You're gonna bite that thumb clean off your hand one of these days."

Blake flushed as if he'd been caught picking his nose. His oldest habit had never been kickable like the rest of them. "I'm thinking, can't you see that?" He shot back a sheepish grin. "What's up?"

"Just thought I'd let you know the latest from the prosecutor on your ex."

"Is she going to put in a plea yet?" Holly had pled 'not guilty' at her arraignment on parental kidnapping charges, but Blake was fully aware that the prosecuting attorney, Gil Rollins, thought all in this situation would be better-served if they could find a plea agreement for Holly. That meant bargaining with her. Blake didn't think Holly deserved any kind of leniency.

"Her attorney has said she refuses to make a deal. At all. She wants this to go to trial," Harv chewed his gum thoughtfully.

"Any idea why?"

"Have you gone to talk to her, Blake?"

Blake shook his head guiltily. A man with his big-boy panties on would have had the guts to face her by now, but he didn't know if, after all this time, he could keep his resentment in check. Her betrayal cut way too deep for him to make any kind of reasonable sense out of it. He couldn't deny his hurt, or his anger, at losing his wife and his child all on one blustery night. Fifty years could have passed and he would still feel the same.

Harv looked Blake fully in the face, drawing his attention back to the now. "I have gone to see her, Blake. I'm gonna need you to answer some hard questions here."

"Okay."

"I remember the scuttle way back when about how your wife had run away 'cause you beat her. Shoot, the story took hold so well, it came back up during your election."

Blake pursed his lips. He didn't like this line of questioning, not from his subordinate.

Harv noticed, and held his hands out palm-up in surrender. "I realize this sticks in your craw to talk about this, Enforcer, but you need to know what kind of defense she's planning to put up. You see, she told me she has x-rays she saved from clear back when, with the date documented as the night she disappeared with your boy."

"So what? She fell on the porch after she left, or she did something else clumsy like that. Why does this always come back to me? We've hammered over this issue a thousand times, Harv. It's my word against hers."

"That's right, Enforcer. It's your word against hers. Your word as one of the most powerful men in the county, with every police resource at your disposal. Your word as an upstanding member of a founding family in this community. Your word as a man with a brand new, loving wife and family, that is the very picture of domestic bliss. What the hell am I thinking, wondering if her word has any kind of credo?"

The room fell silent as a tomb.

"What are you implying, Harv?" Blake asked defensively.

"I am implying nothing. I do this job honorably and I want to know that the man I work for is a man of honor too. A man of honor admits his mistakes. A man of honor figures out how to forgive and to move on. A man of honor does what's best for his children, always. Are you that man, Sheriff Dermot?"

Blake picked up Jonah's clay paper weight and wondered again what it was—Bulldog? Bowling ball? Bust of Picasso? His kids meant everything to him. Otherwise, he might have relegated this to a junk drawer at home. Otherwise, he wouldn't have fought so hard to have Corey back. His intentions were always pure where they were concerned, weren't they? What right did Harv have to question him?

Whatever he and his closest confidant, Minerva, knew wasn't any concern of Harv's or the prosecution's. Whatever he had admitted to in the past did not justify the loss of his child—and he had lost his child, because what he had now was a boy who didn't know or trust him. If he had to withhold this one bit of information from Harv and the prosecutor, Blake took solace in the fact that he had become a much better man since those pool nights at the Watering Hole.

There was no way they'd take Holly's word over his. After all, she was an admitted kidnapper and fraud. She'd grown up on the wrong side of the tracks. She was not a hometown girl. Her mother had pled guilty to aiding and abetting her escape and awaited sentencing.

Harv stood before him with hands on his hips, so Blake replied to his question the only way he could. "I'm a good man, Harv."

"This I know, Sheriff. But are you a good man with honor? This is the question I'm going to leave you to chew on while I scuttle my butt outta here. Last thing I need is a censure for insubordination." Harv sported his most winning smile.

The door clicked shut behind him and Blake commenced mangling his thumbnail.

~~~~~~~~~~

The door of the Sawtooth opened like a leather flap on a cave. It took his eyes a moment to adjust while Minerva made a beeline toward a booth in the back corner. They were having a rare breakfast rendezvous before Blake did his weekly dust-up with the county commissioners. He only wished Minerva had booked a room at the Omak Lodge instead so he could really make the most of their time.

He'd slid halfway into the booth before Blake noticed the petite brunette perched across from him. "Minerva, there's already someone sitting here..."

"Of course there is," Minerva said matter-of-factly as she slid her napkin politely over her lap. "This is Kelly Jones."

"You didn't mention we were meeting with anyone... Did you say Jones? You wouldn't happen to be any relation to Mrs. Jones?"

Kelly's giggle sounded like the notes from a flute. "Of course my mother was Mrs. Jones. The question is: Do you know which one?" She giggled again. "I'm teasing you, Sheriff Dermot. Mrs. Jones' first name was Ingrid, though she never told it to anyone because the missus suited her just fine. She most definitely was my mother."

"You left a message in my office recently. I'm

sorry I haven't had time to return it," Blake covered. Actually, he'd shifted it to the bottom of his pile of pink notes from his secretary several times.

Minerva cut in, "She finally bypassed your mess of an office and called our home. She has information to share with you. She has promised no trouble, so I told her I'd bring you to breakfast."

Just like that. So typical of his wife, he thought, to be trusting of a perfect stranger.

The waitress took their orders and he passed off his menu. Kelly politely declined to order since she'd already eaten. "What can I help you with, then, Kelly?"

A book roughly the size of the Bible and half as thick emerged from the bench beside her. The gold leaf on the cover and edges glinted in the pendant light overhead. Kelly ran her hand lovingly over the cover and then handed it over to Blake.

"It's my mother's diary."

He held it away from him as if to give it back. "You've read it, I assume."

"I have. I've bookmarked some pages you might be interested in. I've also scanned it page by page into my computer in case the actual book gets, um, lost. You see, Sheriff Dermot, I'm afraid to say that my mother has, among its pages, confessed to a murder."

Blake's mouth went dry. He had expected to hear Kelly confess something else, to say that Mrs. Jones had written about him and Holly's mess. He faltered for a moment. "A…murder? Did she, um, say who she killed?"

"My father. In Ireland. But you see, Sheriff, that was forty years ago on a whole other continent. We lived there when I was a child and I always thought he'd gotten drunk and fallen off a cliff. Folks didn't talk about it much around me. I'm sure rumors must have flown about my mother's involvement, but I never heard them. I only knew she loved us and took care of us. You can imagine my surprise when I found out, well, it's all there in black and white, really, when you take a read of it yourself."

"Why did you seek out my help?" Blake asked
while Minerva looked on wide-eyed.

"You knew my mother and I know your
relationship was tenuous. That's in there too. I
thought that fact might help you lend a little bit of…
sensitivity…to any kind of notification of the proper
authorities."

"You would like me to contact Interpol about this?"

"Or the authorities in Galway if there's any way to
do that."

Blake scarcely noticed the plate of biscuits and
gravy the waitress plopped in front of him. "Your
mother is dead, Kelly, God rest her soul. You could
have let this information die with her, you know. You
still could. I don't have to read any of it."

Tears glistened on Kelly's rosy cheeks. "Yes, I
know, Sheriff Dermot, but the man she killed was my
father. Shouldn't he rest in peace also, for all of his
shortcomings?"

Minerva and Blake nodded.

"Besides," Kelly added softly, musically, "there's
much to be learned from her words. You, in particular,
could most benefit from what she had to say. Promise
me you'll read it."

When he thought he'd heard the last he'd ever
hear from Mrs. Jones, she was destined, after all, to
have the last word, wasn't she? He nodded ironically.
"Okay. I promise."

Kelly shook his hand and gracefully took her
leave. Minerva kissed him on the cheek and they
dug into their mouthwatering breakfast sausage and
buttermilk biscuits, with no idea of the shocking
revelations that awaited them.

Chapter Forty-one

Mrs. Jones

Blake cleared his bleary eyes with his fists and picked the journal back up. It neared midnight—hours since Minerva and the kids had gone to bed, but some of this stuff was too juicy to miss. Mrs. Jones' words read like a novel, no less exciting or less insightful either. He kept on, disregarding Kelly's cues. He would read this cover-to-cover. The story had started simply:

> *March 15,1960—You'd think with three children and my full-time job at the pub, that there wouldn't be time for writing, nor inclination. What I have vowed, here, in these pages is to write whatever is true about my life. Misery loves company—it really does. Plus, it is an opportunity to write proper English, something I've always wanted to do.*
> *Where to begin: Those sun-filled days in the fold of my family in one of the most beautiful homes in Europe? The first time bile rose to my throat while I was being molested by the master of the house? The daring strip tease in the labyrinth with Borys while the Mueller children napped? The first, confusing weeks in Ireland when neither Borys nor I could find purchase with a job or a place to live? The search for work that finally led us to sea-shorn cliffs and endless fog and rain? The first week at my job when I found out my melancholy had less to do with*

the weather, and more to do with the state of my belly?

Maybe I should begin with my children, each unexpected, but no less wanted than the last. They're beautiful—Kelly with light eyes like my own and a delightful lilt to her voice, Sean with his square build and rare sense of humor, Rafe the miniature of his father and ever so busy. They give me much joy. Kelly's seven now, attending school and reading everything she can get her hands on. I cannot wait for Sean to go to school, though it's likely his teacher will get nothing done, keeping up with his antics. Rafe, well, he's my baby, and he could never grow, as far as I'm concerned.

I've decided, instead, to make this journal an homage to the only love I've had in my life— Borys Ciszek—my husband and my tormentor.

Our lives together started with all of the passion and exploration of two forbidden lovers in their twenties. We met covertly in the gardens, for he was the son of the Polish gardener; and in the nursery, for I was the nanny. I told him of Master Mueller's fondling, and he promised to whisk me away from all of it. We'd already passed the uncertainty of post-war Germany. The Muellers had been big supporters of the Nazi movement, but had managed to fly under the radar when Hitler was defeated. We were west of the Wall and situated in the country, which meant we could move about Europe more freely than our Eastern counterparts.

Still, emigration was not easy, and we had little food and money for our journey on that September night when we chose to leave our families and the only home we'd ever known and depart for Berlin and the train station. We had fares for the train to Paris and the boat to England and on to Ireland. We'd chosen our destination from an atlas in the Mueller library. Ireland looked romantic in pictures, and very, very green. Little did we know that such greenery required frequent and violent watering.

Never had either of us given any thought to getting jobs or a home. Ireland was in transition at the time and good jobs were rare. There weren't the sprawling garden estates we'd known at home—only impoverished, simple-thinking farmers, and in the city—pubs and gambling. The latter enthralled Borys right away, and I fear that is when I lost him.

I convinced him to answer an ad with me to manage a pub on the coast. We lived out of the pub, yet Borys rarely left. I cooked and cleaned during business hours, but then he and his cronies stayed long into the night to bet on nearly everything—horses, fights, whether Sara Ryan might be pregnant again, whether I might be pregnant again.

Drinking made Borys more friendly at first, but I was disgusted by him—the sour smells, the falling asleep during the act, the snoring after. I began to refuse him in bed after his late nights. He began to push me around more, always out of the sight of Kelly and Sean, and later Rafe. Kelly was three the first time he backhanded me hard enough to make my lip bleed. Yes, I had given him a tongue-lashing and made him feel 'inadequate' as he told me in broken German. (He always spoke German when he was drunk.)

Yet, I've always been a positive person. I've always believed life would right itself, that any bad situation was bound to get better. This is why I can't understand the progressive beatings that have ensued since that time. Black eyes, bloodied lips, swollen nose—I can ill-hide these from the children or anyone else. Each time, in the morn, when he sees what he's done, he spends a day or so making atonement, bringing me flowers, saying he's always loved me more than life itself.

I do not love him anymore. This is the sad case. I will never speak these feelings aloud, for fear of hurting my children. This is my ode to the gorgeous, strapping young man I fell for years ago, this journal; but he is all but lost to me in my ever-increasing sadness...

April 30, 1960—I've always believed my sadness was selfish, especially after reading my first installment. How dreary. You'd have thought I hadn't actually fallen in love with the brackish smell of sea at low tide and the way the fog snakes around my ankles as I gather eggs first thing in the morning. Ireland was not the answer to any of our problems, but it has become home nonetheless. I've built a life here, and the best part of it is the love of my children.

That is why I cannot bear the next words I have to write. I'll rest my pen while I fortify with afternoon tea and contemplate how to put such pain through the tip of a pen...

...I've justified my beatings with the stability of my family, my home, my children. I've never spoken of my pain to them, nor tried to sully their father in their eyes, for they believe him to be the fun-loving man that he is for them. They know nothing of beer-tinged breath and blistering words. At least they didn't know, until now.

Sean spilled his glass of milk at breakfast this morning. As I rushed for the sink rag, Sean took to giggling. Whether it was nervous or silly laughter, I don't know, but Borys balked at laughter that belittled the cleaning up I had to do. That irritated his blossoming hangover. Instead of gritting his teeth and ignoring the breakfast set as he usually did, Borys called his oldest son over to the table.

I still rinsed my rag at the sink when I heard

the all-too-familiar sound of knuckles striking flesh...my sweet little boy's flesh. Sean screamed like a warning siren and held his hand over his angry eye. Borys rose quickly from his chair, knocking it to the ground, and rushed for the shower. I grabbed from the counter the rib eye steak I'd pulled from the ice box that very morning and rushed over to put it on my son's eye.

Kelly and Rafe watched it all transpire, agape. Kelly gathered herself for school, while I wailed with my son and rocked him in my arms on the kitchen floor. Rafe, all of four years old, finished his bowl of porridge, placed it quietly in the sink, and went to play with his wood blocks.

Borys didn't even bother to bid his sons and me goodbye on his way to the pub. He must have sensed every bit of my fury—even more when I didn't show up to help him today.

Sean and I haven't spoken about it again. He's played docilely with his brother today and he's been quite careful with his dishes. None of the mischievousness that is his signature, none of the mirth, just stoicism and an impossibly swollen left eye that seems to change color each time I look at him...

May 15, 1960—I have begun to plot his demise. He's already raised a hand again, though this time he failed to swing it. His verbal abuse and hatred of me has increased exponentially. It's only a matter of time before he kills one of us. It's my job to make sure that doesn't happen to my children...

June 21, 1960—The deed was achingly simple and the opportunity so much sooner than I imagined. Borys was stumbling drunk and the kids were tucked safely into their beds hours before. Instead of rebuffing Borys as I had recently done, I kissed him and convinced him to go for a moonlight walk. It was clear outside, for once, and the quarter moon shone through high clouds. Tangy salt tickled our noses as I held his hand and led him toward the sea. We passed neighboring houses, laughing like young lovers—he because he had no idea why I was so friendly, but it pleased him; and me, because I had every idea what his destiny would be.

The path to the cliff was hairy with so little light to lead us and I feared that I would become more than just a widow. I convinced myself to make sure steps, so my children would not be orphans.

Borys and I kissed again and I faced out toward the sea, breathing in its organic aroma to clear my nose of the beer on Borys' breath. Borys faced the edge of the cliff with me, scarcely able to stand in place after his night at the books. The push held no more force than a stiff breeze. Had I run away at that moment, I'm quite sure he would have died just fine on his own, but I needed to be certain, you see. I couldn't leave our safety to chance.

What I do wish was that I'd worn a cloak to cover my ears against the pitiful sound of his descent. He cried 'no!' the whole way down and the ending thud was quite sickening. There was, for me, incredible sadness those first few moments—and absolutely no regret.

I waited for a while there to assure that Borys wouldn't call for help, in the event that he survived the fall. No calls came and as I heard the surf pound the rocks below, I became convinced that perhaps he'd washed away.

I rushed up the path to the local doctor's home because he was the nearest person from whom I could seek help. I made sure to be breathless as I asked him to please contact the authorities—my husband had taken a fall from the cliff by the sea! I was quite consoled by his wife and the other local ladies who rushed to

my aid with the pub and the children while
arrangements were made.

Borys' funeral mass was lovely in the
graveyard facing the sea. The lie of the cliffs
sent Borys to an outcropping of rock, instead
of washing him away, as I had thought in the
lonely darkness. His body had broken past the
point of survival, but had still been suitable for
burial.

I am, all at once, aggrieved and so relieved.
Life will be harder, and it will be easier.

The children don't understand why I can't
continue to work at the pub. Ours was a team
job that we were hired for anyway, and the
owners didn't think a woman would be fit
to run the whole operation. We will move to
Dublin where I've taken a job as a hotel maid...

February 12, 1965—Life amid the Dubliners
tries my spirit. It's each man or woman for
himself in a race for jobs, education, and status.
The children are miserable—I can tell by
their lifeless eyes. They are dispirited by their
widowed mother, menial jobs, and a pitiful,
roach-infested apartment.

I've learned of an opportunity to move to
America. I have written to a lonely gentleman
through an agency in the States that places
foreign women with husbands. He doesn't
know I have children. I'm only thirty-five—
hardly old by anyone's measure. I have read of
the opportunities that abound in America. My
neighbor, Rose, will watch the children for me
until I can send for them. They are all in school
now, and hardly any trouble, plus they can help
her with her younger children. I'll send them
money, in amounts unheard of in Ireland, that I
promise.

Soon we'll all be together again, as soon
as I can convince Mr. Ike Jones to bring them
along...

June 3, 1965—I never imagined how much I would miss them.

Life is steady here. I'm really not much more than a housekeeper, well, and sort of a man-keeper too! I've married again. Ike Jones and I only communicated for a short time before I made my journey, but we were required to be married within three months or I would lose my visa. We live on a cattle farm nestled at the rainy base of the Cascade Mountains in Washington State, on the western coast of America. So much of Mr. Jones' time has been devoted to his family farm, that he's had no time to seek a wife. When his ailing mother died, Mr. Jones became lonely and sought out a mate through no-nonsense means. He found this service that connects gentlemen with foreign brides. Americans call me a 'mail-order' bride, yet they've been nothing but hospitable and curious about me in the nearest town, a tiny berg called Monroe.

I have yet to reveal the biggest part of myself to my new husband. He's a lovely man, actually—not at all old and fat like I'd imagined from his formal letters. Mr. Jones is only five and a half feet tall, so we see nearly eye-to-eye. He's fair-skinned, but dark-eyed and dark haired. His grandparents were Albanian and they were the first to settle the farm in the late nineteenth century. Everything about him is quiet, from his manner of speaking to his understated clothing. There is nothing threatening about him. We live in a huge, old house, and I'm sure there would be plenty of space for my beloved babies.

But, would there be space in his heart for them? He's only just gotten to know me. How can I tell him that I've been lying to him all along? I've been good to him, cooking and cleaning like a demon. His stomach and house had been neglected far too long before I came here. Plus, he's surprisingly passionate in bed. It *makes me blush to write the words.*

I should be happy, but I will never be, without those souls I've given life to. I will need to tell him soon...

September 1, 1965—Happiness! They are here with me and will be starting school in just a week.

Kelly loves the cows, chickens, and pigs. She says the country air reminds her of Galway, except it reeks of manure instead of sea slime. Sean helps Mr. Jones steadfastly around the farm, which pleases him greatly. Sean is a fast learner and, these days, seems to have his smile back. Rafe has turned nine while I was away, far from a baby, yet he still takes a sit on my petite lap every chance he gets.

Mr. Jones, to my great surprise and relief, was thrilled with the idea of having children to fill the house. He planned to ask me if that was something I would consider with him, but when he found I'd already had that particular adventure, he was eager to bring my children over to the States as soon as possible.

Did he chastise me? Yes. When he realized I'd been stealing money from his wallet for months, he was confused, mostly, and hurt by my deception. Did he get angry or violent? Never. This man would never do that to me. He is the gentlest soul and there is more than enough love in his heart for all of us...

Blake had to look twice at the dates in the journal when he reached this point, because it appeared Mrs. Jones had skipped years in her poignant journaling. Even her handwriting had changed. It became shakier:

December 20, 2000—I never believed my life would be bereft enough to force me to write again in this sad journal of mine. In fact, I've only just found it in the back of my closet.

Mr. Jones died three months ago after thirty-five years of bliss. We raised our children. Rafe received a bachelor's degree in Agriculture at Washington State University and took over the farm in 1980. Kelly and her lawyer husband, Charles, moved to Eastern Washington so he could open a private practice away from the city. They convinced Mr. Jones and me to join them just a year later since we became irrelevant at the farm. Sean soon followed, living with us until he could get an office supply business off the ground.

Mr. Jones took as much joy in our children as I did. I never doubted that he loved us wholeheartedly and without any of the complications I remember faintly from my previous union.

He died of heart failure, suddenly, while tilling under the garden in preparation for winter. With him gone, I couldn't live in the house. It was too empty. I wanted to go with him.

So I sold it, and now I'm moving to a little house closer to Kelly's. Life will be good again, someday, but I'll never rest fully again until I'm resting with Mr. Jones. That I know for sure…

Blake saw that she wrote again, several times, entries about her love lost. Bored, and brutally tired, since it was one o'clock in the morning, he skipped to the first flagged page about two-thirds of the way through the book:

October 10, 2005—Funny, the events that lead me to this leather-bound pity-party. I'll burn it soon, because I'm not getting any younger. There's no sense having Kelly happen upon its revelations. Still, there are things I want to say. For instance: Tonight, more than forty years

melted away, and I almost smelled that wind-
shorn cliff once again.

I watched Wheel of Fortune as usual,
minding my own business, when an unnatural
wail came up from the house next door. I'd
heard the baby cry earlier, a croupy cry that
sounded pitiful, but this new cry, it sounded
like the kind of pain Sean had emitted when his
father layed his knuckles across his left eye. It
pierced me, and before I could think, I flew these
old legs across the sidewalk and up to her porch.

I'd seen him, this abusive husband,
lumbering in and out of the house. We'd been
neighbors for at least six months. In the olden
days, they would have come to introduce
themselves, or I might have gone and done
the same. I hadn't felt compelled in this case,
however—the husband reminded me far too
much of Borys in his carriage, his build.

Turns out I was right about him. She's gotten
her mother, her child, and she's run away from
him too. That, too, isn't handled like it used to
be. Or at least like I handled things, anyway…

October 11, 2005—I've had another encounter
with this Dermot thug. She was right to leave
him. The only thing saving the babe was sheerly
how young he was. He would only need to be
four years older, like Sean, before a little spilled
milk would earn him a black eye. I can only
hope the young mother, Holly, will keep in
touch. I've stonewalled him, thus far, given her
a head start. I'll be ready with plenty of advice,
should she need it…

Blake took a deep breath. Of course Mrs. Jones
had seen him in that light. Whenever had he behaved
otherwise? She had only known him back then. He
took solace in that he had changed, after an enormous
amount of work. He half-wished she was still around
so he could prove it to her. He read on:

January 2, 2007—Perhaps being old gives one better insights into a person's character. Maybe I'm fooling myself, but that big oaf of a Sheriff's deputy actually seemed to have a few chinks in his armor tonight. Of course, he was just doing his civic duty checking on me. I could never have told him I was burning a letter from his estranged wife. Still, though, he seemed so much less threatening than I remembered. Too much sorrow does that to a person—it reduces him to something less than he used to be. It's as if he's shrunk.

That's silly, but then I remember how I felt when I was forced to be away from my children that endless summer. Whether he misses his wife, more than just being angry with her for staying away, or whether it's simply the loss of his child that's done so, he's suffered…

Blake took in a shaky breath and arrested the tear that escaped his eye unexpectedly. So, she had noticed. He wasn't sure why that mattered.

January 10, 2007—Just as I suspected: In the papers today—Blake Dermot has announced his engagement to Minerva Jenkins. Minerva does Kelly's hair. Nice woman. Now I know where that softening came from. Love does that to people.

I wonder, then, if that love makes his ex-wife and child easier to forget, or more missed? Especially the child—if he gets married and has more children, will Mr. Dermot be able to replace Corey? I don't believe that's possible. Obviously, he's had the grace to move on, but the heart can never forget.

Speaking of hearts, mine is being wholly uncooperative these days. Dr. Scot has fit me into his schedule next week, so I shall see what the pains are all about. I haven't told Kelly.

She'd be beside herself with worry. She's my best friend and confidant, after all. If I can't tell her about it, I can't tell anybody. So I'm telling my journal. I really do need to burn this thing, but then Blake Dermot might show up at my doorstep again.

I'm just going to say one more thing about that man, and then I'm going to let him peacefully move on with his life. Holly is about to have another baby. She's living her life on the run, out of fear of a man who may or may not still be dangerous. That's no life for her and the boys. I'm going to reserve final judgment on Blake Dermot for the day they find each other again. Whether it will be years from now, or months, I'm sure Holly and Corey will eventually be found. I hope so, actually, so I can see them both again, whole and unafraid. My final word on Blake Dermot will be issued the day he sees Holly and Corey again. Will he find the forgiveness in his heart that a life of harmony and happiness has blessed him with? Will he need vengeance? Will he forget all he has learned by enduring loss in the first place? That will be the day I know for sure whether the spirit of Borys Ciszek lives on, or whether I really shed the world of it nearly half a century ago in Ireland...

Chapter Forty-two

Holly

Once Stanley bailed her mom out, Holly relaxed slightly, believing that Sissy would fight her battles for both of them. At the very least, the boys would have contact with someone they knew and loved.

Daily life in the jail, though mundane, wasn't filled with the horrors Holly imagined. She broke up time in her cell with outdoor grounds-keeping at the county courthouse and fairgrounds, and doing dishes in the cafeteria. Her hands became calloused and her muscles strong.

Holly's strawberry blond roots shone back at her persistently from her unbreakable mirror, so on her fourteenth day of incarceration, she celebrated by borrowing kitchen shears and snipping her curls away about half an inch from her scalp. To herself, earring-less and make-up free, she looked startlingly like a teenage boy. To guards and fellow prisoners, her cornflower blue eyes suddenly became her face's centerpiece, and she looked nothing like a boy.

She deflected their interest with sharp words and confidence built from life in the big city, and years on the run. Holly Dermot, from years' past, would never have had the tools. She had Blake to thank for that.

Holly's feelings toward Blake were surprisingly neutral. True, he had created the mess in the first place through a cowardly act of violence, but then, she had perpetuated it by running, and then running some more. He'd gotten the far worse part of the deal by losing touch with their child for so long. She couldn't give those years back to Blake, no matter how long a judge put her in jail for. But then, how did you put a price or a jail sentence on any of the pain they'd inflicted on each other?

The one thing Holly had too much of, that she could do without, was time to think. No matter how much she resisted, when she was alone, she thought about Tanner. What would he say if he could see her now? There'd be no hiding anymore. She wondered if Yvonne and Mrs. O'Donnell had given Tanner her letter. Tanner wouldn't even know her now if he saw her on a street corner.

But then, their attraction had never really been about looks. If that were true, she wouldn't have noticed anything about Tanner except the fact that he was in a wheelchair. If all he loved about her had been chestnut curls and dark eyes, he would never have persisted to find out the truth about her. Their passion was more pure than that, and thinking about it now made her blush.

It was with this flush high on her cheeks, that Blake found Holly trimming a hedge outside his office building. Roomy orange prison garb could do nothing to conceal the banging body Holly still had underneath. Holly wanted to disappear into herself when she saw Blake look her up and down the way he had when they were in high school.

Blake looked just as taken aback by his automatic perusal. He was a family man now, and he'd had no idea where her thoughts had been when he happened upon her. He nodded to the guard nearby, who indicated they might want to be left alone. Everyone at the jail knew this was the sheriff's ex-wife.

Blake shook his head, "Nope, Halloway, I think you should probably stay nearby in this case."

Holly looked back and forth between the men. Blake really thought she might be a problem if they were left alone. Interesting.

Blake looked back at her. "Anybody with any kind of sense about his job would not want to talk to his kidnapper ex-wife without a witness," he reasoned.

"Is that how you see me?" Holly wondered aloud. "Well, I guess you would."

Blake scowled. "I didn't approach you to pick a fight. That's the last thing I want."

"I don't want a fight, either, Sheriff. We could argue forever about who started this whole thing, couldn't we?" Holly sighed and held up her hands.

Blake couldn't help but glance at the wrist he'd heard snap so many years ago, as much as he'd denied knowing he'd hurt her. The years melted away as he remembered storming away even though she was hurt.

"I started it," he murmured and looked at the ground.

"What?" Holly's mouth went slack as she watched this man that she'd built up as her big, bad enemy for so long, admit the mistake that had irreversibly altered their lives.

"It's my fault you ran away with Corey," Blake looked into her eyes now in the shade of a hundred-year-old catalpa tree. She remembered for a moment what it had felt like when it was the two of them, young and battling against the whole world.

"Oh, Blake, it's not your fault I ran away. Yes, you hurt me. Yes, Corey was sick at the time, and I was worried for the both of us that you cared so little as to leave us alone in that state…"

"I wasn't thinking…" Blake interrupted.

"…No, let me finish," Holly persisted. "I've had a lot of time to think lately. I think about how I would feel if one of my children had been taken away from me for more than six years. I think about how I would feel now if either of them could never see me again. It's devastating. Plain and simple."

"It *is* horrible." Blake looked near tears as he enunciated those words. The jail guard looked away discreetly at the show of emotion and pretended to watch another of the inmates work.

"I chose to run away. I could have faced you, left

you, and raised Corey somewhere nearby. Instead, by the time I realized I was strong enough to do that, I was afraid I'd been gone too long, and I couldn't fathom telling you I'd made a mistake." Her throat became raw with tears. If only she could undo things that easily.

"I had almost given up finding you both," Blake admitted, taking Holly by surprise. "I found you by accident, on a family vacation. The only reason I went through with finding you was for my other kids. I'd resigned myself to the fact that Corey and I wouldn't know each other. We barely know each other now, and it is not going well, believe me; but I wanted to find him so that Jonah, Camillia, and Sammy could know their brother. They're so close, my kids."

Holly smiled through light tears. "How does Tristan fit into all of that? Mom told me you have him too."

Blake grinned back. "That kid could make friends with a den-full of hungry lions."

She giggled at the analogy. Truer words were never spoken. Her heart lightened immensely knowing her baby was safe and happy, even with Minerva Jenkins. That wasn't fair, though. She'd always liked Minerva. Minerva was spunky and fun, and insanely jealous of Holly, back in the day.

"And Corey? It's not going well, huh?" Holly inquired, instinctively knowing that her oldest was less easy-going with new people.

"He's worried about you."

Holly's heart tugged. That was just like the both of them.

"You need to stop worrying so much. I'm going to fix this," Blake offered quietly, again taking her by surprise.

"How do you mean? Have you taken Corey to counseling at all?"

"He's been a few times, but I'm not talking about Corey, Holly. He'll be fine once he can see you again."

"So, what?"

"Do you remember old Mrs. Jones? I know you wrote to her after you left."

"How could I forget Mrs. Jones? She was my life-line. I swear she's my guardian angel. You wouldn't believe how much her spirit has popped up during these years away."

Blake bit his thumb nervously. "Oh, I believe it. My mom and everybody except Minerva are going to kill me for saying this, but I've decided to ask the judge for leniency for you, and I'm going to agree to shared custody of Corey."

"Because of Mrs. Jones?" Holly asked incredulously.

"She saw something in me that I never expected her to see. I read her journal, just a few nights ago. I thought the old lady hated me. Turns out she was just waiting for me to do the right thing, after all."

Holly wondered again at the spirit of her old friend. "I'd like to read that some day."

"Well, for now, the book is in the hands of the Irish authorities. Did you know she knocked off her husband? He gave one of her kids a black eye, so she pushed him off a cliff."

"What? Wow! I had no idea, actually. She and my mom definitely did encourage me to stay away from you, but I've wondered a lot over the years whether they told me to stay away for them, or for me. The thing is, Blake, as much as I made you out to be a bad guy, I don't think you're either as bad as Mrs. Jones' first husband, or any of my mom's thug boyfriends."

Blake choked up again, momentarily. "I'm not. I was young and angry an awful lot in those days. I never hurt you on purpose, and I would never have laid a hand on Corey. My mistake was not acknowledging that I'd hurt you, even on accident."

"I believe you, Blake. Believe me now, when I say I didn't mean to hurt you either."

They didn't touch, but each knew the truce was complete. Blake cleared his throat to get the attention of the guard and asked him to carry on. Holly turned her attention back to the hedge; as if they hadn't just both added years to their lives after hashing out the mistakes of the last few.

PART III

Between the radiant white of a clear conscience
and the coal black of a conscience sullied by sin
lie many shades of gray—where most of us
live our lives. Not perfect, but not beyond
redemption.

—Sherry L. Hoppe

Chapter Forty-three

Karen Dermot

Karen wouldn't have missed this hearing for the world. Holly had decided to take a plea deal with the prosecutor's office after three weeks of incarceration. Today was the sentencing hearing in Superior Court and assignment of custody, which—she could practically sing—meant Corey would be theirs forever!

Her mouth pinched distastefully when she thought about the other child. She feared her feelings about him stemmed from the fact that he looked and acted so much like his mother. Plus, he had that unsightly birthmark. Karen noticed it, even if hardly anyone else acknowledged it anymore. Minerva, for instance—she took too much interest in Tristan. Well, Karen snorted to herself, consider the source.

Holly could have her other child, as far as Karen cared, and good riddance. But then, how would she ever take care of him in jail?

She hummed as she placed a pearl carefully in each ear lobe. She smoothed down her canary suit with its silk shell. She hoped it wouldn't be too hot in the old courthouse. She hated to sweat in silk.

Winston's nurse swept in at the last minute, so Karen ran hastily to her car and hit the gas to make the hearing. So much for not sweating.

With minimal braking, Karen arrived at the courthouse just in time and took Blake's arm. He looked so handsome in his uniform, though he didn't say much. This couldn't be easy for him. He acknowledged Minerva, who sat quietly in the back of the courtroom with both boys. Minerva hugged Tristan to her while Corey kept a polite distance. Karen frowned. Well, they could fix that too, given enough time.

Sissy, disheveled and gaudy as usual, sat across the courtroom with her derelict husband. Karen glared at Sissy and Sissy responded in kind. Karen wondered fleetingly why such a disastrous woman would look altogether smug as she grabbed her husband's hand.

Holly entered the courtroom in a stunning short-sleeved sapphire suit. Karen barely withheld her gasp as she saw Holly's hair shorn nearly to her scalp. Yet, Holly managed to look sophisticated and, oh so young. She smiled tremulously at her boys. Tristan waved back wholeheartedly and even Corey cracked a rare smile.

Everyone rose for the judge, Her Honor Belen Velasques, to take her seat at the bench. The judge had come all the way from King County, west of the Cascades, to preside over the case because it involved an elected county official.

The rarity of a female judge in such a conservative county, plus the fact that she was Latina, caused surprised deference from her observers. The courtroom went still as glass when Her Honor spoke:

"We are here today to sentence the defendant, Holly Lynn Reel Dermot, for the offense of second degree parental kidnapping with the aggravating circumstance of crossing state lines with the minor child. The defendant agreed to a guilty plea two days ago. Both parents, in this case, have had a chance to enter statements and to have input in both appropriate sentencing and custody issues. Given the sensitivity of the case, and the extenuating circumstances to which both parties have admitted, I'm going to be going outside the usual sentencing guidelines for such a case.

"Sheriff Dermot has asked to make a statement at this hearing and I'm going to let him speak now, before I give the defendant's sentence. Sheriff Dermot?"

Blake rose to his imposing height and went to the witness box to make his statement. He remained standing and addressed everyone in the courtroom. "Thank you, Judge Velasques. I appreciate the consideration you've given our family during this tough time. The 'extenuating circumstances' you speak of are some that I haven't ever acknowledged or taken responsibility for. Yes, the defendant, Holly Dermot, ran with our child, Corey Dermot, for more than six years, with no intention of ever returning him to me or his extended family. She has agreed to take responsibility for her part in that.

"My actions, however, are the reason that she felt compelled to run away in the first place."

He paused, and Karen's blood ran cold. What the hell was he doing?

"That chilly night, so many Octobers ago, Holly and I had a fight. Corey was sick with croup and taking a nap. Holly asked me where I'd been, and I got unnecessarily defensive. During our argument, I shoved her toward the bed. When I shoved her, Holly's arm collided with the bedside table, and her wrist was badly broken."

A collective gasp went up from the courtroom. Karen watched Sissy clap her hands together and put them to her lips while tears swelled up in her eyes.

"Holly has told me only recently the rest of the story. When I stormed out, not having acknowledged her injury, I slammed the door, awakening our baby, who'd only just fallen into the first real sleep he'd had in two days. Holly cried until the neighbor lady heard her and then they called her mother.

"For all of these years, I blamed Holly for stealing our child, but I never owned up to the responsibility I held for making her run in the first place. Of course she was terrified of me. Her wrist injury wasn't the first time I'd pushed or physically intimidated her. She felt her only option was to run. I worked for the

Sheriff's department. I was in a position of power. In fact, I used that power, repeatedly, to search for her."

It was all Karen could do to restrain herself as she watched her son decimate himself at the front of the courtroom.

"When I campaigned for the position of Sheriff, my ex-wife's injury made the headlines as a smear tactic in my opponent's campaign. What did I do when she accused me of spousal abuse? Deny, deny, deny. You believed me. Everyone believed me. I was clean-cut, a family man, dedicated to a job I'd done so well for years. You elected me; and I lied to you.

"That is why I've asked to speak before the sentencing. The sentence and custody agreement that go down today will make news because of exceptional circumstances.

"The far bigger headline today, though, will be this: 'Sheriff Resigns; Admits Lying to Voters.' I will step down after today, from a job that I'm passionate about, and pass my position temporarily to my second in command, Harvey Morris. The county commissioners are aware of this and have agreed with my choice for my replacement. I cannot continue to serve in an elected position when I didn't deserve this position in the first place. My family and I hope you'll respect our privacy and that of Holly Dermot after this hearing today. Thank you for your time."

The packed courtroom erupted in chaos. Karen felt like her head would explode. Perhaps she was stroking out, just as Winston had. She tried to calm her breathing as her son refused to make eye contact on his way back to his wife and the boys.

There was still the sentencing. She hoped that judge would let Holly have her comeuppance with both barrels. In fact, Karen's sanity relied on it.

The judge banged her gavel and cleared her throat. "Yes, then. Thank you, Sheriff. Now, onto the sentencing. The defendant will please rise…"

Holly rose demurely and raised her eyes to the judge.

"Miss Holly Lynn Reel Dermot, you are hereby sentenced to twenty-one days in jail, with credit for time served, and one year of supervised community service. Per the agreed-upon custody arrangement with Blake Dermot, you will be allowed to have shared custody of your son, Corey, so long as you agree to reside within Washington State at least until the child turns eighteen. Your other minor son, Tristan Reel, will be returned to your custody immediately. You, ma'am, are free to go."

Handcuffs were removed from Holly's wrists and she turned to embrace both of her sons and her mother, who had joined her at the defense table. Minerva and Blake stood to the side holding hands and watched bemusedly.

Karen tried wobbly legs and found the floor right where she had left it. Grateful that solid ground hadn't disintegrated with every hope and dream she'd had in the last month, Karen bolted for her car before anyone could see her devastation—or her rage, murderous rage that burned like a tanker truck on fire.

Where could she go? Not home. Home was her penitentiary, never-ending drudgery. She'd left that mess too long to fester, and now it looked like she'd given Blake too much room to blunder too. As if she didn't have enough power to manage her own family, to keep them all on the right track. Well, damnit, she thought as she tore out of the courthouse parking lot, she *did* have power, and like *none* of them, she knew what was right.

Karen would just need to prove it to them all.

Chapter Fourty-four

Tanner

The pixie princess with tear-filled eyes the color
of Liz Taylor's, well, she just couldn't be his Claudia.
Claudia's beauty had always been understated,
her hair long and luxuriously curly, her eyes less
remarkable for their color and more intriguing for the
secrets they held.

Holly Dermot's fine bone structure and her carriage
held remnants of the Claudia he remembered from
just a month ago in New York, but this woman in this
courtroom was far more beautiful. Tanner realized, as
she hugged her boys to her sides, she was a stranger
to him.

At the realization, Tanner felt panic nearly like the
time he was underwater and couldn't use his arms to
swim.

He backed himself quickly away from the corner
he'd positioned himself in to watch the hearing and
waited impatiently for an older woman, her face the
color of a ripe tomato, to exit. He wheeled himself into
the hallway to await the 'down' elevator. Only then
could he finally take a cleansing breath.

The Okanogan County courthouse was a turn-
of-the-twentieth-century concrete and stucco
behemoth with three stories and just one pokey
elevator, an afterthought installed after the Americans
with Disabilities Act was thrust upon the county
commissioners several decades before. Thus, it was
nearly five minutes before the elevator doors opened
and Tanner felt he might be safe from discovery.

What had he been thinking? That he could be her knight in shining armor and sweep her away from all of the pain and struggles she'd finally been made to face? That they could take up where they left off, when where they left meant a life in California or New York that fit his old life perfectly? That she would be Claudia still, when he knew full well that the woman he loved before had never really existed?

That her former beauty wouldn't be completely incomparable to what she really looked like? He'd known there was a blond under there, but strawberry blond? Plus, her short haircut brought out the well-sculpted bones of her face so she looked delicate and vulnerable, two things his Claudia had always been careful not to be.

Holly Dermot wouldn't want anything to do with him now that she was free and could forget the woman she was while in refuge. Tanner was the past, and a life with him came with strings. Plus, right up until her arrest, he'd given Claudia nothing but a hard time, all in the name of the truth.

Just as the elevator doors were about to close, a meaty hand thrust through and the man Tanner recognized as former Sheriff Blake Dermot stepped on board with his striking wife.

"Sorry, man," Blake apologized, "We thought it would be easier to skip the stairs…"

"…and sneak out through the old jail entrance where there's no press," Minerva added and giggled.

Blake grinned back at her and gave her a searing kiss. Their celebratory mood was not something Tanner expected after the speech the Sheriff had given.

"How do you know I'm not press?" Tanner asked cleverly.

Blake pressed the first floor button and cleared his throat. "Bad assumption. Um, are you press?"

Minerva giggled again.

"No, I am not press. But I do take pictures for a living. Name's Tanner Grafton. You gave a nice speech up there. Not that it means anything coming from me, but you did the right thing." Tanner held out his hand and Blake took it.

"Tanner Grafton? Wasn't that the name of the photographer who took that picture of Tristan in L.A.?" Minerva asked.

Tanner nearly swore when he saw the light bulb in Blake Dermot's eyes blink on. He'd had no idea how they tracked Claudia down in the first place. So it had been his picture of Taylor after all. Her worries hadn't been unfounded and he'd placed Claudia right into the hands of her ex-husband when he insisted on publishing the picture.

"Does Holly know you're here?" Blake asked frankly.

"No, she doesn't. It took me a while to find a way to see her. She wouldn't take visitors at the jail; and every time I tried to talk to her mother, Sissy, to see if she could get a message to Holly, I got stonewalled by Sissy's friends and associates. Sissy is an incredibly hard woman to locate."

"You're telling me?" Blake chuckled. "You could have stayed behind, you know, and talked to Holly. She's totally free to do what she wants now. Why did you leave?"

The elevator opened and Tanner considered fleeing before he could answer the question. His wheels were way faster than feet. But then Blake would feel compelled to tell Holly that he'd seen Tanner. He waited for the Sheriff and his wife to exit and he followed them out while he contemplated his answer.

"Let's just say that I probably had a whole lot more to offer her when she was scared and on the run. She needs time to rediscover herself and rebuild her life with her boys before I come and interfere."

"Oh, I don't know about that, buddy," Blake argued. "She's had plenty of free time on her hands lately to think. Plus, I happen to know that she already knows where she'll stay with the boys. And, the last time we talked, a good portion of her planning had to do with how she would find you and make you fall for her again, despite her being a rotten criminal on probation in Washington State."

Tanner couldn't help but smile at that. "She told you about me?"

"We've confessed a whole lot of things over the last few days," Blake admitted. "There are now two things I'm certain of: She did the very best thing for both of us because her leaving meant I got to fall in love with my wife, and Minerva here is…everything…"

Minerva wrapped her arms around her husband's waist and planted a kiss on his cheek.

"…and the other thing is that Holly loves you like she's never loved anyone. Your relationship is probably the most real one she's had, even though everything about her was fake at the time."

"You see, I don't know what to do with that," Tanner reasoned. "How could it have been real if she was never honest with me?"

Blake tucked his arm back around his wife. "When a woman loves her man, there is nothing dishonest about it. Minerva could dye her hair purple and wear cat's eye contacts and I would still recognize the love there. I would know it when our hearts did their dance and my pulse quickened to match hers."

Tanner nodded. That feeling was precisely what had compelled him to chase Holly to Okanogan County in the first place, as absurd as it had seemed when he Googled a map and found out just how far the little county was from civilization in general, and airports specifically. Plus, he was disabled, which took a little more planning, but Holly's love and the possibilities had kept him going.

"Would it help you understand if I told you I'm a coward?" Tanner joked.

Blake shook his head. "Oh, no, I don't believe that. No coward would have found his way to that courtroom. I think you should go back."

"I'm sure she's already left by now."

"I do happen to know where she's going, if you're

interested," Blake hedged.

"This jail entrance," Tanner asked, "does it turn out to have a wheelchair ramp?"

"I don't know, but we're going to find out!" Minerva clapped her hands and led the way down the cavernous hallway to their mutual escape.

Chapter Forty-five

Corey

Corey wondered if joy came in different flavors just like ice cream. There was Bubble Gum, so sweet you wondered if you could make it all the way to the bottom of the cone without puking. The moment in the courtroom where he learned he could go back with his mom—that was like Bubble Gum.

Then there was Rocky Road, also sweet and delicious, but with nuts that you had to take your time to chew. He was happy to be with his mom and brother again for the moment, but he still needed to chew on the fact that he would be shared with his dad, and that his brother wasn't all the way his brother. Also, that his mom still hadn't had a chance to explain her side of the kidnapping story.

Perhaps joy was like Spumoni—a flavor an Italian friend in New York had introduced him to— complicated and not entirely describable.

"Hey, Mom?" he asked from the back seat of Sissy's car.

"Yah, baby?" His mom turned her face to him. She was still a mess from the make-up that smeared all over while she was crying at the courthouse.

"Can we stop for ice cream somewhere?"

Tristan piped up. "Can we? Can we?"

Sissy laughed from the middle seat in the back. "Stanley? Do you think we could manage to scrounge up an ice cream in this town?"

"They have packaged ice creams at the Quik Stop. That's the best we can do unless we go another five miles out of our way."

"Will that work, Corey?" Holly asked. "I know you love *Fudgesicles*."

"Okay," Corey agreed. Then he added, "Hey Mom, do you think Tristan and me could go back to being called Taylor and Cody?"

For some reason, the question wiped the smiles off the faces of everyone in the car, which made Corey think he wasn't going to like the answer.

"That would get kind of confusing for your dad and Minerva when they had you, don't you think, Corey?" His mom offered gently.

He nodded sullenly and looked down at his lap.

"Hey sweetie?"

Corey looked back up at his mom again.

"I want to talk about all of this with you, okay? You must have a ton of questions and I'll answer them as best I can. Let's get home and relax for a while. I need to wash my face and change into a pair of real sweatpants. Then we'll snuggle up proper and have a nice long chit chat. I promise."

He tried to smile, but his stomach did a few flips too. He'd probably have to save a few questions for later. He didn't want to hurt his mom's feelings when she'd only just gotten out of jail.

They got their ice creams and piled back into the car to drive the few more blocks to the house Stanley and Sissy had rented for them. The house was cute—yellow with little flower boxes like they'd had on their apartment building in New York. Sissy had planted purple flowers in the middle and little white ones that trailed off the sides.

They ran inside to explore; and Corey was excited to see that he had his own room, not like at his dad's where he'd had to share with all of the boys except for the baby, Sammy. The only quiet he ever had at that place was in the back yard shooting baskets.

Even more exciting was, as he started to examine the things in his closet and on his shelves, that he had his old stuff from New York! "How'd it get here?"

Corey asked enthusiastically as he held up his favorite book about sharks that he'd had since he was five.

Sissy came and put her arm around his shoulders. "Some very good friends of your mom's packed everything up lovingly and shipped all of this out here for her and you guys. Stanley and I had a great time putting it all away, but you can change the order of things if you want to."

"It's perfect, Grandma," Corey declared.

Tristan came bounding in. "Corey! I have my Rock-em, Sock-em Robots! Do you wanna play? I also found my Battleship game!"

Corey messed up his brother's hair. "Maybe later, squirt."

"Okay!" Tristan disappeared back out the door to his neighboring bedroom.

Corey walked down a hallway and a small set of stairs to his mom's room. He found her in tears, with even more trails of makeup, running her hands over her shelves of textbooks.

"You can still be a nurse, can't you, Mom?" He walked to her side and leaned into her.

"I don't know, Corey. I have a criminal record now and my name will have to be changed. It's going to be complicated. I don't know who would ever hire me."

"They'd have to be dumb not to hire you, Mom."

She laughed through her tears, but Corey knew her dream jobs, the ones she'd tried so hard to choose between, were toast now. That made him sad.

"What will you do then?" he asked.

"I'm not sure. Lucky for us, we have a grandpa Stanley that generously paid for a place to live for us until I can figure that out."

"Hey, watch it with the 'grandpa' thing," Stanley growled from the door.

His mom went over to embrace Stanley. "Thank you so much for doing all of this. I can't imagine a more beautiful homecoming after everything that's happened to me and the boys."

"I wouldn't have had it any other way, and neither

would your mother. Now, Sissy and me are going to meander back to the motel while you get settled in."

"Are you sure we can't find a place for the two of you to stay here at the house?"

"No way. You might eavesdrop and your mom and I have some celebratin' to do," Stanley winked.

Corey didn't know what that meant, but his mom turned red when Stanley said it.

They saw his grandma and Stanley to the door and then his mom plopped in the middle of their old cushy sofa.

"Come here boys," she commanded, "we've got some long-overdue snuggling to do. Should we have some popcorn and take in a DVD?"

"It's the middle of the day," Tristan pointed out.

"What do you mean?" Mom asked as she peered under the coffee table at their collection of movies. "We don't usually have ice cream before dinner either, but today is not your usual day. Let's see what we've got in here. Hmm. Should we watch *Shrek* or *Monsters, Inc.?*"

"*SHREK!*" both boys screamed enthusiastically.

"I'll get the popcorn," Corey hustled over to the brightly lit kitchen and started rummaging through cupboards.

~~~~~~~~~~

They'd no sooner settled with their bowls and the movie previews when the doorbell rang.

"I wonder who that would be. Don't they know they're interrupting?" Holly grumbled.

"I'll get it!" Tristan shouted.

"Me too," Corey chimed.

"Wait boys! Don't answer the door without me…" Holly commanded. Dread blossomed in her core, along with a healthy dose of déjà vu, as soon as she uttered those words.

Unfortunately the sensation didn't have time to warn her before the door was thrown open to reveal their surprise visitor.

Chapter Forty-six

Minerva

She knew Tanner Grafton loathed pity. She could see that from the way he held himself high and proud in his wheelchair, the way he moved through the world confidently as if his chair was merely an extension of his body, and the way he met your eyes while he spoke that made you forget you were talking to someone lower to the ground. Tanner did not feel sorry for himself in the least.

That was why she felt so genuinely bad for pitying Tanner in this moment; but then, she'd feel sorry for anybody whose car had been surprisingly towed from the courthouse parking lot.

He spoke into his cell phone with the other hand gracefully laid over his outer ear to hear over the brisk wind swirling around them. Why, Minerva wondered, was the weather about to go south when this man was obviously stranded?

"I understand that the spot was designated for a particular county official, but I had clearly posted my handicap sign on my rearview mirror, and there was no other place to park that wasn't on a hillside, or a mile from the courthouse entrance," he argued. "I demand you bring it back.

"No, I will not pay for you to tow it back and, no, I do not have the transportation to come and get it. It's not like I can call a yellow cab in the great city of Okanogan.

"We can give you a ride," Minerva offered again. Tanner held up his hand as his demeanor grew increasingly dour.

"Be assured that you people will be hearing from my lawyer as soon as I reach home. You have been entirely unhelpful." Tanner hit the 'end' button with angry finality.

"Blake is momentarily waylaid by the reporters that camped out at the exit, but I want you to know you're more than welcome to a ride in our minivan. It's not exactly sexy, but I think you could probably get in okay." Minerva tried a winning smile, but it fell flat.

"I'm sorry to get you involved in this. I know you were just trying to help me find Claudia—er, Holly."

"Oh, actually, I'm glad Blake and I can help. When he gets back, it'll only take a phone call to the right person, and I'm pretty sure you'll get your car back, with an apology."

"Right. He's the influential Sheriff of this Godforsaken county."

"Well, not anymore, but he still knows people and he knows how to call in favors."

Tanner nodded and the conversation waned for a few moments.

"You all will be okay after he leaves his job, right? I wondered about that when he made his announcement," Tanner observed.

Minerva kept her face carefully neutral, because in fact she'd been asking herself that since Blake made his decision to resign. "Yes. Yes, we'll be fine. Harv will keep Blake on as a deputy since he's a really good cop. There will be a pay cut, but also no voters to answer to."

"Ah, yes, the public can be so fickle. Being a politician is much like being an artist. You try so hard at both to maintain the integrity of the work itself and to please the audience at the same time. It's exhausting."

Minerva nodded agreeably. "I love your photographs, by the way. After we spotted Tristan's picture, I looked up your website. You're a talented guy. I wish I had an eye for that sort of thing."

"I believe everyone has a talent for something. It just needs to be cultivated."

"That's true. Oh, here comes Blake. Honey, Tanner's car got towed while he was inside."

"Oh crap, buddy. You parked in old man gristlc's parking spot. The man has been county treasurer nearly since they built this place."

"Is prime parking by seniority here then?" Tanner grinned despite his predicament.

"Pretty much," Blake laughed. "That's okay. Scheel's Towing owes me a favor. They hauled off my car a really long time ago and they have yet to set things right. I don't think I've ever thanked Sissy properly for that one."

Tanner raised his eyebrows and Blake waved it off.

"Water under the bridge. Too bad there's enough of it to flood an entire town! Can we give you a ride to the tow yard and see if we can talk some sense into them?"

"That, I would appreciate. My bags and camera equipment are in the trunk. I'm anxious to see those somewhere safe."

"All right then. I'll go get the minivan if you and Minerva will wait here," Blake offered.

"How'd your meeting go with the reporters, honey?"

"There's very little that's sacred nowadays. They were right up in my business, but it'll be okay, Minerva. It was the right thing and I think they'll all see that too in the end." He kissed her to erase her frown and ran to the parking lot on the hillside to get their van.

"I hope everyone will feel that way," Minerva murmured so quietly after him that Tanner nearly didn't hear her.

~~~~~~~~~~

An hour later, Tanner's car was sprung from the impound and he followed Blake and Minerva toward a quaint neighborhood with a neatly eclectic collection of houses on generous lots. Dogs with collars and stray kids ran the sidewalks toward home as thunderclouds menaced above increasingly violent winds.

He hoped Holly and the boys were safely inside by now.

They pulled up in front of Holly's home and the poignant contrast to her former home in Brooklyn nearly took Tanner's breath away. This rural beauty could never be matched by the bustle of a city. This was where Holly was from, her roots. No wonder he'd sensed in her something so different he could never nail it down. Innocence and guilelessness were the hallmarks of a small town girl, and Holly was that girl. It made him feel good to finally make the connection.

Tanner put out the transfer board from his seat and hoisted himself onto it from the swivel seat so that he could retrieve his wheelchair. Blake stood back and watched Tanner's incredible arm strength at work, and admired his self-reliance.

"Is there anything I can help you with then?" Blake asked casually.

"Actually, yes. There's a very high curb here and I'd rather not go all the way to the end of the block to get up on it. You can pull my chair over it if you would. Plus, Holly clearly has stairs leading up to her front door, so I'll need you to ring the doorbell."

"I'm on it, boss." Blake pulled the chair up over the curb and as far as the sidewalk and let Tanner take over wheeling toward the porch.

Blake rang the doorbell and waited for one of the boys to hustle the door like he knew one of his kids would. That's when he noticed the door was slightly ajar. Ah, kids—they rarely saw to getting the door shut either. Blake poked his head through the door. "Hello? Holly? Corey? Tristan?"

"Where are they?" Minerva asked worriedly from behind him.

"Maybe they went out," Blake replied, but his instincts kicked in. Something wasn't right. Why would they go out and leave the door partly open, especially with a storm coming?

"You two wait out here for a second. I'm going to go check this out just to be sure," he commanded. Blake slid past the door and into the foyer. He looked toward the living room where movie credits rolled and bowls of popcorn awaited eating. He heard a sob from the hallway bathroom and rushed toward the sound. "Holly?"

"Sheriff Blake?" It was Tristan, balled up by the toilet, where he'd heaved what looked like popcorn and chocolate syrup.

"Tristan? Are you okay? MINERVA!" he yelled loud enough that she would hear and come help. "Are you by yourself?"

Blake looked the boy over. Other than being painfully sick and scared, he appeared unharmed. Minerva rushed in behind him and scooped Tristan up in her arms.

"Oh my God, baby boy. What happened to you?"

He could barely talk over his wretching sobs. "The b-bad lady t-took 'em."

"Corey and Holly?" Blake asked as calmly as he could and the boy nodded. "Which bad lady?"

"The s-smelly one from the a-airport. She's C-Corey's grandma. I've s-seen her at your h-house. She t-took 'em and shoved m-me fr-from M-Mommy. I h-hit my s-stomach o-on the f floor."

"Okay, baby. Okay," Minerva soothed. "Breathe, baby, breathe." She shot Blake a look of terror over Tristan's head. She had seen first-hand the fine-bladed edge Karen Dermot had been walking.

"What's happened?" They heard from the doorway. Tanner had hauled himself up the stairs on his hands and scooted down the hallway to the bathroom. Neither Blake nor Minerva was surprised to see him.

"My mother has gone too far this time. She took

Holly and Corey and she left this five-year-old boy here to fend for himself," Blake could hardly contain his anger. No wonder he hadn't spotted his mom in the courtroom on his way out. She'd high-tailed it here to stir up trouble just when they had things settled.

"You don't think she'd hurt them?" Tanner inquired. "Why would she take them and leave Taylor?"

"It's Tristan," Minerva said through gritted teeth as she held and rocked the poor boy, "and he doesn't belong to the Dermot family. To her, blood is everything. Thank God you're okay, precious boy."

"So? She's your mother. Where do we begin to try to find her?" Tanner asked Blake impatiently.

"I'll call Harv and have him put out an APB. We'll start at the house. Minerva, can you take Tristan home with you and relieve the sitter? You better put a call in to Sissy as well."

She nodded and continued to rub Tristan's back. He'd already begun to fall asleep in her arms. "Be careful," she warned Blake.

"I'll drive." Tanner already hauled himself back down the hallway at a rate of speed Blake could barely match by walking as he pulled out his cell phone.

"There's no way I'm going to argue with that," he stated as he slipped into the passenger side of the car and put in a call to interim sheriff Harvey Morris.

Fat rain drops pelted the windshield as they fastened their seatbelts and headed for the Dermot house.

Chapter Forty-seven

Karen

Karen fretted that she hadn't had more time to pull her plan together. After all, given enough time, she could have cleaned and packed the lodge weeks before departing; and she and Corey could have had a grand time camping and fishing, and *bonding,* as she yearned so much to do with her grandson.

She had, of course, needed to stop by the house and take care of a few…things… before they embarked on their adventure, she and Corey. She hadn't packed his belongings properly in their rush to leave, so she knew a shopping trip would be required on the way to the lodge to get him some spare clothing and a toothbrush.

If only he would be more agreeable about the plan, she thought. She peered in her rearview at her boy, bound, and finally, when he wouldn't quit screaming at her, gagged, and carefully strapped into the booster seat in the back. Nine-year-olds still needed boosters, didn't they? Oh well, she couldn't remember, so she did it anyway.

Corey was surprisingly stout, so she'd had a bit of a struggle getting him in place, but then she'd been well-conditioned, dealing with the dead weight of Winston for years. At least the experience was good for something, she thought, as she turned and gave Corey a winning smile. Daggers shot from his eyes, but she shrugged them off. He'd get to know and love her over time. That, they would have plenty of, she hoped.

After all, nobody in her family knew about the lodge—at least nobody who could still speak intelligibly. She and Winston had run into a bit of a snag years ago with a local client who had turned in an insurance claim on a fire in a defunct business building. The thing was: Winston had seen the client in a neighboring town buying gas cans. A metal dumpster had been pushed against the back door of the building, presumably so its contents could be burned too, but the fire had been extinguished before it reached the back of the store.

Winston had collected the gas cans from the dumpster during the initial chaos following the fire. He confronted the client. The client offered them the deed to the lodge in exchange for their silence and his freedom, with the agreement that they would let the claim go through to their parent company. It was the first, but unfortunately not the only time they'd let their greed override their business ethics.

Winston had worried himself inside-out over these kinds of exchanges, but Karen had proceeded with cool indifference. How else were they to provide their four children with everything they needed? Besides, they were merely the gateway between the client and the insurance company, which had billions of dollars at its disposal. If she and Winston had gotten real estate, favors, even money, in exchange for their discretion, well, she considered these things simply bonuses because they worked so hard.

They'd used the lodge as a vacation rental. It sat near Lake Wenatchee, so they never had any problem renting it out for the summer season through a property management company. After Winston's stroke, though, Karen hadn't wanted to bother paying a property manager anymore and, frankly, she needed the cash, so she'd put the lodge up for sale. Unfortunately, the real estate market had tanked about then, so the property remained sparsely furnished and unused.

It was the perfect retreat for Corey and her. She

knew he'd come around once he saw how much fun was to be had. That was, if the weather held up. She frowned at the steady rain blowing sideways on the windshield. Obviously, they'd need rain gear. They could stop in Wenatchee for supplies and clothing, but Karen didn't want to leave Corey in the car while she went in, for fear he would alert somebody in the parking lot. So, she used the one hundred mile drive from Okanogan to cajole him.

"If you will be agreeable for the rest of our trip, I'll be happy to remove the bandana from your mouth and the scarves from your wrists."

Corey shook his head firmly—no.

"I would like to take you to dinner at a fine restaurant in Wenatchee. Do you think you could be good so that I could take you in?"

This time Corey didn't shake his head. He had to be hungry. Dinnertime had gone with daylight. Yet, his eyes still sang his hostility.

"I'm not going to hurt you, Corey. I've taken you away so you can get to know me better. I'm your grandma. I used to be your very favorite when you were a baby. Nobody could get you to smile and babble like I could. By the time your mom took you, you'd already started to say 'Gama' to me. I'm simply hoping to recapture some of that, to have some fun with you."

Corey's angry eyes turned skeptical.

"I can pull over at the next historical marker and take off the gag if you agree to stop screaming at me."

He nodded finally, resigned.

The first words out of his mouth nearly made Karen gag him all over again—"What did you do to my mom?"

"She's taken care of, Corey. Don't worry."

"You left my little brother all by himself," he accused.

"He's resourceful, isn't he? He could go to a neighbor for help or call 9-1-1, right? Haven't you taught him those things?"

"Mom did," Corey admitted.

"This trip is about you, Corey, and me, and all of the time I've missed with you over the years. Holly took you away for nearly seven years. I'd like just a portion of the next seven."

"You're going to keep me for seven years?" Corey whined desperately. She could see him doing the math—he'd be driving by then. "What about school? Sports? My dad? You care about him, don't you?"

"Blake has been brainwashed by that dimwit wife of his. You didn't like her either, did you Corey? Nope. I didn't think so. He barely made an effort all those years to get you back, and then when he finally did find you, he gave you right back to your mother."

"He didn't exactly give me back. Mom said that 'shared custody' meant that I'd spend time with both of them."

"Well, I'm not so good at 'sharing'," Karen sniffed.

Corey shifted uncomfortably in his seat, his hands still bound by a silk scarf. "I need to pee."

"There is a fruit stand not too far away. I'll stop for you, but you must give nothing away to the clerk. I still have that little handgun standing by if you say anything. You'll be safe, Corey, unharmed just like I told you, but I cannot say the same for either of your parents if you betray me."

Corey shuddered involuntarily, but he was perfectly cooperative for their quick stop, in Wenatchee while they gathered supplies and ate, and the rest of the way to the lodge.

She left him untied after their first stop, yet she watched him carefully for any signs that he would try to flee. The pitch blackness of the night outside the lodge took the fight out of him. Besides, they were both exhausted. Corey fell asleep the minute his head hit the pillow in the lodge's first bedroom. Karen lay down beside him and fell into a fitful sleep of her own only moments later.

Chapter Forty-eight

Winston

He'd been locked inside his body for so long that he'd given in to its treachery. He no longer even tried to move just a finger here or an eyebrow there. He simply rode the rollercoaster of involuntary movement until a moment when movement really mattered. Like the times Karen gave him the same soup on his tray five meals in a row. He got sick of vegetable broth, for shit's sake. So he willed it to fly, and he took small satisfaction when it did.

Karen had never betrayed him the way his body had. He shouldn't have punished her so, but there came a point at which she hated him for her servitude. So he hated her back for letting him live through it. By taking care of him, she'd assigned him to the life of a miserable cripple. The times he found her hovering over him with a pillow, murder in her eyes, his mind pleaded with her to do it. He resented her for being too much of a coward. Would she be able to live this way?

That was why he finally understood when she came and dismissed his nurse on Tuesday afternoon and then walked out and slammed the door only minutes later and left him by himself. She returned for a short time about an hour after and then walked out again, without feeding him, without cleansing him of his waste. She failed to even acknowledge Winston as she hurried about. It was as if she'd forgotten him in her haste to take care of whatever was on her mind.

It made him sad that this should be their departure

after so many years together. There would have
been so much more dignity in smothering him with
a pillow, for him anyway. He would not have sat for
hours in hunger and thirst and acrid excrement.

When the door burst open several hours later, upon
the waning of daylight, Winston didn't know whether
to be thankful, or to wither with embarrassment. He
hoped it would be Karen again, that she'd changed
her mind and come back to make amends, to say
goodbye properly, or to tend to him like she always
had.

Instead it was Blake, Troy, and Tony, Troy and
Tony's wives, and some other guy in a wheelchair.
Winston looked at his sons: Blake's physical size
and proud demeanor reflective of the way Winston
had once stood; Troy, his oldest, slighter and Karen's
doppelganger other than his thick shock of dark hair,
which was like Winston's; and Tony, the bumbling
and funny combination of the other two. They'd done
him proud, his sons.

The women exclaimed all over their father-in-law,
but seemed at a loss as to what to do. Their solution—
when a simple bowl of Jello, a soft toast, and a bottle
of butt cleanser would have sufficed—made Winston
want to die all over again: They called an ambulance.

His eyes pleaded with Blake to keep him here,
to help him, but he could not utter the words. He
wanted to ask where his Karen was, what would
keep their mother from taking care of him, and he
feared the worst for his wife who he both loved and
hated. He willed his hand to grab Tony's arm, and he
managed to, but Tony still helped the ambulance guys
load him onto a gurney.

Before he left his home for the last time, Winston
needed to communicate just one thing to his boys.
Especially if Karen was dead, he needed them to
know something, so he concentrated all of his energy
on uttering one word repeatedly with the hopes they
would get it. His voice was raspy from disuse and
he couldn't move his lips properly, so the word was

completely fouled up, but he repeated it over and over just the same.

"What is that, Winston?" Trish leaned closer as they wheeled him toward the waiting ambulance. "Sheriff? Car off? Far off? Serif? I'm not getting this. Blake, honey? Can you hear what he's whispering?"

"It sounds like he's saying carafe. But that's a weird thing to say. Maybe he's thirsty. Do you need a drink from mom's carafe, Dad? Is that what you're saying?"

Winston could only grunt his approval at his son's understanding of the word, but he couldn't tell his son that Karen owned about twenty carafes. She forever sought to entertain and beverages simply could not go on the table in their given containers. There was only one carafe of concern to him, though. He'd pilfered it from Karen's collection for his own personal use and Winston could only hope his son would go searching for it.

The ambulance doors closed with finality on that hope, shutting out the deluge that left Winston sputtering and wishing, already, for home.

Chapter Forty-nine

Tanner

After Winston Dermot was carried away via ambulance, Blake, his brothers, and Tanner decided to do an all-out search of the house to see if they could locate Karen Dermot and her hostages. Tanner assigned himself to the carafes, since most would be in lower cupboards where he could reach. The four of them figured the whole carafe thing was a long-shot, but it made Tanner feel like he could be of help.

A search of the kitchen and dining room revealed carafes and pitchers of all shapes and themes. Karen Dermot even had holiday carafes stuffed into nooks and cupboards, one shaped like a candy cane, another a shamrock. He put the splendid array on the dining table where even Blake was impressed by the sheer number of pitchers his mother owned.

By this time, they were well past midnight and Tanner had tired of looking and getting nowhere.

"Alright, guys," Tanner inquired of the brothers. "Where else would your junk-loving mother put her carafes?"

"I saw some on the laundry room shelves when I was looking for old papers and keys," Tony offered.

"She has a storage bureau in the bedroom hallway too. You might try the lower cupboard in there."

"Okay, thanks. Hey, does your dad have a thing for carafes too? Would he have put one in his study or anything?" Tanner wondered aloud, his sleuthing instincts kicking in.

"I've been in his study most of the evening, but I

haven't checked his liquor cabinet yet. You could try there," Blake offered. "The key is taped under the middle drawer of his desk."

"Just how do you know that?" Troy teased his younger brother. "You were sneaking nips when you were a kid, weren't you?"

"No, you punk," Blake retorted, playfully slapping away his brother's jibe, "Dad showed me one time where the key was in case I needed to get in there."

"Wait a minute. Why would he lock the liquor cabinet and then show one of his adult children where the key was unless there was something more important in there than booze?" Tanner deduced as he watched Blake's eyes light.

"You should be a cop, Grafton," Blake praised. "Let's check it out."

They found the carafe straight away, made of solid hand-hammered silver, and stuffed to the rim with documents.

"What are they?" Tony asked, trying to make sense of papers that had been set aside for no obvious purpose.

"They're all copies of insurance claims. He wrote a number at the top of each one. They're in dollars, see?" Tanner pointed out the neatly written numeric figures to the brothers.

"Let's look at some of the names and see if they ring a bell," Blake suggested.

"Joy Lerner. I remember that chick," Troy offered. "She showed up at the office so many times over a period of about a month, I thought she was having an affair with Dad. She was all legs, too. This says she made a claim for stolen goods from a storage locker. Huh. I guess she was just there on business."

"How about Koffey?" Tony added. "Wasn't he the guy who just up and left that Shelby Mustang in Dad's driveway one morning? That was right before I started driving and I begged him for that car, man. What was his claim for?"

"He had flood damage to his warehouse," Tanner

answered.

"That dollar amount in the corner. I blue-booked that Mustang years later and that's roughly what it was worth. No wonder the old man wouldn't let me drive it. I was a punk teenager. I mighta wrecked it."

"This one is different," Tanner noted. There's a deed attached to the back of the claim. Do you guys know the name Wilsey?"

"Oh yeah," Blake chimed in. "That was the name of the guy who owned several of the buildings downtown. One of his businesses went under and the building mysteriously caught fire. The firefighters put it out before it could burn any adjacent businesses, but rumor had it for years that old man Wilsey started the fire himself. I didn't know Dad was his agent. That was before my time as a cop."

"So this is just a copy of a deed, not the original, but would you say this 'lodge' on the deed would be worth roughly $75,000 when the fire happened, like we have written on the claim?" Tanner held the papers up for the brothers' perusal. "Look at the deed, gentlemen. Who is that lodge deeded to?"

"Dad!" The brothers chimed in unison.

"Do you think your dad might have been taking favors, cars, and real estate in exchange for filing fraudulent claims?" Tanner asked gently. He could tell this wasn't easy for Blake in particular.

"I just can't see him doing that," Blake shifted uncomfortably. "Dad's always been such an honest man. It would have killed him to hide something that big from everyone."

"Or it may have pushed him into having a stroke…" Tony concluded and they all murmured their agreement.

"Back to this lodge—do you think they still own it? Didn't Harv call in and say he tracked your mom's credit card transactions tonight in Wenatchee? Would they maybe be on their way to…what's this say…Lake Wenatchee? Not that I know where that's at." Tanner handed the deed over to Blake.

"I know it's certainly worth checking out," Blake admitted. "You too tired to drive, Grafton? I could take a squad car."

"That would be too obvious. If they are at the lodge, I would think my civilian car would offer a much more subtle disguise."

"Good point. Okay, you drive. If you get tired, we'll spell you. I don't have the faintest idea how to do those hand controls, though."

"Oh, don't worry, rental cars have a way to disable those so anyone can drive the car," Tanner scrubbed the fatigue from his face with both hands. He turned to Troy and Tony. "You two can stuff yourselves in the back. You're not quite as long-legged as your brother. We'll chuck my wheelchair in the trunk so long as one of you promises to bring it to me. Try not to let it get wet."

"Will do," Tony promised.

"Okay, then. Wasn't Wenatchee that Podunk village with the single runway they called an airport? Where I flew after I left Seattle?"

The brothers laughed and Blake replied wryly, "Don't you worry, city boy, we'll point the way."

Chapter Fifty

Karen

Karen's eyes popped open as the first glimmer of daylight slanted across their bed. Good, Corey still slept peacefully. He hadn't tried to go anywhere.

She unpacked the car and put all of the groceries away in the ample kitchen. This lodge had been built to accommodate conferences and church groups, so there were several bunk rooms and three smaller bedrooms for the cook and the group leaders. The dining nook was built-in and surrounded by log benches fit for eighteen people. She and Corey would certainly rattle around a bit in the space, but at least they wouldn't be bumping into each other.

There was cleaning to do, so Karen readied her supplies. She was about to attack the toilet when she heard Corey stir next door.

"You're awake. It's a beautiful day!" she exclaimed, the perfect hostess, "Can I make you some breakfast, young man?"

Corey rubbed at the bruises on his wrists and scowled Karen's way.

"Yes, well, I'm sorry about those, but if you hadn't fought so much…Anyway, I've got eggs and bacon or pancake fixings. I make world-famous pancakes. Would you like some?"

Karen could hear Corey's stomach betray him from across the room. She smiled. "Pancakes it is, then," she declared, abandoning her cleaning supplies for the moment.

Corey seemed determined through breakfast to

maintain his indifference, though he did clean his whole plate, which pleased her.

She realized how much of a city kid she had with her when she made him get dressed to go for a walk. He immediately donned shorts and flip-flops for the trek through the woods. "Oh no, kiddo. This is a forest. You need long pants and those hiking boots we just bought. Your toes will be thankful the first time they run over a bullsnake."

"There are snakes out here?" Corey asked, his eyebrows flying to the ceiling. Instead of fear, though, she saw wonder. "Will I see a cougar or a beaver? Can we throw rocks in the lake? I could see the moon shining off it when we pulled in last night. I learned to skip rocks at Central Park last year."

This attitude was more like it. If he couldn't accept her right away, he could at least learn to like his surroundings. If he learned to like his surroundings, he could learn to like her.

"Let's go see what we can find," Karen smiled confidently and put on her own hiking boots.

Chapter Fifty-one

Corey

If his mom and brother had been along for the adventure, Corey would have been having the time of his life. Instead, he acted like he was having fun, spotting deer, seeing a fish jump on the lake, eating Grandma's food. It seemed to make her happy. He wanted her to be happy, because if she wasn't, she said she'd hurt his mom and dad.

It would have been a whole lot easier to pretend if he hadn't been so worried about his mom. Tristan had probably thought to call Minerva by now, so he was likely just fine. Grandma had dropped him awfully hard, though, after she detached his monkey legs from Mom. His little brother tried not to let his mom get away easily this time.

Corey had tried the same thing when his grandma pointed the gun at his mom and ordered her out of the car at the Dermot house. He'd clung to his mom as if his knees and upper arms contained suction cups. It was Holly who detached him, pled with him to be good, because she didn't want him to be hurt if the hand gun was suddenly pointed at him.

When his mom hadn't come back, Corey had fought with his grandma bodily until she put a knee in the middle of his back and forced his hands behind him where she tied them together with the scarf from around her neck.

When he started to scream, she ran into the house and came straight back with a navy blue bandanna and tied it around his mouth.

Pretending right now was a ton easier than being bound and gagged.

They'd returned from their walk and Corey decided to explore the attic of the lodge while his grandma cleaned house. He acted carefree so his grandma wouldn't suspect he was trying to find a way out. There could be some kind of weapon in the attic.

He would have to be careful, though. He needed to make sure she couldn't come back and hurt his mom or dad. Did that mean he would have to kill her? That, he couldn't imagine. Well, anyway, he vowed to figure out a way.

The attic had an access in the floor with retrievable stairs, so he got a step stool from the utility room and pulled the stairs down. The attic space was surprisingly clean, with neatly labeled boxes stacked in rows. The pungent smell of mothballs stung his nose. The ceiling height was just over his head, so he didn't have to stoop, but a grown-up would. There was a small window at either end of the attic, hexagon-shaped like a stop sign, which let in enough light to allow him daytime exploration.

Corey went over to the window. He was so high! He looked out over the forest. Movement drew his eyes toward a car in the trees. That hadn't been there before when they took their walk, he was pretty sure. His heart beat faster. The guys in the back seat looked like his dad's brothers, his uncles Troy and Tony. Had they found him and grandma?

His dad and a silver-haired guy in a wheelchair worked their way toward the lodge cautiously, though Corey was pretty sure Grandma would be too wrapped up in scrubbing to notice them. At least she had been when Corey went upstairs.

Corey pounded on the window. Both men stopped and looked around, but failed to look his way. Corey started searching for something to break the window with, but then he thought twice. Grandma would hear that for sure. Instead he crept back to the attic stairs and retrieved them, wincing at the groan they issued as he pulled them skyward. He didn't want Grandma coming to grab him and run when she saw his dad. If he pulled and locked the stairs, she wouldn't be able to reach him at all. He could watch whatever transpired and then go back down when the coast was clear.

"Corey? What are you doing?" She sang from below.

He couldn't give his dad and the other guy away, so he thought quickly. "Oh, nothing, Grandma. I couldn't get around to the other side of the stairs unless I closed 'em," he shouted through the attic floor.

"Okay, but don't you lock them, Corey. I don't want you getting stuck up there."

"Okay, Grandma," he replied agreeably, and muttered under his breath 'yah, right.' He moved back to the window and noticed he couldn't see his dad or the other guy any more, but Troy had taken up position at this side of the attic. Corey walked over to the other window and saw Tony hunkered down beneath the dining room windows. Where was his dad?

Corey heard a knock on the front door. He put his head to the floor to listen.

"Can I help you, young man?" His grandma's voice sounded suspicious, and she obviously wasn't talking to his dad, 'cause she would call him by name.

"The name is Tanner Grafton. I'm from Seattle. I can see from the signs that this place is for sale. I've stopped by before, you see, but it's always been empty. I noticed your car here this morning. Would you mind showing me around?"

"Oh, it's not my place to show the house. I'm merely doing a favor for a friend and cleaning it."

Ooh, Corey thought, Grandma's a pretty slick liar.

"I really would like to have a look around," the man persisted, "I'm only in town for today and then I have to head back home. As you can see, I'm in a wheelchair. This cabin has a nice ramp and it looks like it has only one level of living space. I've peeked through the windows many times."

"It has an attic," his grandma argued.

"Well I wouldn't be interested in seeing that, obviously, but do you think you could show me the rest?"

Corey could hear his grandmother sigh. "I guess there can't be any harm if you want to have a look around. It isn't presentable just yet, I'm afraid. Did you say your name was Tanner? For some reason, it sounds familiar to me. *You* seem familiar."

"I get that a lot. It's because I'm gray-haired," the man replied as his voice moved closer to Corey. Corey was tempted to drop the stairs, because he could hear his grandma hovering below them. They'd knock her a good one in the melon, which she deserved. Corey fingered the latch, tempted by the possibility, when he heard his father's booming voice.

"Mom."

Karen Dermot yelped in surprise. "Blake Dermot, what in the world are you doing here?"

"I'm here to get Holly and Corey and take them home."

"Are you on official capacity? I thought you threw that job in the toilet only yesterday," Karen sniffed.

"I'm with Tanner and Tanner is with me. Thanks for letting him in by the way."

"I found some kid's clothes in the bedroom," Tanner volunteered from somewhere to Corey's right. "There's no sign of Holly, though."

"Where is he, Mom?" Blake demanded.

"I sent him down to the lake to play," his grandma lied. Corey teetered between the need to call her out on the lie and the fear that if he gave himself away, she'd pull the handgun out of her apron pocket and shoot his dad and his friend straight away.

Indecision welled up in Corey's chest so that he almost forgot to breathe.

"By himself, Mom? He's only nine and he's lived in

New York most of his life! He doesn't have any idea how to swim!" Corey could hear Blake's retreating footsteps as he raced for the dock eight hundred yards away, through a thick stand of trees.

Corey could hear his grandmother rustle through her bag in the bedroom, the click of the clip of her handgun which he'd heard only the day before, and her rush to follow his dad. He had to stop her!

Corey flipped the door latch opposite of the way he'd locked it and pushed mightily downward, hanging on, in case the stairs dropped all at once instead of staying on the spring that they'd come down with.

Nothing happened.

He tried flipping the latch the opposite way and pushing. Nothing. Frustrated and now panicked, he tried it again, and again. The lock wouldn't budge! He was stuck!

He ran to Troy's side of the house and pounded and yelled at the window. He looked down. Troy had apparently followed his dad, so he went to the other side of the attic to call for Tony, but he had done the same.

Frantic about the safety of a man he'd hardly gotten to know—his dad—a man who'd been nothing but kind to him, Corey started picking up boxes from the neat piles and upending them on the floor. There had to be something here to break a window with. Box after box of clothing and papers grew into a heap as Corey felt time, and his chance to warn his dad, slip eerily away.

Chapter Fifty-two

Holly

She recognized the Dermot cellar by the dim light seeping through the slats in the wooden door. She could tell the cellar belonged to the Dermots because she and Blake had sneaked down there more than once when they were teenagers to have sex somewhere besides the back seat of a car.

Holly shivered. It might be July, but none of the heat of the new day had reached her subterranean prison. A night's worth of rain and passing thunderstorms had left everything damp, including the sweats she'd so looked forward to wearing. There was a wooden apple box in the corner, so she sat on it instead of the unforgiving concrete she'd passed out on. Karen had clubbed her with something that clanged against her skull before rendering her unconscious. Probably a shovel, Holly thought as she rubbed the sore lump on the back of her head. She couldn't be so lucky as to have that shovel inside the cellar with her, could she?

The cellar sat in the middle of a lavish flower garden, surround by gladiolas and lilies and Holly could smell the sweet blooms mingling with the acrid earth of the cellar walls. She'd already tried to climb the stairs and shove open the door. It was chained shut.

The shelves of the cellar were lined with jars of canned food, but she had no way of knowing which foods were safe to eat, or, in the meager light, if there were any dates on them. The way her stomach growled, Holly was sure that soon she wouldn't care if she got food poisoning or not. She'd crack open those jar lids with her teeth if she had to.

Holly sat contemplating her prison, wondering if Karen had left her for dead. But then, would a dead person need to be chained in? Did that mean Karen would come back for her, then? Would she tell anybody else where to find Holly? What would Karen do with Corey in the meantime? Surely she wouldn't take him from Blake, even if she had clobbered Holly and taken him from her. Blake would make his mom see reason.

It was that belief that kept her calm in that hole in the ground, full of memories, and a whole new crop of fears.

Chapter Fifty-three

Karen

If you would have asked her three years ago if she could harm one of her children, Karen would have answered instantly, 'Of course not. Women who hurt their children are deviant psychopaths. Period."

As she rushed after Blake, handgun loaded, Karen nearly laughed hysterically to think she'd just joined the ranks of Andrea Yates and Susan Smith. She was so caught up in her musings, she didn't even notice when her two older sons filed after her, slipping past evergreens and waist-high scrub bushes, matching her quiet efficiency.

Her physical trials with Winston had made Karen strong and quick. She might have been thin, but she was wiry. Blake's size didn't intimidate her whatsoever. She pressed herself into the last evergreen before the clearing that led to the lodge's dock and watched her son.

He stood at the end of the dock yelling into their lagoon, "Corey? *Corey?* If you can hear me from where you are, yell back."

He waited for an answer. When there was none, he yelled again, "Corey?" His voice echoed back at him. Karen could hear ducks carry on in the distance, but otherwise, silence. Blake eyes began to scan the water in earnest, looking for movement. Karen could feel his distress as his imaginings put his son at the bottom of the murky lake.

She knew how Blake felt, imagining that his son was already gone, that there was nothing he could do to save him. She felt the same way about Blake. In her mind, her son was already dead.

She left the shelter of the tree, her elbows locked, her pistol leading the way, just as her husband and her son, the cop, had taught her. "He's already gone, Blake."

"Gone? What do you mean? What have you done with my son?" His face crumpled.

Karen advanced toward the dock. Blake raised his hands in surrender, as if that would keep her from shooting him. He'd failed on every level to do the right thing for his son. Blake didn't deserve to have Corey. He was here to take Corey back, and he would do so over her dead body.

"He's safe. Safe from you," she hedged as she eased forward.

"Mom, could you please put the gun down? Let's be rational about this…"

"Rational? I was perfectly rational yesterday when I sat down in that courtroom. Then I watched you blow your life and Corey's to smithereens! That whore took him away from you and somehow convinced you it was your fault, so what did you do? You torpedoed your career, handed your son over to her with a smile, and put your arm around your current whore while your first whore and her slutty mother celebrated. It made me sick, Blake."

"Holly and Minerva are *loving* mothers, not 'whores'. You must not think very much of me to put both of my wives in that category," Blake defended.

"You're right, Blake. I don't think very much of you. It was a good family name and luck that put you in the county's top law enforcement position. You've never had a steady sense of direction like your brothers, or any sort of a spine; and you have horrible taste in women."

"So what? You're going to shoot me? Because you don't like my wife? What about your other grandchildren? You're going to leave them without a father?"

"If Minerva is such a wonderful mother, she'll have no problem raising them without you," Karen grinned at her son ironically. That was when she saw the first real glimmer of fear surface in Blake's eyes. *Finally a little respect,* she thought.

The fishing dock was linked to the lakeshore by two stairs made of railroad ties. At the end of the stairs, the dock slanted slightly downward with wooden planks about two feet wide, and led to a wider dock several feet away. Cattails and milfoil surrounded the smaller part of the dock and became fully submerged by the end of the bigger deck, where the water was much deeper. A concrete pile-on stood at each side of the junction between the docks, placed there for the purpose of tying up fishing boats. Karen descended the steps, her gun still trained on Blake.

"You do realize that Tanner is probably calling for help right now?" Blake, ever the cop, reminded her.

"As long as it takes to navigate the roads out here, I'll have you both taken care of long before the authorities get here." Karen started down the incline as Blake backed himself to the far edge of the dock.

"What are you planning to do about us?" Tony's voice boomed from directly behind her, startling Karen just as she took the final step down to the wider deck. She hadn't accounted for surprise, nor the slickness, from last night's rain storm, of the moss on that final board. Her right foot slid from beneath her like she'd stepped on ice. She heard the small roar of her handgun as she fired off a shot in surprise, followed by a loud splash that didn't come from her. The world tilted skyward, and she had time to think, *what a blue sky,* just before her cranium struck a concrete boat anchor, and her troubled mind finally went quiet.

Chapter Fifty-four

Blake

"Where did she land?" Blake shouted as soon as he resurfaced and heard his mom hit the water too.

"Blake! I thought she shot you!" Tony called from the shore. He was already shedding his jeans and shoes to dive in after his brother.

"She did shoot me. It's just superficial. Troy, do you see her?"

Troy gagged when he ran gingerly to the end of the dock and saw the trails of blood coming from both his mother and brother. "She's passed out, Blake, face down right at the edge of the toolies. I can't quite reach her. You're bleeding. Are you able to swim to her? Careful, man, she still has the gun in her hand. She's got a death grip on that thing."

"I've got her," Blake said, turning his mother over in the water. It was that moment that he realized the irony of his brother's words. Karen's eyes were open, pupils fixed and dilated. "Ah, God, Mom, no. Why?... Why?"

Tony's eyes started to run immediately as he joined Troy breathlessly on the dock. "She's dead, isn't she?"

Troy, Karen's eldest, looked resigned. "Push her this way, Blake. We need to get you out of the water too and check you out."

Blake's side burned, but not nearly as much as his vision as tears sprung to his eyes. As much as he hurt, he needed to hold his poor mother for just a moment longer, so he pretended he hadn't heard Troy. He pushed her over-long hair away from her face and closed her eyes for her. A sob caught in his throat as he said, "I never meant to fail you, Mom. Please forgive me."

"Blake, you need to let go. Give me Mom. I'll take care of her, I promise. Minerva would kick my ass if I didn't fish you out of the water before you bled to death," Troy pleaded.

At the mention of his wife, Blake remembered Corey, and the reason they'd come to the cabin in the first place. He pushed his mother's body to his brothers and eased himself onto the dock to assess the damage. He lifted his uniform shirt gingerly away from his bloodied side. He was right about the wound only being superficial, and he'd been damn lucky. The bullet had grazed him at the lower edge of his left rib cage—just below his heart and dangerously close to his spleen.

Blake fashioned his shirt into a bandage and held it against his side to stem the flow of blood. His brothers shared the burden of their mother as the three of them trudged ashore. What they found there was a breathless man in a less-than-all-terrain wheelchair picking his way down the woodland trail.

"Your mom… is she dead? Sweet Jesus, I'm sorry, Blake, Troy, Tony," Tanner offered. "I heard the gunshot. What happened?"

"Where the hell have you been? Did you find Corey or Holly?" Blake quizzed as exhaustion and pain began to kick in all at once.

"Neither. There isn't any sign that Holly's been here at all. Your mom must have dropped her off somewhere before she came out here."

"Corey probably knows where she left her," Blake reasoned. "We need to find him first."

"Your mom certainly won't be telling us, will she?" Tanner asked testily.

"Cut the ironic shit," Troy growled.

"All I'm saying is that she created this mess. Why did you goons go and get her killed before she could tell us where she put Holly?" Tanner groused.

"Okay, okay," Blake winced. "I realize this is all just a gigantic cluster of mayhem. Harv should be here any time with the posse from Chelan County. If this God-forsaken cabin wasn't so damn hard to find, they'd be here by now, I'm sure. Can we just concentrate now on finding my son, please?"

"I've been all over this place, Blake. I haven't seen him."

Blake looked back toward the lake in panic. Surely he wasn't out there somewhere. His mother had said she had Corey safe somewhere. The lake itself would not be safe for a little boy who didn't swim.

"I'll check the lodge one more time," Tony offered as he and Troy moved on up the trail to settle Karen Dermot on the porch swing. Troy covered her with a tarp from the utility box.

"I can check around the out-buildings. It looks like there's an old shed up the road about a quarter mile," Troy suggested.

"Okay," Blake's breath, by now, was coming in pants, from exertion, and from pain.

Moments later, he heard his brother pipe up from inside. "He's here, Blake."

"Where? Oh, thank you, God," he breathed, as he rushed inside and heard his son's cries from overhead. The attic.

"Corey? Can you open the door?"

"Dad?" Corey answered. Blake could hear the wretched tears in his voice. "I thought she shot you. I heard the gun go off. I thought you were dead. I couldn't save you. I couldn't save you…"

"Shhh, Corey. I'm here, buddy. I'm okay. You'll have lots of time to rescue your old dad on future adventures, if you'll go on them with me." Blake's heart tore when he realized for the first time that his son would have actually *missed* him if he had died. They had a long way to go, but at least they had that.

"Can you get the latch?" Blake heard sirens in the distance at last, the sign that Harv had found them with slightly more than a half-hour leeway, which was what the plan had been.

"I've tried, Dad. Over and over. I'm stuck."

"Okay, Corey," Tony offered, seeing that Blake was powerless to help them with the door at the moment, "I'm going to pull on the door while you push. Hang on, though, because those stairs might come down fast. Ready? One, two, three…"

The door latch ripped completely away with Tony's effort and the stairs came crashing down with a little boy clinging for dear life. He no sooner landed than a mountain of boxes and junk came raining down on top of him.

"Corey? Corey!" Blake exclaimed, pulling debris away from his son. Corey's tear-streaked face appeared from beneath the mound, eyes closed, his breathing alarmingly quiet. "He's unconscious." Blake ignored the pain in his side as he lifted his not-so-little replica from the pile of rubble.

Troy burst into the house with Tanner behind him. "Harvey and the posse are here."

"Did they bring an ambulance? Corey's hurt," Blake said as blood began to drip from his make-shift bandage below the arm where he cradled Corey's head.

Tony came up behind him, rubbing his head. "I hope so, 'cause it looks like he's not the only one."

Chapter Fifty-five

Tanner

"I cannot believe you didn't at least ask him if he knew where his mom was before you dropped him eight feet from the attic." Tanner paced as only a man in a wheelchair could, wheeling back and forth at the foot of Blake's hospital gurney.

"Hey, he had a lot on his mind," Troy growled from his chair in the corner. "Our mom had just shot him and died before our eyes. His son was traumatized and stuck in an attic. What do you want, city boy? We realize you're all ga-ga over Holly, but she was not our priority at the time."

"Will Holly ever be a priority to you Dermots?" Tanner asked, furious. "It's that attitude that got her snatched in the first place. For all we know she could be hurt or dead somewhere at the hands of your psycho mother."

Lying on his right side, Blake had an arm over his eyes, shielding them from the light while the doctor stitched him up. He winced. "Watch it, Grafton."

"I'm sorry about your mom, Blake. I really am, but your son is lying unconscious next door and he is, right now, the only one who can possibly lead us to Holly, and you didn't bother to ask him where your mother left her."

"The doc here says he's just staying asleep out of exhaustion. They did a Cat Scan and didn't find anything wrong with his head, so he could wake up anytime. Will you please relax and stop making me seasick?" Blake begged, grappling for the basin on the bedside table.

"Be still," the doctor requested through gritted teeth, "or I'll end up stitching your flank to your left nipple."

"Ouch," Troy laughed. Tanner couldn't help but smirk too, at the thought. He was just mad enough at Blake to think he deserved it.

"It's already five o'clock," Tanner looked at his watch for the thousandth time since they'd gotten to the hospital. "Holly's been missing for more than twenty-four hours. What if she's somewhere with no food or water? It's July. It's muggy and the heat today has been oppressive. She can't last long in those conditions."

"Assuming she's still alive," Tony pointed out as he walked in with a steaming tray of coffee, black, for the exhausted bunch. None of them had slept or eaten much since the disappearance of Holly and Corey.

"She's still alive. I know it," Tanner concluded because he couldn't imagine any other ending.

Minerva swept into the room fresh as spring rain. "Aren't you just a sad-looking bunch of Dermot boys?" Troy and Tony frowned.

Blake laughed and winced at the stab of pain he got in return. "You've got that right."

"All those years as a cop and you never got shot until now," Minerva came over and grabbed Blake's free hand and smoothed his hair off his forehead before she kissed it. Just like she always did with the kids. "How are you honey?"

He winced again as the numbing medication began to wear off the area the doctor was stitching. "I've been better. Have you been in to see Corey?"

She nodded. "He was just starting to stir when I was in there. I thought he'd probably rather see you than me when he finally woke up."

Tanner started to wheel toward the neighboring room, then held up when he heard Blake growl. "Grafton, don't even think about it."

"He has to tell us where she left Holly…"

"I'll get the information. Trust me. Just leave my kid alone." Blake looked at the doc frankly. "Are you very close to finishing?"

"One more stitch," the doctor offered, sounding as relieved to be finished as Blake was to have him stop.

Blake rolled his huge frame gingerly to his back and let Minerva help him sit upright.

The big man walked to his son's bed, his expression as tender as a mother laying her newborn down to sleep. Tanner felt a pang of envy as he wheeled into the doorframe.

Corey opened his eyes. "Hi, Dad."

"Hi, Son. How are you feeling?"

"My head hurts a little. It's too bright in here, but I'm okay. Just tired."

"We're at the hospital in Wenatchee," Blake explained.

"Where's Grandma?" Corey asked tentatively, fear playing around with his face as he scanned the doorway and beyond.

"She's not going to bother us anymore."

"Is she dead?"

"Yes, son, she is."

Corey's head fell back against the pillows. "That's good. I'm sorry if that makes you sad, but she threatened to hurt you and Mom if I tried to run away or tattle on her."

"It's okay to feel that way, Corey. I am sad. I miss her already, like you'd miss your mom if she was never coming back. I'm relieved too, because now your grandma doesn't have to shoulder any more burdens. Her life got a little bit heavy for her there at the very end."

Blake settled back into his chair. Tanner could almost taste his own impatience as he waited for Blake to get around to the big question.

"So, Corey, do you know where Grandma might have dropped your mom off?"

"You still haven't found Mom?" Corey sat up, alarmed.

"Tanner, your uncles, and I have looked everywhere we can think of. Where all did you stop before you came out here to the lake?"

Corey glanced over at Tanner and back toward his dad. "Grandma made Mom get out at her house."

"She's at Grandma and Grandpa Dermot's house?" Blake quizzed.

"That's not possible, Blake. We turned that place inside out looking for carafes this morning. Unless you know about some secret link with an underground railroad, there was nowhere else for her to hide." Blake glared at Tanner for interrupting. Tanner pursed his lips. Blake surely couldn't expect him not to dig a little for the truth.

"That's it!" Blake exclaimed making both Minerva and Corey jump. "She's under*ground!* My mom and dad have an outside-access-only cellar on the outside of the house. We need to go check there."

"You're not going anywhere, Mister," Minerva stood with her hands on her hips, bodily nixing any ideas Blake or Corey might have about leaving the hospital.

"That's okay," Harvey Morris interrupted from behind Tanner in the doorway. "The department can take it from here."

"Not without me, you don't." Tanner turned on his wheel, nearly taking out the interim sheriff.

"Tanner?" Corey asked, as if he knew exactly who Tanner was. So Holly had talked about him after all, with the boys.

"Yes, Corey?" Tanner could hardly stand the depths of fear in the boy's eyes, but he couldn't look away either, for he knew that whatever he did now would count forever with Corey.

"You need to make my mom safe. You love her. Make sure she's safe. Me and Tristan need her. Okay?"

Tanner swallowed a lump in his throat. What if he made a promise now that he couldn't keep? For the first time in a very long time, he felt entirely helpless. He knew the boys needed Holly. *He* needed Holly.

He nodded solemnly to Corey as Harv patted his shoulder to go.

"Okay."

Chapter Fifty-six

Holly

Holly was a nurse. She knew by the scrape of dry eyelids over blurry eyes, by the way her tongue felt like sandpaper on the roof of her mouth, that she was dangerously dehydrated. The crisp morning had turned into searing summer temperatures, seeping through the gapes in the cellar door into her underground lair and turning the damp walls and floor to stifling vapor.

Muggy air stole her moisture like a thick towel, yet she still hadn't heard a peep outside. No cars coming and going, no signs of life in the house nearby. Holly was trapped and she knew she was in a whole lot of trouble if somebody didn't come for her soon.

By mid-afternoon, the contents of the cellar shelves beckoned. Sunshine bore down on the southern exposure and Holly could no longer resist her instinct to survive. She needed to eat. She needed to drink.

She cranked as hard as she could on the lid of a jar that contained what looked like corn kernels. When the lid wouldn't budge, she tapped it on her wooden crate gently to loosen it. When that still wouldn't work, she tried to summon enough saliva to wet the edges of the lid before she tried again. Yet, she didn't really have any spit left. Frustrated, she chucked the jar as hard at the stone floor as she could. She practically hummed when the jar split wide open.

She bent to grab some of the corn from the bottom of the jar when a smell akin to dirty socks soaked in whiskey hit her nose. Botulism? She'd once taken

care of an elderly woman in New York who'd eaten
a bad can of green beans and actually died from
dehydration after all of her vomiting and diarrhea.
Holly backed away quickly, horrified.

Her predicament overwhelmed her for a moment,
so she forced herself to breathe, told herself the jars
couldn't possibly all be bad, and reminded herself
how much she had to live for. She remembered
something about low acid foods being the ones that
were dangerous to eat if not properly canned.

She would have thought Karen a proper canner.
Then again, maybe Karen stored the good stuff
upstairs and *not* in this hell-hole!

Holly looked around for fruit jars, holding each one
up to the light until she was satisfied she had a jar of
canned peaches, surrounded by viscous liquid. The
screw-on lid came off much easier and she used the
edge of the wooden crate to pop off the sealed part of
the lid.

The peaches slid home like a five-course dinner.
Holly smacked her lips like a little kid with a *Popsicle*.
She settled onto the floor for a nap, grateful for the
nutrition—for about two hours.

As the sun began to wane, a wave of intestinal
cramps hit Holly. She fashioned an emergency latrine
out of her same wooden crate and put it in the corner
with the contents of the first jar, which she'd swept
there with her shirt. The smell and the indignity of it
all upset her stomach further and she began to vomit
until there was nothing left but violent retching.

Still dehydrated, her vision blurred by strain and
lack of light, Holly curled into the fetal position and
closed her eyes. She wanted to cry out for herself, for
her boys, and for her mother and sister, as she gave up
the fight, but all that came out was a pitiful mewl, and
not even an echo, in what would become her grave.

Her last conscious thoughts as she gave in to
the night were of Tanner—his arms strong, his hair
impossibly silky, his lips utterly soft as he embraced
her—and she wondered if he would ever know what

became of her. Would he long for her the way she would him, even from the afterlife?

Chapter Fifty-seven

Tanner

Sirens blaring, reaching top speeds of one hundred and twenty miles per hour, it still felt to Harv and Tanner like it took a lifetime to reach Okanogan.

Harv called ahead and they received frequent radio updates along the way: The cellar had been located, the lock breached, and the missing woman found—unconscious, apparently dehydrated, pulse thready, and blood pressure dangerously low. Harv and Tanner were about a half-hour from town when the last bit of news came across the radio, so they changed course for the hospital.

Tanner thought he would go out of his mind as he sat in the passenger seat awaiting the sight of her, awaiting fate, and wondering if he'd lied to Corey after all.

Harv unloaded Tanner's wheelchair. He yearned for the first time in years to have legs that could carry him swiftly and steadily to Holly's side. Instead, Tanner struggled with the wheel locks and fumbled with the foot pedals, his actions uncertain like they never were.

"Can I help you, Mr. Grafton?" Harv offered, sensing Tanner's distress.

"Call me Tanner. I know I haven't said much, but I appreciate everything you've done…" he continued to tussle with the wheelchair.

Harv cut him off. "Well, see, here's the thing: That girl in there? She's caused a whole lot of trouble for a very good friend of mine. It would have been much easier for Blake if Holly had disappeared years ago and left Corey behind. Instead, she took their kid and made his mother go completely crazy. His mom's dead, his dad's in a nursing home, their kid's in the hospital with a concussion…

"Yet, still, inexplicably," Harv continued, holding up his hand as Tanner moved to interrupt, "Blake cares what happens to her. When it boils down to it, the fact remains that she has two sons and a family that loves her. She has you, and you seem like a nice guy.

"So, I can see why you can't quite get a grip on those wheels; and I can also see that you're a very proud man, but if you will allow me to help you, there is a young woman in there who needs you, and a bunch of people who need her."

Tanner nodded and Harv took the handles of the wheelchair and wheeled him up the ramp. Tanner took a fortifying breath when they rounded the corner into the main room of the ER.

Holly, covered to her chin in warm blankets, looked tiny in the gurney. The cellar had shriveled her like dried fruit. Her lips were cracked and her eyelids paper thin, covering sunken eyes that stubbornly refused to open. She looked like a concentration camp survivor. His heart felt leaden in his chest.

Holly's nurse had her IV line cracked wide open, pouring in fluids she needed. She lowered the gurney and gestured to him to go ahead. Take her hand. So he did.

Her hand was warm, thank God. He found his voice, though it rumbled forth quietly, through days of fatigue, "Holly? I'm here. It's Tanner."

Her eyelids fluttered.

"It's taken me an awfully long time to find you, so do you think you could do me a favor and open your eyes? I know they're blue. They're incredible, so much more like you."

She gripped his hand and strained forward, yet her eyes still refused to open.

"Listen, we've got Corey. He's with Blake and he can't wait to see you. Tristan is with your mom and her husband. Everybody is safe except for you, and we *need* you. Will you open your eyes?"

Her eyelids batted once, twice, and Holly finally cracked them open, wincing with the sudden light. She turned them to him, and tears sprung to his own when she uttered, "Tanner?"

"Hi there, Claudia," He teased, his voice tender, "Wanna go on a date with a poor guy in a wheelchair?"

She smiled, despite sore lips, and squeezed his hand. "Well, Tanner, just how could I resist an offer like that?"

Chapter Fifty-eight

Tristan

The spring day felt so warm, Tristan wondered if his mom would let him run through sprinklers after she cut up the cake. Of course, his tux was a lot warmer than a swimsuit would be. She'd probably say no.

This wedding stuff had him confused. Everybody got dressed up and acted like the time they were at Disneyworld and Grandma Sissy got married. In one moment, everyone smiled and clapped each other on the backs, and the husbands and wives, they kissed a lot. Yuck. Next thing he knew, tears ran out of everyone's eyes.

Personally, it didn't make him want to cry when Tanner kissed his mom. He wanted to yell out. Tanner was his guy. He liked him almost as much as he liked Minerva.

Corey liked him too. Tristan could tell by the way Corey gave Tanner a fist bump after everyone cheered. Then, Tanner put their mom on his lap to wheel her back out of the church. Afterward, they all went to the park where Tristan had never seen so many flowers in one place.

His aunt Susan held up her glass full of bubbly and said how she'd never seen his mom so happy. Her little baby boy gurgled and toddled around, but Tristan made sure he didn't go anywhere near the parking lot.

Grandma Sissy held Grandpa Stanley's hand and smiled all day long. She was even nice to his uncle

Blake and aunt Minerva, which was new for her. Jonah, Camillia, and Sammy helped Tristan pass out punch and cake to all the people at the tables. Well, Sammy mostly spilled his punch, but Tristan let him have a couple of cups anyway, because it made him happy.

Tanner wasn't the only man in a wheelchair. Corey's Grandpa Dermot sat at the table with Blake. Minerva fed him Jell-o salad. Grandpa Dermot never said anything and he kind of creeped Tristan out, but Tristan could tell it made Blake happy to take care of his dad. Uncle Blake was still a police officer, but his job was a lot easier now, because he spent his days visiting schools and daring kids to stay good, instead of catching the really bad guys.

Soon it was time to dance. Tanner gave his mom another ride in his wheelchair for their song and then Tanner took his mother's hand. Tanner's mom had hair like polished silver, just like her son. Her name was Lotty. She wore red to the wedding, even brighter than Grandma Sissy's orange. Lotty had brought new baseball mitts and balls for him and Corey when she arrived in town for the wedding, so that made her okay in Tristan's book. Plus, Holly seemed to like her too. Tristan could get used to this whole new grandma thing.

Corey's other grandma had died. Her funeral had been a whole lot sadder, though everyone had dressed up for that too. Corey felt bad, but he confessed to Tristan that he was scared of that grandma, and that she had hated their mom to the point that she banged her over the head with a shovel and left her to die.

Tristan hated stories like that. He couldn't understand why anyone wouldn't love his mom. She was awfully pretty, even more now that her hair was the color of the outside of a grapefruit and fell like springs around her chin. She wore a white gown that hugged her body clear to her ankles with flowers sewn onto it. Tanner spent a lot of time staring at her and kissing her. Double yuck. But then, Tristan supposed he should get used to that.

Before the wedding, Tanner found out he could set up a studio in Okanogan and work with his agent in L.A. That made his mom really happy, because Tanner would only travel a few times a year to the big cities. They could still visit her old friends in New York at Christmas and spend spring breaks at Disneyland. Corey could be close to his dad. Tristan could spend time at Minerva's, which he loved.

They would spend part of their summers with Grandma Sissy and Grandpa Stanley in Montana. His mom took a job working as a nurse part-time, but she wanted to be able to travel with them and Tanner, so she turned down her chance to be the boss of all the nurses at the hospital.

For now, they kept their little house, which Tristan liked because it was close to the grade school and ball field, so he could go play whenever he wanted. They made a ramp on the front porch and Tanner got a smaller wheel chair to fit through narrow doorways. His mom and Tanner had made hints lately about building a house to make space for a baby brother or sister, or both. *As if there weren't enough ankle-biters around to keep him and Corey busy at these big parties,* he thought, as he fished Sammy's cake out of the water fountain.

Then Camillia fell asleep on his shoulder as the two of them leaned up against a shade tree. Maybe being a big brother again wouldn't be so bad. He waved at Corey, who grinned at the two of them around his third slice of wedding cake.

After all, being a *little* brother was the bomb.

Kimberly Ann Freel writes about and lives in Okanogan County, Washington with her husband and four kids. *The Son I Seek* is her fifth novel. To learn more about Kimberly and her other books, visit **www. cmppg.com** or **www.kimfreel.com**.